-RIPPED APART

Quantum Twins Series

RIPPED APART
HUNTED
BETRAYED
REBELLION

RIPPED APART

QUANTUM TWINS

ADVENTURES ON TWO WORLDS

GEOFFREY ARNOLD

Matador
9 Priory Business Park,
Wistow Road, Kibworth Beauchamp,
Leicestershire. LE8 0RX
Tel: 0116 279 2299
Email: books@troubador.co.uk
Web: www.troubador.co.uk/matador
Twitter: @matadorbooks

ISBN 978 1784624 750

British Library Cataloguing in Publication Data.
A catalogue record for this book is available from the British Library.

Printed and bound by CPI Group (UK) Ltd, Croydon, CR0 4YY
Typeset in 11pt Goudy Old Style by Troubador Publishing Ltd, Leicester, UK

Matador is an imprint of Troubador Publishing Ltd

ACKNOWLEDGEMENTS

My thanks go to the team that every author needs.

Naomi Sesay who ran the most powerful workshop I have ever attended: The Human Upgrade. It was there I met the Twins who asked me to tell their story. I never expected that to turn out to be four books!

After the Twins wrote what became the first nine chapters, my (best!) handwriting was so difficult to read that all their other adventures have been put on tape. That those words have made it onto paper is due to the indefatigable efforts of Cecily Wheeler, who also taught me African words like muzungu.

Heather Thomas, editor and playwright, whose comments on reading the first draft of the first part of this book amounted to a marvellous course on the technical aspects of writing.

To the friends who bought my first ebook as a result of whose comments I took it out of publication and engaged a professional editor.

Judith Henstra, my editor, whose advice and comments have been and continue to be invaluable. Caroline Swain who proof reads and copy edits. I have made some changes since she did that, so any errors are mine.

And now, even with self publishing, an author can have a publisher. I have a great team at Matador. Discovering just what is involved to do it properly makes me very happy that I cancelled my first, all-by-myself, eBook.

Trevor Stevens, who built the framework for the Twins' main website and taught me how to fill it. Anna Langa for the website for *Ripped Apart*. Francine Beleyi for marketing instruction. All three and Cecily Wheeler for their support and interest throughout the years, and patience as each tries to teach me aspects of the 'modern communication techniques' of their own professions.

Through it all there is my wife, who gives me the space and time it takes, on holiday and then at home. And from whom, on our nights out, the twins have learnt the dance steps to most of the popular music of the 60s and 70s.

RIPPED APART

Welcome to The Story the Twins have told me. They do not consider this to be a work of fiction.

CHAPTER 1

A MYSTERY

Out of pale blue ovals, two pairs of large, purple eyes stared at each other. They glowed as the twins recalled the previous evening's discussion with their parents. They rolled out of their beds, slipped on their dayrobes and made their way to the main window of their attic domain. The view was what they wanted to see. After five continuous days the snow had stopped falling.

<At last!! We can start on The Mystery. We'll reroute the primary Neutron Emitter then...> Realising how enervated they were becoming they stopped thoughtsharing. They did not dare let their parents overhear their plans, or worse, have them discover that their children had worked out how to disable the security around the attic in Lungunu.

Lowering their energies they thoughtsent to their respective halves of the window to open, and leant out searching for a glimpse of Lungunu, the home of their father's great aunt and great uncle. Living far out in the countryside there were no houses nearby to spoil the view. As far as their eyes could see, everything was covered in a thick white blanket, sparkling under a clear blue sky. With only two days to go to the winter KeyPoint, the longest night of the year, they were expecting to see strange lighting effects in the sky above the house, even though it was several kilometres away. Nothing.

Disappointed, Tullia turned to her twin. 'Do you think it snowed on Auriga?' she asked wistfully. She added the thought that she was just wondering, so as to stop him snapping back asking how did she expect him to know.

'We know almost nothing about our original homeworld and little about the lives of the Auriganii,' Qwelby replied. 'I don't understand why there's so little information in the Racial Memory Archives.'

'It's over a hundred thousand sun cycles since we, well they, left there!'

'But that's it. The records refer to sun cycles. That must be their year. We don't even know how long that was!' he said, adding feelings of frustration to his thoughts.

As with all young Tazii, their genes tightly controlled the release of hormones at the time of each rebirthday. At fifteen and a quarter years old they were at the beginning of the fourth phase of their second era, when the genes that had been activated required them to explore the meaning of home and roots. Whilst they had some special friends, both boys and girls, it would be nearly two years before they would experience the first stirrings of feelings towards the concept of a deeper relationship with a boy-friend or girl-friend.

Lost in thought, they pulled their heads back in and initiated closure of their halves of the window.

The two soft chimes of the halves closing jerked them out of their reverie. They turned to look at each other. Their purple orbs flared, and they raced across the room, threw themselves onto and down the two twirlypoles, across the hall and into the kitchen, a dead heat, as usual.

Their parents looked up, shaking their heads at the exuberance. Shandur, their father took after the men in the family. He was tall and well built with a full head of prematurely greying, dark brown hair that fell to just above his shoulders, as was the custom for men. He was dressed in his usual style when at home in a lightweight, soft round neck sweater and trousers, today's choices being plain olive over tan.

Mizena, their mother was shorter than average with a sturdy build that came from all the time she spent working on the gardens and farms of both her own home and that of her husband's great aunt and uncle. Ready for work, she was wearing a lightweight polo neck in a range of browns and greens, shot through with splashes of orange, and dark green trousers which she would tuck into boots when outside.

'Mum Dad the forecast was right it's stopped snowing the sky is clear its not our day this tenday to be in college and you said can we please??' the twins exclaimed in unison, without a pause.

Tullia was making her eyes go perfectly round, elongating and fluttering her already long lashes and exuding an impression of sweet innocence whilst Qwelby controlled his desire to be sick at her antics.

'Can you what?' asked Shandur, their father, with a straight face.

'Take our sleds to Lungunu!!' they replied in exasperated tones of two voices.

'Will you never grow up?' Mizena, their mother, asked rhetorically.

The twins turned to look at one another, wrinkled their brows and pursed their lips as though giving the question due thought.

'No,' they replied. 'We're not going to be old!!'

Their parents turned to each other, shook their heads, gave up trying to look serious and smiled. 'All right,' they said together, not to be outdone by their children.

'Yippee!!'

Racing to the bottom of the twirlypoles the twins thoughtpropelled themselves upwards, laughing as each tried to force the other to lose concentration and slide down to the bottom.

'Breakfast first,' their mother called after them. 'Just over fifteen years old and they are so childish at times,' she muttered.

'Maybe I'm not being fair,' she added, turning to her husband. 'Working with your Aunt Lellia studying the Azurii, I forget how much slower our children grow up emotionally compared to those humans with their short lives.'

With many Tazii living to be two hundred years old, it was customary to omit saying one or even more "Greats", the speaker's accompanying thought making the situation clear.

'We've done a lot to encourage that behaviour,' Shandur said, taking his wife's hand in his and using the physical contact to infuse her with all his love and support.

His words obliquely referring to their reasoning, the previous existence of another pair of Quantum Twins, stopped any further discussion. In a world where people's energy fields were clearly visible and easily readable, and where the whole race was loosely mentally interconnected, the transmission of thoughts had to be carefully guarded. Husband and wife locked eyes, each knowing that the other was reflecting on the potential tragedy facing their children.

Quantum Twins were unique. Although genetically identical, one was a boy, the other a girl. There was no explanation for that impossibility. According to the Archives only one other pair had ever been born, and that had been several hundred years ago. Surprisingly for such a recent record, it was badly degraded. For the sake of preservation, as with any very old and degraded record, access was restricted to a small group of Custodians known as Preservers. With expressions of sorrow, the oldest and most senior who was known as The Antiquarian, had advised the family of the best interpretation they had been able to make.

Unable to bear being separated in any way, as that pair of Quantum Twins had passed into adulthood their introversion had become pronounced. They had refused to accept help, and their interaction with and contribution to the world outside of themselves had steadily decreased. The world of quantum energy required continuing interaction, symbolised by the Tazii as a constantly moving, three dimensional figure of eight comprised of two dragons swallowing each other's tail. Failing to interact with the world at large, those twins had broken their essential connection with Life. No longer able to receive the energy needed to sustain their existence, their lifelines had ended at a much earlier age than normal.

Just as with that pair, until the age of six Qwelby and Tullia had found it very difficult to acknowledge that they were different. So much so that they could come running into the house with one saying that they were hurt, when it was the other that had been injured. The family had done everything possible to encourage them to see each other as distinct and separate individuals and form good relationships with other youngsters. The twins' constant rivalry and bickering was seen as evidence of success, although their parents in particular hoped it would not last for too many more years.

CHAPTER 2

BURGLARS

The twins were pulled in two directions. By their twelfth rebirthday they had developed their own distinct personalities and a keen sense of rivalry, yet underlying their whole existence was a fierce need for unity. Today, that was shown by the identical, heavily padded, blue sledsuits they were wearing. Physically, they obviously were a boy and girl in their second Eras, equally tall at one metre eighty-five. Yet in the underlying quantum world, they were identical. Occasionally they would play with that by dressing the same in the fashionable unisex style. Although that did nothing to hide Tullia's female features, they were still able to use the power of thoughtsending to pretend to be each other, even fooling their four closest friends.

On their last visit to Lungunu a tenday ago, their father and his great uncle had been deep in conversation, their thoughts safely contained behind a strong Privacy Shield. That was normal. What had not been normal was the almost guilty reaction when the twins came upon them, as though they were hatching a conspiracy. Guessing that the adults were discussing a new invention, the twins had decided to try and listen to their thoughts.

Tazii did not speak words telepathically. Thoughts consisted of images, impressions, feelings and colours. The more that people were in tune with each other, the closer that became to being as clear as actual words.

Unable to break through the Privacy Shield by themselves, the twins had mentally called on their four best friends to help. Invoking their special group, all six had pooled their energies. It was the first time they had tried working as a group when all six were not physically together. There had only been limited success, but the strange and incomplete mixture of impressions had convinced them all that a secret new project was being developed concerning the twins that was connected to their Aurigan heritage. Whatever was being made had to be secreted in the attic as that was the only part of Lungunu the youngsters were forbidden to explore.

What had been overheard was far too tantalising to ignore. If all six tried to break into the attic that amount of energy was bound to set off the alarms. With their unique skills, the twins might be able to succeed by themselves. Ever since that day they had been waiting for an opportunity to return and try to unravel what they were calling The Mystery.

As they stepped outside their home they were just in time to see Snubble sliding through a little doorway into Barn. Programmed by their father, it had just finished clearing the snow away from all the paths around the house and garden.

At the twins' insistence Shandur had made Snubble look like a snowboy and girl, kneeling side by side and sharing one enormous mouth to suck in the snow. To their disappointment that was then blown out through the ears. Glowing garishly with their favourite colours of purple and lilac, red and green, it was easily visible on the darkest night.

'Open Sesame!' Qwelby commanded as they reached Barn.

'Stop giving things Azuran names!' Tullia complained. 'You're obsessed with that planet with its daft name of Earth.'

'Yeah, I know, the people, they're all weirdos.'

'Takes one to know one.'

'Anyway, what about you searching for Azuran hairstyles?' he challenged, not wanting to lose an argument so early in the day.

'That's different, that's *fashion*. You wouldn't understand. You're a boy!'

Barn contained the family's basic transport. Although looking like primitive sleds open to the elements, they were energy efficient and, as with almost all Tazian equipment, equipped with thought controls and energy shielding. All sleek lines, the fronts of the sleds curved up smoothly to form control columns shaped especially for travelling on water and snow. On the right were the twins' single seaters and two more sleds with seats wide enough for two people. On the left rested the large family sled.

Tullia stood for a moment admiring her sled with its multiple shades of pink.

As Qwelby walked to his, he regretted his choice of colour. The variegated shades of orange and lime green had certainly been eye-catching – from a distance. Close up, it hurt his eyes. After their last visit to Lungunu he had resolved to change it at the first opportunity. He could have mentaformed the new colour scheme whilst the heavy and consistent snowfall had confined them to the house, but Tullia would have known what he was doing. He had an idea for some special effects and definitely did not want her to know if that went wrong.

Yet the time spent at home had been good. Mentally sharing with their four special friends they had all worked hard at their various college studies, building lots of energy credits as a result. Relaxation had been a mixture of games playing and exploring the Racial Memory Archives where, with all six working together, they were able to explore areas that were age restricted to older youngsters and young adults.

It had been frustrating watching the snow fall for five days when it was possible to transweave to Lungunu. Most means of travel such as powersleds or Twistors generated their own power, whereas teleportation required a large amount of external power. Although the power to operate such systems was freely available at source, a personal energy exchange was required for the social costs of the creation and maintenance of the Tsela network that distributed the power. To transweave, they would have had to ask permission, and they could not tell the truth. In theory, any Tazian could tell a lie, but that fact always showed up in that person's own energy field. Hence Tazii did not even think of lying, unless they possessed very advanced mental skills, and even then only with great care.

Each seated on their own sled, they powered up the gravity repulsors, engaged the EMtrac drives and glided out of Barn, thoughtsharing that on their last visit Qwelby had taken the inside track so it was Tullia's turn this time.

'Winner chooses our evening HoloWrapper Adventure?' Qwelby said as his twin came alongside.

'Yay-oh!' Tullia agreed.

Gliding a few centimetres above the snow, the twins swung their sleds around to the front of Siyataka, their home. They dialled down the GravReps so the sleds slowly settled with their broad and curved bases coming to rest on top of the snow. They stood up and reset the control columns into their upright positions. Speeding along without the safety harness they would normally use when seated was all part of the excitement of a race.

The front of the house had been grown from living stone of the palest shade of creamy yellow with veins of soft pink. The mentasculpted decoration reflected the family's interests, with pride of place over the entrance being given to the interlinked disks representing the sun and moon, and their energies essential to all Tazian life. With regular and heavy winter snowfalls that entrance was set at the top of a short flight of steps.

The twins inspected Principal Door, which had already garlanding itself for the winter KeyPoint celebrations. Every year the family eagerly awaited the moment when Siyataka revealed its chosen theme. Naturally, the twins wagered. Their guesses were held securely by Siyataka until midnight on the Turn. The winner's prize and the loser's forfeit were decided by their father's great uncle who delighted in playing games with them.

Principal Door opened, revealing their parents. Shandur held up a hand.

The twins waited.

Their father dropped his hand.

'Eat Snow!!' the twins yelled together as they sped away over the crisp snow, laughing as each sent thoughts trying to make the other lose control and fall off, to end up, literally, eating snow.

As always for a race they were using the challenging route that followed the switchback series of curves of a low range of hills. Side by side, the lead changing with each curve, yet never more than a few centimetres difference, Tullia was in the lead as they swung round a gentle curve to see Lungunu spread before them. Around a central dome, the five wings of the house fanned out like the petals of a flower. The sun shone brightly on the sandy coloured stone effect that was Lungunu's current choice.

As their route bent sharply, hiding the house from view again and signalling the final part of the race, Qwelby felt a sense of triumph. With his twin on the inside of the concave bend he would have a slightly shorter path. Overtaking her, he gunned his sled for more speed for the straight run to Lungunu, only to sweep too wide of the final bend and hear Tullia's cry of triumph as she clung tightly to the inside of the last turn.

As Lungunu came into sight they sensed their sleds level with each other. But. Interference with mental perception was all part of Tazian gamesplay, albeit with strict rules to ensure fairness between different age bands. Glancing sideways they confirmed it. They were nose to nose.

Switching vision, they examined the flowing lines of the planet's magnetic field and each selected a line for the best run. The same line. Although intensely competitive they were Quantum Twins – one. Bent low over the control bars as they accelerated to maximum speed, their eyes opened wide as a series of multicoloured auras of electro-magnetic waves spread out from the house. Buried deep within the domed central section, the Stroems had to be SuperXzyling. Although the Stroems were safely contained within the Cavern, sometimes the effects of their Xzyling reached out well past Lungunu, usually copying the form of the house itself with its five wings. Facing them was a great arc of the planets distorted magnetic field looking like a multi-coloured pathway to the roof. Had their parents been with them they would have been commanded to veer aside, stop and wait for the disturbance to subside.

<*We can do it!!*>

Side by side at full speed their sleds raced up the arc.

'*A Window!!*' they thoughtsent to House.

'*Open!!*' they added as it appeared.

Reaching the crest of the arc they shot through into the attic that formed the top section of all five wings. Thoughtsending to the sleds to power down and stop sent everything sliding across the floor. The twins followed, rolling along the short arm of a T-junction in their thick, padded sled suits, laughing with relief, and agreeing that the race had been a tie.

'Phew. That was close!' Qwelby exclaimed.

'Yes,' agreed House in a grumpy voice. 'Two sekonds later and there would not have been a window there.'

'But you'd have saved us,' Tullia said.

'That's not the point,' House replied. 'You must allow Time for your image-into-action to work.'

'It's not our fault if the Stroems SuperXzyle,' Qwelby added, petulantly.

House made a sound like someone clearing their throat. Difficult when there was no throat to clear. 'Apology accepted.'

'But I wasn't...'

'Tamuchly, House,' Tullia said in a loud voice, overriding her twin and thumping him whilst she tight-beamed so House would not pick up her thought: '*You know how tetchy House gets when the Stroems SuperXzyle, even if it's not yet full moon.*'

11

Qwelby howled like a werebeast and looked at the palms of his hands where hair was growing.

'Oh, do grow up, Kaigii!' an exasperated Tullia said, thumping him again for good measure.

<¡Alarm alert!>

'Aw, House,' Qwelby said, mentastroking the image the twins had given House of an ancient and honoured family retainer. 'You know you enjoy playing with us.' It was his turn to wheedle. He did it well, borrowing Tullia's voice. 'If you don't tell... we won't.'

House was in a quandary. It was a semisentient, which was a very useful attribute but not at moments like this. Because of the emergency caused by the Stroems excessive energy, it had taken the decision to override its programming and allow the twins into the attic. Now, about to sound the alarm as required, it stopped to review its options. Over the years there had been many occasions when it had allowed the twins to do things they shouldn't. If that were to be discovered, House could have its enviable array of functions reduced. Yet their entry into the attic was strictly forbidden.

Qwelby felt Tullia making his mouth smirk. Tullia looked at him as his mouth returned to normal, and they grinned. Drawing on their twinergy, she had slid her mind into the controls and erased the data recording their entry. As its data showed that no-one had entered the attic, there was no reason for the alarm to be sounded. A slightly puzzled House withdrew its awareness from the attic.

'Do you think?' Qwelby asked.

'No.'

They shook their heads in agreement. Gumma, as they called their Great Great Uncle Mandara, could not have deliberately created the wave. They knew that the planet's six XzylStroems were the key to maintaining the essential link with Azura, as the Tazii called Earth. Orchestrating their eruptions and determining specific effects was beyond the capabilities of even as learned a scientist as the Arch-Discoverer of the Academy of Discoverers.

'Lift,' called Qwelby. 'Sleds and suits to the usual places, tamuchly.'

Lift materialised, one side opaqued into not-being-there. The sleds and coats slid inside. The side de-opaqued into looking solid. Lift disappeared.

They looked at one another and smiled. No matter how similar they looked: faces, black hair and fashionable, one-piece bodysuits; they had chosen their favourite, bright colours: Qwelby in emerald green and red, Tullia in purple and lilac.

Free of the coat's hood, Tullia let her hair down and vigorously shook her head. Taking a comb from one of the many carefully concealed pockets in her bodysuit, she ran it through her thick, waist long tresses, green light flickering from the ends as she rearranged her hair into that day's artfully planned, casual-looking, Azuran style.

Qwelby contented himself with running his fingers through his equally thick, shoulder length hair, deliberately flicking the ends so as not to be outdone by the green flickering from his twin's combing.

They looked around, not for the first time in their lives wondering at what appeared to be a convenient juxtaposition of events. They were united in their desire to break into the attic. Even drawing on their Quantum Twinergy they might have failed, yet the unrelated Xzyling had created a situation whereby House had let them in.

Gallia, as they called their Great Great Aunt Lellia, would say that events coming together like that were synchronicities, meaningful occurrences. It happened to the twins from time to time when they seriously wanted to achieve something important: by working together. Sometimes it suited what they wanted, at other times it prevented them from achieving their aim: but then that invariably turned out to have been for the best.

<Explore>

They knew from the slowly moving colourscopes of pale browns and greens on the walls that they were in Gumma's wing of

Lungunu. As they returned to the corridor end of the junction they looked both ways.

<Search>

Standing side by side at arm's length they held hands and tilted their heads to the side, one to the left the other to the right, ready to share the results.

After a while their eyes detected a tiny irregularity in the movement of the colours.

<Reveal>

Each twin took one colour, circled it through their linked memories and played the relevant sequence backwards until the flow across the wall appeared to halt. They smiled as they saw down at floor level a little door set well back behind the false image of a solid wall. On hands and knees they crawled to it.

The lock required a key with two opposed sets of trines. They slid their minds into the lock.

'*No temporal sequencer. This is too easy?*' Qwelby thoughtsent.

'*We're not supposed to be here. Remember!*' Tullia responded

They mentapushed the tumblers into the correct alignment.

In a world where children manipulated energy from a very early age, security was usually on a practical level, with quantum level devices being reserved for where exceptional levels of protection were required. Moving several solid levers, each imbued with additional inertia, required a major effort. Although tumblers were smaller and could not be loaded with so much inertia, juggling the usual two opposed sets of ten required intense skill. But not for the twins with their unique mental bonding.

Inside the room they found a big, colourless trunk that wasn't really there.

Tullia bathed the trunk in a thoughtprojection so that Qwelby was able to examine it. After a few moments, they agreed that there was no conversion alarm.

His green body-suit was slashed with bright red patches shaped like flames. Some of them were pockets, fastened with teethless zips called szeames. He unszeamed one and took out one of Gumma's inventions, a Molecular Gadget Reconstructor, which they had shortened to Mogarcon. It looked like a fat water pistol. Turning a dial on the side caused the free-flowing, phosphorescent energy inside to provide whatever gadget was selected. He chose a temporal readjuster, activated the plasma flow and swept it across the trunk. The air shimmered and a solid, grey trunk appeared.

'No obvious lid. No handles. Two locks, one at each end. Two keys, needs Gumma and Gallia to open. But only one set of tumblers in each,' he announced.

<*Too easy, again??*>

Putting a key in a normal lock, irrespective of the number of sets, the tumblers would jiggle up and down until the key was fully inserted. Turn the key: unlocked. A similar situation for thought projection.

Sliding their minds into the locks they exchanged images.

<*Each key a flat blade – Insert fully – Tines project – Sequence inside to outside – Within a set time sequence – Three interlocking quantum alarms flicking between different time frames – Antimatter components extended to link all three*>

'Deactivating the alarms as a start is well beyond us,' Qwelby said.

'Gumma definitely does not want us to open it,' Tullia agreed.

They grinned.

<*The hard way!!*>

The first alarm was in case a tumbler moved without a keyblade having been inserted. The second was for the time sequence. And the third? They would find out.

Holding hands and merging their energy fields into one so as to achieve maximum synchronicity, they started work. As the last two tumblers slid into place the first two alarms deactivated. Freed of the interlocking, the third disappeared.

The trunk hummed. The twins held their breaths, and sighed with relief when the top opened up like the petals of a flower in full bloom. The trunk now looked like a brown and gnarled tree trunk, its sides almost hidden by the fluorescent white petals of an enormous white moonflower.

'Phew!!' Both of them let out long held breaths and wiped sweat from their brows. 'That was tricky,' they said, their minds momentarily too tired to thoughtshare and to recognise the slightly out-of-focus nature of their surroundings indicating a temporal discontinuity.

Searching through the trunk, Tullia took out a shallow round box. It was dusky pink with an eye on the lid, both the oval and the central orb etched in silver. As she examined it, the oval turned pale blue, the orb purple, and the etching around the orb lavender, matching her own eye.

'Neat,' she said, turning the box so that the eye on the lid matched the angle of hers, then tilted the box until it was exactly parallel with her own eye. The lid opened, as she had expected. Inside was a confusing mix of colours which turned out to be produced by three semi translucent disks of varying shades of blue, green and red.

There was an inner rim that looked as though it could rotate, with a series of little openings through which they thought they could see images. Trying to see them more clearly, Tullia discovered that the rim rotated, but in the opposite direction to what she had expected.

Tullia closed the box and handed it to Qwelby, the eye once again a dusky pink etched in silver. He matched the lid to the plane and angle of his eye just as she had done. The colour of the eye changed to reflect his own and the lid opened.

Agreeing with Tullia to call it Soloc, short for colours backwards, Qwelby closed the lid and put it to one side.

They knew Gumma experimented with Time, which slightly elastic in the fifth dimension. It also had its own colouration. Gumma intended the box to be safely locked away. That meant they were not supposed to have it. Yet it was coded to open for each of them.

<Is this a clue to The Mystery??>

At the bottom of the trunk something coloured seemed to be wriggling. Qwelby delved and picked up a blue and green ball. Looking closer, they realised that the colours were on the inside of a semi-translucent surface. It looked like a map of a world that was inside out. They put that to one side very, very carefully. They knew if they thought too hard about what it might be like to be inside, with the power of image-into-action they could find themselves inside.

Then there was a magic lantern. It was black. The sort of black that wasn't really black, but wasn't dark grey either. They knew it was a magic lantern because the controls didn't make any sense. On one side was a dial that had two layers. The lettering was small and they could just make out the words.

Unlikely < OFF > Possibly   Uncertain < ON > Probably

More < ? > Less

There were cone-shaped projections on two opposing sides. There was a cover over what they assumed was the front one, presumably to stop the photons escaping. Tullia thought about that. *What goes in through the back?* Carefully she put it to one side. Something that odd just had to be useful. *Didn't it?*

A faint chiming sounded in the room and everything shimmered.

'Dragon's Breath!' Qwelby exclaimed. 'The third alarm. When the other two deactivated that one must have been in a future timeframe. That future must be now!'

¡Share! Tullia's thought contained no sisterly request.

Opening his mind and shutting his eyes, Qwelby felt like a rubber band that was stretched and then snapped back.

The alarm stopped.

Feeling sick, Qwelby opened his eyes and saw that the room looked normal. 'Now we're in trouble,' he moaned.

Being told off by his older sister was irritating, but it was part of their relationship. He hated it when they were reprimanded by anyone else as it was always focussed on him. Tullia did what he called her "Little Girly Act," fluttering her long eyelashes, making her oval eyes go completely round and projecting totally unwarranted innocence. How anyone could think she was cute was beyond him!

'Temporal readjustment. The time frame had not reached its end.' Tullia rolled her eyes to the sky at his failure to understand what she had done. Then she made her eyes go round, fluttered her eyelashes, and gave him an overdone, sickly sweet smile.

He wanted to strangle her.

Putting her hands to her throat and making choking noises, she stuck out an elongated, bright pink tongue and made her eyeballs pop out.

He couldn't help it. He laughed.

Their quarrels seldom lasted long, usually descending into silliness and laughter.

'Oh, Kaigii, remember what happened last time?' she said, acting the caring big sister, knowing he always fell for that. *Boys. So easy to manipulate!* She hid the thought behind her Privacy Shield.

Qwelby smiled, also hiding his thought as he allowed himself to be manipulated. She had made him laugh. And he thoughtsent an acknowledgment that he owed her one for saving them from being discovered. Some time in the future she would collect on that.

CHAPTER 3

PICTURES

They never had time to sink back into the memory as a swishing sound made them realise that the room was disappearing into whatever alternate timeframe it normally existed.

<¡Gather:Go!>

Hugging each other they were swept into the corridor. When they looked back, no trace of the door remained. As they eased back from one another and looked down between them, they grinned. Competing was fun, cooperating brought rewards. Trapped between them were all the items they had put on one side together with a fawn coloured canvas satchel. Opening it, they discovered a black box inside in its own pocket, and agreed to examine that later.

Having put all their objects into the satchel, they stood up and mentascanned. The emergency created by the SuperXzyling was over and House was returning to normal. They did not dare summon Lift as that would tell House they were in the attic. They needed to find a door and override the security system for long enough to get well away from the attic. Then they would relax and House would know they were there. Everyone would assume that they had got into their own suite by subverting that part of the security – successfully responding to the challenge set by their great great uncle.

The colourscopes stopped moving and they were plunged into the dark. Qwelby got out the Mogarcon and dialled up a torchlight.

They returned to the T-junction and found the top of a spiral staircase. Qwelby set off first, shining the narrow beam on the steps.

'Will we ever reach the bottom?' Tullia asked after a long time.

'We must do,' answered her twin. 'Lungunu is always a bit strange. Okay, never as weird as this, but it can't be so weird that there isn't a bottom to a staircase. After all,' he said with eminent logic, 'it has got a top.'

'Do you think that life on Earth is ever like this?' Tullia said.

'What makes you say that?'

'Don't know, really. Just been thinking about the flikkers we watch.

Their minds scanned their memories of how ordinary Tazii had come to know something of Azura and its people. It had started when Tazian scientists picked up occasional electronic transmissions. As the years went by and the Azurii plunged further into the quantum world, increasing numbers of their transmissions were captured and the images deciphered: Television programmes being beamed around Earth by satellite.

For the Tazii, taking decisions that affected the whole race took a very long time. As was customary, conflicting interests were eventually accommodated. Transmissions were heavily screened for unacceptable levels of violence, first by a few daring Discriminators and rapidly followed by what were to become increasingly complex, self-programming algorithms. When appropriate age-related categories had been allocated they were made available through specially built facilities called Elmits. The quality was poor, so the programmes were called Flikkers.

The idea behind the Elmits was to give the Tazii a flavour of Azuran life. Hence the rooms where the flikkers were shown were small compared to Tazian rooms; the chairs were totally unresponsive, not transmitting movement, feelings or sensations; there were no moving colourscopes on walls and ceilings, and the pictures themselves were watched on small, flat screens.

Most adults displayed little more than a passing interest. But, as with the young of all races throughout the multiverse, something new caught on and became a fad: in many different directions, including clothes and hair styles from a wide mix of centuries. A weekly visit to an Elmit with friends to laugh at the backward Azurii and their impossible lives became a must.

Recently, the most daring youngsters had taken to visiting one of the new LockDown Clubs. Entry was by wearing Azuran clothing that was completely dissimilar to any current Tazian fashion. Heavy energy emitters ensured that once inside no thoughtsharing or sending was possible, and all auras were scrambled so as to be unreadable. Even the strongest youngster was likely to leave within half an ouer, pleading for sanity. The twins had never visited one. The mere thought of not being in mental contact was enough to give them nightmares.

A whole new range of HoloWrapper Kartoons was created. Even young children screamed with the thrill of being cut into several slices, or flattened by a steamroller followed by the brief experience of life in a two-dimensional world.

The twins laughed. It was not just young children who enjoyed what to the Tazii was a quantum-like sense of fun in the KiddyKartoons.

'Their lives seem so, well, restricted,' Qwelby said. 'Take their sports. They're all solid. Kicking balls, throwing things, no mental interference, nothing exciting. What a life where imagination doesn't work. Not even in their space stories.'

'They have some good effects, though. Pretending it does work.'

'But that's just make-believe.'

'Unkh!!'

Looking at his feet as he was concentrating on lighting the steps, Qwelby had bumped into a wall. He dropped the Mogarcon and the light went out. He got down onto his knees and started to run his hands over the floor.

Click. Before he could ask his twin what she was doing, a small circle appeared on the wall. As it grew, it seemed as though the wall was dissolving, a soft light shining through from outside. As the image cleared they realised they were looking down on a sort of desert.

As their eyes adjusted to the bright light, they were able to make out a large expanse of land. Sandy, red brown and fairly flat with a lot of scrubby bushes and little trees. It seemed to go on forever. They thought it must be a desert because it was so hot and dry, but it wasn't what they thought of as a real desert with big sand dunes and an oasis.

A group of figures appeared at the bottom of the picture. They were making their way steadily across the ground. The twins could see them easily as the trees had very thin branches and no leaves. It was a group of dark brown and almost naked men carrying spears and bows. They paused now and then to check the ground as though they were following the tracks of something.

As the men moved through the trees and out into a wide area of low bushes, a group of women appeared, obviously following the men. Tullia noticed their hair. All wore it close to their heads and woven into many different patterns, except for one. She was a lot taller and bigger built than the others with a reddish colour to her tan. She had long black hair that fell below her shoulder blades in many thin plaits.

Tullia thought there was something familiar about her. She stood up to take a closer look. With a shock she saw she had quite a different view of the scene. It could not be a picture she was looking at. It had to be a window she was looking through. She stood there stunned. *What is happening today?*

The big woman turned round and looked up. Tullia's eyes were drawn to the oddity of her wearing what looked like a necklace made of vegetation. The men came running back to kneel in front of the women, shielding them. A slender youth stood up, hefting his spear. To the twins, it seemed as though the people were staring

22

right at them. The big woman frowned, clearly puzzled rather than frightened. Tullia was sure there was something familiar about her. She wanted a better look. With her arm, she wiped away from the window the mist that had formed from their breath.

An older man gestured. The young man pulled back his arm and threw the spear. The twins ducked and knocked the lantern off the step. Everything went dark as the window disappeared.

They sat back down feeling a bit silly.

'We never go that dark brown. Even Tazii who live in the WarmBand still retain our reddish hue,' Qwelby said feeling very puzzled.

'Did you notice that woman with the long plaits?' Tullia asked. 'There was something familiar about her.'

'No, I was looking at the men with their spears and bows. They must be tracking an animal.'

'Can we can wind the pictures back?' Tullia wondered, desperately hoping that they could.

She picked up the lantern. As she turned the dial she realised that what she thought was the projector with the flap over it, was at the back. A light appeared on the wall. *Oh well, simple mistake.*

The light slowly changed into a picture – *or a window* – thought Tullia. Slowly, whatever it was they were seeing cleared – snow! There was a lot of land, a steep hill sloping down to a more gentle slope and lots of trees. They looked very pretty with their branches all covered in thick snow.

Together they moved closer to the wall and looked at the scene from opposite angles. They agreed. It wasn't a picture they were looking at. The different views they had were exactly as if they were looking through a window. Yet they had gone down the stairs so far they had to be underground.

Whatever the answer, the really big question was: what was the point of the pictures or scenes they were being shown? Just as all Tazii, the twins lived their lives intimately connected with the quantum world, where everything was connected in one way or another. There had to be a reason, however difficult it might be to find the answer.

The lantern made a soft humming sound and the scene disappeared.

Tullia turned one of the dials around. Click, click. Nothing happened. Taking a deep breath, she thought: *In for a Quark, in for a Twistor*, and tried turning the other dial backwards. Kcilc. The Lantern shuddered and a window reappeared. It was fuzzy and bright. All they could see was a greyish white colour. Feeling very unsettled, they sat and waited for a picture, or a scene, to appear.

When nothing happened they summonsed up their courage and stood up to look through what they had accepted must be a window. The view was still very fuzzy. Strange shapes were dotted along the hillside. One of them was larger than the others. As they watched, it split into three as they saw two shapes move to either side of the third.

In silent agreement, the twins used their arms to wipe away the condensation on the window, just as two of the figures turned and looked up, right at them it seemed.

'A snowman!!'

'Children??'

'Our sort of age??'

'Pale faces and blonde hair!!'

They turned to look at one another, each seeing the look of amazement in the other's eyes.

'Azurii!!'

Tullia was intrigued by the girl's hair style. A series of multi-coloured rings around the top of her head. How had she created that effect?

'Kaigii?' She turned to look at her twin. His face was pressed against the window, his eyes two violet ovals. Concerned, as he was only a boy, younger than her, and she had to look after him, she moved alongside and gently put her arm around him so as not to disturb his deepstate.

Something was different. She leant her head against his and searched. He was not there! He had left his body and gone travelling. That meant using the seventh dimension. They had done that a few times with full preparation and under close supervision by Lellia in her special Seliya Chamber. And always together.

CHAPTER 4

TRAVELLING

Qwelby was puzzled. A moment ago he had been looking down through a window, now he was only metres away from what had to be Azurii. He tried to move. He was stuck inside something. Inside whatever it was he could just squirm around a little. Then it struck him. He was in the snowman!

Roaring Xzarze! I'm in my energy body. On Azura! 'Busana!' he called, naturally using Tazian as the only language he knew to say "Hallo." There was no reaction. 'Buuuusana!' he yelled. Still no reaction. The youngsters could not hear him.

'Flaming Werebeasts! This is madness. If I go back and tell Kaigii I don't know what's happening, she'll hold that over me for the rest of my life. Xzarze. No!

'Seventh dimension,' his Intuition said.

'Blazing Novas, of course!' he exclaimed, and opened his memory to those studies. Relaxing, he composed his body as best as possible, breathed deeply and steadily and settled into his Kore. Then he expanded his energy field out through the snowman, into the ground and far enough to encompass the two youngsters.

He discovered that it was the first heavy snowfall of the year and the whole village was out for the day celebrating with snowball fights and making snowmen. He was inside one of several snowmen in a row facing a forest at the side of what in a few days time was to become the local ski slope. Midwinter was some time away. That was why there was a fuzziness to everything. He had gone back in time!

How many times had he dreamed of this, played with Wrenden at being slow, clumsy Azurii, stuck on the ground, confined to travelling in boxes on roads and unable to use image-into-action. Alright, he was stuck in the snowman, but Dragon's Breath! this was amazing, better than any deepstate he'd ever experienced.

The boy he'd seen a few moments ago was talking to him. Or that was how it seemed. Wearing a dark blue anorak with the neck of a blue and white sweater showing, Qwelby named him BlueBoy. Unable to hear or be heard he felt frustrated.

The girl appeared. She was wearing a lilac anorak with a white scarf around her neck. Under a multi-coloured woollen hat her long blonde hair fell over her shoulders. It was not as long and thick as most Tazii, but there was something about her that Qwelby liked. He named her LilacGirl.

They looked just like Azurii did in flikkers, except seeing them for real they did not look quite so ugly with their horizontal eyes, small noses and mouths. The boy was a lot taller than the girl and both had white skin with bright red cheeks.

He saw that they were happy, shy, liking each other, not knowing what to say. They must be meeting for the first time. But how weird! How on 'Tazia did they manage without reading each other's energy fields? Then he realised. Their auras did not spread out past their thick clothing, but he was still able to see them!

'Seventh dimension,' his Intuition said.

Qwelby wanted to meet them. Once again he tried to move, wave, call out. Nothing happened. Then they turned their backs on him, looking up into the sky.

Qwelby followed their gaze and saw a faint image. It looked like a small, round blurry cloud with two dark objects in the middle. 'That's me. Up there!' he called out, and felt stupid when they did not react.

Still looking up into the sky, they moved closer to each other. Hesitantly, each reached out a hand, touched, and held. They turned to look at one another, faces pink from more than the cold. Their lips moved.

'You've seen us! That's me and Kaigii, up there, somewhere,' Qwelby said aloud, desperately hoping that something would change and they would hear him.

In an instant, the energies changed. Three boys had arrived, all with pale faces, pink cheeks and short, blonde hair. Two were shorter than BlueBoy, the third was about the same height and bigger built. BigBoy was speaking. His arm lashed out straight towards Qwelby. He did not have the room to duck! The fist passed right through him.

'Roaring Xzarze!' Qwelby exclaimed, for no-one to hear, as an altercation proceed in front of him.

One of the boys made a grab at the girl's hat. BlueBoy stepped in the way. There was pushing, then a fight. The biggest boy stood watching with his arms folded as BlueBoy held his own for a few moments against the other two. Then he and one of his attackers went down in a tangle with BlueBoy on top.

Seeing blood on the face of the attacker, Qwelby was nearly sick. Violence simply did not exist on Vertazia. All Tazii knew how violent the Azurii were. After a lot of persuading, Discriminators had eventually allowed Tazii to see the make-believe violence in Azurii KiddyKartoons. But this, this was real, human to human. He had been stunned to witness that. And now real, human blood!

The other boy drew back his leg to kick BlueBoy. LilacGirl grabbed the attacker's arm. He swung around aiming a punch at her face. BigBoy stepped in between, his mouth working, red anger flaring in his aura. Pushing the girl away, he grabbed the boy's arm, spun him around and kicked him hard. He fell down into the snow. Out of the corner of his eye Qwelby saw LilacGirl fall on top of BlueBoy who had been getting up, bearing him back into the deep snow.

BigBoy walked across to where the first attacker was still lying in the snow. With lots of angry red still flaring through his aura, he kicked him to get up, then turned and kicked the other one.

Qwelby could see from their energy fields that the two boys in the snow were not badly hurt, but there were strong, dirty yellow streaks of cowardice running through their auras. They got up looking shamefaced. Qwelby did not understand why BigBoy was angry with them. From the gestures, it had seemed as if it had been BigBoy who had told one of the others to take the girl's hat. Punishment for their failure? What a weird world!

By the time Qwelby thought to look around, BlueBoy and LilacGirl were almost out of sight, holding hands as they walked downhill. He smiled, thinking that was nice, yet puzzling. Their energy fields were showing soft pinks and pale greens. They liked one another. But he was sure from his energy sensing that had not been present when the girl had arrived. They looked about the same age as himself and Tullia, so too young to be interested in each other. *Ah, but, Azurii. . They live shorter lives so grow up quicker than we do. I can't imagine being interested in a girl.*

He felt dizzy, hollow, was he fainting?

Tullia had become concerned as her twin had gone very cold. She knew it was a sign of travel in the seventh dimension. But was still unable to believe that he had gone without any preparation as Lellia had always said that wasn't possible. She remained there looking through the window with an arm around him. The window was misting up from their breath. With her free arm she wiped it away.

Taking her twin's weight as the window closed and he sagged against her, she spoke to cover up her relief that he had returned from wherever.

'LAIM boy,' she said, but without the usual bite in her voice. Standing for "Look After Idiot Male", it was what she and her friend Tamina used for Qwelby and Wrenden when they had got themselves into a mess by being stupid.

Qwelby shook his head. 'Not my fault, Kaigii. Not this time. I was just looking. Then I was in the snowman.'

As she helped him sit down, she could see his eyes twirling fast, the purple shot through with vivid splashes of red and orange.

'Out of your body?'

'Dragons Breath! But it was exciting,' he added.

Before she could ask him about it, the lantern hummed and the window reappeared. They saw the desert again. They were too tired by everything that had happened to get up and look closely. Slowly their minds asked why, as they were looking up at a picture, they seemed to be looking down on a scene that was outside.

Qwelby was aware that his twin had gone very still. Mentally he felt for her. She was not there. And she was cold. The cold of having left her body! Tenderly, he wrapped an arm around her and pulled her to lean against him. It felt good. However much they competed, underneath it all they were one.

Tullia was high up above the ground, as though looking through the window at the same desert. But there was no window and a different group of people. Expanding her energy field she was vividly aware of everything that was taking place and, just as in a dreamstate, understood what was happening.

Several dark-skinned women wearing little clothing were gathering plants and roots. It was mid-morning and the sun was burning down from a clear blue sky. It was mid-summer and soon the temperature would rise close to forty degrees, far too hot for work.

They stopped working. She saw a skinny girl slump into the semi-shade of an acacia tree. The girl's mother produced what looked like a potato. Oval, white, the size of a small fist, she handed it to the girl, who passed it on to her smaller sister. The younger girl bit into it, wiped her mouth with the back of her hand, and returned the food to the older girl.

Several others were also eating. When they had finished, the whole group gathered up the plants and tubers they had collected and headed for home, carefully wending their way past bushes that carried needle-like spikes. Reaching their village, the women moved to sit in the shade of small, conical shaped huts made of what looked like very long, grey grass.

With a jolt, Tullia felt herself swoop down and land on the red sandy ground inside the village. She looked around for the two young girls she had noticed and a little way away she saw a group of young children sitting cross-legged in a semi circle. Opposite them and almost facing her was a slender young man. All were almost naked.

The man looked up, right at her. She gulped. What to say? Then he looked back down and she saw his mouth move. He was speaking and she could not hear him. He had not seen her. She looked down at her legs. 'Whistling Xzarze! Where are they?' She jerked her head up as she realised she had spoken aloud. No reaction from anyone. They had not heard.

Rapidly she ran her hands down her body, legs and feet. 'I AM here. It's just that I'm invisible! Blazing Novas, that was a shock.' She took deep breaths and calmed herself whilst she reviewed the available data. She'd thought she'd been in a dreamstate, now she was as certain as could be that like her twin she was travelling Out-Of-Body. To be able to feel herself as normal meant she was in her InForming Matrix, the energy body that was effectively the blueprint for her normal, fifth dimensional body, and allowed Tazii to travel in the seventh dimension.

She reassured herself by walking around. There were a lot of footprints all over the sandy soil. She thought she saw the tiniest depression where she stepped, but... she was not sure.

Having moved to the side of the group she saw that various items were spread on the ground between the man and the children. There were nuts, leaves and berries, a small piece of creamy coloured root, a short thin stick of dark wood, a loop of

31

string, a twig and then what had to be jewellery. She recognised a bracelet, two earrings and a necklace, all made from a mixture of what looked like white and dark brown beads. After a while, the man covered everything with a cloth.

It was a memory game Tullia had often played. 'HornsFlute! This is exciting.' She walked up and sat at the edge of the group. When the man took the covering away she was ready to play. When the items were covered again she started whispering to herself as she recalled what she had seen.

A sort of tickle on the crown of her head made her look up. The skinny young girl she had first noticed was looking at her, not straight on, but out of the corner of her eye. Tullia felt a shiver run through her. She licked her lips and, feeling stupid, waved her hand. The girl turned her head to look straight at her. Then turned back again, obviously trying to see out of the corner of her eye.

Movement. Tullia saw the young man turn around and signal to the girl to go away.

'Xzarze!' Tullia cursed him aloud, and saw the girl turn back, look right at her, then shrug her shoulders and continue to walk away.

Tullia was annoyed, she was sure she'd just been about to make contact with an energy sensitive girl. Very dark brown skins, black hair, lovely soft energy fields, a gentle people. The girl's hair, an interesting style closely woven over her head. And the jewellery most wore, simple necklaces and bracelets made from natural materials. 'Native' seemed to be the right word.

Tullia felt herself sinking deep into the energy field of the village, information flooding in. The girl and boy were brother and sister. She was responsible for the younger girls as she was the oldest girl-not-yet-woman.

That must mean she's in her second Era. Tullia thought. *Yet she's much too small to be that old. Can't be more than six or seven.*

Tullia saw sunbeams spreading across the ground. The sand

became darker red and the individual grains grew larger and started to move into a pattern. She felt meaning unfolding...

'Data *overload*,' her Intuition said. And she toppled towards the dark red ground.

CHAPTER 5

A DANGEROUS DESCENT

Qwelby felt his twin sag against him as she returned.

'EPT,' she murmured. 'HornsFlute! It was amazing.' She knew her eyes were twirling rapidly. So rapidly she felt dizzy. 'Tell later.' She snuggled her head against her twin's shoulder. Well, he always wanted to look after her. He could. Just for now.

EPT, Qwelby mused, Extra Physiological Travelling, a fancy title used for travelling out of one's normal body. The easiest way for any Tazian to do that, and all they could manage at their age, was to use what was termed the InForming Matrix: the energy body that in essence was the blueprint for their own fifth dimensional Forms.

Qwelby felt nice, cuddling his twin. She was ten minits older than him, and to his intense annoyance not only believed but acted as though she had to look after him. But it was his duty to look after her, she was only a girl. And he sensed she wanted reassurance that the icy fingers he sensed in her were not premonitions. How could they be?

By itself, using the InForming Matrix for travelling was not a matter for concern. They had done it before with special preparation and as a form of lucid dreaming, but this was completely different. They had only been looking at pictures.

<*Questions for Gallia*>

With that they agreed that they needed to share the detail of what each had experienced.

'I'd like to go there for real, meet the people I was with. Their lives look so different from ours,' Tullia murmured later, still deep amongst her memories from the sharing. Perhaps it was the strangeness of still allowing herself to enjoy being comforted by her younger twin that let her be enfolded in his excitement at the more vivid sensations he had experienced.

Qwelby could not believe his ears. When he talked about visiting Earth, it always started one of their arguments. He never understood why. She enjoyed looking at Azuran flikkers as much as he did. Admittedly for different reasons: he was into adventure whereas her interests were more for clothes and hair styles.

'I like the heat,' he said, turning to look at his twin. 'But I prefer snow and skiing to having sand getting into everything.'

'One world each and we'll share experiences,' she suggested.

'Yeah. Double the fun,' he said with a laugh, knowing it could never happen.

In the dark their eyes appeared brighter than normal. Each saw the others gently twirling. Mentally they shared that each had experienced the same sensation: as though every cell in their bodies had tingled, accompanied by a impossible sense that that had happened before – a long, long time ago.

Tullia pulled herself out of her dreamy state and her twin's encircling arms, and rubbed the centre of her forehead, watching him rubbing the crown of his head. Their eyes twirled faster as they wondered at their actions: as if they had just removed the headgear they had worn for playing Dragons and Unicorns when they were younger.

'Let's find the Morgarcon and discover a way out,' Tullia said, breaking the discomforting sensation.

'Anything useful in the bag?' Tullia asked when the torchlight had not shown any signs of a possible exit.

There was the one item that had already been in the bag. Not knowing what it was, Qwelby decided to try that. He pulled out a box that was about the size of a book. As he showed it to his twin, it didn't look like something that was coloured black, rather it looked so black that it wasn't there. But he knew it was as he could feel it resting on the palms of his hands and see his thumbs on top.

'Here,' he said, passing it to his twin.

Tullia took it in her hands and gasped. It felt alive.

Carefully she put it down on the floor and took her hands away. It disappeared. She reached out a hand and rested it on the box. It reappeared.

They heard each other swallow.

'What are the three E's of Learning,' Tullia said.

'Enquire, Explore, Experiment.'

'So?'

Nervously, Qwelby picked up the Mogarcon and turned the dial, watching the display for a gadget that might help. A picture of an eye appeared in the side panel. He showed it to his twin who grunted her approval.

He pointed the Mogarcon at the box and pressed the trigger. It hummed and the lid lit up with the words:

Unidirectional Transweave Projector
Experimental Prototype

'What?' asked Qwelby as Tullia exclaimed, 'Not possible!'

They knew that for teleportation to work there had to be a unit at either end, and each always had both a transmitter and a receiver.

Holding his breath, he pressed the trigger again and ran the muzzle around the edges of the box, jumping back as it started to move. The lid folded back and the box opened out. Very thin, rigid sheets of duraskin spread out until the twins were looking at a shimmering rectangle, large enough for one person to stand on, with a narrow, shiny, metallic-looking edge. Then, from one of the longer sides, a page sized sheet of duraskin slid out, lit up and turned into a monitor screen. At the bottom was a row of entry fields and a tiny numeric keypad. As they watched, words appeared on the screen.

Enter Co-ordinates
TriNumeric
Or
Visual

They agreed, that was logical. TriNumeric would be altitude, latitude and longitude. Not knowing any of those they would have to use Visual.

Whatever destination they agreed to image, a Darkness appeared preventing them from visualising any of them clearly enough. The Darkness was not tangible, yet it had a foul smell.

'We need help,' Tullia said.

'Yeah. Our friends?' Qwelby suggested.

'Yes. But focus on one,' Tullia said

'Errm...' he thought of Wrenden, but he knew what Tullia would say.

'Tamina.'

'Agreed.'

Tamina was Tullia's elderest, a sort of caring older-sister-cum-guide. Nearly seventeen-years-old and approaching the end of her fifth phase of creativity, she was the most sensible of the six of them, well most of the time anyway.

Into their sending Tullia added an image of a smiling bird, which she knew Tamina would understand. She watched it become swallowed up in a cloying feel of the same Darkness, hoping it would get through.

A few moments later a relieved Tullia was able to pass on to Qwelby that contact had been made and Tamina would return in twenty minits.

About 24 Azuran minutes, thought Qwelby. And wondered why he was thinking so much about that strange planet.

They relaxed, relieved that the end of their disturbing day was near.

Twenty minits later the twins felt the combined energies of all four friends. Tamina had gathered together Wrenden, her almost fourteen-year-old brother and fifteen-years-old Shimara and Pelnak. With the Darkness swirling around, even all of them together found it impossible to hold a visualisation of any specific destination strongly enough. Reluctantly, they agreed there was only one concept on which they could all focus. 'Up, Up, and Away.'

After a few moments a picture of a beautiful blue sky with one or two fluffy clouds formed in their minds. Then the top of a bell tower. *A bell tower, what's that?* It looked so peaceful and ...

A click came from Mandara's machine and the soft humming grew in intensity.

The screen showed a large number *10*

'?'

9

They froze

8

thoughtshared: *We must go!!*

7

leapt to their feet as

6

Tullia grabbed the lantern and helped

5

Qwelby stuff items back into the bag

4

as they stepped onto the base

3
standing on each other's feet as they struggled to get all four
feet inside the metallic edge
2
about to fall off, they grasped each other
1
teetered sideways
0
and fell.

Disoriented, their teeter turned into a painful fall onto a hard surface. They pulled themselves up into sitting positions and grabbed at one another as they gasped in dismay. They had landed on a narrow walkway that ran around a circular tower made of dark stone. Looking up there was a domed, black roof. Around the walkway were several small windows.

Their eyes locked, each saw the other run a tongue around their lips. Slowly, they looked back up. Dozens of bats were hanging upside-down from the roof. The name 'Belfry Bats' slid into their minds. They gulped.

Staying on hands and knees, each crawled to a separate window, grabbed hold of the stone sill and looked over. Far below all was peaceful. A wide expanse of grass that stretched away to a low range of hills.

The twins had never been up a bell tower before. In fact they were sure there was no bell tower at Lungunu. They looked all around. No sight of the house.

'Lungunu must be the other side of those hills,' suggested Qwelby.

'And the snow stopped over there,' Tullia tried to sound as though she believed that.

'Would fit,' he agreed.

'Yeah,' she said, unconvinced.

They could not see any obvious way down from the bell tower.

No lift, no graviton descenders, no stairway waiting to be thoughtprompted into appearance. Thinking that around Lungunu it was always a sensible precaution to have non-quantum items in reserve, their peered over the edge. Not even any ladders or challenging handholds in the smooth walls to be seen.

They looked at the ropes dangling from the bells and shook their heads.

Feeling more unsettled than ever before, not daring to stand up on the narrow walkway they had landed on, they crawled to each other and sat down with their legs dangling over the edge. They merged auras and tried to restore contact with their friends.

Darkness.

With mounting panic they tried Dad, Gumma, Gallia and their mother.

Thick, smelly Darkness.

They looked into each other's twirling eyes, purple shot with greys and browns and even yellows. Whatever was preventing them reaching outside, was not preventing them from sharing. They watched as each pair of eyes settled down and a soft purple colour returned, although still tinged with ochre.

<Down the ropes>

A massive wooden beam about the width of one of their feet extended from one side of the tower to the other. From it hung three bells. Attached to the top of each bell was a much smaller wooden beam sticking out horizontally. From the far end of that dangled a rope. Pulling the rope made the bell swing against the clapper. As the rope was released the bell swung back, the other side striking the clapper.

The bells were a soft copper colour. The ropes were twirls of alternating red and white. The very prettiness making a contrast to the dark walls of the tower was reminiscent of a scene from a HWScary they had wrapped into, with a frightening, brightly coloured clown.

They would have to crawl along the beam from opposite sides, reach out and jump or fall and catch a rope. Looking down the outside of the tower they had seen that it was a long way down to the ground. Looking down the inside, they saw it was just as far. Imagination was not working!

<*If we fall...*>

Looking across and seeing the colours swirling through the other's energy field, they knew this was not a competition. They needed to work together.

'No time like the present,' said Tullia.

'I'd prefer tomorrow,' quipped Qwelby.

'Nutter,' she responded, with a shake of her head.

'About to be,' he said as he started to crawl to one end of the beam.

In position at opposite ends of the beam they looked at one another, licked lips and grimaced.

'Don't look down,' was Tullia's attempt at breaking the tension as they started to crawl towards each other.

They stared into each other's twirling eyes, disturbed by the sight yet comforted that each was feeling the same. Reaching the two end bells, they stopped.

'Do it in two. Go for the bar. Land on your stomach. As the bar tilts, slide down...' Qwelby started.

'And grab the rope,' Tullia finished.

'Don't look up,' Qwelby quipped.

'I'm scared,' Tullia called out.

'Me two,' Qwelby called back, sending a picture with the spelling.

Tullia managed a faint smile.

<*One, two, go!!*>

They leapt and hit the bars. Two massive 'CLANGS' shook the tower as they slid off the ends of the bars, fell, and grabbed at the thick ropes. Swinging, they were jerked up and down as the bells swung back and forth.

Hundreds of squeaking bats launched themselves into the air. They swarmed around, seeking the windows. Too many had awoken at the same time to make their way through those above the bells. A lot of them flew down below the bells, heading for the windows further down. Qwelby was sliding down the rope to get away from them, swinging as several battered into him.

Hanging on to the wildly swinging rope he heard Tullia's scream above the deafening sound of the bells. A bat was entangled in her long hair. Another joined it. Trying to free its companion or attacking Tullia made no difference to her. She screamed again. Waved an arm at them, slipped, yelled, her gyrating form swinging the rope around.

Qwelby was sliding down fast as he batted at the bats with one hand.

A piecing scream of pure, unalloyed panic cut through his annoyance. Looking up, he saw Tullia had used both hands to free her hair of the bats and the rope was swinging out of her reach.

She seemed to hang in mid air.

Ignoring the bats, he gripped his rope with both hands and swung his legs.

Gravity pressed down on Tullia.

Qwelby swung his legs again, desperately trying to make the rope work like a pendulum.

Seeing his twin swooping down on him with her arms reaching out, took him back to a HWAdventure. He had been flying through the air to be caught by the other trapeze artiste. But now he had to catch Tullia. He had to take one hand off the rope. This was real life and there was no safety net.

'ALWAYS TOGETHER!' he thoughtscreamed as he swung his legs once more and stretched out his hand.

She grabbed him and crashed into his body. He felt her hand slipping, saw her eyes twirling faster than he'd ever seen, brilliant purple shot through with crimson and ochre. His fingers were straightening, he could not stop them slowly uncurling, watching helplessly as she slid down.

The rope was running through his left hand. Panic was rising in his stomach as he feared he could not keep his grip. Millimetre by millimetre, in seeming slow motion he watched Tullia slide out of his grip. His mind was frozen, his throat so choked he was unable to cry out.

He watched her long black hair flying out and up above her head as she fell. Felt her arms wrap around his leg, watched as she slid down, gasped as his body jerked as she stopped to hang, swinging from his foot. He reached up with his right hand and grasped the rope. As hard as he gripped, he could not slow their descent.

Running through both hands, the rope was burning, burning. He wanted to use his imagination to ease the pain but dared not. He focussed his mind on sending his twin the image-into-action of her holding onto his foot.

With both hands on the rope he could not look down. Trying to measure how far they had to fall he looked up and saw the bells rushing away from him at a frightening speed. There was a crash and a cry of pain from below, then a jarring smash as he thudded into Tullia. Arms and legs all tangled, they righted themselves into each other's arms, holding fiercely, searching each other's energy fields.

'You saved me!' she cried. 'Gave me the strength to hang on!'

'I wanted a soft landing,' he replied.

'Beast!'

'Kaigii.'

'Yeah.'

It was time to let out oohs and arghs of pain, run their hands over their bodies and search inside. They agreed. *Nothing broken. Lots of bruises and burns.*

'Oh Kaigii, your hands,' Tullia exclaimed, as she gently took them and let them lie on the palms of her own hands. She bent her head and softly hummed healing energy into them, flickers of green light running from the crown of her head all the way along her hair. His hands were badly burnt and she let her soft tears well up and fall, watching the burns start to heal.

'You love me!' Qwelby exclaimed.

'Don't kid yourself,' she replied.

Mentally hugging, they shared their healing energies. As new skin spread over his palms, Tullia helped Qwelby up. With an arm around each other they stepped through the open doorway just as the sun dipped below the horizon and Night threw her cloak of darkness over the land. They looked around. Where were they? Far away there was a faint glow from behind the hills, which they hoped was from Lungunu. They stepped forward and shivered as if they had passed through a waterfall.

Aided by the half moon, millions of stars spread their twinkling light across the snow.

<Snow?!>

They looked behind them. The bell tower had disappeared.

<Home...Where??>

They looked at their wristers. After XOÑOX had been formed, Pelnak had made a special wrister for each of them. Discovering that the Azurii believed they could capture and measure Time in all manner of differently shaped boxes, and wore them strapped to their wrists, a wrister had become a Tazian fashion fad.

Pelnak had made all theirs in the pattern of an eye, appropriately coloured for each of them. Around the edge of the central orb a tiny facsimile of Vertazia rotated, matching its daily passage around the sun. There were a number of thought-controlled functions and a multi-coloured communicator that only worked between the six of them.

A large green arrow on each wrister pointed in the same direction. They swung their arms around and, like compass needles finding North, the arrows continued to point in the same direction. Knowing in which direction to send their thoughts, wearily they leant on each another. Tullia concentrated on sending 'Home *please,'* to their father, whilst Qwelby imaged a fire inside each of them. A few moments later they sagged with relief as they received his thought: *'Wait.'*

They soon heard a swishing sound as he arrived on the family PowerSled. Confident that he could master the necessary energies for a short while, he had not delayed to put on a sled-suit which he could have plugged in to keep him warm, instead, he had draped a bright red cape over his shoulders. He helped his children climb aboard and wrapped them in reassurance as they collapsed onto the rear seat and the energy field comfortably snuggled them in.

They could feel his concern. It was nice. Like his great uncle, he was a quantum scientist. A quiet man who went through life with a slightly bemused expression on his face as though he watched everything from a distance. The twins were pleased that he had come for them. Their mother would be so worried she would have asked lots of questions and drained their energy.

CHAPTER 6

UNSETTLING NEWS

As the twins walked in through the door, their mother surprised them by not asking any questions. Although looking more than usually harassed she gave each of them an energy feed with a big hug. 'Go on through to the gather room. Uncle Mandara is waiting for you. I'll bring hot drinks,' she said.

As they entered the room Shandur sat to one side in an armchair, leaving the twins to sit down together on a settee opposite his great uncle. Mandara was sitting in a comfy armchair in his own study, wearing his usual working tunic: dark green with so many pockets they knew it was easy for him to forget in which one he had put whatever he wanted.

<Why...>

'There is so much disturbance around Lungunu that it's not safe to transweave,' Mandara said, cutting off their thoughtsharing.

The twins liked him. Like his wife, he was over one hundred and thirty years old, and at that age both of them were termed Elders. Two metres twenty tall, he was a big man in every way. His face had lots and lots of lines on it. They looked like the sort of lines that came to a person who had lived a very long time and who had probably seen everything there was to see. His hair had prematurely lost the family dark brown and was white, shining and long. He was a quantum physicist with a very soft spot for his great great niece and nephew. They loved it when he had fun with them in his own way, especially inventing unusual gadgets for them.

With him using so much energy by projecting so as to be personally present the moment they arrived, they knew they were in trouble. Both of them, and equally. They didn't want to reveal how worried they were by holding hands, instead, they casually leant against each other as though tired.

'Are you hurt in any way, on any level?' he asked.

'No,' they replied together

He ran his fingers through his hair. Instead of lying down neatly it stuck out all over. With a light that was artfully arranged to be shining from behind the chair he used for projecting, it looked like he was wearing a large, round, translucent hat. Unusually for him his brown eyes were not twinkling, and all the wrinkles on his forehead made a puzzling frown.

Relaxing at his tone of voice, the twins noticed from his energy field that he was more worried and concerned than angry.

Lellia, his wife, appeared and sat on one of the arms of the chair. Of average build and a little on the short side, she was a marked contrast to her husband. She usually wore flowing robes of a gentle mix of pastel colours, co-ordinating with the seasons as they passed. That day, soft ivories and creams with hints of palest pinks and turquoises. Her hair was more midnight blue than black, with an unusual streak of white that fell to one side. 'In sympathy with my husband,' she would say with a laugh when asked.

'There has been an exceptionally strong eruption of the XzylStroem today,' she said. 'There was a lot of disturbance in the Trans-Temporal Energy field. What happened? Are you all right?' She glanced at Mizena as her great niece entered.

The twins took the drinks from their mother. She usually wore her shiny, black hair in a single or double braid, with the shorter side pieces hanging free over her ears. They could tell how anxious she had been from what the family called the worry-tangles in the sides. They sipped their drinks as they provided a summary of the strange things that had happened. They were excited when Mandara explained the adventure with the Bell Tower as their first experience of the out-of-space-and-time nature of a NullPoint. Yet they could see that Gumma and Gallia, as they called their great great uncle and aunt, were very worried as they openly shared that the room the twins had found should have remained hidden in its own time-frame, and the trunk should have remained invisible.

He was relieved that the third alarm had worked, ejecting the twins before they had been able to find any more of his rejected or unfinished experiments. His biggest concern was that they had found the lantern. It was one of his many attempts to recover long lost Aurigan science. He had never been certain whether or not it was working, and had locked it away, concerned that the whole concept was too dangerous to develop.

That it had worked for the twins raised disturbing thoughts, most of all in Lellia's mind. She felt that none of the others fully appreciated the intense energy the twins possessed at a deep level.

Mandara was staggered at the level of skill the children had demonstrated in opening the locks. He had carefully crafted them so only he and his wife acting together could do that. Behind their Privacy Shields, he shared with the adults his concern that the group of six had the power to create such an extremely rare inter-dimensional rift. 'There are times when you pair are too clever for your own good,' he said, whilst allowing his aura to show a mixture of concern and pride.

<Yah-oh!!>

With the twins too tired to successfully shield their jubilation, Mandara shook his head in mock despair.

'I'm worried about that Darkness that seems to have seeped into the MentaNet,' Mizena said. 'Kumelanii or Shakazii?'

'It must be the Kumelanii, Lellia replied. 'They are ultra traditional and intensely dislike the idea of Quantum Twins...'

'Why??' the twins asked, interrupting her.

'I think it is because it reminds them how far we have fallen since the Aurigan heyday when we had all twelve segments of DNA, fully active,' Lellia said. 'They claim it never happened in Aurigan times. But cannot produce any records to evidence that.'

'And it's because we have three identical segments that Qwelby and I can be... what we are,' Tullia said.

'Yes. It creates your extremely strong bond. And makes you very special to us,' Mizena said.

'And I sense an element of fear in their attitude to the twins, especially from the Custodians to whom the Kumelanii look for guidance,' Lellia continued. 'But not the Shakazii. As you know, our daughter and her pairbond have worked with them for years. They are forward looking and the only, sadly small, sector of the Tazii who see the disastrous situation facing us.'

A heavy silence settled in the room as Lellia mentally tightbanded apologies to the adults for having voiced the last few words in front of the children.

Sending images of restless sleep, nightmares and persistent questioning, Mizena tightbanded her thoughts that it was better that the situation was explained right away

'What is serious is that not just the Kumelanii, but the majority of Tazii won't face the fact that we are, well, dying out,' Lellia said. '??!!'

She nodded sadly. 'Our third segment makes us unbalanced. Through an excessive focus on harmony and cohesion it produces our peaceful lifestyle, but with a serious lack of drive, and fertility. Put simply, as each generation passes we produce fewer and fewer children. Our total population is fast approaching a critical number, below which we will not be able to continue with our way of life. Then there will be a rapid descent spiral and...' She raised her hands in a gesture of despair, whilst thoughtsending images of that being a very, very long time in the future.

The twins were so tired that Mizena had gently slipped into the surface of their minds without them noticing. She squeezed her husband's hand at the insubstantial nature of the images, hoping that tiredness meant they had not noticed what was a sure sign of her great aunt's deception.

'It's not just that we have to recombine with the more numerous Azurii to have the energy to restore our Aurigan heritage, but, if we don't... we will die?' Tullia asked.

Lellia took a deep breath. She had already bent the truth, now she was faced with telling a direct lie. The twins were tired... She sensed a probing. It had Tullia's signature. She glanced at Mizena. She had temporised too long. The probing was stronger, now carrying the twins' joint signature.

Feeling trapped, she had to answer truthfully. 'No.' There was a sense of triumph in their probing as the twins withdrew.

'The Azurii are rapidly driving their world to destruction,' Lellia explained. 'To survive, they need our third segment with all that means. Then together we can work to restore our common heritage. Generations, millennia away. But right now we need to reverse the changes that have been made that stifle us.' She held up a hand. 'This is something we did not want you to know until you were much older...'

'Adults??' the twins interrupted.

'Yes,' Lellia confirmed. 'I am talking about a time several generations away...'

'In our lifetimes??'

Once again Lellia took a deep breath. 'Probably.'

'But I don't understand,' Tullia said, dredging up the last of her energy. 'Why aren't we doing anything about this?'

'Kumelanii, Custodians, have weaved a web that the two are linked. That the way forward is through the carefully crafted development cycles and that the Shakazii need to return to the mainstream patterns before we can progress. But our people are so afraid of violence that most of them have let themselves be persuaded that recombination can only happen when there is peace on Azura...'

'They'll never...' Tullia blurted, her energy field radiating her alarm. '¡LockDown!' Qwelby thoughtsent. Called the ShadowMarket, there was a SubNet culture amongst older youths that the twins had been able to worm their way into. Not only had that to be protected at all costs, the twins knew their parents would never approve of some of the forms of energy exchange they provided for what was very definitely forbidden material: deep access into the Archives and heavily shielded knowledge of the Azurii.

Once again there was silence, this time as the adults stared at the children whose energy fields were quivering as they slammed shut all connection. An essential element of growing up was discovering how to break the rules and not let too much of that show in the aura, be that triumph or fear of being caught. No parent needed to threaten a child with 'bogeymen'. If too much sense of wrong-doing seeped into the individual's aura, hints would slip into the MentaNet and might be detected by Readjusters. The result – a fate far worse than any imagined bogeyman.

'Bedtime,' Mizena said firmly. Her children were exhausted. Their aura LockDown was so extreme as to be unprecedented. That would have to be approached very carefully, and she and her husband had some serious talking to do beforehand. 'You've had enough for one day. Look at your depleted auras. Right now you need something to eat and a good night's sleep.'

'Tomorrow, we'll all get together here,' Mandara said. 'Now, don't worry about today. Tomorrow, we'll make sense of that all that has happened.'

And so, with those reassuring words, he rose from his chair, tripped over, and vanished with a surprised exclamation. Forgetting that he was in his own home of Lungunu, and not actually sitting with his family in Siyataka, he had moved the wrong way around his chair and knocked over a table with his drink on it.

51

Everyone heard the faint hum of a HouseCarl, followed by: 'Tch, Tch.'

Exhausted, the twins managed a feeble high five.

'We programmed Lungunu's HouseCarls to make that sound,' Qwelby explained.

'When they clear up after Gumma,' Tullia added, as they followed their parents into the kitchen.

'Why do they only co-operate when it's to cause mischief?' Mizena thoughtsent to her husband.

Shandur merely grunted, trying to conceal both his amusement at what the children had done to the HouseCarl and his pride at their level of skill.

Too tired to eat, Tullia snuggled up to her mother. Qwelby cleared his plate, looked at his twin's, then pushed it away.

'You must be tired!' his father said sympathetically.

'Mmpf,' his son agreed, flopping onto the table.

A few moments later the twins were settling down for the night sharing a collection of images and feelings, and sad that Tullia had had to leave the lantern behind when descending the bell ropes.

Tullia's journey to Haven with descendants of the Auriganii was logical. Qwelby to Azura was the puzzle. Was that the future, when he was an adult? Was he going to go there as part of a Tazian mission to reunite the two races... whilst Tullia was on Haven... bringing all three races together... setting in motion the restoration of their full Aurigan heritage?

Tingling with excitement, they imaged a strange mixture of a scene: half Azuran flikker, half HoloWrapper Adventure of imagined Aurigan times. Flanked by a dragon and a unicorn, they were two Venerables, each known as "Purple", and wearing totally over-the-top robes, presiding over the celebrations of the restoration of the Aurigan Dynasty...

CHAPTER 7

A GOOY MESS

The day after the twins' disturbing adventures started well. Washed and dressed, they stood looking out of the bedroom window. They were trying to adjust to the fact that they had spent a large part of the previous day not merely working together, which was not unusual, but openly admitting that they needed to rely on each other.

That had been their life until they were twelve. From then on, each establishing their own identity had become very important. Even so, that had to be within the structure of their intense and unique genetic relationship. For a time they each had had their own bedroom-cum-study. More often than not they had ended up together in one room or the other, often squashing their four best friends in with them.

Eventually, they had persuaded their parents to let them have the attic as their domain for everything: a combination of individual spaces and sharing spaces. One large room artistically, or not according to their mother, divided into spaces for sleeping, studying, playing and a separate room that Qwelby called GirlySpace. Even Tullia agreed that she spent far longer in that corner then he ever would.

One day they would discover that Siyataka's roof had been changed to its unusual shape shortly before they were born, that their extensive wheedling, carefully explaining how easy it would be to convert the attic, had been unnecessary, and that their parents had so enjoyed the twins' inventiveness that they had made them wheedle for longer than originally intended.

Recalling how good it had felt when Tullia had cuddled up to him, wanting to be cared for, Qwelby decided to humour her by letting her arrange his thick hair into her latest style for him. As he watched in Mirror the green lights flickering around the comb and brush, they thoughtshared their feelings about their Out-Of-Body experiences.

Their Images quivered and their faces grew older. Tullia's hair became full of thin plaits interwoven. A style she had never effected. Qwelby's hair had grown so long that it was pulled back behind his head in a mane. They sensed each other trembling with anticipation, and saw the dull yellow of fear flickering at the edges of their auras.

Tullia pushed her twin's hair into a fringe, then swept it away as she broke eye contact and steadied her anxiety. 'Breakfast.'

Feeling excited, a little fearful and in need of reassurance, instead of sliding down the twirlypoles they walked down the stairs side by side, careful not to hold hands. They were fifteen-years-old. Togetherness was one thing, getting mushy for a second day running was not on.

Their mother was very much a homemaker, taking pride in managing the family farms at Siyataka and Lungunu, giving instructions to the domestic appliances, and occasionally even cooking by hand. Full of living wood, Kitchen looked and felt old and rustic. 'An energy balance with the all the hi-tech equipment in my husband's part of the house,' she would say to surprised guests. As she moved around Kitchen it filled itself with a sound like branches happily rubbing together in a soft breeze.

As they all sat down, the miniature twistors in Tullia's earrings broke away from their restraining gluons. Chaos resulted. The kitchen ended up looking as though a whirlwind had swept through it.

Mizena was so upset at the mess in her kitchen that she turned the clock backwards. Back upstairs Tullia adjusted her earrings, then the twins went downstairs, and the whole morning dissolved into chaos for the second time.

Time-travel was both theoretically possible and believed to be actually possible in the eighth dimension. In their worlds of the fifth and seventh, it was as though anyone that went back in time found themselves in a cocoon and unable to step outside of reality. Going forwards in time never happened.

In desperation, their mother reversed the clock again, further back in time. The twins awoke and this time Qwelby tried to help Tullia firmly fix the twistors in place. Try how they might, the family was unable to avoid what fate had in store for them that morning, and Mizena fled from the kitchen in tears.

Shandur sent the twins to Barn, correctly judging that the twistors could not go too far away from their homes in his daughter's earrings. He needed them all out of the way whilst he thoughtsent to the Helping Hands Agency. In no time at all several "Pairs of Hands" as the young Apprentices styled themselves, arrived and helped clear up the mess.

When order had been restored, and Shandur had the earrings safely locked in a box, he patiently coaxed his wife out of yesterday and reminded the family they were going to Lungunu. As a treat, he said they would all fly their twistors and go the long way round.

Riding what looked like a permanently revolving, elongated corkscrew the size of a PowerSled required a very sophisticated saddle and a lot of skill. Twistors chose their own colours to reflect their personality. Against his father's suggestions Qwelby had chosen his favourite: bright red with orange stripes.

CHAPTER 8

TULLIA LECTURES

As they were nearing Lungunu, ignoring his father's thoughtsending, Qwelby swooped low over a forest, looking pretty with its mass of yellow winter berries standing out against the snow. Unfortunately, they were not berries but the crests of SentryBirds. Startled, the whole flock rose up, shrilling their alarm calls. The large aegiele with its bright red breast was their most feared predator. Seeing the bright red swooping down on them, they attacked, shooting streams of ochre coloured goo like semi-liquid chewing gum that they used to trap the small rodents that were their favourite diet. Qwelby and his twistor were covered in it.

As the family arrived at Lungunu and settled their twistors into the cradles, Lellia appeared with TAC, the third assistant cook. To Qwelby's surprise, Lellia was happy. She was working on analysing the SentryBirds's goo and was delighted to have so much to use. The downside was that he was not able to use the neutron shower for his clothes and helmet which would not be cleaned until much later in the day.

Qwelby was sulking. Like his twin, he had been wearing the flying suit given to him on their rebirthday three months ago: emerald green with bright vermilion slashes that looked like flames.

With 'one on him', as Tullia described his childish moods, rather than go to their suite and find some more clothes, he stomped into the Gather Room wearing what any Tazian boy wore underneath a flying suit: snug shorts and a tank top. He consoled himself with the fact that the satchel with their uncle's gizmos in it was clean, having been safely stored in the twistor's saddle box.

Designed by Lellia, the Gather Room was a charming blend of furnishings in a modern angular style within a traditional room, the soft pinks and oranges of the gently moving colourscopes on the walls giving a feeling of warmth. Set against one wall which, with tiny lights twinkling against the deep blue represented the enormity of space, pride of place was given to a series of Living Statues of those Uddîšû whose genes were borne by the various members of the family. In any other setting that would have been ostentatious, but the Gather Room was used almost exclusively by the family. On the rare occasions when other people were present, the Statues disappeared into the seventh dimension.

At the other end of the sofa, Tullia was still happily wearing her flying suit. They were so stylish that youngsters often wore them even when not flying. Hers was a rich, deep purple with flame-like patches of bright violet. Like any flying or body suit, many of the bright patches contained artfully hidden, teethless zips, called szeames.

Tullia was always very careful only to put in her pockets the tiniest things that she might ever need. There was no way she was going to spoil the look of her suit by having bulging pockets like some boys did.

'With the KeyPoint only a day away, the latest experiments being conducted on Azura are stressing the XzylStroem,' Mandara said. He nodded to his great nephew who knew that the Academy of Discoverers was becoming increasingly concerned by the successes Azuran scientists were having on practical levels.

'That is dangerous,' Lellia added, her eyes looking from Tullia to Qwelby. 'To remind you. A key function of this, the first XzylStroem, is to maintain all other five in balanced harmony, and the link with Azura.'

'Oh do stop that!' snapped Qwelby at Tullia, who was absent-mindedly playing with her szeames. 'It's really irritating.'

'Don't blame me!' Tullia snapped back. 'It's not my fault you got bird shit all over your flying-suit.'

'It's not...'

'Enough!' Mandara said. 'We have a lot to talk about. Seriously.' He thoughtsent to the twins to concentrate. The brief flaring in the their energy fields settled, he focussed his attention on them

'In order to discuss what happened yesterday,' he continued, 'you will need some background information. Knowledge you will not be taught on your college days, but left for you to discover for yourselves when you are much older. Knowing how much you have asked all of us about yourselves, and that you have searched the Archives, will you tell us what you have learnt about Auriga, and our race's background. It will save boring repetition.'

'And correcting anything that needs...' Lellia added, with a smile.

Tullia glanced at her twin who nodded. No point in them mindmelding as each knew exactly the same as the other. She uncurled her legs, then curled them back underneath her the other way round. She felt a humorous tickle in her mind. It had Qwelby's signature.

'Are you sitting comfortably?' Tullia asked, in her best imitation of her favourite Assistant Educationer, thoughtsending her twin a smile. 'Then I'll begin.' She smiled sweetly at the adults. 'This is with all six of us working together.'

'Each Essence emerged from the primal chaos onto Auriga in the third dimension, a baby bounded by Form and Time, just like on Azura.'

The room went cold as the adults withdrew behind a Group PrivacyShield to share their shock that the youngsters had been able to discover that. How? It was so securely shielded.

Looking smug at their obvious consternation, Tullia waited until their auras settled.

'Evolving over increasingly longer periods of time, the Essence moved into successive higher, faster, vibrations of the other dimensions.

'Four. It acquired consciousness and became a proper human being. No real change externally as it was still bounded by Form and Time.

'Five. It gained a very limited elasticity of Form and Time. Just like us today.

'Seven. She or he learned how to exit Form and adopt any appearance they liked. Again just like we can. We think that the Auriganii were able to remain in the seventh for much longer periods than us.

'Eight. Time-travel is said to be possible in the eighth, so, and we are...' Tullia's lips quirked in a smile as she received her twin's clear thought: *'Not guessing'* 'predicating that life in the eighth was totally without Form.

'Nine. The Space Wars suggest that Auriganii combined into amorphous groups. That must have been there, because:

'Ten. We know that is where we go to merge into The All.

'Our two biggest assumptions are.

'That all the way through that life, the Auriganii had increasing numbers of sequences of DNA being activated on each transition.

'The sixth level of vibration, or dimension. No direct information. We think it might be like Kaigii and I wrapped into in an HWAdventure, where it's a sort of tunnel that enabled the Auriganii to move across dimensions.'

<*Yah-oh!*> Qwelby's thought arrived. She glanced at him. His right hand was raised, making it look like he had only three digits. It was from their favourite Azuran Space flikker, a gesture they had adopted

59

from a man who was made to look a little bit like a very pale Tazian.

Tullia smiled. Sulking was childish. But, well, he was only a boy. And always Kaigii.

'We don't understand how they were able to use a space ship to leave Auriga and travel across several galaxies in only forty thousand sun cycles, when they had to take life in the third dimension with them. Even if they could warp space-time-consciousness, we know they had to travel within planetary systems because of the fighting. And that must have been to search for a new home planet and get food and stuff for the people. Unless...' She felt her twin's encouragement.

'We know the Auriganii lived for at least two thousand years, so there would be an awful lot of older, faster ones compared to those in the lower dimensions. We think those of the highest vibrations were able to wrap their energy fields around the space ship. And.' She took a deep breath.

'They lived on some sort of space food. Energy from distance suns, well stars really.' She finished talking in a small voice, expecting, hopefully polite, derision. The last part was all so fanciful.

'Well, Chief Educationer Tullia Rrîl'zânâ Mizenatyr, that is impressive,' Mandara said, smiling, whilst Tullia's face split from ear to ear with a big grin. She was mindbathed in approbation. She felt Qwelby join her. '*Fair's fair Kaigii. What I've explained is what all six of us worked out,*' she thoughtsent. Full of confidence she continued.

'There was great Darkness that was difficult to penetrate around how the Auriganii DNA sequences degenerated from twelve down to three segments for us and two for the Azurii. And...' Not liking what they had sensed, she sent a pleading thought to her twin.

'We are taught that there was a terrible war amongst the Azurii that caused the separation,' Qwelby said as he took up the story. 'From the feelings we got in the Archives it was like around the Space Wars but much worse. There were these terrible feelings of guilt and shame. Why, if the war was amongst the Azurii? We think there must have been war here on Vertazia as well. No facts. It was like the Darkness was trying to cover up that "we" were fighting. With the Space Wars the feelings of the violence were bad, but always there was the sense of it wasn't "us" that was causing it. We know from our history that we were only defending ourselves in those times, don't we Dad?'

With the DragonRider genes that he had passed onto his son, and because of their unique relationship, also to his daughter, Shandur nodded. 'Yes. Always only in defence.'

'And we've never found any more information about us. That's weird,' Qwelby said as feelings of frustration ran strongly through the auras of both twins.

'Very weird,' Tullia added, looking almost accusingly at her parents.

'Tullia, Qwelby,' Mandara said. 'I have to tell you that I found it very difficult to discover all the data you must have uncovered. From which, by the way, I have drawn very similar conclusions. Except. The war was entirely amongst the humans. It was the side effects of that destroyed our bases, and thus our ability to translocate to Azura.'

He shielded his thoughts that it had been so difficult to drill down to find some of the data that he suspected a deliberate attempt had been made over the centuries to hide the more revealing aspects. Around those areas there had been an unpleasant, dark, energy. What was of even more concern were the stories that over the centuries a handful of researchers had been mind damaged. That was attributed to Aurigan defences around ancient and forbidden areas.

Recently, Mandara had very reluctantly come to the conclusion that the dark energy he had experienced was not Aurigan in nature, but indicated Antiquarians or Custodians. It was a worrying discovery in a supposedly open society that that made him wonder exactly what more lay concealed in the Archives beyond even his reach.

61

The twins looked at one another, wondering if it had been a mistake to let the adults know what they were able to do. But, to tell only half truths was almost as bad as lying – and both clearly showed up in the speaker's aura.

Since Qwelby had become elderest to Wrenden and they had formed XOÑOX, a lot of exploration was done as a group of six. The more difficult it was to access the information, the more fun they had in winkling it out. Except there were times when they had come across an exceptionally strong, foul Darkness that seemed to be at the root of the Kumelanii's fears. They hadn't wanted to try to penetrate it. It had been forbidding: full of foreboding, guilt and shame.

They had chosen the name XOÑOX from their mantra: "xátuyé osiy nola nola osiy xátuyé". A lot later they were to discover that they could make XONNOX from several of the Azuran languages, but that it didn't quite work in the most common one: six all one one all six.

Shandur and Mizena were relieved that their children had not discovered anything about the short lives of the previous pair of Quantum Twins. They had a lot to discuss with their children and wanted them relaxed and at home to do that with no more worries on their minds. As they thoughtshared that with their great uncle and aunt it seemed as though everyone was plunged into an HWAdventure: immersed in an enormous fish tank as a wave swept through it, rippling through their bodies and distorting their vision.

'The Stroems are Swirling strongly this KeyPoint,' Lellia said, standing up and walking to the door. 'They've started earlier than normal and, as you know, the effects will continue until the solstice is past. I'll come back as soon as they are settled for a while.'

'Tullia, Qwelby, what you have discovered is nothing short of amazing,' Mandara said as the door closed behind his wife. 'You must have gone very deep into the Archives. Just with your four friends?'

Two grinning faces nodded.

'Please make me a promise. None of the six of you are to

explore those areas again, until I have had chance to discus this with your parents.' He looked across to Shandur and Mizena. 'I am very concerned about the Darkness that surrounds some the sections they must have explored, and again that mentally isolated them yesterday.' He turned back to the twins and raised an eyebrow.

'We promise,' they said, looking puzzled.

'Don't worry, You haven't done anything wrong. Far from it. But there are dangers, and we need to ensure your safety for future exploration.

The twins nodded, relieved that no-one was asking how they had managed to dig so deep. There were matters best kept from parents.

'Now, with the Stroems so excited, I don't want you exploring Lungunu today,' Mandara continued. 'Please use the Elmit Room. We'll all get together later and sort out what happened yesterday. Another day we will talk about Aurigan times in detail. Meanwhile,' he added with a grin. 'I've got a new invention for you.' He produced a small box from one of his pockets and opened it.

'Wow! Miniature squigglesnakes!' Qwelby exclaimed as he peered into the box.

'Don't be daft,' Tullia scolded, pushing him aside to get a closer look. 'They're not real snakes!'

Mandara took a compact neutron magnifier from another pocket and placed it on top of the box. The twins could see what looked like two incredibly small spirals. As they looked closer they could make out arrays of wriggling wires at each end.

'Nano technology!! What do they do?.?'

'Guess.'

'Nose de-bogeyfiers?' asked Qwelby.

'Urgh! Revolting child!' Tullia exclaimed.

'Try again,' said Mandara quickly, stopping Qwelby from responding.

'Miniature karaoke sets?' suggested Tullia.

'No.'

'Miniaturised twistors?' Qwelby contributed.

'No.' He laughed. Their guesses had given him ideas for more experiments. 'Personal, Self-Learning, Interactive, Language Compilers, incorporating Pseudo Tetraquarks.'

'Ehh??'

Lellia gave her husband a despairing look. 'Try speaking Tazian, Mandara. Not your techno-babble!'

'It is what they are,' he retorted.

'What are they for?' Tullia asked.

'For the Elmit Room,' he replied, looking smug.

'Gumma! You haven't?' Tullia almost squeaked in her excitement.

'Yes. I've managed to put together enough extracts from flikkers to create several Viewings. I am confident that each Viewing is put together from the same, unique series of Azuran programmes, and that there is consistent Azuran language in each one.'

The twins goggled at him, speechless.

'These compilers are intuitive programmes. As well as Tazian, each contains Reduced Aurigan as a comparator. They will interact with your memories and thoughts as you learn the different Azuran languages.'

'We learn?' Tullia asked.

Mandara raised an eyebrow.

'Compiler, airhead!' Qwelby crowed.

Tullia grimaced as she realised that her twin had picked up her thought that what Gumma had created was a translator, as opposed to software that would store vocabulary and syntax in their brains.

'But why do we need to learn their languages?' she asked, flashing her twin a look that said: *'You didn't think to ask that, did you!'*

'Have you never studied Reduced Aurigan?' Lellia asked, certain the twins had never studied the old Living Aurigan which encompassed multi-dimensional images and feelings.

64

'No.'

'If you had, you would know that as you learn a different language, you discover how those people think differently,' their mother explained.

'You mean that if we learn an Azuran language, we will not just understand the flikkers, but also how weird the Azurii are?' Qwelby asked.

'Something like that,' she replied with a smile.

The twins looked at each other. <Scary!! *Surely everyone thinks the same??*>

'Not so,' Mizena said, thoughtsharing with her husband that no matter how advanced their children were at times, they still had a lot to learn about Life.

Mandara turned to Tullia. 'Inside your left ear?'

She nodded, eyes wide with surprise, and gave a little shiver as it slipped inside and said *'hullo.'*

He turned to Qwelby. 'Right?'

He nodded and twitched his head as it tingled inside him.

Mandara smiled as he noticed their reactions. 'Good. That's the Self-Locating element safely anchoring inside your ears. Try them out...'

'Race you!' Tullia called as she headed for the door.

'If necessary, I'll explain ...'

'No way!' Qwelby exclaimed, as firmly clasping the satchel under his arm he followed his twin.

'...how to use them when you come back...' Mandara finished, looking at the closed door.

CHAPTER 9

WHEN IS A DOUGHNUT NOT A DONUT?

The twins raced around the semi-circular entrance hall and up the twirlypoles located in the centre of the main, bifurcated wing of Lungunu, Qwelby following Tullia into the Elmit room in their suite. He stood undecided, go into their bedroom and put on some more clothes or try the compilers? As Tullia turned to him with a drink in her outstretched hand, the fish-tank effect happened again.

He raised his left arm with his fist clenched. Tullia immediately damped down her thoughts, and raised an eyebrow as she put her head close to his.

'You know that room that's not in this timeframe?' Qwelby whispered.

'Where Gumma's trying an experiment with Azura?' Tullia whispered back

'Yeah.'

'And we're forbidden even to try to go there.'

'We'll never get a better chance.'

'How d'you mean?' Tulia asked, sounding dubious at what he was suggesting.

'They want to talk about us. They'll establish a Group PrivacyShield, so we can't listen in...'

'Meaning they won't hear our thoughts either...'

'And with the Stroems Swirling so strongly, that'll cover us up even more,' Qwelby said.

Tullia continued to look uncertain.

'Afraid of your DragonRider genes when you Awaken?' Qwelby taunted.

'Nothing to do with BigMan!' Tullia spat back, referring to the myth that all boys pretended not to believe, that the more adventurous a boy was before puberty the bigger his emerging masculinity would be.

'Kaigii,' Qwelby responded, reminding his twin that as they had identical genes he was just as concerned as to what would happen to him when he Awakened.

'Come on, Sis, just a look,' Qwelby wheedled, using their code to acknowledge she was older and offering her the decision.

'Just a look,' Tullia agreed, mollified.

They left their suite and headed to where they knew that special room had to be, as that part of Lungunu was missing from the fifth dimension. Holding hands so as to maximise their energy sharing, they waited, facing a wall they knew wasn't there, Qwelby hoping for another Swirling, Tullia beginning to regret having agreed.

Tullia was just about to speak when the wall wavered. Holding in their minds as strongly as possible the concept of a room containing an experiment with Azura, the twins stepped forward and found themselves in a corridor. Everything, even the air itself, was shimmering. They walked to the end and turned the corner. In a dark alcove was a door that looked like an airlock from an Azuran space flikker: dark grey metal, bevelled edges and a large central wheel in a lighter grey.

'There are twelve bolts connected to the wheel,' Tullia said as she withdrew her mind from the door. 'All in light grey and heavily loaded with inertia.'

Qwelby tried to turn the wheel. His hands slid around it as though it was not really there. 'Temporal discontinuity. We need to adjust the timeframe,' he said.

'Backwards to latest opening,' Tullia suggested.

'No. Forwards. To when we will open it.'

'Yeah, of course.'

With all four hands on the wheel, they focussed on imaging it and the mechanism inside changing into dark grey in a very near future.

The fish-tank effect happened again. All the metal was dark grey. They heaved on the wheel.

Nothing happened.

Eventually, with aching muscles, they stood back and examined the door.

They heard humming

'Why does a door hum?' Tullia asked.

'Because it's happy?' Qwelby replied.

'What does a door want to do?' Tullia asked.

'Open!!' they said together, grabbing the wheel, bracing their feet and heaving. The wheel spun and the door swung away from them. With their hands all tangled together they were dragged with it. Hands slipping free, they fell to the floor.

As they untangled themselves and got to their feet, the door swung to behind them. They were mesmerised. One moment they were in a brightly lit room, all chrome and white like an operating theatre. The next moment they seemed to be standing in a total blackness that seemed to go on forever. They hoped they were still in the room and not out in space. As the room morphed to and fro, they were showered with a kaleidoscope of colours.

They hadn't intended to enter the room, only have a look, but, now they were in it, well, looking couldn't do any harm, could it...

Slowly their eyes focussed on the only object that seemed constant. It looked like a permanently shimmering, hi-tech, chromium Jacuzzi, large enough to take the whole family. On both sides it was connected to pipes big enough for the twins to crawl through. When the room wasn't there, the whole setup became translucent and they could see great streams of colours circling through the pipes in opposite directions. When the room was actually there, the colours fountained out of the Jacuzzi-like thing. What the twins did not know was that the energy streams were from an Azuran machine, everything safely isolated and contained in a different space-time continuum – but one which they had just entered.

The Large Hadron Collider as the Azurii called the machine, had been warmed up and the latest series of experiments initiated. Two streams of particles were shooting towards each other. When they had accelerated ten thousand times around the ring of what was called the Big Doughnut to almost the speed of light, millions of collisions would happen every second.

All the twins could see were two amazingly beautiful streams of colour flowing like miniature comets in opposite directions.

Tullia mindslipped into one as Qwelby examined Mandara's array of controls and monitors. They were the most complex he had ever seen and it was going to take him ages to understand them.

'Dragon's Breath!' he exclaimed as he realised that the two streams were going to collide. His urgent thought did not reach Tullia. Every quantum particle of her self was immersed in the beauty and splendour of being what to her was a comet soaring through deep space.

'Xzarze, Tullia! Why do I have to keep on rescuing you?' he muttered. He ignored his Intuition's tart comment that she rescued him just as often, as he mindslipped half into the other comet and half into the controls.

'Eeyooowww!' he exclaimed as the power of the comet ripped his half mind from the controls.

<*¡HELP!*>

Seeking the transdimensional strength of the Stroems, his panicked thought reached them in the microseconds before the comet quantumwrapped him just as the other had done to Tullia.

The twins found themselves hurtling through space, or was it Time, or did they remain still and everything hurtled past them? Whatever, it seemed as though they found themselves inside a great big tunnel hurtling along at almost the speed of light. Around and around they went, in opposite directions. Strange buzzes not so much ringing in their ears as vibrating through their bodies.

Shooting around faster and faster, they felt their bodies getting longer and thinner. Two streams of energy sweeping past each other. Where was the end or the beginning of a line of infinite length?

Sending out powerful thoughts of their desperate need to be with each other, the twins' electro-magnetic fields interacted and became part of the powerful magnetic fields in the Big Doughnut. The shock ripped through their whole beings.

It felt like a fizzy drink. Not drinking one. Being one.

Scattered throughout the length and breadth of their bodies, each managed one thought. *I have fifty trillion cells in my body. Every single one HURTS!*

Uncountable numbers of fundamental particles showered in every direction.

? WHERE AM I ?

? WHEN AM I ?

? am i ?

? ?

?

CHAPTER 10

WHERE ARE THEY?

'They're growing up so fast since their crystals were attuned to their EraBands,' Shandur said as the door closed behind his children.

'It started before they were fourteen, ShahShah,' his wife pointed out. 'It's since Tamina became elderest to Tullia. And that's well over three years ago.'

'But I still don't understand how they can have reached through that adult energy banding,' Shandur protested.

'You don't see them like I do when they are around Siyataka,' his wife replied. 'I see how very strong they are. It frightens me at times. Their power. What they can do. Just look how they created that Bell Tower.'

'Right!' Mandara said forcefully. 'Let's discuss yesterday. We can talk freely without them here. Lellia can add her comments later.'

Lellia had returned and they were well into the discussion when House shook and quivered. Ornaments rattled and a phlock of photons swooped around the room. Unprecedented numbers of electrons swopped places all at once so that everything seemed to flicker in and out of solidity.

Mizena called the twins. She could not locate them mentally. Shandur tried. No luck either.

'Don't worry,' Mandara was quick to say, 'I have the perfect answer for that. My latest gadget. I haven't told you about it because I was waiting until the twins were back with us. It's part of the Compiler I gave them. I can't speak with them, but I will be able to say where they are. First though, we have to go to my study.'

Mandara summoned Lift. After being shaken about as Lift bucked to the after-effects of what they assumed was another XzylStroem eruption, it dissolved and left them standing in Mandara's study. He sat behind his desk and explained.

'I'd been thinking about how much the twins enjoy going to the Elmits to see the strange things that happen on Azura. Flat screens, not being able to actually be there in the film, fuzzy pictures and time differences, but, you know kids. And watching those incomprehensible flikkers with the twins, we agreed that most appear to be mixtures of two or more transmissions.

'Well. Shandur and I decided to capture some transmissions ourselves. Obviously we needed to develop a programme that would decipher any language. Then I thought: why not go one better and enable the twins to speak the languages!'

Lellia and Mizena looked at one another and shook their heads. *'Who's the biggest child!'* they thoughtshared

'And I couldn't help it,' he added with a smile. 'Because I am a genius, I built-in a tracking device.'

Shandur nodded. His great uncle loved creating his gadgets as much as the children loved using them.

'I used a meson and its paired anti-meson. The up or down quark is in the compiler, the down or up anti-quark is here, in what I call the locator. The screen will show where they are on a scalable map.'

When all that appeared on the screen was a fuzzy blur, and no map, Mandara ran a diagnostic. He turned to face the others with a strained look on his face. 'Both anti-quarks have gone. They must have paired with the quarks.'

'How's that possible?' Mizena asked.

'Something must have interfered with their interaction separators,' he replied, his mind already sorting through possibilities.

Lellia took her great niece's hand in hers. 'There are other ways of checking on the twins and making sure they're alright,' she said in a gentle tone of voice. 'The men can deal with the mechanical side of quantum physics. We'll go and explore in a different way.'

When Mizena had married Shandur, in true Tazian tradition they had been taken fully into each other's families. In the eyes of Mandara and Lellia, Mizena had become their great niece, just as much as Shandur was Mandara's great nephew by birth.

With heavy hearts, Lellia and Mizena left Mandara's study, walked down the stairs and crossed over to Lellia's personal wing on the opposite side of Lungunu. Walking side by side up the stairs, the thick, woodland green carpet muffled the sounds of their feet and all was silent. The soft colourscopes on the walls helped them relax and discuss how to proceed.

Reaching the top of the staircase they walked along the corridor and entered what Lellia called her Homely Room where they changed into GeleleSilk robes of midnight blue. The silk had been mistakenly named after the Gelele tree before it was discovered that the fine threads that appeared on a hot sunny day in the spring were the result of the rainbow-coloured Wenkosi butterflies dropping from their cocoons before taking flight.

Lellia led her niece out of the room and further along the corridor to a very special room at the end. The door was Night, and in the Night stood a beautiful Isuna wearing robes that were both so black and diaphanous that she hardly seemed to be there at all. Did they sparkle with starlight, or were the stars behind her? Mizena could not tell. In her hands the Isuna held a Moon. As the two women neared the door, the Isuna smiled and the door opened.

Mizena stopped with amazement. She had never seen the door before. Her mind told her she was looking at an ordinary door with a painting on it. Her eyes and all her other senses told her it really was a woman holding a Moon standing somewhere in the middle of Night.

As the door closed behind them Mizena saw six walls forming the hexagonal shape of a cell in a honeycomb. She smiled at the impression that she was entering a hive of her beloved bees, how important they were to life on both planets, and hoped that some Azurii still followed the Path of Pollen. Bathed in soft light from the alcoves that were set at different heights in each wall, the golden colour slowly turned to black, different shades of black. As Lellia led her niece to the centre, Mizena felt as though she was walking through a field of black grass.

The centre of the room was a large, sunken circle. In the centre of that circle was a low, round table, on it a dome of the blackest black, so black that as Mizena tried to focus on it, it seemed to disappear. Large cushions were set all around the table. Whilst Lellia was used to sitting in the lotus position she knew that would not be comfortable for her niece. She sent a thought to the floor. Behind one of the cushions a curved segment of it rose up to form a comfortable chair. They settled themselves comfortably, opposite each other.

'Let's begin with Tullia,' Lellia said softly, leant forward and removed what Mizena then saw was the cover over a round ball of pure, clear crystal. The ball had been handed down through generations of Seekers, always female, always members of the family. Sianarrah would serve only as long as she wanted to, but always faithfully, of that there never was any doubt.

The two women looked into the crystal ball, holding in their centres their love for the twins.

A soft mist appeared, swirling slowly. After a while it seemed as though there was a faint hint of lilac in the centre. The mist thickened and Lellia sent gentle, calming energy to her niece. As the mist thinned, they saw a small cloud of lilac being swept along, all round the globe. Lellia leant forward stretching out her hands. Her niece took them and they merged their energies. The swirling calmed and the lilac contracted and deepened until it was a clear purple, gently pulsing. Mizena gave a soft sigh as her daughter's favourite colour established itself as the messenger of her well-being.

Suddenly it was ripped apart as a series of colours mushroomed out. Mizena gasped with dismay as shades of grey and slashes of black intermingled. Then gasped again as streaks of vermilion shot through, followed by brilliant flashes like bolts of lightning.

She wanted to pull away and cover her eyes, but felt her aunt gripping her hands tightly, maintaining the connection.

A small spot in the centre grew into a mouth with gnashing teeth. It filled the whole crystal. The tiny patch of purple was in the centre of it. The mouth shrank. The ball filled with swirling grey mist as the mouth twisted and turned, chasing the tiny speck of purple.

A thin brown spiral unfolded around the outer edges of the crystal. Rapidly it grew in size, changing colour to a rich dark red, glowing with streaks of emerald green and sun-kissed yellow, bright violet sparkling from its wingtips. It stretched wide its jaws, a tongue flickered and the mouth was swallowed. The dragon grinned, then disappeared, leaving a tall, thin streak of vibrating purple in the centre of the swirling mist that slowly faded away, leaving the ball empty.

As they left the Seliya Chamber, Mizena thoughtsent Cook. The two women had scarcely settled themselves comfortably in the Homely Room before a big pot of Cook's Special Restorative Chay arrived.

They were half way through their second cup when Mizena saw her aunt's eyes return to focus and the grim look leave her face.

'Well?' Mizena asked.

'From the size and depth of colour of the purple column, she must be well.' Her aunt heaved a sigh. 'But I am sure she is not on Vertazia.'

Mizena choked back a sob. 'What makes you say that?'

'The lightning bolts and the mouth. They did not have Tazian energy signatures. I have only rarely seen that energy before. They are what we call the Dark Denizenii. But the dragon. That was a much older energy and protecting Tullia.'

'But, the Dark Denizenii, they don't really exist?' Mizena queried.

'It's all the repression of our era,' Lellia replied. 'We have come so far from our Aurigan days that negative energies such as fear and hate have become powerful archetypes that not only influence people but can even be used between dimensions.'

'It was all so confusing. No image of Tullia or even her whereabouts. It was almost as though Sianarrah could not get a good focus?' Mizena asked.

'Yes,' Lellia agreed. 'There was an unsettled energy with her I've not experienced before. She usually knows where we are working. This time all I got from her was that we were both near and far, and what we were seeing was happening now. Yet she didn't know when 'now' was!' Lellia shook her head, clearly perplexed. She held up a hand to forestall any questions. 'Remember the strength of that purple. She is alive, well, vibrant. And protected.'

Mizena nodded. 'Through the male line Qwelby has the genetic inheritance of the Hero of olden days we only know by the name of his dragon: Zhólérrân. Do you think?'

'Possible. I suppose.'

'The dragon grinned. Not smiled. Grinned. It's just how Qwelby looks when he's got one up on Tullia. She smirks. Sometimes they are different,' Mizena said as she smiled faintly, feeling the first touches of hope. If they were alive and well, anything was possible.

'Do you feel strong enough to search for Qwelby?' her aunt queried.

'Yes. We know Tullia is alive and well. I must know that Qwelby is.' Tears trickled from the corners of her eyes.

They returned to the Seliya Chamber and settled into their meditation. As they did so, the crystal ball filled with swirling mist.

They waited.

The mist continued to swirl.

Both women felt their energy being drained into the crystal.

'No, Sianarrah. No!' Lellia cried out, reaching for the cover and dropping it over the crystal.

Mizena looked at her aunt dumbfounded. 'What? Sianarrah cannot find him?'

Lellia looked troubled. 'I don't understand. She has never tried to draw that amount of energy from me before. But then, this is the first occasion I've used her to scry for people.' She gave her niece a sympathetic look as she got up. 'I'm sorry, no more scrying now, you look drained and I know I can do no more today.'

'No sense of Qwelby?' Mizena asked.

'Siahranah must have sensed his energy somewhere...to want to draw so much power from me.' Lellia decided not to add "somewhen," her niece had enough to worry about.

They returned to Lellia's Homely Room. Checking with House, they discovered that their husbands were still working. Feeling in need of comfort, they descended to the kitchen where Cook started to prepare meals for everyone.

Earlier, Lift had deposited the two husbands at the door to Mandara's communications room. They entered and sat side by side at a massive, U-shaped work area.

Hours passed as they worked feverishly, trying idea after idea, testing and rechecking the equipment. Finally, defeated, they slumped in their chairs, staring at each other vacantly. They had tried everything they could think of to get a signal to either of the twin's communicators. They might have succeeded. They didn't know, because the other half of the problem was getting a signal back. They had even tried devices similar to Azuran radar and sonar, all to no avail.

When Mandara explained exactly how he had managed to persuade the two mesons to co-operate, the two scientists agreed. The anti-quarks would never have rejoined their quarks unless they sensed permanent dislocation. Neither the mesons, the compilers nor the twins were any longer anywhere in the fifth or seventh dimensions.

They did not need to speak or thoughtshare. There were only two possibilities.

'House,' Mandara asked. 'Correlate the time of when you last were able to monitor the twins' presence with the shockwave.' He knew the answer. When he had first heard it hours ago, it was not what he wanted, now it was the only remaining alternative to the termination of their lifelines.

'A gap of thirty seven minits and nineteen sekonds.'

Mandara thought. What question did he need to ask?

'House. Correlate loss of monitoring with any other potentially relevant event.'

'I recorded what appeared to be a faint echo of what I deduce to have been a Spatio-Temporal discontinuity at that precise moment in that part of Lungunu that lies outside my frame of reference.'

Mandara grimaced. When he had first questioned House he should have asked for a complete physical presentation of all records it considered relevant. After all, it was a semisentient.

Shandur looked at his uncle sympathetically. 'I didn't want my thoughts to go there until, well... there was no alternative.'

There was silence as the men considered the possibility of what might have happened.

'Uncle, we're drained and I certainly am hungry. I don't suppose you noticed your wife's thought about eating: in the Garden Room?'

Mandara shook his head.

'Lets join our wives. They may have had more success than us.'

Some seasons ago, Garden had decided to turn a section at the back of the rear wing of House into a room, and had carefully grown various plants into the right shapes to provide things that could be used as tables and chairs. House had added energy fields for walls and a ceiling. Garden was still working on how to replace those fields with translucent plants.

As the men reached the Garden Room, Mizena got up, ran to her husband and threw her arms around him.

'Tullia is alive and well. But we don't know where she is. And we, I, think Qwelby is, but...' she wailed as she burst into tears.

Clear blue sky, with the sun close to setting, throwing long shadows. House resealed the energy fields and added warmth to the air as everyone found somewhere to sit and Lellia briefly repeated what she and Mizena had experienced.

'You've had more success than we did.' Shandur said sadly, hugging his wife to him, as much for his comfort as hers.

'They are not in the fifth or seventh dimensions. There is no way any Tazian can elevate to the eighth at present, not even Quantum Twins,' Mandara explained.

He turned to look at his wife. 'The third, but hopefully the fourth dimensions are a possibility. We need to explore the Accelerator room.' He shrugged apologetically at his nephew and niece, they both knew that there were areas of Lungunu that were only accessible to people who had lived in the building and worked with its energies for a great many years.

'Yes,' Lellia agreed. 'Right now, we all need to rest and restore our energies. Cook. We're ready for our meals, in the Garden Room please.'

CHAPTER 11

FRIENDS GATHER

Shandur and Mizena were getting ready to return to Lungunu to continue searching for their children when the CommViewer chimed. Mizena sighed. It was the twins' group of four best friends. This was a moment she had feared, but she had not expected it to come so soon. She knew that she could not conceal the amount of worry in her auras.

Taking a deep breath she said: 'Welcome.'

The swirly cloud in the viewer slowly cleared and four faces bearing puzzled looks appeared.

Tamina spoke first. Three months short of her seventeenth rebirthday she was entering the most powerful trimester of her phase of creativity. In a nervous voice she said: 'We haven't had any contact with either of the twins for almost a whole day.'

'We've lost contact with them,' Mizena said baldly.

Tamina tilted her head to one side. 'Mngnh?!'

Mizena's shoulders shrugged. 'We don't know exactly where they are.'

'They're not... on Vertazia?' Tamina asked. Given the hive-like mental linking across all Tazii, for their parents to have lost all mental contact with the twins was impossible – if they were anywhere on Vertazia. Had their lifelines been terminated, their parents would have felt the shockwave, as would Pelnak and particularly Tamina and Wrenden through their special relationships.

'We've lost them!' The words were out of Mizena's mouth before she could stop them.

'Uh-huh,' Tamina murmured, glancing around her brother and friends.

'How could you know?' Mizena asked weakly.

'Ever since I have been able to MentaSynch with them,' Tamina explained. 'even if they didn't want to be contacted, I've always been able to sense them. Now it's different. And Qwelby's not there at all.'

'What can we do to help?' asked Tamina's younger brother Wrenden. Forever asking 'why not?' when he was young had earned him the nickname of Yknot, which they pronounced "Why not" and which his sister had later shortened to Eeky. A little short of his fourteenth rebirthday, he was the only one of the four friends not to have a crystal for his EraBand: a torc or necklace given to every youngster on the occasion of their twelfth rebirthday.

Mizena sighed. 'Switch to TransWeave, transport mode and come on through,' she said. She wanted this sorted quickly and was content to use the family's energy credits for the short journey rather than wait whilst the youngsters made other arrangements.

Tamina stepped through gracefully. Almost two metres tall, her height was accentuated by her slim Form. With her heavily slanted eyes, slim nose and generous mouth, for many years her young brother had expected to discover that she was not really his bossy sister but a domineering alien in a Tazian body. Her rich coffee-cream skin with a coppery tinge was matched by auburn hair, its naturally golden highlighted wavelets so long she could sit on it.

She was followed by Wrenden. Like his sister he was slim and, at one metre eighty, also tall for his age. Skin like his sister's but with dark brown wavy hair, the top cut 'en brosse'.

Pelnak and Shimara arrived together, stumbled, and only just managed to stop each other falling over. Although a few months older than the twins, the boy and girl were markedly shorter than them, rounder in build with a stronger red cast to their skin.

Their mothers were twins. Submitting to an imperative that they only vaguely understood, they had insisted on bringing forth the new lives together, in the same Incarnation Reception Suite. The two babies had been born at exactly the same moment. They were inseparable and acted more like twins than did Qwelby and Tullia. In that they were helped by the fashion amongst youngsters for unisex clothing and the identical, pageboy styles each had chosen for their red hair. They were often referred to as the 'not-twins', and sometimes called Pelnmara.

Aware of the mental communication, Shandur arrived in the kitchen and thoughtshared with his wife. She agreed.

'Mizena will check with Uncle Mandara. Whilst she does that, I will get the Omnitor out.'

'????'

'With what happened yesterday, it's not safe to transweave to Lungunu at present.'

Made up from six twistors representing the five basic directions and one that doesn't, it lived all by itself in a green, space-time-consciousness continuum, called gesticc for short. The Omnitor didn't have a name. Every time someone tried to give it one, the Omnitor handed it straight back. It was just called Ing. If anyone suggested that Ing was short for 'inanimate thing', it disappeared in a microsecond. Even in the quantum world, trying to winkle an Omnitor out of a microsecond was almost impossible.

Shandur's call brought Ing to the door. It had a soft spot for the youngsters. Even when they were squabbling they were always polite, often thoughtsending capital letters with their 'Tamuchlies.' Picking up the feelings of worry, sadness and concern, Ing decided they needed cheering up. It arrived looking like a cluster of six, four dimensional stars gathered around a fifth, bright in a mixture of fluorescent colours. As each person entered a different star they found themselves seated inside the central one.

Ing always enjoyed taking people on journeys because it confused the logic out of every brain. It worked on the same principle as a twistor, instantaneously becoming five lines of infinite length, each in a different direction, except the one that didn't.

Shandur had to locate which line passed through where they wanted to get off, and then stop. Ing took them through all five directions, one after the other, before allowing itself to be located at Lungunu. The four youngsters were left at the front door where they were greeted by Aunt Gallia, as they called the twins' great-great aunt.

'Why don't you go down to the kitchen,' she said. 'I'm sure Cook can find you something nice to eat. Mandara and I need to talk with the twins' parents.'

The not-twins didn't really want to, because they wanted to do something useful. As usual, Wrenden thought: *'Why not?'* Tamina took charge.

'That's a good idea,' she said in a loud voice to cover up thoughtsending: *'Cook likes twins. We winkle truth.'*

'Come to the Welcome Room when you're ready,' Lellia said, smiling at Tamina's innocent belief that she was old enough to securely tightband a thought to three other people. That the youngsters would get the broad picture from Cook suited Lellia. She would not have to relate the distressing events and she wanted her nephew and niece to have privacy for the news she had for them about the Accelerator Room.

Cook had what she considered the perfect image: round and jolly with cheery red cheeks. The four friends knew that the way to her heart was through their stomachs.

Twenty minits of happy munching later and winkling successfully concluded, they knew all there was to know. Despite searching in every manner possible the adults had not been able to locate either twin on Vertazia, or in the seventh dimension which the friends had not thought of. Yet they had found sufficient evidence to indicate they were alive. Due to serious damage in a special part of Lungunu, Lellia and Mandara had not yet been able to pursue a theory that the twins might be on Azura.

'If anyone can find them. We can,' Tamina said with certainty. The others nodded. They knew how powerful the bond was between all six of them. 'If they are on Azura, a group mentasynch, using the power of the Stroems,' she announced into the silence.

They all knew that the basic function of the six Stroems was to maintain the link with Azura, but not even the twins had ever been allowed to go into the Cavern because of the potential danger. The others paled, licked their lips, then nodded: the six were BestFriends. They rose as one, gave their honourings to the animals and crops that had provided their meal, their thanks to Cook, and headed upstairs.

As they entered the Welcome Room, the friends had to admit that they were forever impressed by Lungunu's skill. As the door closed they found themselves on a beautiful tropical island. Like most Tazii when indoors, none of them wore shoes so as to experience the variety of effects most floors enjoyed displaying. The beach felt like luxurious sandy coloured grass.

Disappointed to find four loungers waiting for them, they were pleased as their thoughts were recognised and the loungers moved together and transformed into a curved sofa, whilst retaining the multicoloured stripes of the loungers.

Lellia scrutinised the youngsters as they settled down and sent their 'Tamuchlies' to House.

Pelnak and Shimara were as quiet and self-composed as usual and living up to their nickname of 'not-twins'. Both were wearing long-sleeved tops over trousers cut-off at mid calf. One with a top in shades of pale yellow over trousers with swirls of dark green, the other with a top of shades of pale green over trousers with swirls of dark yellow.

Wrenden had chosen plain colours to suit his sombre mood. A dark green sweater over brown cut-offs.

Tamina had shot up early to be much taller than usual for her age. Her discomfort at being head and shoulders above her contemporaries had been exacerbated when she developed a generous bust line. Lellia was pleased to see that she had at last got over her embarrassment which had caused her to badly round her shoulders, and was now celebrating her Form. A steely determination in Tamina's aura was reflected in a figure hugging, sleeveless snuggy in shades of pale blue-grey over fashionable cut-off trouser-tights in electric blue with silver threads.

'Aunt Gallia,' Tamina started, 'we know about the twins being missing. We ourselves think Tullia is all right, but we can't reach Qwelby. We thought a group mentasynch using the energy of the Stroems?' Although it was originally her idea, the others had agreed, so all four now owned it.

All three adults were taken aback. '*Tamina had not been that explicit earlier,*' the twin's parents thoughtshared, then remembered her exact words which they had not followed up.

'I know none of us have been into the XzylCavern,' Tamina continued when no one commented. 'We need more power. And. Well. The twins have told us of the Stroems. And, I thought...' Tamina finished in a small voice, deciding to take the blame for what she was sure was the forthcoming criticism.

'I think my husband needs to hear this,' Lellia said, thoughtsending him to join them.

Lift noted the urgency in Lellia's request, and acted.

Tamina had only just had time to share her feeling of relief that Mandara's being summoned meant they were being taken seriously when Lift arrived and dissolved, depositing him into a striped armchair. He arched one massive eyebrow.

'Tamina,' Lellia said. 'Please start with why you contacted the twins' parents.'

At sixteen years and eight months, Tamina was the oldest by a year, but she was not the leader. In true Tazian style the group had no leader. Being in Lungunu with the twins' family, she wished they were there to explain. But. She was Tullia's elderest and thus also a sort of older sister to Qwelby. *And to my own irritating brother.* She sat upright and folded her hands in her lap.

'We all tune in to each other every day, even if only for a light touch.' Set in soft, straw yellow ovals, the unusually large emerald green centres of her eyes went pale as she flicked into her memory, and she decided to summarise what had happened.

'When none of us had reached either of the twins, we got together at our house. We formed our group in the usual way. And searched. I found a faint trace of Tullia. But she was only half there.'

'I found no trace of Qwelby,' Wrenden added, sadly.

'Your group of four?' Mandara asked. 'How do you form that?'

'Our ritual is really for all six of us. Sometimes we do something similar when we are... erm, experimenting with the twins...' Tamina paused. She was having difficulty in keeping away from voicing any untruths, as that fact would be seen in her aura. She was also struggling with her emotions as she recalled the part they had all played in helping the twins to penetrate Mandara's and Shandur's Privacy Shield, which had led to them exploring the attic.

'We did that when we helped them the other day,' she finished brightly, thinking of the Bell Tower. Relieved, she went on to explain the ceremony used by all six of them.

'We based it on one of the HoloWrapper adventures of Aurigan times,' Pelnak added. 'The twins suggested some changes to make it really ours and not just a copy of an HWFantasy.'

The youngsters were puzzled by the solid feeling of amazement issuing from Mandara.

Lellia was sending forth a strong feeling of encouragement, so it was natural for Wrenden to volunteer more.

'I felt a bit left out as all the others have their fourteenth rebirthday crystals. So Qwelby made this for me.' He slipped a hand down his sweater and pulled his EraBand into view. It was a torc made of a series of linked metal ovals, each striped gold and silver on a dark grey base. One oval was larger than the others and would be the home for whatever crystal was chosen and attuned to his torc. Attached to that oval by a short, invisible cord was an oval of green simujade. Everyone could see engraved on it were two, interlinked circles.

'Your ceremony. You mentioned using a... plaque?' Mandara asked.

Tamina reached into a pouch hanging at her side and held it out on the palm of her hand for all to see. There was a profound silence as the adults studied it.

Completely covering her hand everyone could see a slightly convex object with twelve straight sides. Fine grooves etched onto it created twelve isosceles triangles marked with the ten colours of the rainbow plus infra red and ultra violet. Joining the corners of each pair of adjacent triangles was a pair of intertwined lines, forming six larger isosceles triangles.

'This is the result of all the time spent in my laboratory?' Mandara asked.

Grins and nods were all the answer required.

The adults' desire for further explanation was so strong there was no need for anyone to ask.

'The twins designed all this,' Tamina explained. They were very insistent it was done exactly as they said. Each of us applied two of the colours to adjacent triangles. Then we engraved the six sides of the inner figure. You will see that each side bridges exactly two segments. In this sequence.' She pointed as she spoke. 'Me, Tullia, Shimara, Wrenden, Qwelby, Pelnak. And we engraved those sides in opposite pairs. So Wrenden and I each engraved one line on both of our segments, and so on. The twins said its name is Óweppâ.'

Tamina leant forward, extending her hand and the object.

'Right in the centre you can see seven semi-circles. No particular pattern. The twins said they represented the seven dimensions of life. Three, four, five, six, seven, eight and nine.' She looked around the adult's faces. 'We've never heard of the sixth dimension but the twins said it was there.'

Mizena held out her hand and received the object.

'Heavy!' she exclaimed. 'And old.'

'No, we made it less than two years ago,' Pelnak said.

'No. I mean the energy is old,' Mizena replied. Noticing her husband's raised eyebrow she turned to him. 'I'm not just a happy farmer, mother and house-wife. Don't forget my genes,' she said in reference to the genes she carried of Rrîltallâ Taminûllÿâ, the great healer-heroine of Aurigan times.

'It was all very strange,' Wrenden explained. 'We just did what they said. No discussion at all. And the twins were... different.'

'It was their eyes,' Shimara said. 'All the time we were working the fine rims around their purple orbs were silver, instead of their usual, you know, Tullia lavender and Qwelby violet.'

'And their ovals were rimmed with silver,' Pelnak added.

'It was like *Invaders from the Nebula*,' Wrenden said, referring to a Sci-Fi HoloWrapper popular amongst the younger children, 'and they'd been taken over by the aliens.'

The object was passed round to Mandara.

'You have created a very powerful Talisman,' he said, feeling the energy. 'This one interfaces with the sixth level of vibration. What do you know of that?'

The youngsters and Mizena shook their heads.

'We know so little of the time before the Great Divide. Our researches,' he indicated his wife and Shandur, 'indicate the sixth dimension to have been a vibratory band on the side, so to speak. Not a level through which the Auriganii lived in what seems to have been the long journey through all the levels.' He paused.

'Keep it simple, my dear,' his wife said, reaching out to rest a hand gently on the big mans' arm and using the contact to ensure tight-beaming of an accompanying thought. *This is not the time to mention the inner hexagon and the power of its links.*'

'*No. Your expertise. But you worry me. How much power are they unconsciously tapping into, and where did the twins learn all this?*' Mandara tight-beamed back as he appeared to take time to consider his words.

'In the manner in which you have explained that you formed your group, you have managed to reproduce what I believe was a powerful Aurigan ceremony, by which you have created a separate and distinct energy entity capable of accessing the sixth dimension. One that has far more power than all six of you put together. I think that explains how you were able to create the Time Bubble and the Bell Tower.'

The youngsters shared looks of surprise, amazement and excitement.

'What do you use this for?' Mandara asked.

'There is so much information in the Archives that is age restricted,' Pelnak answered. 'Since we formed our group, all six of us exploring together, we can access well beyond our age limits.'

'Such as?' Mizena asked

'Science for me,' Pelnak answered.

'Azura, for me and Qwelby,' Wrenden said.

'Dance and fashion for me,' Tamina added. 'And fashion for Tullia, of course. And she explores healing and what it would mean to devote her life to that.'

'I like bits of what the girls explore,' Shimara explained. 'I like the idea of combing them to create new energy schemes of interior decoration, houses and furniture that can adapt themselves to people's needs, emotional as well as physical.' She blushed as she glanced at Tamina. 'And asking you to help make them beautiful.'

'And Quantum Twins of course,' Tamina and Wrenden said together.

All four adults nodded their understanding. Given that the whole race lived in tune with the underlying energies of the cosmos they were convinced that there had to be a particular reason for the existence of Quantum Twins. Hoping to find information amongst the very old and degraded records, Mandara and Lellia had devised powerful and discrete search protocols. They had not been able to discover any more than they had already been told.

'And we all want to know more about the lives of our ancestors,' Pelnak added to nods from his friends.

'It sounds like you have accessed knowledge several years ahead of you, at least into the tenth and eleventh phases,' Mizena said in admiration.

'And beyond,' Wrenden added. 'But that's adult stuff and it's, well, boring.'

The adults laughed as a feeling of relief spread amongst them that the children still were, at least sometimes, children.

'How do your Educationers react to the knowledge in your work?' Mizena asked.

'We don't put any age restricted stuff into our college work!' Pelnak replied in a horrified tone of voice.

'The Educationers are all adults and they're... boring.' Wrenden's voice tailed off. 'But you're not,' he added quickly.

Everyone could see the 'Why not?' hanging in the air above his head.

It was as though the room itself sighed as Lellia received thoughts of permission from the other adults. The lighting dimmed and the sky turned to night. Instead of the sun, hanging above their heads was a planet streaked with dark reds and blacks and with a purple ring around it. The traditional image for Auriga in its last days.

'I will save you a long and technical history lesson,' Lellia said. 'It appeared that the basis for the violence was in some of the exploration, creation, achievement and reward sequences of our DNA. Now, by the time adulthood is achieved, each Tazian has been calibrated and, dependent upon the individual, certain restrictions are applied as part of the ceremony. Putting it far too simply: the calibration is on a peace/aggression index related to co-operative effort/personal achievement.'

'Oh, great. I'm in for a full dose then,' Wrenden said bitterly, referring to his genetic inheritance from the Uddîšû Ngélûzhrâ Khèrñîszón.

'Surely we need adventurers and explorers,' Tamina said, tightbanding her brother her thought that it was about time he let go of that Hero's other attribute of Trickster. It had only been a few days ago that he had played his latest trick at a family meal with the twins present.

Black hens laid eggs larger than all others, and occasionally even larger sky blue ones with a lot of rich yolk at the narrow end. Tamina loved those soft boiled. As she had gone to crack the shell the egg cup had morphed, turning the egg narrow side down. By the time she had discovered that it was glued in position and had had to eat though the white, the yolk had gone hard, totally spoiling her special treat. She had grimaced and shaken her head, as if in sad dismissal and deliberately disarming her brother. She had then mentaformed an arm into a snake and hissed.

All Tazian boys had a degree of snake phobia before their Awakening and becoming men. At times Tamina used that to get back at her brother, using real snakes. On that occasion Wrenden had jerked back and succeeded in partially blocking the energy. Qwelby had gone pale and rushed from the room. Tullia had groaned, clutched her stomach and bent over.

'He's terrified,' Tullia had said. 'I never send snake images, no matter how much he annoys me. I feel his fear. Kaigii. Identical twins.' She had given Tamina a lop-sided smile. 'You couldn't know. We hide that very securely.'

Tamina had only recently experienced her Awakening and was coming to terms with what it meant for her. How she was going to help Tullia through that when her youngerest reacted as a boy as well as a girl was a question she had filed away to explore later.

'We do need them.' Lellia's words cut through Tamina's reminiscing. 'It depends on their level of co-operation.' Her accompanying thoughts were expressing her long-standing concern about the basis on which such decisions were made.

'Oh, he can do that all right,' Tamina said, in a sour tone of voice. She was remembering one of the more audacious tricks that her brother and Qwelby had pulled off. Entering her bedroom she had seen a sphere of water balanced on the top of the door. It had taken her too long to think through the unbelievably advanced level of skill of 'the pair of pests' as she and Tullia called them. It was not even real water that was being released from a mental force field. She was being made to imagine the water. By the time she had realised that, she had allowed herself to feel soaked through.

'It was only several centuries ago that it was considered that one more change was needed to maintain total peace and harmony,' Lellia continued. 'To have adulthood achieved at the end of the second era rather than the third. That deliberately denied to most Tazii what used to be twelve years of active exploration and personal, individual development.'

'Why?' all four youngsters asked.

'It was feared that as increasing numbers of Tazii espoused the philosophy of the Shakazii, and equally many other Tazii were pressing for implementation of the more extremist interpretations of The True Aurigan Teachings, there would be conflict.'

There was a long silence whilst the youngsters absorbed what they had learnt.

'Did you sense any opposition when searching for the twins?' Lellia asked.

A variety of 'no's' and shaking of heads provided her answer.

'That would be most unlikely,' Mandara commented. 'If I am correct, they were linking, or trying to link, within the discreet boundaries of their own energy entity.' Not normally given to seeking reassurance, he glanced at his fellow quantum scientist. Shandur nodded his agreement.

The youngsters felt a chill as the adults withdrew behind a Privacy Shield to share their thoughts. As Orchestrator of the First XzylStroem, responsible for maintaining the planet's six XzylStroems in balance and thus the link with Azura in the third dimension, the final decision had to be Lellia's.

Warmth returned as the adults finished their discussion. Lellia carefully searched each youngster's aura. She acknowledged that their EraBands were holding well to their developing selves. She stilled a sigh. Twelve was so young to be considered mentally developed. Yet it had been so for millennia, with emotional maturity being achieved over the next twelve years, before growth was dramatically slowed. Momentarily, she allowed her regret to surface at the change from the original Tazian timing of three eras totalling thirty-six years. *At least three have their crystals and Wrenden will have his soon.*

'We have thoughtsent your parents. They know how keen you are to mentalink with the twins. They have agreed with a visit to the XzylCavern. With the sixth dimensional energy of the talisman linking all six of you together.' She flicked a quick thought to her husband, and received his confirmation. 'You four stand the best chance we have of making a connection with the twins. Tamina and Pelnak, you are elderests for Tullia and Qwelby...'

'And Qwelby's my elderest,' Wrenden said. 'We have fun together,' his voice breaking as he shot a glance at his big sister, who was the butt of many of their jokes.

'So that's what you call it, you little squirt.' Tamina's repartee lacked any bite. She knew that Qwelby was not only her brother's elderest but also his BestFriend who he hero-worshipped.

Taking a deep breath, Lellia got up from her chair. 'I will introduce you to the Stroems. We'll have to walk. Lift doesn't like going there.' Door closed quietly behind them.

'Don't you think its strange, wrong, that we know more, far more, about the Azurii than we do about our own history?' Mandara asked Shandur and Mizena rhetorically. 'Not just Auriga and that incredible journey, but even the early years here, before we separated into... what? Two watered-down offshoots of the same race?'

The friends followed Lellia to the top floor of the central and rearmost wing of Lungunu. There was a small bridge that spanned the two halves of the largest of the five wings. From the centre of the bridge a door opened onto a short corridor. At the end was a doorway that looked like an ordinary, semi-translucent, three-layered iris. To one side was a neat little booth with a door. It looked like the sort of object that just demanded Tazii youngsters to discover how many they could cram into it at once.

Lellia explained. 'One at a time, relax back into Chair. When asked why you are here, you will say: 'First visit.' You will be fitted with a XzylStroem helmet and insulshoes. If you cannot see or hear, just think that and the helmet will adjust itself.'

One by one they went into the booth and came out looking like bug-eyed, steel grey hedgehogs on Bad Hair Day. No-one knew how it had started, but the annual Bad Hair Day had become a cult anti-celebration for youngsters in their second Era between the ages of twelve and twenty-four. Twiyeras as they were called. The winner from each category, short hair or long hair, was known as "The Mary". They were presented with a miniature facsimile of a traditional shepherd's NeutrinoCrook, and wore an outfit made of simuseashells for that night's party.

When Lellia came out of the booth with her own helmet, she explained. 'The visuglobes will act like strong snowshades. Inside the XzylCavern everything will seem to be in varying shades of grey, except the Stroems. There is a much greater exchange of neutrons than normal. Everything will appear to be flickering in and out of reality. Don't think about it! Enough of what is there, and is there for long enough, for everything to act as though it is solid.'

She made eye contact with each youngster in turn and waited until they nodded, nervously.

Knowing how much Tazian children enjoyed watching Azuran transmissions, she bent over, grew a hunchback and walked through the door with a heavy limp saying: 'Walk this way.'

'Wasn't that hunch on the other side?' asked Wrenden.

Lellia smiled. He had picked up her reference to one of his favourite Azuran flikkers.

The triple iris was the first part of the StroemLock. Mandara liked his little bits of showmanship. When all five people were in the Lock and the third iris closed with no other doorway to be seen, the walls of the Lock shimmered out of existence.

Four young voices gasped. They were in the XzylCavern, round and with a domed ceiling it appeared to be larger than the entire house, which it was. They were high up on a gallery. It ran around the dome and took them with it. Far, far down below, there was a great seething mass of swirling colour, noise and vibration. Every now and then a piece would leap up like a wave, curl over at the top and fall back with a strange glooping sound.

As the gallery brought them back to the entrance, Lellia asked: 'Have you had enough for your first visit, or do you want to try a mentasynch with the twins now?'

There was a pause as the friends realised that they were no mind contacts. Lellia heard the faint sound of four pairs of lips being moistened, followed by four subdued yeses.

'Walk around this gallery. Take your time. Look around and get used to the fact that you have to speak aloud. Get used to the vibrations you can feel and the sight of the Stroems. Do not be afraid. I will not bother you with all the technicalities that are built in for safety. However strongly the Stroems Xzyle, they cannot reach you up on this gallery.'

The friends did as instructed. The longer they walked around, the more they peered into the depths, the less afraid they became.

With a great, jagged sound like a thousand strips of calico being torn, a mighty scarlet Stroem reared up towards them. They leapt back against the wall. A contorted, orange head appeared, a long snout extruded and sharp fangs curved down from the top of its mouth and over the lower jaw. Drool dripped from the sides of its mouth as its jaws opened wide enough to swallow them all. A forked, black tongue flashed out between the two rows of yellow teeth. Four pairs of tiny, bloodshot eyes focussed individually on each youngster. They gleamed with anticipation. Bright lines of coruscating colour reached out from all around the walls and held the horror well below the gallery. Shoulders appeared as it dropped its head. Muscles in the shoulders and neck strained. It was obvious it was going to try to leap up past the barrier and devour the friends.

Trembling and too frightened to move, the four reached out, held hands and merged energy fields.

The beast's head lifted up almost to a level with the gallery. Bright light exploded in a ring all around it, momentarily dazzling the youngsters before the visuglobes darkened. With a scream the visage collapsed and disappeared in a mass of swirling Xzyls.

'Let's go,' Lellia called, deciding that they had experienced enough for their first visit to the Stroems. She pointed towards the exit.

With the Stroemlock firmly closed, Lellia told them to enter the both and say: 'Visit ended.' When she came out of the booth she led them into a cosy side room and asked House for a large jug of multijuice and several bowls of craklesnax.

Fifteen minits of happy munching later, Tamina sent a private thought around the other three. They agreed. She turned to Lellia.

'I'm sorry Tamina, your Privacy Shield was not strong enough. I heard your thought.' Lellia smiled. 'If all four of you really are sure you're ready to return?'

All four nodded, looks of determination on their faces.

'Now you have just spoiled your appetites...'

Lellia was deluged by a horrified exclamations.

'And Eeky's ALWAYS hungry,' Tamina added.

Lellia laughed and a sound of violins, cellos and muted horns filled the room. 'Thank you my dears. That's done me the world of good. Come. Let's find what Cook has got for us.'

CHAPTER 12

IT'S COLD

Cold. Numbing cold assailed Qwelby from all sides. Eyes opened. *My eyes?* The world was white. Buffeted by harsh wind, he wrapped his arms around himself as the snowstorm battered him. As the winds swirled the snow there was a brief gap. He caught a glimpse of buildings, grey in the half-light. Then the snow blotted them out.

Shelter. Must find shelter.

He staggered forwards. A building loomed up before him. As he stepped into the lee of the wall, the wind eased. Rubbing his torso to keep warm he remembered his training and rapidly built his inner fire, letting the inner furnace pump the heat around his bloodstream.

The shivering stopped. He looked around. He did not recognise his surroundings. Through the snow he made out several tall buildings but no sign of any doors or windows. They were bland, uniform and grouped close together. Nothing like he had ever seen anywhere on Vertazia. The complex had the feel of a strange working area, closed for a celebration day. Behind him there was only the driving snow, thick, white turning to grey, impenetrable.

He turned back. The way ahead did not look promising, but somewhere there had to be doors and people. He started to walk, remembering to keep his inner fire burning brightly. Without seeing any doors or windows it was difficult to think of what he was passing as buildings. A brief lull in the winds and through the steadily falling snow he was able to make out more towering walls on the other side of the road. As far as he was able to see, more stretched away in front of him. There were occasional gaps wide enough to allow large powersleds to travel two or even three abreast. *Surely they must lead to where there are people? Perhaps access is through tunnels from a central area. A plaza with shops and cafés. Hot drinks!*

Trying to work out where that centre might be, he stopped at a crossroads and turned all around. Behind him, half masked by the falling snow, were two shapes. People. He took a step towards them. Sensed danger. Stopped. They were dark, colourless. Where were their energy fields? Again the winds shifted, momentarily parting the snow and giving him an almost clear view. They did have energy fields, but they were as dark as their shapes. A man and a woman. They felt like predators.

He hastened down a narrow passageway to his left, moving quickly between the tall buildings that loomed menacingly over him.

Where are the entrances? I know. If I walk all around one building I must find the way in. He quickened his pace even more and turned right at the next corner. There at the end of the street were the two figures, coming towards him. Frightened, he turned and ran back the way he had come.

CHAPTER 13

DICING WITH DEATH

The meal finished, the four friends returned to the cosy room where Lellia told them more about the Stroems and how they would work with them.

Back inside the XzylCavern the youngsters were startled by the difference. Although well below the gallery this time, the myriad streams of coruscating light holding down the vigorously Xzyling mass of colour made it look as though the Stroems were again eager to reach out to them.

'This is not good.' Lellia's voice came clearly through the speakers in their helmets. 'It is far too dangerous to work with them today. I've never seen them this disturbed.'

'They want to talk to us,' Wrenden said.

'Don't be daft, Eeky,' Tamina said. 'You know what Aunt Gallia has just explained to us.'

'But they're energy. And energy can talk,' he said in a petulant tone of voice.

'Your sister is right, Wrenden,' Lellia confirmed. 'Remember, the Stroems are a trans-dimensional vortex. Lungunu is built over one of the six focal points that bind us to Azura. They are energy of a very different nature to the semi-sentients like House and Lift to which you are accustomed.'

'Look!' called Pelnak excitedly. 'Faces.'

He was right. They could all see the rearing tops of the Stroems forming into impressions of faces. This time they saw several. Eyes and mouths were not in the right places. Noses appeared where ears should be. The more the Stroems fell back and rose again, the more realistic were the faces they formed.

The youngsters were drawn to the railings around the gallery, peering over, mesmerised by the uncanny likenesses to real faces that developed.

Lellia nodded to herself. The youngsters had passed the Stroems' test on their first visit. Now the Stroems were trying to interact.

'Qwelby!' Wrenden cried as a face appeared immediately below him. He bent over the railing around the gallery. Peering down he saw that everything had changed. He was looking through the colourful Stroems at a dreary collection of tall buildings, swathed in snow. They made a uniform grid-like layout. As he scanned the scene, indistinctly through the snow he saw what looked like a long ladder, some distance away.

Qwelby stopped and looked around. No-one in sight.

'Up here.'

Looking up he saw a figure on top of a roof. Was it? Yes, surely.

'Wrenden. Is that you?'

'Yes.'

'How do I get to you?'

'Go that way,' Wrenden called, pointing in the direction Qwelby was heading.

As the wind swirled the snow around, Qwelby momentarily saw a long, wide passageway that seemed to go on forever. On the sides of the buildings past the next intersection were open stairways reaching from the tops towards the ground. Weird. He was sure his eyes were not deceiving him, but the stairs seemed to stop several metres off the ground.

Comforted that Wrenden was there for him and assuming the others must be around, he headed for the first of the puzzling stairs.

He came to a side passage. Looked up. Where was Wrenden?

'I'm here,' his friend called from the top of the next building.

Puzzled as to how Wrenden had managed that, yet at the same time relieved that he was still there, Qwelby continued to make for the first stairway. Horror! Through the swirling snow he saw dark shapes coming towards him. *How can they move so quickly?* He turned to look back the way he had come. Now they were close behind him. No! He shook with fear as he realised that there were four people following him. The word 'corralling' came into his mind, followed by 'capture.'

'Quick, Qwelby, this way,' Wrenden called, gesturing him back to a side passage he had just passed.

A sudden shiver of cold reminded Qwelby he had forgotten to keep his fire going. He focussed on that as he turned back and ran down the sideway. As he reached another crossroads a gust of wind knocked him into the corner of a building. He cried out as pain shot through his arm, looked up for Wrenden. Another jolt. He saw what he assumed were windows. All shuttered with blinds or something similar, the same grey colour as the walls.

'Qwelby!' came the urgent cry. Up on the top, Wrenden was pointing around the next corner. Stepping around to his left, Qwelby saw one of the strange flights of open steps. He ran towards it, jumped but could not reach the bottom rung. Tried again. No good. It was several feet out of reach. Weird. It looked as though there was a ladder attached to the bottom. Stairs you could only go down, or up, if someone came down first?

He felt a sense of foreboding and looked back. All four people were coming up behind him. Two men and two women, spread out across the street, like safety wardens trying to herd a dangerous animal into a trap. There was something scary about the way they walked so steadily. No sense of hurrying, as though they knew whatever he did they would catch him. It reminded him of an

HWScary he had experienced. With those he could always get out and back to the comfort of the HoloChair. He never did. But he could. Now there was no such escape. But at least he was not cornered, there were three more passageways he could run down, and his four friends were here to help him.

Tamina was struck dumb. She was looking at Qwelby's face. It had his energy. As Tullia's elderest she always had a strong link with Qwelby, but it was through Tullia. This felt similar as though the link was coming through the Stroem.

The face dissolved as the Stroem fell back into the seething mass.

The Stroems Xzyled even more vigorously than before. They were swirling around, faster and faster, forming a deep whirlpool. The deeper the centre, the higher up the walls of the Cavern the edges reached until the light beams were pulsing all around the gallery, holding the top of the whirlpool down. With a great roar, the whirling edges sank back and a single giant Stroem reared up, past the net of light, hovering almost at the edge of the gallery. This time the face was perfectly formed.

'Qwelby!' Tamina cried.

Looking up, Qwelby saw Tamina, Tullia's elderest and Wrenden's older sister. As well as their esting relationship, he and Wrenden were BestFriends, and enjoyed playing-up Tamina as she was so serious and a definite bossy-boots, made worse for Qwelby by the fact that she was a lot taller than him. He would never admit to it, but with Pelnak only four months older than he was, he did look up to Tamina in some ways as a sort of elderest for himself. Her presence there on the roof was reassuring.

'Quick! Run,' Wrenden called from further along the roof. 'They're getting closer.'

'Down here,' came Wrenden's command as Qwelby reached the next corner. He stopped and looked up to see Wrenden signalling him round yet another corner. A few moments later another shout.

Everything was too surreal for either Qwelby or Wrenden to stop and wonder how the latter kept on being on different roofs, in the right places at the right times.

'Stop!' Wrenden called.

As Qwelby looked up the end of a rope fell by him. He could see Tamina behind her young brother with her arms around his waist. He assumed the not-twins were behind her. He grabbed the rope.

'Okay. I've got it. I'll tie myself on,' he called, looking up. The top half of the building disappeared behind thick, driving snow. The climb up did not look inviting.

'No time,' came Wrenden's voice. 'You walk, we pull.'

Qwelby glanced to his left. Two dark figures, a man and a woman were almost upon him. A glance to the right. The other man and woman were faintly visible through the snow that was now falling faster.

A pull on the rope jerked him into the wall. He almost lost his grip. Quickly, he leant back, put one foot high up the wall and started to walk.

The shuttered windows had thin ledges. He must have failed to see them because of the thick snow. He would have liked to rest on the ledges but the rope had been dropped down between the lines of windows.

The higher up the wall he climbed, the more the wind battered at him. Thick snow was concealing his friends on the roof. His arms were aching and it was difficult to keep going as there were unsettling jerks on the rope.

He was wondering how much further he had to go. Unable to see the top he had no way of measuring the distance. Having to concentrate so much on walking up the wall he had no energy left for his inner fire. He was freezing and was afraid his hands were about to lose their grip on the rope. He saw ice forming all along his bare arms and down his bare legs. Ice was glistening on his red tank top and his black shorts, the only colour in the whole scene.

An extra strong gust of wind opened a clear view through the snow.

What was happening? He could see Wrenden holding the rope, Tamina's arms still around him. He could not see Pelnak or Shimara. His arms were trembling with the cold. His fingers were freezing. It looked as though streams of ice were running down the rope. He saw the ice flaking off. No! It was the very strands of the rope itself coming apart. His eyes were watering.

He was almost at the top. He was stuck. Angled out from the wall his feet could go no higher. He needed his friends to pull the rope towards them. He tugged at it, trying to pull himself closer, saw Wrenden start to topple towards him, Tamina's arms sliding down her brother's body, down his thighs. The rope slackened and Qwelby dropped, swung, and crashed against the wall. Cries of pain from above as brother and sister crashed onto the roof.

Momentarily stunned, Qwelby stared at the rope, mesmerised as he saw strand after strand snapping.

'Qwelby!' It was more of a gasp than a shout.

In the StroemCavern, well above the coruscating light beams that were supposed to keep the Stroems in check, an ear extended from the single, enormous Stroem to become an arm, reaching out towards Wrenden. A hand formed at the end.

Wrenden threw himself down onto the floor of the gallery, stretched through the railings, reaching for the hand.

'EEKY!' Tamina shouted, throwing herself at his legs as he was pulled through the barrier.

Looking up, Qwelby saw Wrenden's body halfway over the roof, one hand on the rope, his other arm extended, hand held out.

Using every last drop of strength Qwelby hauled himself up the rope and saw the strands turning to ice, snapping under the strain.

'Qwelby,' Wrenden pleaded.

Tensing himself, gripping the rope with his left hand as hard as possible, Qwelby gave one mighty heave, felt his body rise, stretched his right arm up and seized his young friend's wrist. He felt a hand grip his own wrist, heard a series of sharp cracks, and watched as the rope fell out of sight. Then felt a second hand grip his wrist.

No sooner had he believed himself safe than he dropped, heard cries of pain, then stopped, swinging. Looking up, he saw that Wrenden had slid half way over the sheet of ice that edged the roof. Bent at his stomach he was hanging upside down.

'EEKY!' Tamina shouted.

Qwelby heard the panic in her voice and watched helplessly as her brother slid right over the roof and he himself dropped further down, almost losing his grip as he crashed into the wall again.

'TAMINA!!' Qwelby heard the not-twins cry, followed by the sound of their bodies slamming into the StroemGallery as they hurled themselves at her as she headed over the edge of the roof.

Qwelby looked into his BestFriend's face, seeing the mixture of horror and panic written all over it. Another slip as Tamina was pulled further over the roof edge. Panicked cries from the not-twins out of sight on the roof, and a cry of alarm from Wrenden as he swung in the air. Tamina had slid so far that her stomach was on the edge of the roof. She was hanging upside down, her face to the wall with only her brother's feet in her hands.

Qwelby knew if he did not let go, Tamina would slip again, and all three of them would fall, to be lost forever in the NoWhenWhere. He looked into his youngerest's rapidly twirling eyes: red, yellow and black. And released his grip.

'NO...O...O!' Wrenden screamed.

Too numb from the cold, and with the wet from the snow turning to ice, Wrenden's grip was not strong enough. Qwelby watched as his friend let go with one hand, using it to make a grab for Qwelby's free hand. With a shake of his head, Qwelby made a fist so there was no hand to be seized. Eyes locked together. The two boys felt Qwelby's icy wrist slide through Wrenden's grasp.

Qwelby smiled ruefully. This time Tullia could not tell him off, accusing him as she usually did of leading Wrenden astray. For once he was being a proper elderest.

'Never apart!' Qwelby called as he fell.

'QWELBYYY!' He heard Tamina's scream as he tumbled backwards, the snow beating into his face, blotting everything from his vision

He fell in slow motion, arms and legs stretched out in front. 'There is more colour than red and black,' his mind said. 'There are my red-brown arms and legs. They will save me. If I can twist around and be a cat. Land on all fours, just like in a HoloWrapper.'

A flurry of snow was dashed into his face. He closed his eyes against the stinging. Felt it on his checks and his forehead as he plummeted down

down

down...

Lellia was beside herself with fear as she spoke to Control Panel, beseeching it for more energy into the safety beams, then changed her mind. Wrenden had completely disappeared from sight and only Tamina's feet were visible above the Stroem. *What if Wrenden is below the safety level, he will be cut off, lost in the Stroems, sucked into the NoWhenWhere. And Tamina. Could she be cut in two?* Leila punched the emergency alarm that would bring Mandara. For an emergency like this, no matter how much it would be disturbed, Lift would make the journey.

Rejecting all thoughts of Temporal Consequences, Mandara overrode Lift's counsel and they Timeshifted, Lift setting Mandara and Shandur down at the end of the corridor. They ran to the StroemLock, Shandur grabbing insulshoes as Mandara opened the outer iris. Even with Timeshifting they dared not waste precious moments acquiring helmets.

A frightening scene greeted them. Shimara and Pelnak were half way through the railings, their legs partly wrapped around the stanchions as they slipped further over the edge of the gallery. Their heads and the top halves of their bodies were lost from sight in the throbbing Stroem, its bright emerald green and streaks of vivid red clearly saying "Qwelby."

The two men ran and seized the not-twins' legs.

'We're going to pull you back,' Mandara said in a steady voice. 'Hold on tight!'

They pulled. With a roar of despair the Stroem collapsed back down into the roiling mass below.

Tamina was revealed, holding onto her brother by his feet, and he was still gripping one fine StroemThread in his outstretched hands.

As the Stroem released its support on their bodies, brother and sister swung back to hang vertically upside down and the light beams ceased flickering. Their unsupported weight made Tamina's legs slide through the not-twins' grip. Mandara and Shandur let go of the not-twins and hurled themselves forward, only to see Tamina's feet disappear from view, her empty shoes held in the not-twins' hands. Screams filled all the helmets.

A faint cry of 'Why...?' ending in a sob seemed to rise from the depths, followed by the sound of bodies crashing.

Instead of hearing the hoped for '...not?' everyone's helmet was filled with Mandara's voice.

'Lower the height of the safety beams,' Mandara commanded. 'Cancel all but this sector. Then full power here. Emergency Tachyon Transmission. Engage!'

Lellia did not need to speak to Control Panel, it had heard. Travelling faster than light and thus backwards in time, the Tachyons reinforced the selected sector.

'Raise this sector!' Mandara shouted, fear racing through him. It was the ultimate safety device, but only designed to catch a small object.

Just then the inner iris of the Lock opened and Mizena appeared. She was just in time to see Wrenden's body come into sight, then his sister prostrate beneath him.

Having been told by House that the Stroems were exceptionally excited and her husband and great uncle were without helmets, she had taken the time to be fitted with one. So it was that a few minits later four very shaken youngsters and two suffering men had been helped into the cosy room. Wrenden had turned grey. He looked like an old man, a very old man. His face was haggard and his hair had gone white. Tears were streaming down his face.

'He was climbing up one of the Stroems. It was slipping through my fingers. Then it thinned away to nothing. We had a wrist grip. I was pulling him up. We were all sliding into the StroemWell. He let go of me! I couldn't hold him. I wasn't strong enough. He's gone and it's my fault. I should have saved him.' He choked. 'I could have saved him... he let go.'

An anguished look was plastered all over his face. 'He shouted "Never Apart" as he fell... That's what the twins say.' He looked around, appealing for an explanation.

'I think it was his way of saying he'll always be looking out for you. Wherever he is.' Tamina wrapped her arms around her brother, hugging him as he howled his heart out. With tears in her eyes she looked around the room at the others. 'We were so close.' She looked down and pulled her brother tightly to her. 'If Qwelby hadn't let go, we would have been pulled over into the Well.' She ruffled her brother's hair. 'We weren't going to let go. We couldn't.' She sobbed and buried her face in her brother's hair.

'No. We weren't. We couldn't,' Shimara and Pelnak said together, holding hands and looking at each other, shaking with shock as they remembered the terrible moments when they had heard the anguished cries and then almost immediately they thought they had also lost Tamina and Wrenden forever.

A long time was to pass before everyone was sufficiently recovered for the whole story to emerge.

Eventually, as life on Vertazia changed, the whole event was made into what was to become a famous HWFantasy: containing a serious question: What is Reality?

That was followed by a game playing follow-up whereby the various players, know as 'GamesWrappers' could act together to rescue the Qwelby character in one of several different and challenging ways.

CHAPTER 14

BETWEEN
WORLDS

Qwelby was sweeping down through the blackness of space, a black that was shot through with lines of bright light, sudden flowerings of mixtures of colours, bright reds, oranges and yellows. Shining shapes were moving across his vision. The lines of light were coming from them.

'*Focus. Remember where you are,*' a sharp voice inside his head said. A sensation swept through him as though he had stepped under a waterfall, but the water was flowing through every cell in his body. His senses cleared.

He was astride Zhólérrân, his fire-breathing Dragon, leading a group of DragonRiders in yet another battle against space ships flown by the Solids who were intent on destroying his HomeSphere. *Mine? Of course it is. I am the Dragon Kèhša.* Signalling to his Wing of Warriors, he whirled Zhólérrân into a spiralling dive towards the last target, intent on using the Dragon's "Fire" to mindblast the crews of the remaining few attacking ships.

Oh, but he was weary. Aurigan life began in the solid, third dimension, then progressed over some two thousand years through to the ninth where they existed as pure group consciousnesses free from all constraints of Form, and needing only the energy from distant stars to survive. Extending outwards though a series of concentric orbs from the central third dimension three hundred kilometres in diameter, the whole space ship was finally enwrapped in the energies of those existing in the much faster vibrations of the ninth dimension.

Although designed to be as self-supporting as possible, the HomeSphere still needed to enter planetary systems. Advanced scouts had said that there was no planet suitable for a future home. All they had wanted to do was to pass slowly through the system, re-energising the whole race as they cruised close to the sun, and replenishing stocks from any uninhabited planet of nutriments essential for those existing in the lower dimensions.

Dropping down into the third dimension they had made contact with the inhabitants of the fourth and fifth planets and explained their simple needs. The HomeSphere's course had been at an acute angle to the ecliptic and on a heading to keep it at a great distance from the inhabited planets. Yet once again they had been met with suspicion, mistrust and an almost overwhelming assault.

It was inevitable that a few warriors were lost in each round of fighting. More serious was that the mental anguish all Auriganii experienced from sensing the destruction of so many sentient life-forms was taking its toll on the cohesiveness of the whole race, and threatening to destabilise their DNA. This latest conflict was bringing to a head deep-seated divisions that were threatening to turn into a disastrous schism. Even though by now battle-hardened, he was tiring from the repeated death and destruction. And he was beginning to wonder not only how long he and his warriors could continue, but whether the race would survive.

Its handful of small escorting ships drifting lifeless, their energy projectors silent, a lone battleship was still heading for his HomeSphere. *There it is again, that strange feeling that I created it. But that was thousands of years ago. And who was she that led our people on board?*

Although he was only just over six hundred sun cycles old, already all his DNA was fully activated and he existed at the highest level of the seventh dimension, making sliding between dimensions easy. But maintaining a presence in the solidity of the third for long periods, whilst also using to the full his energy capabilities of the higher levels of vibration, was extremely fatiguing. He was fast approaching the point where he would have to let go his Form and return to the seventh dimension to recuperate and re-energise.

With a great effort of will he summoned his flagging reserves for the final dive. In a blending in which Rider merged with Dragon they Harnessed the minds of Warriors and Dragons. As they launched a mighty, concentrated blast to end the battle, the young Dragon Kèhša shuttered his mind in a vain attempt to blot out the anguished, mental screams of the dying Solids.

A lone gun turret flared from the crippled ship. Excruciating pain seared all down the right side of his body. Helplessly, he tumbled out of the now destroyed harness, the mind shattering scream of his beloved Dragon ringing through every fibre of his being.

Flaming DragonBreath, sparkling laser beams, the mental screams of mind shattered Solids: through it all and as always, the Dragon Kèhša had seen a beautiful, golden-maned, silver Unicorn accompanying his Wing. Now she was speeding towards him.

He cursed the Rider for the dangers she took, time after time, following him and his Wing so closely into the thickest of the fights, regardless of the danger to herself and her Unicorn. His people could not afford to lose her. She was the pre-eminent of all healers. It was only through the application of those skills to people's minds that the Auriganii remained united and continued to thoughtpower the HomeSphere on what had become an interminable quest.

'The people cannot lose their Dragon Kèhša. Nor he his Zhólérrân!' His Dragon thoughtsent a reminder of its own need for healing. A healing that came especially from the almost symbiotic relationship that existed with a Unicorn, that engulfed the Riders of both and left him uncertain in his pain deadened mind of whether he was man or Dragon and loved the woman or the Unicorn, or both.

Surely there will be a day when there is no more war and I will be able to allow my love for her to unfold.

Tumbling through space, feeling sick as a variety of images revolved around him and unbelievable weary, he surrendered to what he thought was the inevitable. *My last fight. The HomeSphere has been saved.*

A comet was roaring towards him. *So much noise in the quiet of deep space?* It looked like a Stroem with an elongated tale. It had a face. *Kaigii!* He stretched out an arm and was swept into its fiery wake...

A feeling of peace swept over Tullia. The blackness of deep space was restful, the myriad tiny pinpoints of stars. But? Some were much larger, moving as she watched. They were not stars. Spaceships? She was in an HWAdventure? A sensation swept through her of being under a waterfall, the water flowing through every cell in her body.

Everything came into focus as a sharp pain lanced though her mind. She felt her heroes' screams and urged Trellûa, her winged Unicorn, towards the tumbling DragonRider. Merging with her Unicorn, she poured all her energy into Trellûa. Golden light sprang forth from the Unicorn's horn, spiralling towards their heroes, the young Dragon Kèhša and his Dragon.

The HomeSphere itself had dropped into the third dimension in order to feed that level of the sun's emissions though to its own, central core where the Seed Generation lived. The unicorn mounted healers operated from the fifth. It saved them the exhaustion of having to maintain third dimensional Form and made them invisible to the attacking Solids.

Right now he needed more than energy healing. Calling up all her skills, she mindmelded with her Unicorn and cloaked them both in Form. Dipping down into the path of his 'fall', freeing herself from the harness and steadied by Trellûa's strong wings, she stood up, stretched forth her arms, caught the unconscious Rider and slid back down onto the Unicorn's back.

She wrapped her arms around the still burning man and cradled him to her breast, focussing every iota of energy into her love for him. Half aware of the whinnying being replaced by the high pitched, almost bleating sound of her Unicorn's pain for the moments it took to quench the fire. With Zhólérrân circling them, they carried the Dragon Kèhša back to the Sphere where many Healers were working.

Born within the same sun cycle, the race's need for her healing abilities had propelled her much faster than normal through the life cycles. As with her hero, all her DNA was already fully activated and she existed at the highest and Formless level of the seventh dimension.

In the early days of the wars she had fallen in love with the young Warrior through his impetuosity and daring in leading the defence of the HomeSphere when the Auriganii had nothing other than a few Dragons with which to protect themselves. She had promised herself that she and Trellûa would always be there to care for all the Warriors and Dragons, and particularly the Dragon Kèhša and his Dragon as they plunged into the thickest of every battle.

Just as his daring and disregard for his safety had resulted in his becoming the leader of the Warriors, so had her skills resulted in her being accepted both as Unicorn Kèhša and the Chief Conciliator. That evolvement had been a surprise to all. Not only were both so young, previously their race had had little concept of or need for leaders.

She longed to be able to stay with him, but could not. Because she was the most powerful Healer, now that the fight was ended her first duty was to see to all the Winged Healer pairs, then tend to the most seriously wounded Dragons and Riders. She would find time for the young man later, and when she was certain of being able to conceal the almost overwhelming love she felt for him. She must not let anything distract him from the onerous burden he carried, responsible for protecting the people she had led onto the HomeSphere he had created.

I had lead...? He had created? That's thousands of years ago...

Cutting off that train of thought and returning to the present, she refused to allow herself to recall the number of times she and Trellûa had gone to the aid of Zhólérrân and his Rider, or the times when he had saved her from her rashness in following him and his Wing of Dragons so closely into battle. They owed their lives to him, and although she would never let the thought escape her, once again, both Dragon and Rider owed theirs to her and Trellûa.

Willing hands reached out as her Unicorn alighted in the HomeSphere. As he was taken from her arms, the six long fingers of her left hand gently caressed his dragonsuit, reassuring the baby scales that people would care for them until Zhólérrân had recovered.

A brief pang at the parting was replaced with the feeling of relief that flowed through her as she discarded her blue skinergysuit and returned to the freedom of the seventh dimension. The battle had been short, her energies were high and she was able to maintain her Impression of Form that gave her an apparent physical presence that she knew was an inspiration to all her Healers.

Even at that high vibrational level she could not but help grimacing. Started by a child's simple drawing, she was faced with what had become a popular symbol displayed throughout the several dimensions. A simple curved line representing a smile, above that in a typical, Aurigan V-shape, a pair of eyes, pale blue ovals with large purple centres, both limned in silver.

She knew it was to honour the Auriganii who had created the HomeSphere and launched them on their momentous voyage. And she knew the Dragon Kèhša shared her own discomfort in that it represented their own, extremely rare colouration, a mark of their genetic inheritance from the QeïchâKaïgï, the identical, man-woman twins who had created the HomeSphere then encouraged the whole race to travel with and around it. Nevertheless it was disconcerting. Along with the half whispered thoughts of *'Kèhša'* that seemed to follow both of them, it was as though the symbols were saying: 'Your ancestors saved us when our sun was dying. Now it is your turn.'

A comet was streaking its way towards her. It looked like a Stroem with an elongated tale. It had a face. *Kaigii!* She reached out an arm and was swept into its fiery wake...

CHAPTER 15

REFORMING

BETWIXT AND BETWEEN

Tazian mathematical theory stated that there must be a boundary between each of the definable nine dimensions, the tenth being The All and thus encompassing everything and without definition or boundary. Having existence meant that a boundary must possess space-time-consciousness, yet without depth or it would form a separate and distinct dimension itself, its spatial component therefore evincing only two dimensions.

In theory, the Twins had to be trapped between the third and fifth dimensions, within the boundary that was an infinitely convoluted plane, warping through space-time-consciousness.

With each and every individual component of their selves reduced to the ultimate constituent of all matter and consciousness, the Kwozakubezeninii, all their multitude of wave forms were spread across the whole universe, in the Timelessness that was the ineffable signature of The All.

Far out at the edge of a minor galaxy an energy rippled. Like a seed crystal dropped into a supersaturated solution, nucleation occurred and the wave forms collapsed. Uncountable numbers of Kuznii raced inwards from the furthest corners of the galaxy as recrystallisation occurred. Combining, Forming, the now particles recreated their original energy-lattice and each twin returned to sentient awareness. Painful awareness. Scenes seen from inside the stairwell ripped through their minds.

Scenes, seen, seeing. The words tumbled through their minds. Their minds played with the words. Timebled?

Yesterday all my troubles seemed so far away: now they're here to stay. Am I in yesterday?? And where is yesterday now that it's today??

? where or when am i ?

? AM I ?

! I AM !

CHAPTER 16

WHERE AM I?

FINLAND

Qwelby was seated astride the Stroem, whooping with excitement as though he was on a DareDragon Ride on an KeyPoint FunDay. Only a few more minits to go. He had already lasted longer than Wrenden and their other friends. Just Kaigii's time to beat. The Stroem disappeared, sending him spiralling down towards... *towards?*

All was pitch black.

He was being scraped on all sides.

Fifty trillion cells in my body and every one of them hurts!

The awful scratching ceased. Moments later it seemed as though he slid into a cold tube and slowed to a stop. He opened his eyes. Nothing to be seen. Was he still in deep space? But where were the stars? However few, he knew there were stars at the very edges of the universe.

He tried to move. That was frightening. His arms were pinned to his sides by the coldness. Panic set in as he struggled. Realisation! His legs were moving. The panic lessened. Another fact slipped into his mind. There was no ground beneath his feet. He took a deep breath, and coughed on the cold air. Now his nose was running. But? Controlling the rising panic, his senses told him he was upside down. He waggled his fingers. *Good. Whatever this cold is, it only goes as far down, or up, as my wrists. I can move!*

He lay still for a moment, checking all his sensations. *I think I am me again.*

As he started to wriggle he discovered that the tube was not solid. The more he pushed with his arms, the more space he was able to make around him. It was like the time when he had fallen off his twistor and gone head first into a snowdrift. Old, packed snow, partly frozen and semi-solid had made a tube with icy walls.

As he flailed about with his feet they hit something solid. *Great, leverage.* He pushed, relaxed, pushed again. Whatever the cold was, the hole was widening. Several more heaves and something slid down by his head. It was his bag, *Fill Me.* With one hand he pushed it to the bottom of the hole, tilted his body the other way, brought up his other arm and pushed against the bag with both hands. It moved a little way then held firm.

As his arms extended, pushing him along the hole, he tilted and realised that he was moving more backwards than upwards. His waist passed the edge of the hole and he slid down, closing his eyes against possible damage.

The sliding stopped and he opened his eyes. It was very dim. Everything was white. Cautiously he lifted his head. Darkness all around. Carefully he moved on the hard but yielding surface. He started to shiver with the cold. As his eyes adjusted he made out... trees? With sloping branches covered in white!

Where were the buildings? His pursuers? His friends?

A torrent of thoughts assailed him. Pictures flashed through his mind. He put his hands over his eyes. 'NO!!' he cried out, slamming the doors on all the intruders. His shivering increased. Panicking, he scrambled to his feet, falling over as the ground gave way. Finally, standing almost knee deep in softness, he looked around, saw a lump at the edge of the trees that looked different, trudged over to it, pushed at the covering and found a fallen tree.

He cleared the cold white stuff from it and sat down. More thoughts were hammering on the doors of his mind, trying to force their way in.

He shoved them aside. *Must get warm.* Skin-tight tank top and shorts, normal wear under a fashionable, figure-hugging bodysuit, were no protection from the cold that was penetrating to his very core. He took a deep breath, coughed and spluttered as the icy air reached his lungs. Eyes watering, nose running, he yanked up the bottom of his red top. By bending over and tugging he just managed to blow his nose, then ducked, gave a wry smile as he realised his twin was not there to give him a slap. Panic rose, was quickly squashed. *Must get warm first. Then find Tullia.*

Tullia? I'm alive!

Covering his mouth with his hand he breathed carefully and settled into his well practised rhythm. As he relaxed, he imagined his heart a furnace, pumping warm blood around his body. He was to discover later that Azurii did the opposite: imagined themselves colder so their bodies would become warmer. It was one of the many ways in which Azuran lives seemed so contrary that he would wonder how they managed to survive on their planet.

Warm at last, he had a good look around. The white stuff was indeed snow. He must have fallen through the trees, but there was no sign of his passage. *Surely I would have knocked snow off the branches? Ah, but not if I was still all those kuznii and didn't become me until I landed. So where was I with all those grey buildings? And where are the others? Too many puzzles!* He firmly locked them away. He would have the time to find answers when he was with Tullia. *Where is my pesky twin?*

The only marks in the snow that he could see were from the hole where he had landed in the snowdrift to where he was sitting. That meant that she had not got up and wandered off. Calling out 'Tullia!' he got up and looked around, becoming more and more worried as he continued calling yet there was never an answer. Trembling with dismay he finally accepted she was not there.

Then a shock hit him so hard he gasped aloud and collapsed back onto the fallen tree. Not only was he alone, and didn't know where or when, his twin was not in that special place that each of them had in their mind where the other lived. For the first time in his life he did not have a mental connection with her. He put his hand to his torc, feeling the chunky, interlinked metals. Its energy was muted. Fearfully, he grasped his crystal of red Drakobata. There was no tiny tremor. The final confirmation. There was no contact with his twin's necklace. They were totally apart.

He felt completely bewildered. *I panicked when I had no need. Normally, I would MentaSynch with her and she would come to help me. Why didn't I do that? Did I try?* He stood up and pounded his chest with his fists. After everything he had been through, hurting himself made him feel real, physical, solid. But. He was a Quantum Twin. Without Tullia in his mind he was not complete, only half a person. He roared into the night, a mixture of rage and anguish.

Feeling exhausted, drained, hopeless, he stared blankly at the snow and trees. A picture came to him of a sandy, scrubby sort of desert. The lantern had shown them two scenes, snow and desert.

I am in the snow. Is Tullia on Haven? He felt panic welling up inside him again. *What have we done? What have I done? If I'd not sulked. If we'd gone to the Elmit room. Can my wanting so much to explore Azura really have caused this to happen?*

He took a deep breath. The freezing air swooping into his lungs turned into a coughing fit. He got up and stamped around, putting his hand over his nose and mouth to warm up his breath. As he wiped away the tears the coughing fit had caused he realised something was missing: the bag. He had left it in the hole. Reluctantly, he squirmed inside, grasped the strap, and laboriously heaved himself out.

He was now thoroughly wet. That reminded him to focus on his inner fire and feed more energy to it. *This can't go on for long. I dare not run out of energy and fall asleep. I will die in this cold.*

Trying to force a sense of calm on top of all the panic, he sat back down on the log and opened the bag. As he bent over to look into it, everything went blurry. He lifted his hand in front of his face. It was expanding and contracting. The trees were circling around him. A big hole opened up inside. He felt his body shrinking. Unable to stop himself he toppled onto the snow.

He was cold, Xzarze! he was cold, and wet. Memory came to him. Feeling dizzy, he used the fallen tree to pull himself up and sat on it, hunched over. One hand over his mouth he breathed steadily and focussed all his weak energy on building his inner fire. As his vision cleared he noticed that the in-side out globe had fallen out of the bag. As he bent down to pick it up he saw that it was brightly coloured and no longer in-side out.

It looked like a map of a planet. There were two patches of white on opposite sides. Holding it so one was on the top, he turned the tennis ball sized globe around. It looked vaguely like Vertazia. *Vaguely?* There was some small lettering on the white patch. He peered closely and read out: 'Third Planet.'

Normally, he would have been sure that Vertazia was the third planet from the sun. Just then he didn't feel sure of anything. He certainly did not want the answer that he was afraid he was going to find. He counted on his fingers. *First planet from the sun is Little Friend, second is the Joker, third is Vertazia, fourth is Haven.* Panic overwhelmed him, made worse by the lack of contact with his twin.

'Tullia! Where are you?' he yelled aloud.

Recovering, he remembered the previous day's weird adventures. They had been in a NullPoint Bubble. What if he was in one now? Or what if he had jumped into a HoloWrapper? Sometimes you started in the middle of an adventure, not knowing where you were, what was going on or even what characters you and your friends were.

'Yes, that must be it,' he said aloud. 'An Azuran style one where there is no mental contact.' He had never experienced that before but, that had happened in the staircase. He felt reassured that he knew what was happening.

Right. Let's get on with it. Find the others. Or at least Kaigii.

It had been dark when he had first opened his eyes. Then as he got accustomed to his surroundings it seemed lighter, now it was dark. Fortunately, the skies were clear and the waxing moon was almost full, its light reflecting off the snow set the landscape in a clear contrast of black and white. Millions of stars twinkled at him. He recognised Orion and several other constellations. Even so, without any of the usual inner sensations of a HoloWrapper, he felt very alone. Covering his mouth, he took a few slow, deep breaths to calm himself.

He looked back at the moon. It was a quarter older than at home. He sighed, reassured. He must be in a HoloWrapper. Admittedly it was unlike anything he had previously experienced, but it linked with the previous frightening scene in the snow.

The fallen tree he was sitting on was at the side of a large area of snow. Shaped like a long, thin triangle, the trees met in a point near the top of the hill. Downhill they formed what appeared to be an impenetrable barrier. Looking behind, through the trees where he had arrived, he thought he could see another expanse of open snow. He would go that way and hope for the best.

Progress was slow as the snow was deep and soft. He concentrated on keeping himself warm and being very careful where he was stepping. It was with relief that he found himself at the edge of the trees, looking over a very wide, steep slope, glistening in the moonlight. Feeling too disoriented to think what it might be, worn out from the effort of trudging through deep snow, seeing a smooth path downhill, he stepped onto it and immediately slipped over. Wow! That was like glass.

He lay for a moment recovering from yet another shock. Everything was so solid and he had not been able to use his energy skills to prevent the fall. As the cold penetrated his thin and wet clothing he rolled onto his hands and knees and crawled to the safety of the thick snow underneath the trees.

Using a tree to pull himself up, he looked downhill and saw what had to be houses with cheery lights. People and warmth! But there was something wrong. What were those little lights on stalks? Nervously, he swallowed. They looked just like buildings in Azuran flikkers. An insidious thought said that since his arrival amongst the trees there had not been one single sensation like in a HoloWrapper adventure.

He was trembling again. He wrapped his arms around his chest, trying to hold himself together and fight off the Memories that were clustering on the fringes of his consciousness.

Lights appeared over to one side. They were moving, more or less in a straight line. They seemed to be moving across the snow. As he watched, they passed underneath the stalk lights. They were followed by a dark green box. A box-on-wheels. An Azuran car! The scene cleared in his mind. There must be a road hidden by a long bank of snow. That was why there was the row of lights. Of course! Azurii used roads to get their clumsy vehicles to houses.

Then it struck him. Slowly, not wanting to, but having to, he looked down at his arms, his body, his legs. Of course he was not in a HoloWrapper, he was in his own body. The only time you could be in a real person's body was when you were there to watch and learn. You had no control, just like when he was in the snowman. And even then, it could not be his body, even if he was ever to be a HW Character that would not happen. The globe was correct. He was on Earth!

He shivered. Again he has stopped concentrating on his fire. *I must get warm! What to do? Well, at least I look like an Azuran. Mostly. They have all sorts of colours. And even if my face is different, well, we all have the same bits! And I have seen them wearing clothes like mine. Shouldn't frighten them. I hope the compiler works!*

He dug deep and found the courage to continue downhill.

CHAPTER 17

A CONFUSING WELCOME

FINLAND

Up in his bedroom, sixteen-year-old Hannu was just about to close the curtains. He stopped to take one last look at the slope on which he would ski the next day. He thought he saw a figure. Surely not at this time of the night? He blinked and looked again. Indeed, someone was coming down the snowy slope. Dressed all in black with long black hair and a handbag over her shoulder. What was a girl doing out on the slopes at this time of night! No-one he knew had hair like that. He shrugged his shoulders and settled down to do his homework.

At the bottom of the slope Qwelby arrived at a steep and very slippery bank. Making his way to the top he saw a long strip of black stretching to the left and right. *I was right. This is what the Azurii use for their stuck-to-the ground transport.* Looking across to the other side he saw three people. *Real Azurii!* Nerves made him tremble. The desperate need for warmth before his energy ran out gave him the courage to cross the black strip and through a gap in the icy bank on the other side.

The three men they were speaking as he approached.

'Busana?' he said

Louder voices, sounding nasty, he was not able to detect their energy fields. Did they not have them? Were they so weak they did not reach out past the thick clothes they were wearing?

'Ghilusa ezwaqondawen eyaghi. Ghikuluma limiwena eya,' he said.

That brought loud guffaws and one of the men pushed him in the chest. Suddenly he was being pushed from one to another, thrown harder and harder. All the time they were calling out words, yet his compiler provided no Tazian.

Taken aback, confused, flailing his arms to keep his balance, he struck one of them. He was hit on the side of his head. He staggered, clutched at a man to stop himself from falling, and was violently pushed away, spinning. The motion called forth a memory of the movements he and Wrenden had practised whilst watching Tamina. He swung an arm around and struck one of the men on the head, heard an exclamation, but still no translation.

A fist came towards his head. As he watched and ducked he realised that everything they were doing was slower than at home. He swivelled and struck out with his foot. As he caught a man behind his knee, saw him fall to the ground, pivoted away and swayed backwards to avoid another fist, realisation struck him. Tamina's dance routine was more than just dance!

Another memory came to him. A few days after she had danced for his recent rebirthday, when he had called her 'Lightning', he had asked her in all seriousness to tell him about her training. She had explained that what she enjoyed most was a demanding form called Active Body Dance, where two or sometimes more people performed fast, complicated movements together. She had tried to get him and Wrenden to try a couple of dance steps as she called them. They had felt silly. It came as a shock to realise it was a lot more than girly dancing.

His leg was struck from behind. He stumbled and was kicked

again. His leg gave way and he fell to the ground. As he rolled onto his back he saw a patch of light high up on the wall of a house some distance away. A window. A head poked through and a voice called out. A boot came swinging towards him. He grabbed it, heaved and rolled away. As the man fell to the ground he continued rolling, fear and cold engulfing him. *It is true. The Azurii are as violent as we have been told.*

Trying to rise, he was felled as he was kicked, then again. Light glinted off something in the hand of the biggest man as he again tried to rise. *A knife!* Bright light flooded the scene as a door was opened and another voice called out. With a shock, Qwelby recognised the face of the man holding the knife. It was the man he thought of as Big Boy, who had smashed in the face of the snowman that day. The knife disappeared.

His attention taken by the fact that another person was standing silhouetted in what had to be a doorway, Qwelby did not see coming the kick that landed in his stomach. He doubled over in pain as another from behind sent him sprawling headlong onto the hard surface.

Curling into a ball he was relieved to see feet walking away as his attackers sauntered off, calling out over their shoulders, waving their arms and making strange gestures with their hands.

Hannu's concentration had been interrupted by noises outside, sounding like a fight going on. He pulled back the curtains. There was a fight. He recognised Erki, the school bully. The other two had to be his idiot companions. As he opened the window he realised with a start that the figure on the ground had black arms and legs. *That explains the attack!*

Whoever it was, she was wearing only shorts and a tank top. He opened the window and called out. 'Leave her alone!' He saw a shaft of light from a door opening in the house right by the affray and a deep man's voice calling out.

As Erki and his mates jeered, swore and moved away, still

shouting abuse and making rude gestures, Hannu did a double take. The figure on the slope had not been wearing all black, it must have been that black girl. What on earth was she doing walking down the slope, and dressed like that. No-one in their right mind would go out of the house dressed like that in this cold.

The figure on the ground uncurled. The movement jolted Hannu out of his wonderings and he switched back to what was happening. Leaping down the stairs, he ran through the kitchen and out of the back door, calling to his mother. 'There's a girl outside, wearing summer clothes, being beaten up!'

He ran down to the footpath and a short way along it, coming up to the tall girl who was on her hands and knees. 'Hello.'

Qwelby jumped with surprise as he heard the voice, rolled over to get away and scrambled to his feet, ready to defend himself from another attack. This time he saw a boy about the same size as himself in dark trousers and a brightly patterned sweater, looking like many Azurii he had seen in flikkers.

They stood looking at one another. Qwelby, wary, half crouching with his arms extended, waiting and watching. Hannu taking in that the black person was a boy with black, shoulder length hair with green highlights.

The Azuran spoke.

Still nothing from Qwelby's compiler. Again, he tried the usual greeting. 'Busana?'

The Azuran cocked his head on one side and spoke again.

Qwelby heard a tonal quality that sounded questioning, and not at all threatening. What to do, what to say? He tried to explain.

'Ghilusa ezwaqondawen eyaghi. Ghikuluma limiwena eya.'

The Azuran spoke again, then tapped his hand on his chest and Qwelby heard: 'Haa - nnu.'

Qwelby guessed that was a name and tapped his own chest saying slowly: 'Qwel - bee.' Then he shivered. His energies were totally gone, he was freezing.

The Azuran smiled and again tapped his chest saying: 'Hannu.' Then stuck out his right hand.

Qwelby took a half pace back in surprise and stared at it for a moment. Then he laughed as he remembered Azuran flikkers he had seen, put his hand out and then they shook hands. Then Qwelby shivered hard. Hannu gripped Qwelby's arm, tugged and gestured behind him to an open door, talking rapidly.

Qwelby understand the gesture and let the boy pull him towards the door. A person was coming towards them wrapped in a thick coat, carrying something large and soft looking. As a coat was held out to him, he guessed the new arrival was a woman. He was shaking so much he almost dropped the coat. The woman stepped up to him and draped it around his shoulders, pulling it together in front as the two Azurii hurried him towards another door that was standing open, casting welcome light onto a path cleared of snow.

They entered a room with a lot of objects around the walls that Qwelby could only guess at, then through into what he recognised from the flikkers as an Azuran kitchen. Qwelby felt himself taken by his shoulders and led to stand by a large, iron object. From the heat coming from it had to be a cooking device.

Hannu said something to the woman who looked closely at Qwelby and went out through another door. She returned a few moments later carrying some clothes and beckoned him to follow as she went into the small room where he had entered the house. She handed him a large, warm towel, and put the clothes on a piece of machinery Qwelby did not recognise.

He understood her gestures. 'Ghikabonawena.' He smiled and started to take off his top. Made of a silky material, skin-tight and wet, he had no strength left in his arms and was stuck.

She spoke and gestured.

Qwelby understood the gesture, felt silly and nodded.

Seija was below average height and with a comfortable, motherly build. As she reached and started to tug up, Qwelby realised her difficulty and bent over, allowing her to pull the tank top over his head. Standing up, he saw the surprise in her eyes as she looked at his chest. Then she turned him round and he felt gentle hands on his back. He sensed her energies: concern, caring, motherly. Ripped from his own world, arriving on Azura without his twin and attacked by the first people he'd met! Coming from a world where violence just did not happen, the woman's caring touch was exactly what he needed. He opened the floodgates of his feelings, seeking security and to be looked after, letting his fear and tension drain out as he felt her caring spreading though him. When he felt her hands leave his body he turned to her with tears in his eyes.

'Ghikabonawena' he repeated, as she gave him an odd look and returned to the kitchen, closing the door behind her.

'He's a... Red Indian,' she said to her son with a perplexed look on her face. Not realising that the red patches were radiation burns, Seija assumed everything was the result of his having been beaten. 'He's badly bruised all over. Lots of bright red patches on his skin. Those devils gave him a bad beating. Just as well you heard.'

'Better than that, they were right outside the Ylönen's house. He opened his door. That's when they went.'

'A good job too,' she said as she busied herself at the stove.

She was just setting hot drinks on the big pine table when Qwelby entered, wearing her son's sweater and tracksuit bottoms. She gestured and Qwelby sat on a chair alongside Hannu.

'Just as well you take after your father,' Seija said to her tall son. 'Your clothes fit him nicely.'

Qwelby's senses were all awry. The trees and snow, so similar to parts of Vertazia that he might have been at home. But the house. In its layout the kitchen was similar to how a Tazian house might be, yet much smaller and everything in it felt odd. The wooden table: old, worn, cared for, yet the solid pieces were from different trees and only half alive.

The drink was an unusual taste, yet it was delicious and he

could feel the heat flowing through his body. Sipping it as he watched the blonde haired boy talking to the equally blonde woman he guessed to be his mother, he noted their energy flows. Although very weak compared to Tazian auras, the colours revealing their surprise, excitement, puzzlement and doubt were a welcome confirmation that he was amongst human beings. As his shock lessened and a corner of his mind told him to relax, he found himself easing into the reassurance of understanding without words that there was a good relationship between the two Azurii, and there was no sense of danger.

Unaware of the power of his thoughts on a world whose inhabitants lacked the mental collectiveness of the almost hive like existence of the Tazii, Qwelby unconsciously flooded the two Azurii with his need for help and protection and a feeling of family. Energies that took root in both.

Mother and son stopped talking. Hannu turned to Qwelby, speaking and gesturing.

Qwelby was fairly certain he was being asked where he had come from. He tried to explain. Hannu was shaking his head, clearly not understanding. He gestured and led Qwelby to the back door, opened it and they stood inside in the warmth. With gestures, raised eyebrows, some nods, and Qwelby starting to learn some Finnish words, he thought that Hannu eventually accepted that he had arrived at the top of the hill. The two went back into the kitchen. As Qwelby sat down it was clear from Hannu's gestures that he was explaining to the woman what he had learnt.

As Qwelby relaxed, he became more aware of the pain from his beating. He wanted to lie down, but was desperate to communicate. Having finally remembered how the compiler worked, he started asking the names of all the things around him.

For a while it worked. Then he picked up the mug and showed that he wanted a word to explain drinking. The answers sent sharp pricks into his head.

He held his head to ease the discomfort. In the silence it struck him that Hannu and his mother were not frightened of him. In fact the boy was actually very excited, and he felt kindness coming from both of them.

Wanting to make faster progress than slowly learning lots of words that would not help him explain who he was and where he came from, he looked all around the room for anything that could help. There was a pretty picture on the wall with a sheet of numbers. That was an exciting find. It reminded him of one of those weird similarities between their worlds, that Azurii used almost the same shapes for numbers as did Tazii. He guessed he was looking at a calendar.

Then his brain made more connections. Pictures. Drawings. Excitedly, he made signs showing that he wanted something to draw on, and grinned at Hannu's equal excitement as he leapt up from the table, speaking rapidly and gesturing for Qwelby to follow him upstairs.

CHAPTER 18

IT'S HOT

KALAHARI

Tullia was seated astride the Stroem, bent forward and murmuring encouragingly to it as she inched ahead of Kaigii and the others in the final DareDragon Race of an KeyPoint FunDay. She was about to shoot through the ColourDash that marked the end of the race and have her flying suit over-painted in the winner's musical colours when the Stroem disappeared, sending her tumbling head over heels in the pitch dark.

She jerked to a painful stop as something large hit her in the back.

A voice said 'Ooowwww!'

My voice? Where has it come from?

Silence.

Fifty trillion cells in my body and each one hurts!

She opened her eyes and quickly closed them as bright sunlight blinded her. Slowly she opened them again, peering out below her hand. She found the source of the pain, a large white stone. Cross with it, she turned around and pushed it out of the way. Something small and black waved at her. Politely she waved back, then stopped, her hand suspended in mid-air.

I recognise that. It's a scorpion. A deadly, black scorpion. She used her hands to lever herself backwards. The scorpion followed, its sting arched high over its body, two large, vicious-looking claws stretching towards her bare foot.

It stopped moving and swung to the side as the ground trembled. A black and white leg appeared before her, rapidly followed by more. They were attached to black and white bodies. *Oh, what beautiful ponies!* A small herd trotted past.

She looked around as the dust settled. No sign of the scorpion.

She did not remember settling into a HoloChair. In fact she could not recall anything since being with Kaigii when their father picked them up on the family PowerSled. As she looked around, the scene shimmered. *Heat Haze.* There was sand on the side of face from where she had been lying down.

She went to unszeam a pocket. Her fingers fumbled. It was right there but she couldn't open it. But she had two sets of fingers. *Very strong heat haze?* Carefully she aligned two sets of fingers with two szeames and undid them, or it. A cramp hit her stomach. She gasped and bent over. The cramp got larger and larger until it engulfed her whole body. She keeled over onto the sand.

As she regained consciousness she heard a strange 'pat, pat' sound. It was getting louder. A pair of long, thin legs came into view, topped by a large, oval-shaped body. A long, thin neck stretched up to a head seemingly high up in the sky. *That's a head. A beak. The body is made of feathers. Feathers? It's a bird! Virtual reality. I'm in a KiddyKartoon!*

So who or what is Kaigii?

Unsteadily, she sat up and looked around. The ground was just dusty red sand. In all directions there was an endless vista of scrubby bushes with lots of small, spindly trees dotted about, unlike any that she knew.

Except.

It was all very similar to what they had seen from inside the staircase.

And the sun.

Shielding her eyes she looked up. It was lower in the sky. She had been asleep, but her inner clock was all awry and all she could do was guess that had probably been for a whole ouer. She was hot. Her winter body suit was a basic AutoReg that would adjust to a normal range of temperatures. She was a sensible girl and saw no point in wasting hard earned energy credits on the SuperLux model when she was sure to have outgrown it by the following winter.

As she reached up to her throat and unszeamed her suit a short way, she puzzled. Nothing fitted. She would not enter a HoloWrapper Enactment in the summer, in a winter flying suit. She would not waste time by falling asleep. *And why am I in my body? I would have chosen to be one of those lovely, black and white ponies.*

My body!

She felt herself shaking. Her brain was at last passing on the messages from her eyes. She was looking at her own body, dressed in her favourite bodysuit. It was impossible to be in a HoloWrapper programme as one's self.

And where is that pesky twin?

She got to her feet, brushed sand from her suit and looked around. Although there were a lot of different marks on the ground, there were no footprints. That meant he had not got up and wandered off.

She called out 'Qwelby!' several times, becoming more and more worried as there was never an answer. Finally, she accepted he was not there.

A long, long silence followed as the truth slowly dawned. Definitely this was not an HW adventure. It was real. Frighteningly real. Worst of all, not only was she alone and didn't know where or when, her twin was not in that special place that each of them had in their minds where the other lived.

For the first time in her life she did not have a mental connection with him. She put her hand to her necklace, running it through her fingers. The three strands of intertwined metals felt soft and silky, but its energy was muted. Finally, fearful of what she was going to sense, she stroked her purple crystal of Kanyisaya. There was no tiny tremor. The final, frightening confirmation. There was no contact with her twin's torc. They were totally apart.

She sat down with a bump. Tears welled up, she sniffed, swallowed, couldn't hold them back and they burst forth. Slowly, her crying calmed down and turned into a few snuffles. She pulled a tissue from one of the many pockets in her flying suit, dried her face and finished with a good blow of her nose.

Tucking the tissue back into a pocket, she stood up and looked around to see in which direction to put her best food forward. Through the leafless bushes she thought she could make out a track. That was heartening! Tracks had to lead to places or, better still, between places, so there should be something at either end, and that, she really hoped, would be people.

Right. My wrister. Why haven't I thought of that before! She pulled back the sleeve of her bodysuit.

The facsimile of Vertazia indicated early afternoon. That was all right. Nothing else was on display. She tried all the other functions. None worked. Her legs went wobbly and she sat down. Surely, here in the WarmBand, there should have been an arrow pointing her in the right direction. Or at least words should have appeared saying: 'You Are Lost.' But nothing? It was lost!

Taking a deep breath, she stood up, lifted her head and looked further away. In the distance on the right hand side she could see a low range of hills. She stared at them for a long time as there was something special about them, but she wasn't sure what. There was a definite shimmering around them, which she knew could just be the effect of the very hot sun, but it felt a lot more than that.

The path did not seem to lead that way and she could not see that it went anywhere in particular. Looking to her left she saw that after a little way the track curved off between the trees. *Ah well, let's see if there's anything round that bend. Best foot forward in that direction.* She looked down at her feet.

Neither of them volunteered, so she selected her left foot and set off to follow the path. As she did so, she realised with excitement that there were a lot of footprints on it.

As she walked along she noticed that several footprints had toes. She wasn't really surprised because it was hot. Almost as hot as she was used to in summer at home, when she and her friends did not bother to wear shoes even when outdoors. The hope of meeting young people like herself gave her a warm feeling.

She was starting to feel a little more relaxed and happier, and naturally she shared those feelings with Qwelby. But she didn't. She couldn't. He wasn't there! It's not just that he wasn't there with her physically. He wasn't there in her mind! That had never happened before.

They were not ordinary twins, they were Quantum Twins. It wasn't that they were always talking to one another in each other's minds, it was just that whenever either one of them thought of the other, they could feel that the other was there in the corner of their mind.

Between themselves they did not bother much with privacy of thoughts. They knew each other so well it was usually obvious what each was thinking anyway, but when they deliberately wanted to think or feel with each other, they always knew that the other was there, even if that twin wasn't immediately able to share. This time there was absolutely, totally, completely nothing!

Tullia felt weak at the knees and stopped walking. She took a couple of steps to the side of the track and lent against a tree while she recovered from her biggest shock yet: the possibility that she was no longer on Vertazia.

The adventures on the staircase played back through her mind. *I have arrived in just the very sort of desert we saw at the bottom of the staircase!* As the next memory popped in of slipping into the comet, her legs trembled so much she had to sit down again. She gave an anguished cry. 'It's all my fault!' *And where is my twin? I cannot feel him. He must be at home. I hope. No. I need him here!* She burst into tears.

She wiped her eyes, blew her nose, and put the tissue back in her pocket. Taking a deep breath, she got up and stepped back onto the track. Looking down at her feet, she thought this time it would only be fair if the right foot had its turn to be her best foot forward.

She was getting hotter. She had left Vertazia dressed for a cold winter's day. She thought of stripping off her bodysuit but did not have the energy. She settled for unszeaming it down to her waist, revealing an iridescent turquoise cami. Thinking of Vertazia reminded her of the one big lesson that they all learnt: 'Use your mind'.

Okay, she thought. She enjoyed most of her time at college because it was fun. You were required to go out to explore and discover all sorts of things all for yourself. In spite of the age differences, for the last couple of years she and Qwelby had done that a lot with their four BestFriends, XOÑOX.

She stopped in the middle of the track, stood still and thought to herself: *'Eyes are for seeing, ears for hearing, nose for smelling, mouth for tasting, hands for touching, quieting for sensing and Intuition for quantuming.'* She did not like the last one because it reminded her that she could not connect with Qwelby. She decided to put that on one side for the moment and just use the other six.

First she looked around more carefully. Nothing to be seen except an endless vista of spiky bushes, small trees with bare branches and a pair of much larger trees. Although there was plenty of space between individual trees, lots of them grew in small groups and there were so many spread out all around that in some directions they eventually formed a barrier to seeing anything further away. Then she listened and became aware of occasional, faint noises. She felt the slightest touch of breeze on her face. When the breeze dropped the noises disappeared. Smelling the air and tasting it did no more than confirm her other senses: warmth, dryness and perhaps a little bit of dust.

As she walked on, the track curved and gently dipped down as it started to descend what she decided to describe as a wide and very shallow valley, that stretched a long way to both left and right. She expected to find a river bed at the bottom but there were no such signs. Feeling disheartened, she stepped off the track and leant her hand against a tall tree which was very different from all the others. As she did so, she felt a gently energy flowing into the palm of her hand. Oh that was a nice, familiar sensation! *Thank the stars, at least that's like it is at home.*

She moved closer to the tree and rested her forehand against its grey and peeling bark. She felt more energy flowing into her and put her arms as far around the trunk as she could manage. Resting her cheek against the comforting feel she relaxed into the flow and felt as if the tree was reaching its arms out around her.

Whilst she was doing that she also started to use her seventh sense without realising it. She received the impression that at times life would be very challenging. As a feeling of despair grew another sensation enveloped her: as long as she remembered to Trust in herself, everything would turn out as it was meant to. Half her mind said sarcastically: *'Oh, thank you very much.'* As the other half acknowledged a typical Tazian reminder about where the source of her strength lay, she gave the tree a big hug and genuinely said: 'Thank you. Thank you very much.'

Feeling very much better, she stepped away from the tree. With a last lingering hand running down its beautiful grey bark, she opened her eyes. To another shock. Two people were standing a few paces away, holding hands and staring at her. Dark brown skin, short black hair, and wearing brightly coloured, heavy clothes suitable for the winter. A slim young man the top of whose head did not quite reach her shoulders, and a shorter, younger looking girl. There was something about them that told her they were brother and sister.

The two young Meera had recognised her. Or they thought they had. They knew that beings known in Africa as Siskas who belonged to the race of the Goddess Nananana were the most human looking of all Extra-Terrestrials.

Whatever had happened to Tullia as she was hurled from Vertazia, her energy field was visibly vibrating, making the flame like patches on her body suit appear to be moving. That the dazzling colours were not the reds and yellows of the fires the Meera knew emphasised Tullia's otherworldliness. She had to have come from the sun. Yet within the flames the Goddess looked more human than they had ever imagined possible.

The young girl could not believe her eyes. In front of her was a figure who was so like the Siska who had appeared in her dream. A dream she had not shared with anybody, not even her brother. It had followed an amazing evening when her tribe of Meera had been celebrating with their special healing dances.

CHAPTER 19

A GODDESS IS BORN

KALAHARI

That night it had been close to freezing. A group of young Meera boys were continually adding branches to the fire to keep the flames leaping high into the air, providing warmth and light. As the healers danced around the fire, a deep groove was cut into the sand. The dancers were almost naked, sweat pouring down their bodies from the mixture of physical exertion and the energies that were channelled from the universe by their ancestors, through them and into those in need.

There was a sudden stillness in the air. The flames stopped their flickering dance. They leapt upwards in a coruscating column and seemed to hang as if suspended from the stars, spinning around like a miniature whirlwind, casting an eerie light across the whole scene. There was no sound, no movement. No-one breathed. It was as though the air had been sucked out of the whole area.

With a loud thunderclap, the flames fell back down to the alarmed cries of the women as pieces of burning wood showered onto their clothes. The men dancing close to the fire fell down where they stood. Those healers who had been moving amongst the onlookers rushed back to pull their colleagues away from the fire.

Slowly, the clearing emptied as people drifted back to their huts, wondering what the omen meant.

Together with Xashee, her sixteen-year-old brother, Tsetsana had helped one of the healers back to his hut. She had returned to stand by the fire, wondering. With his long, black coat wrapped around him, Xameb, their Shaman, was sitting at the other side of the fire. He beckoned her to join him.

'Relax,' he said. 'Breathe as you have been taught. Open to the world of Spirit. We will speak no more.'

Together, they sat close to the fire until a chill breeze pushed away the little heat that remained in the fast dying embers.

She looked at the Shaman.

He nodded.

'Did you see her?' she asked in a small, uncertain voice.

He waited.

'The flames. I thought I saw a figure. A woman made all of flames. Her hair so long it seemed to wrap around her whole body as she spun around.' She bit her lip. He was the seer, the visionary, not her, an eleven-year-old girl not yet become woman.

'You have clear sight, Tsetsana.'

She saw him smile at her sigh of relief.

'What does it mean?' she asked.

'A visitation. Do not speak of this to anyone. Even me.'

She frowned, puzzled.

'Keep it within. In that way you may discover more. If Spirit wills it.'

He nodded to her. They rose and walked back to the village, he to his hut and she to the one she shared with several other girls.

That night, Tsetsana's secret fantasy came alive as she dreamt of meeting the most human-looking of all extra-terrestrials.

Surprisingly, that Siska was wearing the traditional Meera costume of loinskin and bead necklace appropriate to older girls and young, unmarried women. Apart from the green lights flickering throughout her amazingly long hair, she looked like a member of one of the tribes of red-skinned San.

Now, right in front of her with the same face and hair, was a Goddess made of fire. Tsetsana trembled, her legs went weak and she felt herself break out in a sweat. She grabbed hold of her brother with both hands, staring at the apparition, her eyes unfocussed, seeing the two images as one.

Her brother was equally transfixed, overwhelmed by the beauty of the Goddess. His heart was pounding. He could not tear his gaze away from her purple eyes. They seemed to be looking right through him. Half aware of his sister's trembling hands on his arm, he put his other hand on top of hers.

Having been totally open to her Intuition whilst she had been cuddled up to the tree, Tullia realised that they were looking at her with more than just surprise at the sight of a stranger. Their energy fields showed that it was awe. She controlled an urge to have an hysterical giggle as a HoloWrapper phrase: *"I request an audience with your leader,"* sprang into her mind.

She took a deep breath and slid a hand to her throat, feeling her necklace. *I am fifteen years old. I have Thathuma, my EraBand, for my first era. Kanyisaya, my crystal for the completion of my second phase of being. I have completed my third phase of thinking: so THINK!*

Again she had to suppress a giggle. *Are they wondering whether I come from the moon or some other planet? Perhaps they think I'm an Extra-Terrestrial!* Suddenly, she felt very strange. *I AM an Extra-Terrestrial, aren't I? Our planets share the same space, but really we are two completely separate worlds.*

How to communicate? Her mind recalled a fun game she played with her friends, pretending they could not speak Tazian. Now that she knew what she was going to do, she took a deep breath and held herself erect. Thoughts of coming from a different planet, in peace, of being in command and wanting to be friends were coloured by memories of participating in HWAdventures as Aurigani making contact with other races. All that flooded through the two Meera and found homes in the unconsciousness of each youngster.

She pointed at herself and said: 'Tullia.' Then opened her hand, pointing to them in a gesture that she hoped would mean she wanted them to speak. She did not need her Intuition to tell her of their fear and confusion. She smiled, hoping it would mean the same to them as it would to a Tazian. She saw the young girl lose some of her fear and hug her brother's arm.

'The Goddess smiled at us!' Tsetsana said to her brother, looking up at his face,

Relieved they were not too frightened to speak, Tullia gave them another, encouraging smile.

Taking a deep breath, the boy spoke.

Tullia was so relieved. After a strange sound as though he was urging on a horse, she heard: 'Ashee'. She flashed him a smile as she relaxed.

He was thunder-struck. Never before had he seen such a beautiful smile. And those purple eyes. He felt an uncontrollable trembling in all his limbs.

Gripping her brother hard, the girl said: 'Tset – sar – na.'

That was perfect. Although Tullia could see how nervous the girl was, she had heard the sounds so clearly. 'Tset – sar – na,' Tullia repeated. Then added: 'Ashee.'

She saw the boy tremble. His eyes darted around as though he wanted to be anywhere else but where he was. She could see him taking deep breaths, the young girl hanging onto his arm. Puzzled, Tullia could sense the girl was trying to calm the older boy.

'CH – ashee,' he said, looked down at the ground, then back up. 'CH – ashee.'

Ah. That sound. It is part of his name. '"Click" – ashee,' she stumbled over the sound.

He gave a faint smile and nodded.

Making similar gestures as before, she tried to encourage them to say her name. That was difficult. She could not understand why they were so hesitant, so shy. She thought about the girl's name, the breaks in it as though it was three names all together. 'Too – lee – ar,' she said clearly.

'Too – lee – ar?' Tsetsana said.

Tullia beamed at the girl, and was rewarded by a big smile and a sense of relief and, something she could not identify. Recognition? Impossible! The girl was definitely less in awe than the boy. 'Tooleear,' she said, making it one word.

'Tooleear,' repeated Tsetsana. 'Tooleear,' she said again as she turned to look up at her brother.

Tullia could see the girl was excited, but the boy had gone a deep red under his brown skin. Some of the colour shading in his energy field and the way it was fluctuating puzzled her. *Awkward, uncomfortable, but what else is affecting him?*

He took a deep breath and licked his lips. 'Tooleear,' he said.

She felt her shoulders drop. She had not realised how tense she had become. She smiled with relief as the last vestiges of fear drifted away.

She saw the boy tremble. The girl clinging onto his arm as though to steady him. *Is he ill?*

Silence.

Now what to do? A memory arose of important Tazian ceremonies she had seen at home on the HoloReceptor. She licked her lips and swallowed. *I don't remember the exact words, but here goes!*

She brought the palms of her two hands together level with her heart, bowed her head over them, then as she lifted her head she swept her arms down to her sides with the palms facing out towards the two young people, and said: 'Tullia is honoured to meet you, "Click" – ashee and Tset – sar – na.' With the blank looks on their faces reminding her that Gumma's device was not a translator, she added: 'I'm whistling happy to meet you!'

She remembered to complete the greeting in the correct manner by bringing her palms together level with her heart and making a slight bow with her head. She dropped her arms to her sides looking less formal, and smiled.

Being nervous, Tullia's voice had dropped a register below its usual, rich contralto as she clearly enunciated her words as if in an KeyPoint LiveShow. The only words the Meera had understood were the three names. That did not matter. Nor did the fact that her gestures were not like any their own people would make. They had just been sung to by a Goddess! Clearly it was a greeting.

Xashee knew he had to return a similar greeting. He licked his lips. Although he spoke Afrikaans and some English, what was the point? This was a Goddess, not a tourist. He addressed her in his own Meera. 'Goddess from the sun.' He swept his arm up in an arc as he pointed at the sun.

To Tullia it was clear that the boy was accepting her as coming from another planet. That he thought it far out in space did not matter. What incredible luck. His people must be so like her own. She felt her eyes twirling with excitement and relief.

As the purple eyes of the Goddess seemed to be on fire, Xashee dropped his arm and looked at his sister. She gave him a faint but encouraging smile. What should he say? Yes. They had exchanged names. Licking his lips again, he continued. 'I, Xashee, and my sister Tsetsana, welcome you to our village.'

The two Meera were seized with panic as Tullia's mouth dropped open and her eyes went the palest shade of lilac. What had they said? They stood, rooted to the spot as Tullia closed her mouth and took a deep breath and seemed to pull her shoulders back as though to launch herself into an attack on them. Her eyes returned to their deep purple, and a purple light was pulsing from the centre of her necklace.

They could not know that she was recovering from her shock at having recognised them from her unseen visit to the village and that she was fighting an urge to burst into tears. Her momentary euphoria had passed as the full impact of her realisation struck home that she probably was on Haven, and without her twin.

She was almost overwhelmed by the feeling of being desperately alone. As she stood there, obviously struggling with emotions they could only guess at, she also felt a sense of being comforted rise within her. She knew where she was and even had an understanding of how she had got there.

The two Meera had taken a pace back, awaiting the outburst from the Goddess they had so badly offended. As Tullia shook her head, stilling the emotions swirling through her, they gripped each other, rooted to the spot in fear. They almost collapsed with relief as Tullia restored her sense of being in charge and they heard: 'Busana, "Click"ashee. Busana, Tsetsana,' as Tullia smiled and nodded at each in turn.

Whatever it meant, it clearly was a friendly greeting. Tsetsana relaxed her grip on her brother's arm as she turned her face towards him, eyes wide with delight and relief.

He gave her a wan smile. He had been just as afraid.

Heart pounding, his whole body still trembling, Xashee gently pulled his sister to the side of the path. He did not trust himself to speak. Instead he made a big, sweeping gesture with his arm, pointing in the direction from which they had come. Tullia inclined her head, smiled and started to walk forward. The path was not wide enough for them to walk three abreast, so she gestured for them to lead the way.

So many thoughts wanted to run through her mind that she focussed on what she guessed was happening. The youngsters were taking her to their home to meet their mother and father. Was she looking respectable? As she looked over her bodysuit and brushed away traces of sand she realised that the pulsing of her strongly excited energy field was making the lilac patches look as if they were flickering flames. *No wonder they think I come from another planet!*

CHAPTER 20

CONFIRMATION

FINLAND

As Qwelby stepped through the door into Hannu's room he stopped in amazement. Everything was so cluttered, to Qwelby it was a tiny room and it looked as though Hannu had packed into it as much as he and Tullia had in a space that was several times larger. As his eyes roved around he stopped, unable to believe what he saw. On the wall over the bed was a big poster of Earth as seen from space.

Slowly Qwelby's brain sorted into order the various images, providing him with a running commentary. A bed for sleeping. A chair for sitting, books and clothes tumbled over it. A table for writing. A flat screen electronic device: purpose unknown. Objects hanging from the ceiling: space rockets, space plane, space station. Curtains half open. Window.

Qwelby walked across to the window and looked out. Hannu joined him and pointed to the slope. They stood there for a few moments, the compiler steadily increasing Qwelby's database of Finnish, as he discovered that Hannu had seen him from this window, walking down the hillside, then being attacked.

Solemnly, Qwelby offered another handshake. Naturally, he infused the grip with his energy of appreciation. He learnt an important lesson about Azurii as he watched Hannu's amazed expression as he stared at their hands. Azurii did not exchange energy as did Tazii.

Hannu later said to Anita that it was as if the Alien had actually poured friendship into him. What he could not know was that his strong desire to meet an alien allowed that feeling to infuse his whole being. He became bonded to Qwelby at an unconscious level.

As they turned back into the room Qwelby was trying to absorb his amazing good luck. He had travelled through a space-time warp to arrive in the home of a boy of about his own age who shared his own dreams. Not just any boy. A boy whose aura showed that he wanted to be a friend. Qwelby's hand went to his Torc and he caressed his crystal of Drakobata as he thanked the Multiverse for his good fortune.

Then he caught sight of what had to be a Portal. An oval, about thirty centimetres high, against a background of tiny silver specks representing stars, set on the black of deep space was a beautifully proportioned spiral. Eyes wide, trembling, he walked towards it and dropped to his knees, breathless with wonder. Purple eyes sparkling, he turned to Hannu, pointed at him, then at the Portal, raising his eyebrows.

Hannu nodded.

With a sweeping gesture with his right hand, Qwelby touched his crystal, his heart and finished with a finger pointing at the Portal. 'Ghibukuyaalanama bulakuizilwekiti gana esta yangana.'

Hannu looking at him, excitement colouring his whole energy field and shining from his eyes. He was mesmerised. Anita had been strongly drawn to his creation, but this alien's gesture was so evocative it touched Hannu deep inside where the inspiration for the Portal had been born. And there was an energy in the weird sounding, almost musical words, that drew him into Qwelby's feelings. It was as though he had been sucked onto those deep purple eyes and was being invited to travel through his own model and onto the boy's homeworld.

Those eyes! Rich purple, revolving spirals! And set in what a face! The weirdness of the reddish-brown colour, the slanted eyes, the wide mouth: all was forgotten. Hannu was looking at a young boy who had just been given the biggest treat of his life. And a wise old man. Both at once. He felt goose pimples all over his body. If he had had any doubts, they were gone. This truly was an alien. His Alien!

Qwelby saw the look on Hannu's face. So lost in his good fortune of meeting someone like himself, he had forgotten that the Azuran would not understand his words, yet it seemed as though he had. As they remained looking at one another, Qwelby felt a deep connection at an energy level, beyond any words.

Hannu felt a momentary chill run through his whole body, shivered, pulled away from the connection, and finally managed to break eye contact. His shook his head to clear his thoughts, turned to his desk, opened a drawer and took out paper and pencils which he handed to Qwelby, glad of something practical on which to focus.

Qwelby went to the desk with a mixture of anticipation and fear: fear that the globe was correct when it said he was on Earth. He took a sheet of paper and drew a series of concentric circles, then a tiny circle on all the circles except for the smallest one. Carefully looking at what he'd drawn, he tilted his head to one side. He was not satisfied. It was not clear. He looked at the pencils he had been given. Pleased to see a red one, he took that and made the small centre circle look like a lot of flames were springing from it.

Qwelby made a show of counting on his fingers to three and pointed to the third circle out from the centre, Earth's orbit. Hannu reached up to the shelves above the desk. Qwelby could see his hands were trembling as he searched through the books, finally taking one down with a picture on the front of a planet with rings around it. The Tazii had named it Companion, after a friendly race with whom the Auriganii had travelled for some time, and whose spaceships looked a little like that.

Hannu opened the book and quickly turned to a map of the solar system. They looked at one another, and in silent agreement, each with a finger on the page, moved through the planets, outwards from the sun. One, two, three. They agreed. They were on Earth.

Qwelby's stomach lurched as he went weak and dizzy with the confirmation. He sat down on the bed with a thump, holding his head. After a while he looked up and gave Hannu a faint smile.

He got up, took another piece of paper, picked up a blue pencil, and drew a much bigger circle. He looked at the book and carefully copied what he assumed was the name alongside the third planet: EARTH. He then drew what looked like a house and a person, gave the pen to Hannu, pointed at the house and said: 'Ha-nnu.' Hannu wrote down his name.

Qwelby continued to draw on the same piece of paper. This time with a red pencil and using broken lines, he drew a circle in more or less the same place, then added another house and person on the opposite side from the blue ones, gave the red pen to Hannu and said: 'Qwelby.'

Hannu wrote down 'Kwelby,' looked at the drawing, thought for a moment, then wrote 'Kwelby' again, this time using broken lines.

Qwelby was feeling steadier, nodding and smiling in his relief that they were communicating. So far so good. Now, how to draw a girl for a boy on Earth to understand? No matter how confusing Azuran flikkers were, Qwelby knew that Azuran girls often wore the same clothes as boys, and their hair could be as short as Hannu's.

Thinking of Tullia, he automatically flicked to her corner in his mind. He crumpled in on himself with a terrible empty sensation. She was not there! He had forgotten. Then it hit him, hard. The last time he was with his twin: possibly, frighteningly, the last time ever! He had been in such a bad mood. He felt sick inside. He hurt, badly. He almost doubled over as he clutched at his stomach, sat on the bed and hid his face in his hands.

Hannu's mouth dropped open. He felt helpless, puzzled, frightened at the thought this stranger was ill. The Alien was clutching his stomach. Was a voracious beast about to leap out, attack him and devour his family? Hannu was paralysed with fear.

Qwelby straightened up, rose and looked around the room.

Slowly, Hannu's fear subsided as a new puzzle presented itself. *How can the Alien look so pale when he was red-brown a few moments ago? He looks like a haggard old man!*

He watched Qwelby look at a photo that was pinned to a board on the wall. Hannu and a group of friends. Qwelby studied it carefully, nodding to himself. He pointed to two girls, both wearing skirts and the shorter one with long, blonde hair.

'Girls,' Hannu said.

Taking a fresh sheet of paper, Qwelby took a red pencil and drew a stick person with short hair, and copied 'Kwelby' alongside. Then another stick figure with long hair and a skirt. He joined their hands together. Pointed at the girl and said 'Tooleear.'

Hannu nodded and wrote 'Tullia' alongside the stick girl. He saw tears came into the alien's eyes, and guessed it had to be his sister.

Qwelby grabbed another sheet of paper, more pencils and started drawing excitedly, talking incomprehensibly, gesturing wildly around the room and at his drawings. He was getting so excited that Hannu eventually grabbed his arms, held him still and sat him back on the bed, relieved that at least his visitor was now looking like a normal boy, flushed with excitement, but not an old man.

Hannu was in a complete whirl with so many emotions flooding through him, all trumped by unbelievable excitement. Of one fact he was certain. His visitor definitely was an alien. He had to be. Hannu had never seen anyone's face change like his visitor's had done, from a reddish brown teenager to a pale old man. Best of all: they really were able to understand one another.

Now there was the added excitement of another person being involved as well. Perhaps they had to find her, or perhaps she was back at home. With shivers running up and down his spine, his hands trembling at the enormity of what was happening, he searched through his pockets, then stood for a moment lost in thought.

With an exclamation, Hannu scrimmaged through all the papers on his desk and found his mobile phone. He had to share his excitement. There was only one person: his fifteen-year-old girl-friend. As he pressed once and put it to his ear, Qwelby nodded, recognising an Azuran communication device.

'Anita. You've got to come round. I've something exciting to show you. Well, tell you. No, meet you. You won't believe it. I mean him. Well, you will...'

'Not right now, Hannu. I'm with Dad in the workshop.'

'Please, Anita. It's really important. Please. I need your help. Well, he does. Well, I do as well, but he needs it more...' He ran out of words.

There was a pause. Should he say more?

'O... k... ay?'

He liked the long drawn out way she said that with an intrigued tone in her voice.

He pointed to the mobile. 'Anita. Girl. She comes here.' He gestured with his arm.

Qwelby nodded and watched as Hannu sorted through the drawings, putting them in order. He had just got them into a sequence he seemed happy with when there was a call from downstairs.

Hannu looked at Qwelby. 'Say: "Ha-llo A-nee-ta",' he said, turned and ran out of the room and down the stairs.

As he arrived in the kitchen, Anita had just finished removing her outdoor clothes and was stepping into the ubiquitous slippers that were kept for visitors.

'Good. You're wearing a skirt and your hair's down.'

'What?'

'You wait and see,' he replied with a big grin.

'This better be good,' she said with a frown.

'You bet!' he said, unable to take the grin off his face as he led the way upstairs.

He stepped inside his room, turned to Anita, made an extravagant gesture as he said: 'Anita, this is Qwelby. He's from another planet.'

CHAPTER 21

MAKING
FRIENDS

FINLAND

Anita looked at Hannu and shook her head in annoyance. She had been working with her father on a science project and was not in the mood for a silly practical joke. Obviously, this boy was not Finnish. With his strange, dark, reddish-brown colour, black hair and high cheekbones, she assumed he was from a part of Russia far to the East. She opened her mouth to tell Hannu how annoyed she was...

'Ha-llo, A-nee-ta,' Qwelby said slowly, relaxing as he took in that the girl looked like the Azurii he had seen on flikkers. And there was a comforting feel in that the lilac blouse, black skirt and multi-coloured leggings she was wearing were the sort of things that Tullia would wear.

Her head swung back to the stranger. She was intrigued by the almost musical way he pronounced her name. Like most Finns she spoke English and some Russian, and knew that was not an accent of either language. Confusion! She saw the stranger's gaze switch between herself and Hannu, his mouth drop open as he staggered back to sit on the chair, amazement written all over his face. He dropped his head in his hands.

'Is he alright?' she asked.

'I don't know. He's done this before.'

Anita's irritation disappeared. She didn't believe what Hannu had said, but there was a puzzle to be solved. It felt intriguing. She liked that.

After a short time, Qwelby raised his head. He had gone pale again and looked to be in shock. Anita glanced at Hannu who reassured her.

'It's okay. He changes like that.'

Qwelby reached for another sheet of paper and a book, resting them on his lap. He started to draw. A slope, trees on one side, a snowman, a stick figure with short hair, another with a skirt and long hair. He pointed to them and the drawings. Anita and Hannu looked at one another, and nodded. The stranger was drawing them.

Qwelby drew a circle in the sky. Anita clutched Hannu's arm with a mixture of excitement and disbelief as she guessed what was coming. He added into the circle two heads, short hair for one and long hair for the other. As he reached over to the desk again, several sheets of paper fell to the floor. He bent down, searching through them.

Anita was trying to make out the drawings. The suspense was killing her. Finally the strange looking boy sat back and put another drawing on the book. With his tongue sticking out of the corner of his mouth, he slowly wrote on the picture with the circle. In spite of her impatience and tension, Anita smiled. The newcomer looked just like Hannu when he was concentrating.

Qwelby looked up and offered them the picture.

With one hand each, Anita and Hannu held it between them, and stared. He had written 'Kwelby' next to the head with short hair, 'Tullia' next to the head with long hair. And drawn a line from himself to the snowman

Anita was stunned. She had half anticipated what was coming: that he was one of the two figures they had seen in the circle in the sky. But this! She looked at Qwelby. He pointed to the snowman, then himself and pretended to look through his hands, as though using a pair of binoculars. He had been in the snowman?!

She turned to Hannu and guessed the look on his face was mirroring hers. Turning back to Qwelby, she saw his face had changed back into that of a teenager and a big grin had appeared.

He had realised that she and Hannu were remembering that occasion, and the looks on their faces were telling him that they were totally mind-blown. What he was to discover later was that day had been the first time they had talked together. Girls at school had warned Anita that Hannu was "weird". Seeing him talking to a snowman was a weirdness she liked. In spite of saying things they wished in that moment they hadn't said, blushing and mumbling, they had eventually got into a serious conversation about space travel, exploring inner space and Extra Terrestrials.

Pointing to the other figure in the circle, Anita stroked her long hair. 'Girl?' she asked.

Qwelby nodded. 'Yes, girl,' he said in Finnish, to Anita's surprise.

Hannu gave her a nudge. 'He wants to learn Finnish. He's good with names of objects but after that, it's difficult.'

Qwelby had dropped to his knees, searching through the drawings on the floor. He picked up the one of a boy and a girl with joined hands, where both the names Kwelby and Tullia were written. He drew a taller man and woman either side of the boy and girl. He pointed to the female and raised his eyebrows.

'Mother,' Anita said.

Qwelby pointed to the stick man.

'Father,' Hannu said.

'Brother and sister?' offered Anita, gesturing between the two children and the adults.

Qwelby cocked his head to one side and gave her a long look. Taking a pencil he drew a line around the two children, then linked it to the mother and tapped his wrister.

Anita looked at Hannu, their eyes went wide and they cried out together: 'Twins!'

'Twins,' Qwelby repeated. 'Yes, Tullia, Qwelby, twins.' He sat back down, looking both tired and happy, and as though he had done all he could.

Anita knelt down on the floor, looking through the drawings. As she found the one with all the circles, Hannu joined her on the floor bringing the book of the solar system with him, and explained how he and Qwelby had used it to confirm that their visitor was on Earth. He went on to try to explain the blue and red drawings.

'I'm confused. You can't think he means the two planets are in the same place?' Anita objected.

Hannu shrugged his shoulders. He did not understand either.

They sat back on the floor, looking at Qwelby, wondering how to ask questions.

Qwelby joined them on the floor, searched and found the blue and red drawing. To the dotted red house and himself he added a stick girl and slowly wrote 'Tullia'.

Anita and Hannu nodded, they had realised that.

Qwelby found a blue pencil and added a stick man standing on the rim of the planet, labelled it with his name and then joined it to the red dotted figure of himself.

'That's obvious,' said Hannu.

'Yes, but where is that the red planet?' queried Anita.

'Mars? It's always known as the Red Planet,' suggested Hannu.

'But why broken lines?' Anita asked.

The three youngsters sat in silence, looking at each other, puzzled how to proceed. The silence got longer. Anita was thinking of all the discussions she had with her father about the sort of work he did. She was sure he could help them. *But. First we will have to teach the alien to speak Finnish, and that could take forever! Alien... Space travel... Teleportation...*

'Another dimension!' exclaimed Anita. 'The broken lines because we can't see it?'

160

'But how...' asked Hannu.

'Can we...' continued Anita.

'See him?' they said together.

Qwelby laughed, or that is what they thought it was. It sounded like music, Anita thought like a trombone or an alto sax.

They watched his wild gestures and turned to one another.

'That's what...' Anita started to say.

'Twins do,' Hannu finished her sentence.

Suddenly all three were on their feet, hugging and laughing, tears streaming down Qwelby's face. Qwelby's excitement and happiness flowed into the two Finns, binding them all together. It was to be some time before Qwelby started to realise the power of what was to him normal reactions, and that he had to be careful how he broadcast his thoughts and feelings.

As they quietened down and stepped apart and Qwelby bent down to the drawings scattered over the floor, Anita was remembering the day on the ski slope. How she had had a sensation she could not describe, that in the future they would meet the people from the 'window in the sky.' It was sort of like what she had just experienced. Someone else's feeling coming into her. Feeling dizzy and disorientated, she sat on the bed.

Qwelby picked up the paper on which he had drawn himself in blue standing on the outside rim of Earth. He drew with blue, solid lines a stick girl and wrote 'Tullia' alongside, pointed to her and looked all around the room with his hand above his eyes as though he was shielding it from the sunlight.

The two Finns understood. Tullia was on Earth and Qwelby didn't know where.

What they could not know was that the big question in Qwelby's mind was: was she on Earth? With the two pictures seen from the staircase, their casual agreement to explore one world each and his memory of their last few moments together as two passing comets, all made him both fear that she had arrived on Haven, and hope she was safe and well. The alternative reason as to why she was not in his mind was too terrible to contemplate.

Anita beckoned to both boys to sit on the bed, one either side of her. She did not want one of them on the chair. It felt right to be together. She did not know how important that feeling was to become in their lives.

They sat in a companionable silence, each lost in their own thoughts and interplay of conflicting emotions. Occasionally, one of them would raise their head as though about to speak, shake the head, or shrug the shoulders and say nothing.

Anita remembered how Qwelby's face had changed, quite dramatically. Was it really his physical face she wondered, or was it some strange alien energy? Could it be that his feelings made it look as though his face was changing, working on the outside, sort of like how she had felt his happiness inside? She was about to ask Hannu what he thought when the silence was interrupted by the noise of doors opening and slamming, hearty greetings and many voices downstairs.

Hannu got up, looked at Qwelby, pointed downstairs and said: 'Faa-ther.' Then pointed to himself. 'Faa-ther of Hannu.'

Qwelby nodded. 'Faa-ther,' he repeated.

Hannu smiled and pointed at Qwelby. 'You say: "Goood ev-en-ing Faa-ther of Ha-nnu".'

'Goood ev-en-ing Faa-ther of Ha-nnu,' Qwelby dutifully repeated.

'And you shake hands,' he added, holding his own out to Qwelby

'Goood even-ing Faa-ther of Ha-nnu,' Qwelby said, shaking Hannu's hand, as they had done outside the house.

They looked so serious that Anita giggled and all three burst out laughing.

Anita felt a sense of relaxation once again coming from this interesting stranger.

Just then the door opened and Mr Rahkamo walked in. A big, solid man with blonde hair and blue eyes, wearing heavy, yellow coveralls, his face reddened from working outdoors. His energy seemed to fill the room. In spite of the puzzled look on his face, his whole demeanour gave the impression of a steady, practical man, not given to flights of fancy.

Hannu gestured to Qwelby who walked politely up to the new arrival and held out his hand. Paavo automatically took it in his big hand and was startled to hear a musical voice say: 'Goood even-ing, Faa-ther of Ha-nnu.'

'Good evening, errr... Qwelby,' Mr Rahkamo replied. Having heard from his wife about the boy who had arrived and who spoke no Finnish. 'You do speak Finnish!' he exclaimed.

'No.' Qwelby put both hands to his head and closed his eyes. 'Not... yet.'

Mr Rahkamo was so surprised that he did not move. Which was just as well as without warning Qwelby collapsed straight into his arms, was supported and helped to sit on the bed. The big man knelt down and looked into the stranger's face. He saw drooping eyelids, pale eyes and a look of exhaustion. He put the back of his hand against at the youngster's cheek. It was cold.

'Hannu,' he called over his shoulder to his son. 'Call your mother. I'm going to put him in the spare bedroom. Anita. Come and help.'

As he picked the boy up in his strong arms, Qwelby looped one arm over the man's shoulder. Paavo swiftly carried Qwelby the few steps into the guest bedroom. Anita pulled back the duvet. Paavo slid Qwelby onto the bed and they settled the cover over him. Qwelby's eyes opened, still looking pale. For a brief moment they darkened, the large orbs changing to a rich purple and the ovals to a bright violet. Almost before Paavo could register what he was feeling, Qwelby rolled over, curled up and fell fast asleep. Paavo remained standing there holding his arms out, staring at them.

Just then Seija came into the room, gently pushed her husband aside and sat on the edge of the bed. She listened to and watched Qwelby's breathing and gently felt his cheek and forehead. He appeared to be sleeping well, with slow, steady breathing. She took one of his arms out from under the duvet and felt for his pulse.

She sat up and looked at her husband. 'His pulse is slow, but it's steady and strong. He looks very flushed, but he has got quite a red hue to his brown skin, so I can't really tell.' She paused, letting his hand rest in hers. 'I think he's alright. Certainly he seems sound asleep. Wherever he's come from and however he's got here, he's tired out. The best thing is to let him sleep and stay warm. But he's going to get too hot with those clothes on, and he has been badly bruised.'

'Okay. Downstairs you two,' Paavo said to the children standing in the doorway. 'We'll be down in a moment, and then we'll have a good, long talk.'

The two parents removed Qwelby's sweater and tracksuit bottoms. Seija gently smeared cream over the mixture of red patches and darkening bruises. As she pulled the duvet back over him, Qwelby gave a little sigh, rolled onto his side and curled up again.

CHAPTER 22

MEETING THE MEERA

KALAHARI

As Tullia followed the two youngsters along the path they climbed the other side of the little valley. Emerging from a thick screen of trees she saw some way ahead, sheltering behind a tall fence made of a mixture of branches and bushes, a collection of small, conical shaped, thatched, grey huts. Through a wide opening in the fence she could just make out the glow from a couple of tiny fires, but no discernible smoke. As she stood there trying to take it all in, she realised that people were gathering behind the entrance, looking in her direction.

It all looked very peaceful. It was so very different from anything she had expected, yet there was a soft impression of an overall energy from the people that reassuringly felt a little like on her own world. Everyone was dressed as if for a cold winter's day. The bright mix of colours was also reassuring, even if they were not as vibrant as hers. As more people clustered in the entrance, she realised with surprise that no-one was anywhere near her height.

Xashee said a few words and gestured with his arm.

By the time they reached the village, a large crowd had gathered. Two men stepped a few feet onto the track and stopped. Slightly in front was a stockily built man wearing brown trousers and a dark green jacket over a brightly patterned woollen jumper. No taller than Xashee, yet he had a commanding presence. She could sense an energy of leadership.

A slim man, about a hand's-breadth shorter than Tullia, was standing a little behind and to one side. He was wearing grey trousers topped by a long, black overcoat buttoned up to the neck and a woollen hat. He had an energy signature that radiated kindness and concern.

Tullia felt a bundle of nerves. The clothes the two men were wearing were so dissimilar to each other and to anything worn on Vertazia that they gave her no clues. *I have to rely on my energy sensing and Intuition.*

She was aware of a faint smell of wood fires and cooking. Somewhere behind her the sharp, staccato call of a bird emphasised the silence in the village. Seeking reassurance, her hand slipped to her neck and she stroked the rich, purple Kanyisaya, set in her triple-coloured metal necklace.

The time she had spent discovering Xashee's and Tsetsana's names, followed by the exchange of formal greetings, had reminded her of Aurigan times. She swallowed nervously at the memory of history lessons. The difficulties that had accompanied some of her peoples' "First Contacts", when they had been forced to abandon their old homeworld of Auriga as their sun had started to show the signs that it was entering its terminal phase and eventually would turn into a white dwarf star.

She knew that what she was going to do in the next few moments was very important. As she tried to relax into her energy centres and allow her Intuition to guide her, a feeling came that the shorter man slightly in front was probably the village headman. She was not sure about the taller man on the left. There was something different about him.

Being in her fourth phase of exploring her roots, with family, race and the Multiverse, the village with all the meanings of home was very comforting and stabilising.

Everyone was still, waiting. *Okay. I have to move.* Once again she swallowed to settle her nerves, and steeled herself. She walked forward and stopped close to the two important men. Unable to repeat her previous greeting as she did not know their names, she settled for pointing to herself. 'Thallangi Tullia Rrîl'zânâ Mizenatyr. Busana.'

The whole village gasped. The shorter man pointed to himself, said 'Ghadi,' and gave a slight bow of his head.

Tullia noticed a slow smile spread across the face of the taller man. There was something about him that made her think of Great-Great Aunt Lellia. '"Click" amab' was what Tullia heard.

Ghadi beckoned to Xashee and they exchanged a few words. He then turned back to Tullia and with words and gestures invited her into the village.

The crowd of villagers stepped back with a mixture of politeness and just a little fear. They were accustomed to speaking with their ancestors. They were used to seeing them. But to find walking amongst them a Daughter of the Goddess Nananana was something that never had happened before.

As Tullia walked through the two lines of villagers, on her right hand side she saw the shorter man speaking to a woman with intricately plaited hair. She gestured, and two women accompanied her as she walked away.

That was rather nice, Tullia thought. If someone arrived at her home and asked to stay, her mother would ask her to help, perhaps to make sure the guest room was ready. What was happening looked very normal and made Tullia think of food, drink, and somewhere to rest.

At the same time she felt pleased with herself. She was managing to communicate before the compiler had created a database in her brain. If Xashee thought she came from the Moon, well it wasn't that far from the truth.

167

By this time they had arrived at the entrance to a hut. Although she did not understand their words, their gestures were clear. The hut was a place she could rest. There was a short piece of tree trunk by the door to sit on. More gestures indicating food and drink. She nodded vigorously and in a few moments two women appeared with a plate of food and a pitcher of cool, clear water.

She looked at the food. Some of the items looked like foods she knew, but would they taste the same? She was fairly certain there were raw vegetables or possibly fruit. Cautiously, she nibbled. Oh, good. A different texture and taste but that was nice. A fruit, sweet and juicy. Then something that tasted like a raw potato, but a sweeter flavour and very juicy. The water was cool and delicious.

With a gesture, the tall man, who her Intuition was suggesting was a sort of Wiseman, asked if he might leave and she nodded her agreement. The other man who she felt certain was the headman, had taken Xashee on one side and it seemed that he was about to send Tsetsana away. Tullia called out and with a gesture asked that the young girl should come and sit beside her.

She smiled at Tsetsana's response of half fear and half excitement. Tullia did not know why her smile had such an effect on people. Whatever it was, it had the right effect as Tsetsana came up a little nervously and sat down on a log on the other side of the doorway.

As she ate and drank, Tullia felt herself slowly relaxing and the tensions slipping away. She was returning to being what she was, a very frightened youngster, not an Ambassador from another planet. She was also aware of a headache starting. It was not so much an ache but lots of little pinpricks inside her brain.

She was feeling hot, tired and sleepy. For a moment she sagged back against the wall of the hut. Immediately Tsetsana got up and spoke to her. Tullia saw the girl's aura radiating concern, and spread her hands in a gesture which she hoped would show she did not understand. When the girl's gestures clearly asked if Tullia would like to go into the hut and lie down, she nodded and smiled.

Tsetsana rushed off to return a few moments later with three women. Later Tullia learnt that one was Deena, Tsetsana's mother, and the others looked after the guest huts.

The women were speaking and gesturing. The gestures Tullia understood and she chose a simple garment to sleep in. As they left the hut she sat on the bed with relief. Whilst they had been talking, her head had been increasingly filled with little stabs of pain. Slowly they disappeared. With an effort, she got her clothes off, put the robe on and slipped into bed.

Her sleep was not an easy one. Her mind seemed to be chattering to itself. She asked it to stop but it ignored her. She rolled onto her front and tried to lever herself up out of bed. A hand rested gently on the top of her head. The chattering eased, then stopped. Oh! That was blissful. She relaxed as she felt soft, cool energy flowing into her head. She felt another hand gently travelling down from the back of her neck to the base of her spine. The two hands remained there until her whole body was full of a beautiful, soft energy. She gave a great big sigh, curled up into a ball and fell into a peaceful sleep.

CHAPTER 23

X Õ Õ X

The day after Qwelby had almost been rescued from within the Stroems, Wrenden was still at Lungunu. He was so distraught at his failure to rescue his BestFriend that he had been moved to the Caring Room. Not only would he not speak, Cook was unable to get him to eat even her most tempting treats. Tamina refused to leave his side. She had confided to Lellia: 'Most of the time he is a thorough-going pest. But I'm used to that. Qwelby will never forgive me if I let him come to harm.' Feeling she was beginning to sound mushy, she had hastily added: 'And who else will I have to boss around!' Shimara and Pelnak had returned to their homes.

The parents of the four youngsters had come to Lungunu that morning. They were all very unhappy at the danger the children had been in, but each was torn in opposite directions. They accepted that the aeons-old esting traditions, the relationship of elderest and youngerest, bound together Pelnak, Qwelby and Wrenden. Then Pelnak and Shimara had their own bonding, which their parents had to accept was due as much to them as their offspring. Finally, Tamina was elderest to Tullia, who was quantum twin to Qwelby.

They agreed that the buildings that Wrenden and Tamina had described seeing were definitely not Tazian. Various explanations were offered but none sufficed. No-one had the desire to mention the terrible possibility that Qwelby might be trapped in the NoWhenWhere.

It was only after much soul searching, and with heavy hearts, that the friends' parents agreed that their children could make one more visit to the XzylStroem to search for the twins. But only one, when Wrenden was fully recovered, and only after Mandara had installed further security precautions. It was the mothers of Shimara and Pelnak, twins themselves, who summed up the situation: 'Xátuyé osiy nola nola osiy xátuyé. *(six all one and one all six)*. XOÑOX they are,' they said together.

Hearing TwinSpeak, Mizena fled from the room in tears, followed by her husband.

When the friends' parents left, Mandara and Lellia returned to the damaged section of Lungunu to continue with repairs. Exploring the Accelerator room was their top priority.

CHAPTER 24

TRACES

It was late the following afternoon when Mandara and Lellia returned to the main part of Lungunu, satisfied that they had completed the final element of such repairs as could be made. They were exhausted and settled to rest in Mandara's study while everything settled into place. They agreed to wait until they had definite news before contacting their great niece and nephew.

Some time later a soft tinkling of bells presaged House's announcement. 'The Portal has been re-established.'

Thanking House, Mandara got up from he was sitting and turned to a section of the bookcase. It swung open at his request and he stepped through. Lellia followed and the bookcase swung back as they started to walk along the staircase in the pitch dark. They were very careful not to allow their feet to tell them whether they were going up or down, because the stairs weren't really there in that dimension. 'Along' was a much safer thought to hold.

After a little while the darkness faded and they saw that they were now walking along a corridor. The walls were still badly marked as through flames had ripped along them, peeling paint off. Yet the walls never had been painted. The apparent burn marks were slowly sliding down the walls like so much coloured rain down a window, whilst the seeming peeling paint, carried on peeling down in strips, revealing underneath a soft magnolia colour that just begged to have a pretty colourwash applied to it. A corner appeared. They turned it. Set back in a dark alcove was a yellow and red streaked, dark grey door.

'That wheel should be light grey,' Mandara said in a hoarse voice. Taking a deep breath he pushed the door. It moved. 'Impossible! The locking mechanism is in a different timeframe to the door. Or rather, it was.'

He pushed the door wide open. The draft caused a cloud of red dust to blow about and scattered a few pine needles and snowflakes across the floor. The room was in chaos. Half of it was there and half flickering in and out of existence. A sharp tang of ozone overlay the burnt smell. The Jacuzzi-like container had turned black with vivid orange streaks along its sides, the liquid colour trickled down, puddling on the floor like mercury.

As a form of safety cut-out, House possessed a number of discrete subs-routines that covered potentially dangerous parts of Lungunu. After the twins had created a personalised Image of House as an aged and trusted Retainer, with Mandara's permission, they had personalised its sub-routines, naming them Guardians. Mandara spoke to the Guardian of the Room. With tears running down its disembodied, blue face, it explained how the twins had disappeared.

'As you know, I can only control energy at the quantum level. I cannot control the multi-phasic supra-dimensional energy that is the core of a human being. I could not stop them sending their thoughts in and...'

Finally admitting that the twins were no longer on Vertazia, Lellia sighed and leant against her much bigger husband. Really, she had known all along. Since the moment of the major disturbance in House, wherever she was she had been aware of the Stroems' energies: exceptionally strong and steady, calming the other five Stroems. And underneath that, an unusual hint of almost personal disturbance.

She was an hereditary Orchestrator, but only because she had the skills. Even though she worked well with the Stroems, like all other Orchestrators she knew little of what they really were. Aeons ago in what was termed 'The Golden Era' there had been twelve StroemWells, none of them shielded in Caverns. For the first time she wondered if her researches into the lives of the Azurii would have been better devoted to exploring what had caused the loss of the six Wells.

Mandara closed the door as they left the room. 'I will need to come back and restore the timelock,' he mumbled half-heartedly.

Looking at their clothes, Lellia noticed they were speckled with a mixture of red sand, pine needles and snowflakes that were melting now they were out of the room. She brushed a few specks of red sand onto the palm of her hand. 'Feel how heavy these pieces are,' she said proffering them to her husband.

He picked up a few grains up and grunted. 'Not really heavy, lighter than I would expect but...'

'You're right, my dear. More solid. More 'there' somehow,' she said slowly, not liking where her thinking was leading her.

'It's all my fault,' Mandara said. 'Playing all those games that challenge them to develop their innate skills.' He gave a mirthless laugh. 'Breaking into forbidden areas of House.'

'We have all helped them to become who they are,' Lellia said, taking his hands in hers. 'Hoping to avoid the introversion and short lifespans that we are told affected the previous pair of Quantum Twins... and discover the reason for their existence.'

Mandara nodded, accepting what his wife had said.

'Getting them back will be a challenge worthy of the Arch-Discoverer,' she added.

Her husband grimaced. He was the best. He had no false modesty. It was why he had been acclaimed as Arch-Discoverer when he was still so many years away from becoming a Venerable. Together with the different skills of his wife and nephew, supported by Mizena's solidity, if anyone could do it, they could. And then there was the whole of the Council of Discoverers to call on.

CHAPTER 25

CUSTODIANS

The Custodians were Traditionalists who considered themselves to be the successors to the Guardians of Aurigan times, and Keepers of the True Aurigan Teachings

In essence, all Tazii were traditionalists, accepting that they needed to energetically combine with the vastly more numerous Azurii in order for both sub-races to reactivate all their DNA and thus recapture the amazingly beautiful life of the Aurigan era. Yet they were also fearful of any connection with the Azurii, accepting what the Custodians taught, that the endemic violence on Azura was due to a Violence Virus.

On the position of Arch-Custodian becoming vacant, the chosen successor underwent a secret initiation, spending a complete lunar month in The Fount of All Knowledge and Truth. That month was to allow each new incumbent to come to terms with the contents of a secret DataStore within the Archives. And to become reconciled to having to bear for the rest of their life the burden of knowledge which, if revealed, would destroy the Custodians and mean the certain end of the prevailing Tazian way of life. A way that had been inculcated over the millennia by generations of Custodians.

The secret DataStore had been created millennia ago by otherwise forgotten Aurigan technology that totally concealed all indications of its presence. Having been established in the era before the substantial degradation of DNA it also contained its own defences: the Labyrinth.

Since he had been chosen as successor to the then Arch-Custodian, Ceegren had been manoeuvring to have the unique, month long initiation result in the holder of that office being accepted as the undisputed leader of the Custodians. A marked departure from Tazian tradition whereby the titular head of any organisation was just that, without any more power then was conferred by their personality. Then through that acceptance, be appointed as Arbiter of the Spiral Assembly, the very loose form of Tazian government. In view of the situation posed by the twins, he now saw both as essential and urgent.

At one hundred and sixty-two, he was a Venerable. Two metres fifteen tall, broad shouldered, his physical presence matched his personal power. As was usual at his age, his orbs had expanded to completely fill his eyes, giving him two ovals of deep sea green, and his cognomen of Ceegren.

Amongst the secrets revealed to him over twelve years ago had been the nature of Quantum Twins. Over the millennia there had been several other pairs, all of the same type as Qwelby and Tullia. Although vastly different from the QeïchâKaïgïï, it was clear from their uniform difference to all other Tazii, including all other twins, that they had the potential to display greater abilities and power than any other Tazian.

Ceegren was not the first Arch Custodian to fear that eventually a pair might develop whatever the full range of those extra abilities might be, with potentially devastating consequences for the Custodian's grip on Tazian society if that power enabled them to access otherwise embargoed records in the Racial Memory Archives. That fear had been the hidden agenda behind the eventually successful manoeuvring by several successive Arch Custodians to have the age of adulthood, along with the increasing limitations applied to most Tazii at that ceremony, moved from the end of the third era to the end of the second.

From early on he had taken a discrete interest in the twins and their family, especially because of the presence of powerful Uddîsû genes. Inspired by Lellia's interest in Azura, the family had researched Azuran myths, discovering how many were derived from distorted memories of the early Aurigan period on Earth. As knowledge of the twins' disappearance and how that had happened spread through the MentaNet, what had been faintly amusing now gave him cause for alarm.

Ceegren knew that if the children were to be away from Vertazia for any length of time then, freed from the millennia old, tightly age-governed developmental pattern that was an integral part of Tazian society, they were likely to at least start to develop their innate Quantum skills much earlier than normal. Frustratingly, he could only guess at what those might be. The worst case scenario was that on their return to Vertazia they would discover the Labyrinth, would find the Tazian equivalent of Ariadne's Thread, defeat the Aurigan equivalent of the Minotaur, discover and then broadcast the secrets.

That would end all his dreams. He had convinced himself that those were not about personal ambition. Rather, he saw his plans as merely the necessary means to enable him to fulfil what he had come to believe to be the purpose of his life: to return the errant Shakazii to the fold of Traditionalism. He accepted that to achieve such a worthwhile goal would require the "persuasive" efforts of Readjusters. To that end he had been carefully cultivating Dryddnaa, at one hundred and twenty-four a comparatively young yet already formidable Chief Readjuster.

Added to his own personal prestige, being Arch Custodian gave his views great weight but, in true Tazian tradition, he did not have the power to rule. He would have to find very convincing reasons to persuade all Tazii to accept that the twins must never be permitted to return.

He could not even start by revealing the truth to his most

trusted supporters. He had been so terrified of the consequences should he ever let slip anything of the terrible secrets to which he had become privy, that at the end of the month-long induction period he had decided to swear an oath of silence, naming his hero, the great Traditionalist Insûmâne Haa-Zeyló as witness. That oath was binding: physically, mentally and psychically.

Achieving a planet-wide consensus would take planning and time as he would have to work slowly through the inevitable layers of Tazian society, starting with the Inner Council, then the Senate, and as they in turn worked with the Convocation of all Custodians, he would start discussions with the upper echelons of other key groupings of Tazii. And, at the same time, find ways to frustrate the attempts the family would obviously be making to recover their offspring. A family which included the Arch Discoverer, Vertazia's greatest inventive scientist.

As my plans are for the future good of the whole race, maybe Life will respond. Given the Arch Discoverer's scientific link with Azura, it is possible that the children are on that planet where violent death is an everyday occurrence. An accident may befall them. A lasting accident... He abruptly stopped his thinking. Some thoughts were never, ever to be contemplated

A few days after the news of the twins disappearance had been disseminated, the family spread the tidings that both were considered to be alive and one of them was believed to on Azura. Ceegren immediately summoned a meeting of the Senate, a large group of the older and more powerful Custodians. Full of sympathy for the plight of the twins, he played upon the fears of the almost certainty that they would be infected by the Violence Virus.

With the discussion becoming bogged down with no clear agreement in sight, Ceegren owed much to a timely contribution by Dryddnaa. The highly respected Chief Readjuster explained she was confidant that she would be able to establish sufficient protocols to ensure the necessary quarantine, treatment... and cure if necessary. The connotations attaching to the words "treatment" and "cure" falling from the lips of such a powerful Readjuster sent a shiver through the assemblage.

The treatment provided by a Readjuster, variously called a Psych or Psi Doctor, generally ranged from gentle counselling to mentally adjusting individuals to enable them to happily conform. At the extreme end of readjustment were the almost automaton-like consequences of being "Cured". When Dryddnaa requested that, in order for each child to be adjusted as little as possible and especially to avoid the extreme consequences, she needed to work without their twin-link being restored, a unanimous decision was reached.

With genuine expressions of regret, the Senate agreed that in order to reduce the chances of infection, and maximise the children's chances for their future lives, they should be kept apart both mentally and physically. And, sadly, the family had to be prevented from communicating with them, as successful communication would also enable the twins to link.

No references were made either to time or quarantine. It was a typical Tazian decision, dealing with the immediate situation and avoiding the more serious decisions that almost certainly would have to be made in the future.

How the children were to be brought back was a mattert for the Academy of Discoverers. Although that was headed by the twins' great-great uncle, Ceegren knew there were members of the Academy who would see the advantages to be gained by agreeing with his suggestions.

Ceegren returned to his estate with mixed feelings. He had achieved only the minimum he wanted, and that only as the result of an eloquent address by Dryddnaa. He had allowed himself to be carried away by his own prescience and almost overreached himself. With the situation regarding the twins providing the perfect lever, he needed to accelerate his plans. For that he needed powerful help, and Dryddnaa had already made her bid to be included. It was a bid he had to accept as she could be a key ally, yet he was troubled by her obvious ambition.

He needed to tie her closely to him. Having been a member of the Senate for several years, four years ago he had brought her into the Inner Council when she was accorded the status of Elder, at the earliest possible age of one hundred and twenty, disconcerting several other older and longer serving Custodians. At some point soon he would offer her the co-ordinating role of the team to be established to deal with the Shakazii. Taken together with his obvious support, that should set her on the path to eventually becoming the Arch-Readjuster.

Given her support for him and his projects, the energy exchange balance would be neutral. Neither would owe energy to the other. Rather, the mutually beneficial working partnership that had started years earlier when Dryddnaa had persuaded the younger Custodians to support his appointment as the chosen successor would be firmly cemented in place.

There was a delicious irony. The consequence of the restrictions imposed on most Tazii at the time of achievement of adulthood at the end of their second era, was the resultant inertia of the majority of adults. For his plans to succeed, Ceegren had always known there would come a time when he needed to harness higher vibrational energies: those of twiyeras between twelve and twenty-four. With their focus on each individual annual phase of development they were so much easier to manipulate than adults.

With events now requiring him to accelerate his plans, the biggest problem he faced was the lack of a charismatic youth leader. The LifeLine of the boy he had chosen, who had been serving as his acolyte for many years, had been terminated in an unfortunate Omnitor accident. The replacement he had chosen and who was now serving as the younger of his two acolytes was far too young.

He would visit the Custodians' base where there were many youths under training. But. He shook his head. None had ever stood out as having the qualities he needed. It looked as though he would need Dryddnaa's assistance to find a suitable individual. Taking her at least part way into his confidence at this stage would make him vulnerable. Equally, it would commit her to him.

As I sow, so do I reap!

CHAPTER 26

REFLECTIONS

RAIATEA

Late on the evening of December the twenty-sixth Professor Romain was sitting on his patio on the island of Raiatea gazing out at a world divided in two. A black dome full of twinkling stars above the unbroken black expanse of the South Pacific. Wearing cream chinos and a brightly coloured, island shirt, he was savouring a fine cognac and looking back on a satisfactory year's work.

David Beauregard Romain was a tall slim Englishman in his late fifties with a neat moustache. One of the world's leading quantum scientists, he had left CERN to pursue his own research. Using his personal fortune he had built the complex on Raiatea. Mathematics indicated that there had to be at least ten and possibly twenty-six other dimensions in order for the observable three to exist. His passion, he refused to accept the word obsession, was to prove their actual, physical existence.

He had an inquisitive and inventive mind. Ever since a teenager he had produced commercially viable ideas. Since having learnt early on that his father's approach to business was all take and no give, everything was legally wrapped up, tightly. The royalties together with dividends from his steadily increasing shareholdings in his father's companies, his own identity hidden though a variety of shell companies, provided him with the necessary money to fund his research into the quantum field.

Financially, the previous year had been good. He had been right to engage the couple, the three of them made a good team. Between them in that year alone they had produced two ideas with definite commercial prospects, sold as was customary to one of his father's many companies.

His musings took him back to his decision to engage assistants.

During the course of refining his equipment, inexplicable anomalies arose. It seemed that interference was being caused – by a source that was not there. No matter how hard he tried, he was not able to detect what was causing the problem. One evening he remembered the paradox of Schrödinger's cat.

The Copenhagen interpretation of quantum mechanics required that the theoretical cat in the box was simultaneously alive and dead. Yet if one were to look in the box, the cat would be seen as either alive or dead. The act of looking having caused the observable reality to collapse the quantum superpositioning into one possibility or the other. With that possibility being dependent upon the viewer's preconception of the outcome of the experiment.

That took him to the previous interpretation known as the EPR Paradox concerning entanglement, named after a paper produced in 1913 by Albert Einstein, Boris Podolsky and Nathan Rosen.

In exploring the Earth's quantum field Romain had slowly and very reluctantly come to the conclusion that his thinking about his experiments seemed to be influencing the results far more than was considered the norm for the acknowledged "observer effect" as epitomised by the famous double-slit experiment. At the back of his mind hovered the thought that it was precisely because he believed in the EQF that he had discovered it.

He pondered on the alternative paradoxes of Copenhagen and EPR, and that quantum entanglement across dimensions was his ultimate goal. The result was that he decided to follow what he termed the "excessive observer effect" in looking for the anomaly: was he somehow creating the anomaly, and why?

Eventfully, that approach led him to discover a fourth neutrino. Like all "particles" it was paired with its anti-particle. The crucial difference was that it was uniquely pair-bonded. As a result each half cancelled out the other making it undetectable, except by the interference it was causing. And implying that it had not even the minuscule mass attributed to other neutrinos or photons.

Creating a beam of neutrinos normally required a massive amount of energy and large physical structures. Inspired by the success of several young teenagers in creating miniature Colliders, he chose graphene for the container and designed and built what was in essence a miniature particle accelerator – that produced a stream of the new neutrinos.

Once again he was left with the thought – because he believed that he would succeed. Or rather, he slowly came to the even more outrageous conclusion: that those neutrinos "wanted" to be found. He knew he was verging on – even had overstepped – the boundary into psychosis. But. He was producing those new neutrinos in his laboratory!

It was as he was questioning his sanity that he knew he needed to engage doctoral assistants. And they had to be the right ones. He remembered being impressed by a postgrad student who had attended several of his lectures at the university in Los Angeles where he was Visiting Professor of Quantum Mechanics. There had been a quiet determination and an energy of subdued intensity about her and her probing questions.

Satisfied with the enquiries he made, he decided to follow his intuition. His contract required him to give a series of lectures every semester. At his next visit he took the opportunity afforded by the various dinners which he enjoyed attending to ask about the progress of specific past students, including a petite Japanese-American. He mentioned to one particular professor that he was looking for two assistants who would need to be able to work in a small team in a somewhat isolated location. Shortly thereafter that professor contacted him with the names of a married couple who might be interested.

A few days later, after the obligatory initial exchanges, Romain met the two applicants at the Uturoa airport in Raiatea and drove them along the coast road to a little patisserie where they relaxed and soaked up the feel of the island.

Miki Tamagusuku-Jefferson was the petite Japanese-American who had impressed him. She explained that her unusually dark skin came from an unknown mixture of races in her family's history. At one time fisher-folk living on a small island off the coast of Japan, more than one of her distant ancestors had been the result of liaisons with passing sailors.

Honouring the sacrifices her parents had made for her education, Miki had kept her family name on marriage to Dr Tyler Jefferson. A solidly built man of average height, he liked to say that he was a very genuine Jamaican-American, as the unusual reddish cast to his skin was due to one of his recent ancestors being a Native American.

After a while, Romain pointed out the laboratory complex high up on the mountainside.

'All camouflaged, it's like something out of a James Bond movie,' Miki had said.

'All steel and glass reflecting the sun would have been a monstrosity,' Romain snapped his reply. 'One of the many reasons for its location is peace and quite. Essential for relaxation. I do not want my home to be an attraction for gawping tourists.'

They returned to the Ranger. 'Think of Raiatea like a hat,' Romain explained as they travelled the road up the side of the mountain. 'Odd Job's perhaps.' Annoyed with himself for his over-reaction he tried to lighten the atmosphere in the four-by-four.

'The brim is the coastal rim, heavily occupied by the small population, and the tourist trade. The rest is the mountain. Up here we are away from all that fuss and bother, the vibrations of traffic and the variety of electromagnetic waves being received and generated.'

They came to the end of the metalled road. 'As you can see we are almost isolated here. A four-by-four is not really necessary but it makes easy going of this track. And that may be improved if the planned observatory is ever built. Social concourse with other scientists will be a welcome diversion.'

He pulled up outside a long, low building on their right. 'There is the communication mast,' he said, pointing to the left at the sheltering mountain crest. 'Permanently in line of sight with one of the several telecommunications satellites. Essential for my international travelling.' *And crucial for my secret link with CERN.*

As they entered the building, then the lift, he pointed to the buttons and explained. 'This is the first floor, then numbered down to four. I am not going to say that I live on the ground floor and work in the basement! Not after all the years underground at CERN.'

Exiting the building on the fourth floor, stepping onto the large patio with its swimming pool, both visitors gasped at the beauty of the view across the Pacific Ocean some seven hundred metres below. Turning to face the building they saw that the front was almost entirely glass. The windows and doors in varying shades of green, the supporting structure in shades of brown and the dark blue-grey of the mountain rock, and the whole edifice crowned off by a large conservatory that ran across most of its width, but was not apparent to anyone entering the first floor.

'The whole building is my own design. What I call the securaglass in the windows, one of my inventions. From inside: a completely clear view with solar filtering as necessary.

'This floor: a stretch of modular accommodation. Currently including guest rooms and facilities where you will stay tonight.

'To the right, the steps leading up to that small balcony, domestic staff accommodation and main kitchen. To the left, the steps to the small patio, accommodation for my assistants. Specifically designed for a couple, of whatever persuasion. Further to the left the emergency stairs. Caged in for safety if it has to be used in high winds.

'Above, third floor, the main research laboratory. Behind that, tunnelled into the rock for the same reasons of shielding as at CERN, the key to all my research. It contains my equipment which is unique, in the true meaning of that word. I call it the Fifth Room.' He paused for a moment. Silly maybe, but a little test.

'The four dimensions of space-time-consciousness, then another one you want to prove is as real,' Miki said.

Romain smiled as he nodded. 'Shielding and security is so much better and easier to create here than digging down into the exorbitantly priced land of the coastal strip, even if I could have found the right location.

'Above, second floor. What I call the working laboratory where ideas with commercial potential are developed. To the left, the West room: fully equipped for work outside the main labs. To the right the East room.' He turned to make eye contact with both, momentarily lingering on Miki. 'Also with equipment that is truly unique.' A decade younger than her husband, it was not long since she had been awarded her doctorate, yet he sensed she was the driving force of the pair.

'Finally, top floor, my own suite. As you can see, the roofs are almost entirely covered with solar panels. Back up generators of course. Never been needed.

'The design. Not ideal perhaps, but it works. The gently curving facade and several levels largely determined by the shape of the mountain face and the outcroppings of solid rock. No need to dig down and lay foundations.

'Enjoy the view,' he said and walked a few paces away, giving them time to discuss their initial reactions.

He disagreed with Professor Eysenck about interviews not being necessary. In this particular situation they were essential. Whoever he chose, the three of them would be living and working closely together with little outside socialising. With no intention of revealing his mutually beneficial negotiations with the Island's President and the High Commissioner, he realised that he had spoken abruptly in making it clear that the whole edifice and its location had been designed for practical reasons.

He liked their CV's. He needed to sooth the initial contact before they settled down for serious discussions. As he walked up to them, Dr Tamagusuku was standing nearer to him than her husband.

'Well, what do think, Miss Moneypenny?' he had asked with a slight smile.

As she had turned to face him he had seen her blink her eyes in surprise. A momentary pause.

'It is impressive, Mr Bond,' she replied with a straight face.

After a short break to allow the couple to unpack, freshen up and change, they met for a light lunch and the commencement of serious questioning and discussions.

Satisfied that their scientific background was what he needed, Romain found himself more than content with the philosophical exchanges with Miki as she was happy to speculate outside conventional boundaries. Tyler's rigidly practical responses were causing him concern. How could he cope with where Romain's thoughts had taken him?

The following morning he offered them a tour of the laboratories, subject to completion of tightly worded non-disclosure agreements. Tyler was clearly excited to see the miniature linear accelerator. When Romain was questioned by Tyler on his reasoning, and the possibility of constructing an equally miniature collider, the professor was guarded with his replies and said nothing about his discovery of a new neutrino.

Sure about engaging Miki, unsure about Tyler, yet impressed by the obvious enthusiasm for the practical side of quantum mechanics he had shown during the tour, Romain offered an unusual trial engagement. They would take the maximum holiday period they were permitted that summer and come to Raiatea where they would work with him.

During those few weeks they ran a series of trials using the linear accelerator. Tyler failed to produce any of the new neutrinos whilst, working together, Romain and Miki succeeded – as long as Tyler was not in the same room.

The key element in the experiments with the psien was that they had to believe in what they were seeking to achieve. Romain had slowly come to that realisation over the years. With Miki's personal philosophy she had been willing to suspend a hard, practical scientific approach, give it a go – and succeed.

Tyler was too good a scientist to ignore the evidence, especially when it passed the essential test of being regularly repeated. He accepted Romain's definition of an 'excessive observer effect' as a neat description to cover the fact that he really could not accept that he was mentally influencing sub-atomic particles.

Most quantum scientists believed that too many sub-atomic particles existed for the ultimate building block or blocks of the universe yet to have been discovered. When Tyler eventually achieved limited success and produced a few of the new neutrinos, he became excited by the prospect that he might actually have seen the first particle at that level. Were they exploring sub-quantum mechanics? Was there a whole new set of 'rules' to be discovered? Could he and Miki be part of that adventure?

Offered contracts, the two doctors returned to America to hand in their resignations.

Romain had been right about Miki. Unlike with Tyler, there was a good connection at a deep level. Amongst many things she understood why, whatever important function to which all three were invited for the Solstice celebrations, Romain always carried a flask containing the local, illicit, hooch for them to drink their own, personal toast. And why it was special to Romain that the drink was obtained from Kaikane, their housekeeper's husband who brewed his own.

Gently twirling his glass now drained of the Tesseron Lot No.65, Romain got up and took the glass into his small kitchen where he washed, dried and put it away before settling down to sleep: blissfully unaware that the next day was to start him on a trail to a discovery beyond his wildest imaginings.

CHAPTER 27

RIPPLES

EUROPE

A core of scientists at CERN had been working all through the Christmas holiday, trying to establish what had happened on the twentieth of December to cause the fields of two magnets to collapse and the circuits protecting the monitoring equipment to rupture as though submitted to a massive overload. The consequent damage requiring repair had been minimal, fuses blown and some wiring burnt out. When after exhaustive exploration, theories and tests they were still unable to explain what had happened, they decided to make a test run of the LHC.

Over the years CERN had run a variety of experiments with the Laboratories at Gran Sasso near Rome, MonKiw in Tasmania and Firmilab in Illinois, USA. They had asked for skeleton staff at all three to set up and run monitoring equipment in case anything went wrong and might show up on the monitors. The same had been asked of the institute at Jyväskylä as it lay to the North, whereas the others, although spread wide apart, were all situated to the South.

Using satellite links, a conference call was set up between all five with a scientist at CERN advising of progress. Late on the afternoon of twenty-seven December a very short test run was completed. The monitoring equipment in the Institute at Jyväskylä flickered momentarily at the same time as interference overrode all conversation on the call. Subsequent short test runs produced no interference anywhere.

Satisfied that all seemed well and glad that the long night was over, the four monitoring sites closed down and the staff returned to their homes to continue their interrupted holidays. Meanwhile, puzzled scientists at CERN shut down the LHC for another maintenance check. In due course that reported all was satisfactory and the planned series of runs was recommenced.

A small team was established to review unusual results and look for any clues to the two odd occurrences, especially that of the twentieth.

In an office on the third floor of the Lubyanka an elderly, bored clerk of the FSB, the Russian Federal Security Service, was cross-indexing computer records with very old paper files. Working through the alphabet, Feodor Ivanovich Demidov opened the records of a famous operation by the then KGB where double agents had been working at the highest level of the British Secret Service for nearly twenty years. He became engrossed in his reading.

With a start, he realised how late it was. Not wanting to be locked in the building overnight, he rapidly finished the computer entries, closed down the case files and signed off with a nod and a muttered: 'The good old days, eh, Comrade Colonel Philby.' As he did so, a new file with the name Kwilby was created. An accidental mistake in his hurry, or the effect of the twins' arrival? No-one would ever know.

Seeking to cross-index the new file, the computer searched databases. Finding nothing, it was classified as a new case and automatically flagged for attention on a low level circulation list.

Over in the Yasanevo District of Moscow it came to the attention of the SVR, the Foreign Intelligence Service. It was with a mixture of glee and derision at the failings of their hated rivals that a young agent, Andrei Petrovic Kurochkin, called to his colleagues: 'FSB incompetence. Can you believe it? A new file and no source data. Nothing!'

Scornfully he made a brief note: "Novvy Chelovek." Which simply meant "new man", and was used by both agencies to indicate a new surveillance target.

Feodor and Andrei had nothing in common except their hatred of each other's branch of State Security. That hatred was soon to turn personal when each was dismissed over their part in the creation of the Kwilby file. The first of the casualties of the twins' sojourn on Earth.

CHAPTER 28

AN UNLIKELY EXPLANATION

FINLAND

Having closed the door to the bedroom where Qwelby was sleeping, Mr Rahkamo went down to the kitchen where his wife was preparing hot drinks. Working as a maintenance engineer on all the equipment at a large ski centre, his job required a methodical approach. The same applied now. Before he could decide what to do, he wanted to have all the facts.

Hannu and Anita came into the kitchen clutching the book on the solar system and sheets of drawings which they started to spread over the table.

To Paavo, the drawings looked like the sort children did when still in nursery school. Right then he thought that nothing would surprise him. He was a big man in every sense of the word. His very stillness made the whole room feel calm and relaxed. He waited until everyone was settled, then leant forward, drawing them all together.

'I will start by repeating what my wife has told me. Tell me whether I've got it right. Fill in any gaps if need be. At least then we will know that we are starting from the same place.' He gestured to the drawings. 'It looks as though you two have got a lot more you want to tell us?'

The two youngsters nodded, eyes bright with excitement.

Paavo then briefly summarised what he understood had happened from the time that Hannu had called out that he had seen a stranger, until the two boys had gone to Hannu's room.

'That's it, Dad,' Hannu said approvingly, as his father sat back in his chair.

Seija smiled and rested a hand on her husband's much larger one.

Satisfied that he'd got the facts straight in his own mind, Paavo smiled at his wife, turned his hand over and gave hers a gentle squeeze.

'Right. Your turn.' He looked at the two youngsters, their faces full of eager anticipation.

'He's a nice boy,' Anita said. 'It's a funny thing to say when we hardly know him.' She looked at Hannu. 'But he "feels" nice.' She blushed.

'You mean it's like, sort of, you can feel his feelings, you mean?' Hannu asked.

'When we three hugged, I could feel his happiness, somehow as if it was me feeling happy,' Anita confirmed.

'Yeah. I had that, sort of, but different, when he showed me how much he liked the Portal. It was like, you know, there was power in his words. And I understood what he was saying. I felt, like a bond between us, as though we were space explorers. Together. That was weird.' He laughed, feeling silly.

Anita put a reassuring hand on Hannu's arm, looking at his parents. 'He spoke a lot whilst he was doing all the drawings. His language sounds very musical. It carries you with it.' She gave Hannu an encouraging glance.

Between them, Hannu and Anita explained what they understood of the drawings.

They saw Paavo nodding and heard the occasional grunt as they

195

took him through step by step. The blue world of Earth. Qwelby's red world. They thought it might be Mars, but Qwelby seemed to be saying that it was inside Earth. Then moving from one world to the other.

He had a sister named Tullia, almost certainly a twin. They laughed as they related that incident, repeating Qwelby's gestures and seeing him nodding his confirmation. Then Qwelby's uncertainty. Was Tullia on Earth or still at home?

Paavo had been leaning forward, looking at the drawings with obvious interest. As the youngsters stopped talking he sat back in his chair, shaking his head with a look of doubt on his face.

'Dad! He is an Alien!' Hannu said as he searched through the drawings. 'Well not really, he doesn't come from another planet, well, he does, because he doesn't come from our planet but it's not one that's like out there, it's like it's out here, or in here, but I suppose that means he is a sort of an alien but he is not an alien-alien ...' Hannu had run out of breath.

'We think he comes from an alternate reality,' Anita said. Her words reminded Paavo that her father was a scientist.

Hannu presented the drawing of the two planets again: one in solid blue lines and the other in broken red ones. He took a deep breath and looked to Anita for support.

'We think he is trying to tell us that his world occupies the same space as ours,' he explained.

'An alternate reality doesn't have to be as solid as ours,' Anita added rapidly. 'It probably has to vibrate at a different frequency. That would allow it to occupy the same space.'

Paavo shook his head. He had followed every step, even the last one. It was all eminently logical. But. There was one big problem. He knew that what they were saying was totally impossible. Lovely theory, fun for the Science Fiction films he knew his son liked, but not here and now, in this world. No. Definitely, absolutely, not.

'Like the waves for mobile phones. We don't see them but

they're there, or here. Well you know, they go right through us, don't they?' added Hannu, desperate to convince his father.

That really was too much for Paavo. His world revolved around solid mechanisms, ski lifts, cables, drums. Electricity. *Which can't be seen. No-one knows why it works. We know how it works, but not why the electrons stream through the cables.* He was glad to have that train of thought broken as his wife returned to the room, having slipped upstairs to check that their guest was still sleeping peacefully.

Paavo had never believed in UFO's, and was convinced that there always was a rational explanation for any claimed "sighting". Yet there was a strange boy asleep in his house who didn't speak any language the children had been able to recognise. Then: why was he wearing summer clothes in winter, and: how had he arrived on the slope opposite their house? He liked that thought. It told him there was something practical he could do.

'Right. There's one way of solving this. I'm going over there and find out just where he came from.'

'Dad, can we come as well?' asked Hannu.

'Why not. Then you can see for yourselves he's no alien from outer space.'

CHAPTER 29

THAT'S NOT A DESERT!

FINLAND

All three wrapped up in warm clothes, picked up torches, and took stout walking sticks to help with the ice that had formed over the surface of the snow.

They got to the top of the bank on the far side of the road and looked out over the crisp snow. The almost full moon shining from a clear sky made everything so bright it was easy to see that a fresh trail had been made through the trees. It led to a fallen one where it was clear that someone had brushed snow from part of the trunk. From there, more tracks led back into the forest. They followed them to the foot of a snowdrift where the snow was all messed up by a large hole.

'That looks just like that hole I made that day when I went out skiing before the ice crust had melted,' Hannu said, more excited at what he thought it meant than the embarrassment of that morning. He turned to Anita. 'I couldn't stop and went head first into the bank at the side of the road.

'That was deliberate, rather than shoot over the bank and across the road!' he added, defensively, as Anita smiled.

'And you think that's where he landed,' she said.

All three of them looked around the whole area very carefully. They could find no other marks of any kind.

'Look, Dad, it's like this,' Hannu was sure he could explain. 'We agree that he arrived just here, in this hole, slid out and walked to that fallen tree. All the other marks are him going downhill. I saw him.'

'Yes,' Paavo said reluctantly.

'Right. If he had arrived by parachute, either we would find it caught in the trees or footprints showing where he landed or buried it. There are no marks. So, no parachute.' He waited.

'All right, no parachute,' his father agreed.

'If a helicopter had landed, there would be marks in the snow. There aren't any. If instead of landing, he had been lowered from it, jumped or whatever, again there would be marks in the snow. The downwind from the chopper blades would have swept snow from the branches. If he had fallen through the trees then snow would have been knocked off the branches. Look.' Pointing his torch up, he shone it all around the trees.

'That hasn't happened. And he would have scratches all over his body and his clothes. Mum says there are bruises but no scratches.' He glanced at Anita, impressed with his own clarity for once, then looked at his father.

'So. How did he get here?' he asked. 'Not by any natural means, that's for sure,' he finished with a sound of triumph in his voice.

'If he lives in another dimension he could have arrived here by stepping through a space-time warp or a wormhole,' Anita said, offering a logical explanation.

There was a long silence.

'Let's get back,' Paavo said. He was feeling worse than he had before. He had been so certain that he would find a logical explanation and would not have to worry any more about the strange ideas that had been put into his mind. He led the way home, too many thoughts rushing through his mind for him to pay any attention to the excited chatter between the two youngsters as they continued to debate just how 'Their Alien', as they were thinking of Qwelby, really had arrived.

Entering the house through the back door, they stamped the last remains of snow from their boots, hung up their coats and went into the kitchen to stand around the stove and warm themselves.

Hannu excitedly told his mother what they had found, or rather, hadn't found, proving that their visitor was an alien.

She didn't seem to be particularly concerned.

'Qwelby's still sleeping soundly. The best thing for him is to have a good, long night in bed. Besides which, we haven't had dinner and it is about time we all sat down and ate. We can talk about everything again in the morning. I've telephoned Anita's father and he said she can stay for the night. He'll bring some clothes around for her.'

Dr Keskinen was a scientist working at the nearby Institute in Jyväskylä. Although the family had only moved into the village from Helsinki that summer, Viljo had met Paavo on the ski slopes and they had quickly struck up a friendship, which extended to their wives. Both Anita's parents were happy that their daughter had found a friend who shared her mixture of interests.

'Mum...' Hannu started, afraid she might have explained what had happened.

'All I said was that you two were having so much fun with some science stuff, you'd probably want to stay up late. He wasn't surprised. After all, there's no school tomorrow so...'

The fact that Mrs Rahkamo was taking everything in her stride as though nothing unusual had happened at all, and they just had a new friend staying overnight, eased all the tensions. A few minutes later she put dinner on the table. They all sat down and ate quietly, each lost in their own thoughts.

Some time later Dr Keskinen telephoned and asked if it was

convenient to call round at that moment. Seija suggested that Taimi should also come along, saying it would save telling the story twice. Seija did not allow herself to be drawn on the nature of the story.

The Keskinens arrived, kissed Anita goodnight, and said good night to Hannu as the two children went upstairs.

'Make yourselves comfortable,' Paavo said, as Seija headed into the lobby, followed by the Keskinens to divest themselves of their outdoor clothing and put on the guest slippers every Finnish house kept. The Keskinens looked like the typical image for Scandinavians. Tall, slim, blonde hair and rosy cheeks from the cold. Taimi was wearing a rainbow coloured sweatshirt over black trousers, Viljo a more conservative dark green shirt over brown trousers.

A few moments later all four were settled comfortably in the living room, beers to hand. Paavo threw on more logs and soon there was a blazing fire for them to sit around whilst they sipped their drinks. The Keskinens had seen their daughter and knew there was nothing wrong with her. So, whatever it was, they waited patiently, puzzled looks on their faces.

Twenty minutes later they were no longer puzzled but totally taken aback by the story that had just been told. They had to agree with the sense that the children had made of the drawings done by the visitor. Viljo could understand the logic and he certainly understood the science that could show the logic was true. But to accept that it actually was true and that the boy was the proof? That was something else.

To discover that this strange boy had escaped from a hospital would be a nice easy solution. But even that would not explain how he had arrived in the middle of the forest.

Viljo accepted the mathematics of String Theory that showed that in order to have a planet like Earth with its three dimensions plus time there had to be at least ten dimensions, some scientists argued for twenty-six. He knew that photons, and it was assumed other weightless particles, could travel across the universe, slipping through other dimensions before arriving at their destination. But to accept that a person, a humanoid, living in one of those other dimensions had travelled to Earth? That was too much to accept in one evening.

There was a long silence. Viljo could feel the growing tension. Surely, he thought, we should contact "the authorities". He put quotation marks around that in his mind. Exactly who should they contact?

He looked at Paavo and raised an eyebrow, tilted his head to one side, saw Paavo grimace and guessed he was having similar thoughts.

Spreading his big hands out in front of him, Paavo looked at them, recalling what he had experienced when he had picked up Qwelby. 'He placed all his trust in me,' he said to no one in particular.

'He asked you to trust him?' Viljo queried.

'No,' Paavo replied. 'As he put his arm around my shoulder I felt him giving me his trust. Much like that time when Hannu was eleven, fell over and hit his knee on a large stone I was using to prop the gate open. He couldn't walk right away. I picked him up and carried him indoors.' He smiled at the memory.

Paavo turned to look at his wife. She was nodding. A practical man not much given to displaying his emotions, Seija knew that was one of her husband's precious memories. 'But this was stronger,' he added.

'I had to help him take off his tank top, it was so tight and slippery,' Seija said. 'You saw how badly bruised he is.' She looked at her husband who nodded. 'When his top was off I rested my fingers on his back.' She gave a little embarrassed smile. 'It's what I would do with Hannu,' she added defensively. 'His skin. It felt like velvet. I felt him relax... and more than that.' She turned to Viljo, 'It wasn't trust he was giving me. But it was like a cry for help, to be protected, looked after. It reminded of a kitten I had when a child. It had had a terrible fright. When I picked it up it was mewing pitifully and shivering, I could feel its little claws through

202

my sweater. I know it sounds stupid, but he felt like that. All trembling inside and wanting to be reassured that everything was okay.'

'All this was in your minds?' Viljo said, more as a statement than a question as he switched his gaze between husband and wife.

'No,' Paavo and Seija replied together, switching their gazes between their two friends.

'Feelings,' Paavo said.

'Strong feelings,' Seija added, looking to Taimi for understanding.

Viljo had said that Anita could stay the night, but that had been before he knew the full story, now he was concerned. Having received Seija's permission to examine Qwelby, Taimi went upstairs.

The others sat in silence. Viljo was turning over in his mind what he had felt when he had shaken the boy's hand. It was as though Qwelby was pleased to meet him. His wife was a Yoga teacher. Exercise and relaxing by breathing: he accepted that was good. Meditation. Well, it kept her group of friends happy. But a Transpersonal Psychotherapist. 'Transpersonal.' His wife was an intelligent woman, he did not see how she could believe in all that mumbo jumbo. They avoided discussing that as much as possible.

Taimi returned after several minutes. 'I checked on Anita first. She said that if I hugged Qwelby I'd understand.' Taimi smiled. 'I didn't go that far, but I did sit on the bed and rest my fingers on his temples. That boy is full of one big hurt. Yet there was also a sense of a deep core of serenity under that. In all the years I've been practising Reiki I've never experienced anything like that.' She was confident of what she had felt, and knew Seija would accept her opinion.

'That boy was dead to the world. I don't see him waking before any of us,' Seija said, reassured by her friend's professional expertise.

'Lock him in?' Viljo asked, realising he was the odd one out and feeling it was the least he could do to protect Anita.

When that had been done and the key placed on a hook in the kitchen, although still not entirely reassured, Viljo gave Paavo a half smile. 'Time we went,' he said, gesturing to his wife who followed him thought to the lobby.

The Rahkamos followed. As they said their goodnights, Paavo added 'See you tomorrow?'

'Yes. I would like to meet this "alien" you've found.' Viljo's smile faded as his gaze switched between his two friends and his wife. 'There's got to be a logical explanation. We just haven't found it yet.'

Being also a Reiki Master, Taimi was the only one to think she might have an understanding of what had happened. Alien or not, the boy had so strong an aura that she had sensed it as she sat on his bedside. And physical contact had made deciphering his strong feelings surprisingly easy. But only because she was aware of the process. The overwhelming impression she had received on gently touching his head was that underneath his surface feelings there was an old soul. A powerful old soul. She wanted to talk with him, when the time was right.

Anita lay awake for a long time wondering what it would be like if she were in Qwelby's situation. And where Tullia might be. With "Their Alien" sleeping in the spare bedroom, she was tucked up in a snug, loft room. She decided she liked that more than the guest room she had used before. It felt cosy and reminded her of fun times in the summer, camping. For a time she imagined that the sloping sides of the roof made the walls of a tent, and tried to imagine what it would be like to be in a country where they lived in tents.

That night she dreamed of a desert where small, dark-skinned people lived. It wasn't a desert like she had seen in films with deep sand, piled by the wind into great big dunes, and an oasis with wild tribesmen charging around on beautiful horses. This was very different. Fairly flat, with the sand looking more like hard earth and lots of small bushes and spindly trees.

She could not make out clearly what clothes the people were wearing. Brown bodies wearing almost nothing seemed to elide into the same people wearing ordinary clothes. There were bows and spears. She could not make out which people were carrying them. What she was sure about was that none of them were wearing flowing robes and turbans, and there was no oasis. In her dream she said to herself that it wasn't a real desert. But the brown figures dancing around a big fire said it was.

Meanwhile, Qwelby slept on, whatever else was disturbing him, and being without Tullia was his biggest problem, he knew from the energy responses of the three Rahkamos and Anita, that he was being looked after.

CHAPTER 30

BREAKDOWN

RAIATEA

Twelve hours behind events in Finland, Professor Romain arose early as usual. December twenty-seventh was for him and his team the start of their New Year. They had started their midwinter break by joining with the islanders in celebrating the Earth's turn on the twenty-first. The calendrical New Year had no meaning for them.

Whilst he showered, shaved and dressed he ran through the thoughts he had been having during their break. The unresolved question in his mind was whether he had let his determination to prove the actual, physical existence of other dimensions cloud his judgement of the broader perspective. In his mind he had been discussing that with David Niven. "Sir David" as he thought of the man.

Romain looked on him as the epitome of the quintessential Englishman. A colonel in the Second World War, a consummate actor and a perfect gentleman. Romain had felt that it was only his early death that had prevented him from receiving the knighthood he so justly deserved. When Romain had changed his birth names, he had specifically chosen David for his first name as he so admired Niven and aspired to reach the standard he had set.

Romain's development of the only equipment in the world capable of detecting the Earth's Quantum Field, thus proving that it existed, had been many years ago. That had been all his own work. Once that was made public, he was certain that would earn him the Nobel Prize he coveted.

Miki shared with him the fear that their work could have military applications, to which they were vehemently opposed. Sadly, they had to accept that once the science was out there, how it was used was out of their control.

Early on, Romain had realised just how brilliant a mind Miki had under her self-affacing manner, and how Tyler's more practical bent made all three into a perfect partnership. An unexpected side discovery of a form of biological glue had led to a radical new approoach to surgery. Initially they had developed products that could repair and restore damaged spinal disks, then created full-fuctioning replacements.

The final step had been the creation of what they called the MiniMax. Inserted into the patient, fibre optics provided a large and perfect three dimensional model of any area requiring intervention. The surgeon worked on that whilst the miniaturised robotic equipment carried out the same procedures on the patient. Roman expected to make a lot of money, even hoped for a Nobel Prize.

His fear, at times leading him to the edges of paranoia, had always been that someone would copy his work and beat him to his ultimate goal – quantum entanglement across dimensions.

Turning to check his appearance in the mirror, he shook his head. On his bedroom wall hung a photograph of David Niven playing Sir Charles Litton as the Phantom in the Pink Panther films. Unconsciously, he had dressed the same: black shoes, trousers and a black, silk, polo neck sweater. As a young man Romain would have laughed at anyone who claimed that emulating David Niven was in any way scientific. Having devoted all his adult life to the study of quantum science, he knew that the energy that pervaded all the universe was not exclusively limited to material items and included consciousness.

'Well, Sir David?' he asked the photograph.

'You are a scientist. An explorer. Is it right to conceal so much knowledge of advancements from your community? Is it honourable?'

The voice was clear in Romain's head. The language pricked his conscience. *I am years ahead. Truly, I cannot envisage anyone catching me up, yet alone overtaking me. And by the time that might happen, I may have three Nobel Prizes. But. Is that what I want? No! What I dream of is having tangible evidence of another dimension. Something that I can almost hold in my hand, like my data returning, intelligently reorganised.* He took a deep breath and looked Niven in the eyes.

'I will publish concerning the ELF when the Nobel announcements have been made. Then for the new neutrinos: two or three years after. My assistants deserve the recognition and, hopefully, honour.'

He felt his muscles relax as previously unrecognised tension flowed out of him. He had made a good decision. Feeling lighter than he had done all holiday, he deliberately flicked the end of his hair so that what was usually an annoying piece fell over his forehead, like a forelock ready to be tugged to one's Lord and Master. With a soft smile he tugged it to Niven's photo before descending to join his two doctoral assistants to start the new working year with their usual late breakfast.

Over the years they had developed a set pattern which suited them all. It combined their scientific interest in the changes that took place in the Earth's quantum field as a result of the solstice along with a celebration of the year's turn. They followed that with their own Christmas celebration. In spite of the different personal views of the three scientists it seemed appropriate given the weight of history in the island.

Raiatea had been and still was the religious centre of Polynesia.

The Moai of Rapa Nui were designed to maintain the Polynesian religious order of Raiatea. There, the Mara'e Taputapu-atea faced the Moai in the sky. But now the majority of islanders were Christian.

Romain did not believe in God in any religious sense. Rather he believed in the universe, the multiverse as it really was comprising the whole of everything, as alive. Tyler had been brought up in a community that believed that God saw and ordained everything. After a series of tragedies had struck the community including his family, he had totally disavowed any concept of an overarching deity. Yet both men had a long tradition of celebrating Christmas, and Miki, who described herself as loosely following the ways of Shinbutsu Shag an ancient Japanese tradition, was happy to enjoy the festivities. For all of them it was not just a mid-winter break but the celebration of a year's work.

The small staff, principally a housekeep and one of her daughters, had returned to the family home after serving dinner on the twenty-third. Originally, Romain had provided a cold collation for Christmas Eve based on a variety of European traditions from his many years working on the continent. He was never sure quite how it was that Miki, now in her mid-thirties and still looking like a beautiful doll, had swapped from preparing the meal on Christmas Day to providing a Japanese meal on Christmas Eve. This year it had been two fish dishes: Sushumi followed by an exquisite Kaiseki Ryori. Wine with the meal had been Wakatake Daiginjo with Fu-Kii Plum for the dessert of multi-coloured steam cakes known as Uiro.

Romain had risen to the challenge and served a traditional English Christmas meal. Turkey with stuffing, chipolatas, roast potatoes, a mixture of vegetables, and his own home-made Christmas Pudding with brandy sauce. Older than her by a clear decade, Miki's husband had provided a traditional West Indian meal the following day. Salt Fish and Ace with breadfruit, dumplings, plantain and salad; followed by his variation of a traditional Jamaican Christmas Pudding which included prunes, cherries and dates and, of course, served with rum sauce.

Romain provided the other drinks. The Solstice toast made in the local hooch had been the usual: 'A good year past, a better year to come.' Champagne Bruno Paillard Rosé was used for a very different toast on the twenty-fourth: 'Stellar Thinking', a five-year-old Chablis from Daniel Etienne DeFazio for the turkey and a four-year old Puilly-Fumé from Louis Chevalier for the Salt Fish, with sake, port, brandy and liqueurs to follow.

As Romain said as they relaxed on the twenty-sixth: there was no point in his having spent a large part of his career in France, the country that invented good food and wine, and not passing on the benefit of his education.

'If all else fails we can always open a restaurant here,' Tyler had quipped.

'A "peak" tourist attraction,' Miki had added, teasing Romain with his dislike of tourists.

The two men had groaned at Miki's pun and all three had clinked glasses to a toast of: 'To us.'

The patio on the fourth floor being the most convenient for communal eating, it was there that they were partaking of a leisurely breakfast of fruits, cheeses and freshly baked fougasse with black olives; 'ladder bread' as Tyler called it. Angelique, the fifteen-year-old daughter of the housekeeper who had been driven up early that morning by her older brother, was proving to be as good a cook as her mother.

In their lines of research 'Blue Sky Thinking' was normal. Over the winter break business discussions were supposed to be forbidden. As that had turned out to be impossible they allowed themselves to indulge in what they called 'Stellar Thinking'. Sharing crazy and impossible thoughts that sometimes drilled down to ideas with practical and commercial application.

The meal finished, Romain leant forward. 'Planning meeting this afternoon. Anything in our Stellar Thinking worth pursuing, and remind ourselves where we are with our various experiments. Now that our new year's underway, let's go and make our usual checks and ensure all the equipment is ready for action. Hopefully CERN will be restarting any day now. Tyler, please clear the dishes and thank Angelique for the fougasse, it was perfect. Miki, let's go and start a diagnostic.'

Having seen teams disrupted by favouritism, often unconscious, he was always careful to treat his two assistant equally as he spread around tiresome, menial or challenging tasks. To him, the staff were part of the team. He could not abide the thought that they might feel, or worse, be treated as servants. Yet he was blithely unaware of how embarrassed Angelique was going to be when Doctor Jefferson arrived in the kitchen bearing a tray load of dirty dishes.

Once Tyler and Miki had settled in, Tyler had rapidly rationalised the situation with the neutrinos. As various types of brain waves were well known and easily measurable, he hypothesised that a highly concentrated sub-set of beta waves acted on the psien's energy signature as in a binary system: yes/no, on/off.

With his full commitment, it was not long before the three of them discovered the neutrino's full potential: it could be 'encouraged' to work like a sandwich. A toasted sandwich where the edges were sealed, totally enclosing the filling. Keeping to standard scientific nomenclature they allowed their sense of humour full play by choosing the symbol Ψ , the Greek letter 'psi', to represent two slices of bread and a filling.

Tyler drew the line at Romain's suggestion they should round off the word by adding 'in' for 'intelligent.' Instead, they compromised on 'en' to stand for 'envelop', and agreed that it would remain the same in the plural.

Tyler had been in his element when it came to building the new equipment required. First, what was in effect half of the donut structure of a miniature collider was constructed and situated on the other side of the mountain, opposite the laboratory. The aim being to trap the psien and send them back the way they had come. At first individual psien were sent to align the system. After that, increasing lengths of chains of linked psien.

Next they constructed a data accelerator, whereby the data to be the filling of each individual sandwich was fired into the stream of psien emerging from the accelerator. After a lot of trial and error, a sandwich chain was successfully created, sent through the mountain and returned via the half donut. That evening they had celebrated with a bottle of vintage Mumm Champagne.

Following the successful transmission of substantial amounts of information data as far as the Moon and back using photons, the next goal was to transmit something solid. It did not matter how minuscule that might be. Teleportation, as the media would call it, would be the realisation of an age-old dream. That required a vast amount of power. Way beyond anything that Romain's laboratory could ever produce.

They had one hope for success: to use the power of the Large Hadron Collider at CERN. The initial experiment being to piggy-back a chain of data-carrying psien onto a stream of protons, 'encouraging' them to return as in the trials on Raiatea.

There had been a long period of trial and error before the first, individual psien returned. Once again Tyler was in his element, working with Romain on designing and constructing detection equipment, calibrating, recalibrating and monitoring. As he said in all innocence, it was not feasible for Romain to contact his colleagues at CERN as often as their experiments required.

After that first individual psien had returned, they had steadily sent chains of increasing length and eventually increased the successful return rate to more than fifty percent. Romain was able to advise that CERN had not detected anything amiss. The psien remained invisible.

Finally, on December the twentieth, they were ready for their first trial with a data-carrying chain. To their intense disappointment CERN had shut down, saying that two magnets had failed. Romain was able to report that his contacts had confirmed what CERN had announced. An as yet unexplained surge in the LHC which had caused the failure of two magnets, with the opportunity being taken to close for a short period of routine maintenance.

In a way the timing was fortuitous. They had hoped to start their customary mid-winter break that evening on a note of success. Had they failed and had CERN remained open, they would not have taken the rest they needed.

Having reached the third floor, Romain and Miki stepped into the pre-chamber and changed into pale green coveralls and bootees. With Romain in the lead they stepped through the inner door, walked through the main laboratory and along the short "L" shaped corridor that thus maintained the mountain's maximum shielding of the Fifth Room.

Surprised, they both stopped just inside the door of the latter. Something was wrong. What, was not immediately obvious. The large screen that was a map of the world was jumping about. That could be an ordinary glitch. A red light on the panel covering the data storage system was flickering. That should never happen.

The equipment was so delicate that from time to time it picked up variations that were not in the quantum field itself. Those were stored for checking. The red light came on with a steady glow to show that had happened. It did not flicker.

Damping down his mixture of concern and excitement, Romain issued his command. 'Miki, see what you can do with data retrieval. I'll run a systems diagnostic.'

Miki swept her long hair behind her head, tying it into a knot as she sat at the other large screen and called up the latest data.

Romain went around behind the two large screens. He unlocked a drawer and pulled out a curved keyboard with numeric touchpads at either end. Another of his inventions. The left-hand set of numbers and symbols all carried special programming.

'David, the data is all jumbled up. This is weird.'

'Let me see what I can find.' He nibbled at his moustache in agitation.

The soft humming of equipment and air conditioning. An occasional grunt a '?' or a '!'

'You've found something?' Tyler asked as, similarly clad in green, he brought into the room a container of cold drinks, its round shape adorned by a picture of an array of colourful plants.

Miki looked over her shoulder. 'Problems. Too big a data feed. It's all over the place.'

'Tyler,' Romain called out, ensuring he kept his agitation out of his voice. 'Will you check the connections. I can't make sense of what I'm finding.'

The Jamaican-American went in to a small room that was buried even deeper into the mountain. He returned a few moments later, the streaks of grey in his curly, dark hair seemed to add to his puzzled expression. 'It looks like a fuse has blown.'

Romain's heart leapt. 'A purple spiral?'

'Yes.'

'Please bring it here. It disconnects easily. Don't try to reconnect the ends of the cables, just leave a gap,' Romain said as he turned to Miki.

'The garden,' she said, smiling in acknowledgment.

It was said that NASA had a quantum computer with a power of five hundred and twelve qubits which was used to explore for exoplanets. How that had been created was still a secret. Developing work done by Nobel prize-winner Richard Feynman, Romain's design comprised eight perfectly balanced groups of eight qubits operating sequentially, and was dedicated to exploration of the quantum field. Its capability was derived from a magnificent array of healthily photosynthesising plants that covered a large part of the top of the building. Miki loved her time tending the Quantum Garden. Although at times a hard-nosed scientist, she found the spooky and weird world of quantum mechanics often reminded her of ancient teachings on human life.

'Konnichiwa, Benten-Ro'o,' she said softly as she entered the garden and greeted her colourful friends. She was sure the plants rustled a little more than the gentle breeze required as she added to her "hullo", the name she had given the garden: the Japanese Goddess of good fortune and the Polynesian God of Agriculture.

For a few moments she let her gaze rest on the vivid red flowers of the several Caricature Plants. As she examined the others she was concerned at the drooping red stamen of a group of white-petalled Hibiscus Arnottianus. Using her fingers, she checked their soil moisture and gently inspected their leaves. It was clear that the quantum computer had been shut down unexpectedly. 'Shitsurei shimashita,' she said, expressing her sorrow that the plants had suffered, and left the garden, promising to return as soon as possible.

Meanwhile in the laboratory, Romain had walked round to where Miki hasd been sitting and examined what was showing on the monitor screen. Pouring a glass of juice, he sat down on an adjacent chair, taking deep breaths to calm himself.

Tyler returned holding what looked like a child's toy. A rounded pyramid that seemed to be made of translucent acrylic. Inside was a purple tube that spiralled from the base to the summit. Running through the centre of that was a fine thread of silver surrounded by multi-coloured streaks, with the whole device ending in a black, burnt top.

'As you know, that's the Logic Filter,' Romain said softly, taking it from his assistant. 'I suppose it is a sort of fuse. I've never thought of it like that.' He waived to Tyler. 'Sit down.'

Romain's mind went back to the first time he had shown his assistants the intricate workings of the Fifth Room, and the key component.

'This contains a series of seven mathematical formulae,' he had explained. 'When the Detector receives a signal that data is passed though this Filter. If, and only if, the data passes all seven tests, is it accepted as a fluctuation in the Earth's quantum field. It then goes into a discrete part of the storage system and only then is the alert triggered.'

'How...?' Tyler had asked.

'The formulae are contained within a nanomatrix. When the data passes the first test, red, the nanos act like tumblers in a lock and allow the data to pass to the next test, orange.'

'Then on through to violet,' Miki had added.

'Just so.'

'Why the spiral?' again Tyler had asked .

'Each test is another Logical Level. I liked the idea of a physical setup that looked like that. Also I found it easier to organise the nanos that way.' He lifted it up to look at it more closely. 'My Purple Python.' He smiled, at himself, as his fantasies.

'A David Niven film,' Miki had commented.

'Yes. He was in the first two of three films, "The Curse" and "The Trail", about a diamond called the Pink Panther. When held up to the light you could see a Pink Panther within. The spiral shape reminds me of a python all coiled up. Purple to rhyme.'

'And the Sahasrara, the Crown Chakra,' Miki had added gently.

'Yes,' Romain had agreed softly. He had nodded to himself with pleasure at the connections that were rapidly growing between them.

'Space-Time-Consciousness,' Tyler had almost whispered, voicing what was to become a mantra.

Romain had nodded. He was happy. He knew that Tyler had a definition of consciousness that was different from his own. That did not matter. The connection with his team was deepening, and Romain needed that as much as he needed to keep his secrets safe from them.

Miki's return brought Romain out of his reverie. 'Look at the pattern of discolouration,' he said, holding out the Python and slowly turning it around. 'See the clear channel through the centre, right through all the logical levels. Our psien arrived and passed all the tests. Hence the screen data. But something massive followed so close behind that the Python was ruptured before the alert could be triggered.'

There was silence as all three looked at the Logic Filter, then each other. The message was clear. The psien had passed through the seven levels meaning there had been a perturbation in the Earth's quantum field. With the time delay the only conclusion was that they had travelled through another dimension.

'The white Hibiscus have suffered a serious shock,' Miki said. 'I will spend time in the garden. They will recover.'

'The Tiare Apetahi?' Romain asked after the unique white flower that in the whole world grew only on Raiatea's Mount Temehani, yet had self-seeded in the centre of the quantum garden.

'They are well,' Miki replied with a serious countenance. She shared Romain's belief that it was the presence of that plant that ensured the unbelievable success of the botanical quantum computer. An opinion they agreed never to share with Miki's very prosaic husband.

'Thank you, Miki,' Romain said. 'Now, we need to find out what we've got and why it burnt my poor Python. You two work with the data from storage. I'll carry on with my diagnostic.'

Time passed and they called out to one another as discoveries were made. The biggest problem was the ghost imaging, badly affecting the screen showing the world map.

'The ghosting's gone,' Tyler called out. 'The map is stabilising. No, not really, it's flickering. I think it's trying to show two locations.'

'The co-ordinates for one of them are at CERN,' Miki explained.

'OK. I'll cancel that data stream,' Romain said.

'The map's now stabilised,' Tyler said. 'The other location is in Finland.'

'Miki. Input the other set of co-ordinates manually. That should not cause a problem.'

Romani heaved a sigh of relief. He had been aware of three streams of data. He had concentrated on the ghost image as that had been the most puzzling. The location had been dithering around an area fairly central in the southern part of Africa. But there was something else, he couldn't say what.

He walked around to the map. If the ghost image had been a little to the left of where he was guessing, then it was due south of the mark in Finland.

'That ghosting was due south. A reflection. Undoubtedly that's a computer glitch. I never designed this to handle three different streams of data at once. I'm delighted that it has almost managed two. Remember, this detection system is working at the very fringes of quantum energies. The second set definitely is for CERN.'

Fully in command of his emotions, his natural secrecy asserted itself. He filed away in his mind what he had glimpsed as the coordinates of the ghosting image for further thought and research. It had faded so quickly he was not sure that he had been able to capture all the data.

The basic information would have been stored in the main database. What he had been able to extract with his special keyboard was locked away in special storage. If necessary in the future he could transfer that into the main database.

'I'll go and see what I can find from my contacts at CERN. What we are seeing does not accord with their explanation that the Large Hadron Collider was shut down because of the failure of a pair of magnets and incidental damage to monitoring equipment. In the meantime, find out everything you can about the new location and anything, no matter how small, that might be relevant. I don't need to tell you how thorough to be.' He turned to leave, thought for a moment, then turned back.

'As I've mentioned before, there was more than one scientist CERN who used to support my ideas. They would not say so publicly for fear of ruining their careers. They are prepared to provide what help they can so that if, and when, I succeed...' He smiled. 'They hope that I will remember them favourably. If I were to return to CERN, they would become part of my team.'

His two assistants exchange glances. Working with him they had come to realise just how far out on a limb they were going with some of the research. They feared they could damage their own careers.

'I realise your concerns. Let me reassure you. The system I have set up whereby you are grant-aided from a university in the USA is perfectly valid. The Americans are as keen as anyone to provide research grants where there is a proven track record of commercial products being developed as a spin-off from the research.

'As we've agreed, your names only appear on papers that relate to mainstream research. That is to protect you and your futures. When we are successful, you will not be excluded from credit for all the work you are doing. We shall have major projects to work on here. And, if I do return to CERN, you would be the key members of whatever team I build there.'

He paused to let that fact sink in. 'I presume you have taken the precaution of recording work you have done on my, shall I say, more adventurous ideas.'

The two doctors exchanged meaningful looks.

Romain smiled to himself. He would certainly not value their intelligence and acumen had they not done so. 'Right. Let's get to it.'

CHAPTER 31

BREAKTHROUGH

Romain was buzzing with excitement as he headed for the room he and Franz had carefully concealed so many years before. Franz had been the chief maintenance engineer at CERN whilst Romain had been working there. They had become good friends when Romain had discovered the engineer's interest in the newly developing field of Noetic Science.

Romain's whole body was taut and he felt as though he was vibrating. He just knew that something different had happened this time. The trace on the computer screen that marked CERN was not unusual. It was the trace in Scandinavia that caused his excitement.

His assistants knew nothing of his secret room and how he obtained the information from the research centre. His explanation about former colleagues and their hopes was all very logical and accepted by his assistants. Yet far from the truth.

It was with difficulty that he kept to a steady walk as he made his way to the elevator and ascended to his suite. One wall in his study was used for storage of all sorts, the only indication being the lines of the discreet panelling and the small infra-red receptors that opened the doors.

Having locked the door to his study, Romain opened one of

the panels, revealing a bookcase. Inserting his signet ring into one of the many depressions in the trim, the whole bookcase swung open, revealing a very small room carved out of the bare rock.

As Romain stepped onto the floor, it descended noiselessly to the third floor. Once again using his infra-red key and signet ring he opened a door into a room behind the Fifth Room. That was as much a geek's delight as the main laboratory. The walls were full of the equipment that monitored what was happening at CERN, recorded what was displayed on their monitoring equipment, and enabled Romain to time his experiments with absolute precision.

Sitting at a console, he ran his fingers lightly across the screen as he keyed in the secret encryptions that accessed the equipment he and Franz had so very carefully installed and concealed a few months before Romain had left CERN. A series of different displays flickered across the screen, accompanied by the soft hum of printers spewing out reams of technical data.

He did know one thing for absolute certain. The information he was seeing had to be totally wrong, or...

His practised eye rapidly scanned the print-outs. Impossible! The data said exactly the same thing. Amongst an unbelievable and inexplicable background event, CERN had lost two streams of photons! The sheets of data fell from his hands as he slumped back in his chair, his mind a complete blank. The old joke of: "The impossible on demand, miracles take a little longer," running around inside his mind.

Miracles did not happen in the world of science. There was always a rational explanation. Each time there was something inexplicable, a scientist eventually found an explanation. Newton, in the world of everyday things like apples falling from trees, Einstein, at the level of the atom, and now himself and hundreds of other scientists descending deeper into the sub-atomic world.

Slowly his thoughts marshalled themselves into order. A lot of the exploration of quantum mechanics was by pure mathematics. Physics, the testing of it, the seeing of it, followed long afterwards. This was magnitudes greater than knowing that, by travelling faster than three hundred thousand kilometres per second, photons must slip between dimensions.

The experiment was all his own idea. He had left CERN because the directorate had refused to listen to him. CERN was only involved because he needed the immense power of the LHC, many magnitudes greater than anything he was able to produce, onto which to piggy-back his own experiment. There was no way they could know that he had found the missing streams of photons in Scandinavia.

In the far corner of his mind another fact was added to that ghost image. If CERN had lost two streams, had one arrived in Scandinavia and another in southern Africa?

He asked the computer to repeat the variety of screen shots. What he had was the same raw data available at CERN. It still made no sense. He told the computer to run the special programmes he had designed for a very different series of experiments.

As the results flowed, it began to look as though a lightening bolt had ripped around what was affectionately called 'The Donut'. Impossible. Further analysis revealed two bolts, trillions of protons in coherent streams shooting in opposite directions and disappearing – to where? Scandinavia? And no collisions!

Slowly, very slowly, he dared to admit to himself the possibility that he might have found signs of the first ever matter transportation. He had to clear his throat to repeat clearly his commands to the computer to run programmes he had only ever dreamt of using.

He could hardly contain himself. He fidgeted, he sweated. Nervously chewed his pencil-thin moustache.

Finally the data stopped scrolling across the screen. The humming of the printers died away. His eyes widened at the headlines on the main screen telling him that, after running the algorithms extrapolating the extremes of what was theoretically possible, there was a statistical chance better then fifty percent that the first stage of his dream had come true.

'Beam me up, Scottie,' he murmured to himself, smiled and shook his head. Since his youth, he had been drawn to the Sci-Fi genre that dealt with possibilities of advanced science and the superconscious. For decades, scientists had been successfully experimenting. Electrons changing places across astronomical distances, photons carrying meaningful amounts of data between Earth and the orbiting space station, neutrinos eventually travelling faster than the speed of light between CERN and the Gran Sasso National Laboratory in Italy, thus demonstrating that other dimensions must exist. But his psien carrying a massive amount of – what?

He was angry with himself. Because of the very reasonable explanation for the closure of the LHC for the short period over Christmas and the New Year, he had accepted the surface displays on his equipment confirming what CERN had announced publicly. He had not carried out a deeper analysis. He calmed down as he pointed out to himself that it was this morning's event that was the real excitement and not that of the twentieth.

It was difficult to accept the possibility that had been revealed. His algorithms were designed to calculate the probability of a mathematical theory. In many ways a dream. No-one really knew whether the maths was actually valid in practice. That was why places such as CERN, Firmilab in the USA and many others had been built. Yet here, before his very eyes, there appeared to be hard, physical proof of those theories.

Publish his results now? When he was so close? The word 'honourable' played through his mind. He took a deep breath and steadied himself. *'I made a commitment to you, Sir David... I will honour that... I may even have my proof before the next Nobel announcements!'*

He looked at his watch and was surprised at the time that had passed. In a calm and reflective mood he returned to the laboratory to be greeted by the puzzled looks on the faces of his two assistants.

'CERN has been more than economical with the truth,' he said. Whatever happened on twenty December was more than they announced. Something went very badly wrong. My contacts say there is total confusion and no-one yet knows exactly what happened.' *I bet there is confusion. They don't have my programmes and they won't even have thought of that possibility. Their minds will be so focussed on what they are researching.* 'What have you found?'

His calm mood almost deserted him as he heard his two research assistants say that they had not been able to find anything of use. Lots of basic facts about Finland, the village of Kotomäki and the Research Institute at Jyväskylä. Nothing at all about any major event, or even freak happening, apart from an exceptionally vivid display of the Aurora Borealis much further south than usual.

'Impossible. It must have been a major event. Late afternoon, someone must have seen something. They needn't even have taken a mobile out of a pocket!' he said as he swung his left arm up, wrist turned so his RonaldSon watch faced his assistants. 'Film,' he said, swinging his arm around steadily. 'Play,' he said as his arm stopped swinging.

The video he had just taken with a watch of his own design played clearly on the wall. He had previously demonstrated how, with a few verbal commands, the video could be uploaded onto any one or more of the video channels in The Cloud and that communicated via whatever social media he choose.

'We've rechecked the data. The two locations are clear. But...' Tyler said.

'What we've detected at Kotomäki occurred some ten hours ago. Four am our time, four pm in Finland,' Miki said. 'We've checked and can reconfirm what we already know. The event which caused CERN to shut down was mid-morning on twenty December. The same time as our first data-recovery trial run.'

'And there's nothing on the internet to say that the LHC has restarted,' Tyler added.

Romain sat down. *Quantum entanglement across dimensions. A difference in time – why not!*

Miki hesitantly offered: 'There are reports on the internet of meteor showers over north Finland at Lakes Lappajärvi and Karikkoselkä, not expected at this time of year. It seems more than a coincidence that they were over those lakes where gravity is different to normal as a result of major meteor strikes so long ago.'

'A combination of meteor showers and the difference in gravity disrupting our experiment so that the transmission failed,' Tyler suggested.

'Or the coincidence that CERN restarted the LHC at four pm their time,' Romain dropped his bombshell to open-mouthed silence. 'I did not tell you at first as I wanted to hear what you had discovered. And for all of us to keep open minds.'

Mouths now closed, Miki and Tyler nodded their appreciation. At times, being in ignorance was the best way to work.

'We know our experiment worked to the extent that some of the psien returned from another dimension and that was registered. If our theories are correct, that is because they had been successfully attached to a stream of protons. Presumably those protons also returned,' Miki said, starting with the basics.

Romain narrowed his eyes, the cool scientist in control. 'Not all the psien carried data as we used the first few without data as a hook onto the proton stream. If they returned first as expected then, as you say Miki, it is those which were registered. But why should those carrying the data have ruptured the Python?'

'Because a lot more data was returning than we had loaded,' Tyler said.

'An inference being that the psien without data were travelling faster than the others,' Romain said slowly. 'In fact, several orders of magnitude faster as they had travelled several thousand kilometres to here in the same time as the sandwiched psien travelled only a few hundred to Finland.' He turned to the computer monitor where the map had been changed to display the immediate area around Kotomäki, and pointed to the bright green light. 'To here, on the edge of this little town?'

'Because what was returning was not merely the chain of sandwiched psien we sent, but something more. A coherent package. Which dropped off when the carrier wave ceased,' Miki suggested.

'But if that data-package arrived here, why is the event not showing here but at that village?' Romain knew he was floundering. However extraordinary they might be, one logical hypothesis was contradicting another.

'A dimension rift,' Tyler said thoughtfully 'The protons returned from that other dimension. The first few psien they were carrying passed through the filter. But there were not enough. Insufficient energy to trigger the alert. What was following was additional data, outside the sandwich psien. That overloaded the Python at almost the same moment. That severed the link to the other dimension and the rift closed. Whatever that data represents... it coalesced around something like an energetic centre of gravity, causing the disturbance by that village.'

For a moment Romain had a crazy picture of olden days when mail was dropped off from trains into nets at the side of the railway tracks. His mind reasserted itself. 'Or a version of the double slit experiment where one electron goes through both apertures. Here, the psien travelled across dimensions emerging at different times? And carrying vastly more data than we've ever tried?' He shook his head. 'Too many theories.' But if one of them was true? With great effort of mind, he stopped himself from clenching his hands and teeth and almost groaning in anger at the thought that someone might get there before him.

'I must think,' he said in a harsh voice. 'Take a break.' He left the room, his whole body was quivering with inner turmoil as he went to his study. It was with sweating hands he picked up the telephone and called the agency he used for all his travel arrangements.

He had been so surprised at what his equipment had revealed that he had set the system to run a set of self-diagnostics. He returned to his secret room and ran off a print-out. He checked carefully. Everything with his system was correct. That was not surprising. He had designed, built and programmed it himself. He had no false modesty about his skills.

He turned to the print-outs from his equipment at CERN. Again everything checked out. Had someone interfered with it? He ran a check looking for that. No, again all was satisfactory. That was not surprising. Any engineer checking the systems would find what appeared to be, what in fact was, a third back-up.

They would realise that it was overkill. Administrative errors, not unknown in any large organisation. Perhaps authorised by a scientist with a background of rocketry, where three back-ups were standard procedure. Those were just two of several reasons why that might have happened. Only if it was completely dismantled and someone decided to explore further might it be discovered that the system relayed its data outside CERN. But even then not the destination.

The phone extension from his study rang. The travel agent had good news, he could get Romain to Helsinki by late on thirty December, then a flight to Jyväskylä. It would be a circuitous route with several changes and taking longer than usual. And it would cost. Romain was delighted. He'd feared a much longer delay and was happy to pay what he guessed included the agent's extra commission for working during his holiday.

Heaving a sigh of relief he returned to his suite of rooms where he stood for some time under the shower, letting it wash away all his tensions. Calmer, he slipped into fresh clothes, this time settling for a pale green, short-sleeved shirt, tan slacks and brown loafers. He called his assistants to find that they had returned to the West Room, where he joined them.

'I'm leaving for Finland tomorrow morning. We need to discuss what needs to be done whilst I'm away, and talk through all our thoughts about what we've just discovered. And what I might be looking for in Finland.' He looked at his watch.

'Miki. It's too hot and humid outside for serious discussions. We'll dine in my suite. I'll speak with Angelique. Let's make that six thirty.'

The two doctors grinned, caught up in the excitement.

Seated on board the Air France flight to Los Angeles the following morning Romain reflected on all the ideas they had discussed: logical, practical, possible, some fantastic and even pure flights of fantasy. Intending to jot down some thoughts, he powered up his RonaldSon tablet. He had endeavoured to persuade his father to use the name Reginsen as a reference to the very old, Norse family name for all of what were in effect their joint products. Eventually he had had to settle for a hard-won compromise for those products that he had devised. The "s" in "Ronaldson" being capitalised to emphasise "Son."

An image appeared on the screen of what he thought of as the traditional alien face: a silvery white, domed head with heavily slanted, dark, oval eyes lacking any pupils, small nostrils and a wide mouth. He had developed enhanced facial recognition and replication software that did not need the complexities of multiple cameras or lights. It was becoming widely used in video surveillance and in his father's words: "A nice little earner."

He stared at the excellent 4D image standing out of the tablet as he realised that he had never thought of his search for proof of the existence of other dimensions as meaning a search for an actual alien. Embarrassed at what he had done, and before the passenger alongside noticed and tried to engage him in conversation, he erased the image with a quick gesture and a soft laugh at himself.

Far below, he saw islands drifting by as if sailing the ocean and wondered if that was symbolic of a wild goose chase. There were rare occasions when islands were created by sudden and unexpected volcanic eruptions. His equipment was unique. There were no precedents. Could it be that occasionally there were exceptionally large fluctuations in the Earth's quantum field and this was the first since he had started his experiments? Was that all he had detected, and the faint image in South Africa merely an echo? Or was it indeed the first step on the path to discovering the answer to his dreams?

He would search for evidence of quantum entanglement across dimensions. In his own mind he was sure that would explain the time difference. But the lack of publicity even now more than twenty-four hours later? His equipment indicated a very major event: an unbelievable mass of data. The echo? The lack of publicity understandable. A small event in the middle of an uninhabited desert.

Poor old Purple Python. I shall enjoy repairing you when I return. And I'll make you stronger. Next time we'll capture all the data.

Looking over the deep blue sea he let the scientist within him speak: *Facts first, last and always. No selective hypothesis.* 'But I can still dream,' he muttered to the creamy wake of a cruise liner far below.

He had no idea of just how astonishing a discovery he was to make. Nor what a surprise awaited him regarding his assistants, and how that revelation would become a key to realising his dreams as he submitted to the thrall of his Viking heritage.

CHAPTER 32

A LAST CHANCE

VERTAZIA

For eight days Lellia and Mizena had repeatedly searched through Siahranah until Lellia called a halt as they were exhausted. All the crystal had revealed was an impenetrable, black, fog that slowly sapped the women's energies the more they tried to see through it. When Wrenden had recovered, the four friends repeatedly tried to link through Óweppâ. Although there was no hint of any energy connection, each of the Twins' sections retained their individual colours.

'Good news and bad news,' Mandara explained on one of the evenings when all had gathered together. 'The strong colours in their segments on the Talisman confirm they twins are alive. The barrier shows that the opposition knows that. As there have been no more attacks over eight days, it appears that the opposition is content with a barrier. Barriers can by circumvented. I am certain that the lack of contact through Óweppâ tells us that the twins do not have the power to link. Which has to mean they are not mentally connected. And.' Mandara's shoulders sagged as he looked grim. 'As their friends encountered neither opposition nor any barrier, that reinforces the fact that they must be fully involved in any plans to rescue the twins.'

Lellia and Shandur nodded, grim smiles on their faces.

'I will look after them,' Mizena said.

Lellia had also spent time with the Stroems, her overriding duty as Orchestrator being to restore calm and balance and maintain the essential smooth linkage with the other five Caverns: and Azura. Several days had passed before she had considered it safe for Mandara and Shandur to be able to work in the Cavern. Even then the Stroems had been unhappy.

'It is as though they feel that by increasing safety precautions as all the parents demanded, we are blaming them for what happened when they were actually striving to rescue Qwelby from the NoWhenWhere,' Lellia explained 'The music of the Xzyling is difficult to decipher. The best interpretation I can provide is that at the end they Xzyled the equivalent of a drum roll, pitched well below the level of human hearing. That countered the whirlpool effect to hold Wrenden and Tamina up for long enough to allow the tachyon field to reach back in time and project the strengthened safety shield.'

'But they didn't support Qwelby,' Wrenden complained.

'He wasn't there in the same space-time-consciousness as you and your sister,' Lellia said. 'As The Stroems' purpose is to bridge the divide between Vertazia and Azura they feel bad that... in effect they let Qwelby slip from their grasp. That's why they have been so unsettled and it's been so long before the men could work in the Cavern.'

When all else had failed, the youngsters' parents had honoured their agreement and the four were permitted to make one more visit to the StroemCavern. They were sitting with Lellia in the cosy room alongside the StroemLock as she was finishing her run-through of the procedure they had to follow.

'Wrenden. You are so close to your fourteenth rebirthday and receiving your crystal, you must know your personal shade of colour, and probably what crystal will be yours?'

'Lazabatanzii, I expect.'

Lellia nodded. It was what she saw in his aura. The green crystal vibrating to the elements of Air and Earth were the perfect compliment to Qwelby's red Fire and Earth related Drakobata. She sighed. Tamina's multicoloured Fire and Water related Bula'kabilii, Tullia's purple Air and Water related Kanyisaya. Each with a rare twin power Crystal, firmly binding all four together through the elemental associations. Her fears for the safety and stability of Tamina and Wrenden increased.

'Each of you is to imagine a thread of your principal shade of colour going forth from your centre. Weave all four into a strong cord. Hold in your minds the thought of each twin in turn, and that strong cord will search for them.'

'Search for Qwelby first?' Wrenden asked with a catch in his throat.

The others nodded their agreement. Through Lellia's crystal, she and Mizena had found that Tullia was well. Everyone hoped to discover that Qwelby had survived his fall though the StroemWell.

She looked into each of their energy fields and saw their concern, caring and determination.

'I have to warn you. You must keep your awareness on where you will be. On a gallery above the XzylStroem. From there you just watch the cord on its journey. Do NOT go into your threads and search yourselves. If you do that, the whole of your Kore energy will be pulled out of you into a place between dimensions. You will be in a realm of energy forms of the same level of vibration as your energy bodies. Meeting them would be as if you were in your normal bodies. It would be very real. So real you could be hurt, physically.' She looked into each of their eyes. 'Or worse. Do you understand?'

She saw fear flickering through their energy fields as they absorbed her message. Shimara & Pelnak were subdued. They held hands and nodded. Their energy fields combined and a thought reached her. *'Pelnmara,'* it said.

Strong energy flowed between brother and sister with reassurance going both ways. Tamina tried to hold back from smiling with surprise at her usually exasperating younger brother. Unsuccessfully, as she saw a corner of his mouth twitch.

As tears started at the corners of his eyes, Tamina took his hand in hers. He was still blaming himself for failing to rescue his BestFriend.

'We'll find him, Eeky,' she tried to reassure him.

Getting up from her chair, Lellia led them to the preparation booth and then onto the gallery around the top of the XzylCavern. She turned to Control Panel at the side of the door and spoke nicely to it. A smaller, circular gallery appeared, jiggling about as it hovered right over the centre of the XzylStroem. As they watched, a series of walkways shimmered into view, leading from the gallery on which they were standing to join the central one. Everything was shifting, buckling, clicking, groaning and looking less substantial than on their previous visit.

'We are standing on what we call the viewing gallery,' Lellia explained. 'The circular walkway you can see in the centre we call the interaction gallery. It always keeps itself directly above the energy centre of the XzylStroem. Since your last visit Mandara and Shandur have added emergency energy fields to all the barriers. Now there is no way you can slip through them.'

Once again the Stroems were very different. As the friends watched what had been one gently swirling whirlpool slowly reformed into five. A central one surrounded by four others, equally spaced and which not merely rotated but whirled around the side of the Well. All four seemingly going in both directions at once in a mad blur of colour that was nevertheless distinguishable: as long as the youngsters let the images bypass their surface thinking and slip into their deepminds.

'Do you really want to try to MentaSynch with the twins?' *One last chance to back out. This is so dangerous, and they are so young.*

Four nervous, bug-eyed, hedgehog heads nodded.

'To do that you will have to walk out to the interaction gallery.'

Their helmets swivelled as they looked at each other, the absence of mental connection increasing their nervousness.

'To maintain an energy balance, each one of you will need to walk along a separate path. When you get to the central gallery you will all hold hands.'

'But that central gallery is much too large for four of us to be able to hold hands,' objected Tamina.

'Not when you are there,' Lellia replied.

'Ready?' she asked. Four heads nodded slowly. 'Shimara and Pelnak, go left and right, Tamina to the far side.' She turned to Wrenden. 'This one for you. As you don't yet have a crystal, this way balances up the energies the best we can.' She looked around all four. 'When you walk along, do not try to hold on. Walk as though they were not moving. Remember: Imagination!'

She moved back to the control panel. 'Take up your positions and wait for my signal.'

When the four had moved to the ends of the walkways, they heard her voice through the speakers in their helmets telling them to start walking.

Careful not to hold on and let their imaginations make them even more frightened, they slipped and staggered over the jiggling pathways and reached the interaction gallery safely. Surprise, surprise, it was small enough for them to reach out and hold hands.

Spending more time acting like twins than real twins did, Shimara and Pelnak could find it difficult to reach out and connect with other people. Tamina gentled their energies out of their loop. As she linked all four of them together she reminded them that this first search was for Qwelby.

Swaying to keep their balance, all the weaving movements added a hypnotic effect as they focussed their energies on manifesting their own coloured threads. With a sudden shweeesh! that threw them off balance and made them grip hands tightly, Tamina's orange thread looped around and shot off down into the spiralling centre of the XzylStroem.

She struggled to rein it back and let the others catch up, reached out with her mind and coaxed the other threads to twine around hers, plaiting all four together. Relaxing her control, she watched as the rope spiralled around then plunged into the centre of the Stroems.

CHAPTER 33

DEATH DEFIED

VERTAZIA

Brilliantly coloured energy Xyled along each of the threads, the counterpart to their own colours. With a shock like diving from the highest springboard into a swimming pool, Tamina felt herself pulled headfirst along her thread, and knew the same was happening to the others. Despite promising not to, they had gone out of their bodies. For the first time in their lives each was in their InForming Matrix. They knew the theory, but it was still confusing to find that it seemed to be no different to normal life.

Tamina felt the fear flickering out from the others, calmed her own, absorbed theirs, felt it churning in her stomach. *Please, stay there. Don't let it get into my thoughts*, she asked the Multiverse, as they plunged into a swirling torrent of colours.

She felt like a rocket shooting into space. Clutching onto her legs, Pelnak and Shimara were the big boosters. With his arms wrapped around her waist, she felt as though Wrenden was riding her as if they were in a HoloWrapper Kiddy Kartoon.

A thick, grey mist appeared in front of them. Buried deep within were tiny flecks of red and green. As they headed into the mist, Tamina extended her arms and dropped her head between them, carving through the mist like a diver piercing the water.

Small specks appeared in the distance. As they rapidly grew larger they could be seen to be birds. As birds were used on Vertazia to carry private messages, they all felt joy at such a welcome sight of a message from Qwelby.

Their hopes were shattered as a ghostly face half appeared, wreathed in the mist. Lines of energy could be seen flowing from its mouth and eyes as if it was controlling the birds like animated puppets. The birds dived down and landed on Wrenden's back. Gripping with their claws and flapping their wings, they tried to pull him away. Others landed on Shimara and Pelnak striking with their beaks, seeking to loosen their hold on brother and sister.

'*Grip my legs,*' Wrenden thought to Pelnmara. Even as he remembered that his mind could not reach out past the helmet, he felt the not-twins move so that each had one arm wrapped tightly around one of his calves holding each tightly against his sister's legs. *Out-of-Body. Thoughts work!*

Releasing his grip on his sister, Wrenden rose to his knees and battered at the birds attacking the not-twins. In turn, they used their free arms to strike at the birds on his back. One after the other the birds were pulled free and thrown into the mist, squawking with anger. But there was no respite.

Their claws remained, ran down Wrenden's back and tried to burrow beneath the not-twins arms. Wrenden was bending this way and that, ripping them away as fast as he could. Cries of pain resounding through all four helmets as each claw was torn away from the youngsters' increasingly blood-streaked arms and legs.

Wrenden was struggling with two that were almost hidden out of sight under Shimara's arm. Twisting around to his left and feeling Pelnak's grip on his right leg slacken, he got both hands onto the birds and heaved with all his might, wincing at Shimara's scream as he pulled them away. His mind stored away the impression that tiny points of green and red light clustered around her bleeding arm.

Finally, they were through the flock. Wrenden heard sighs of relief mingling with his own as he dropped down to lie along his sister's back, shaking with fatigue and anxiety. It seemed to him as though tiny waves of green and red colour ran along his back and legs, easing the pain from the many cuts.

Their rest was short-lived. With thrumming wings, yellow spotted, brown beasts dived on them. Again Wrenden rose up, flailing his arms at the new attackers. Shooting long tongues at his arms, they looked like grotesque caricatures of flying chameleons.

As the friends sped through the attacking flock, the fine, saw-toothed surfaces of the tongues slashed his arms. His lovely coffee colour was slowly turning red from the blood that was flowing from the myriad tiny cuts. A beast landed on his left wrist and wrapped its tongue around his forearm. He swung that arm at another approaching chameleon. The two beasts smashed together and pain seared through him as the tongue was wrenched from its grip. He ducked as another attacker sped towards his face. It cannoned off his shoulder and spun off into the distance.

He felt the not-twins tightening their grips. He knew that if he was torn from his perch he was lost. And if their grip on brother and sister was broken, none of them would ever return to Vertazia. What had started out as an exciting adventure had become a very real fight for their lives.

Turning to his right as he heard Pelnak's cry of pain, he saw him tear a beast away from where it had just landed on his left arm, its claws tearing at his flesh, blood spraying into the grey mist. Blood with green streaks? His mind asked.

Hearing the sound of more thrumming, Wrenden turned to the front and saw a cluster of beasts diving from his left. He punched one in the face, sending it crashing into two more behind it. Then that group was gone, whisked past by the speed of the friends' headlong dive down through the mist.

A last remaining group swooped in from his right. He ducked to his left as they flew past, their claws missing him by centimetres. The grin was wiped from his face as tongues whipped out and two wrapped around his forearm, digging into his flesh.

As the beasts fell behind, he was jerked to his right and felt the not-twins straining to keep hold of him. He watched in disbelief as the chameleons folded their wings and wound their tongues in, pulling themselves ever closer, claws on their front legs preparing to grip him. He could not bear the thought of any more pain. His whole body was on fire from all the torn flesh and cuts.

In spite of himself, he screamed loudly as they sunk their claws into his forearm. He was almost fainting with the pain. Desperate to tear them from his arm, yet more frightened of falling from his sister's body, he bent forward and sought to grip his sister with his left hand.

Tamina felt herself flooded with his fear and the panic rising within Pelnak and Shimara.

'Hold on tight!' Tamina thoughtsent. 'Pelnmara, focus on getting us through. I'll help Eeky.'

She twisted her supple, dancer's body around and back and felt her brother's hand grasp her left shoulder. Yes, she could just reach. Gritting her teeth, with her hand held open she slashed her right arm at the nearest chameleon and felt her nails rip across its body. Black blood sprayed out and fell, sizzling onto her brother's arm. Again she slashed, a nail broke; she felt the biting pain as black blood splashed onto her own arm.

Again and again Tamina slashed, feeling more nails break. It was not working, the beasts' skins were too thick and the cuts too shallow.

Her last blow had made the chameleon nearest to her struggle to maintain its hold. It flapped its wings and was plucked away by the wind tunnel effect of the four friend's passage through the mist. It had not left its claws behind. Instead, it reached out with them and gripped its companion. The shock of the collision tore that beast from its perch on Wrenden's arm.

Time seemed to stand still.

The tongues of both beasts were still wrapped around Wrenden's arm. As they reached their full extent a massive jerk was felt by all four friends. His terrified scream resounded through all their helmets as his left hand slipped from his sister's shoulder and his left leg was pulled out of Shimara's grip. He was about to plunge into the mist. Death faced him.

He was an annoying little squirt of a brother, forever playing her up. But he was HER brother. Tamina raised her arm up high above her head and with a viciousness she didn't know she possessed, swung it as fast as possible toward the tongues, felt her hand judder as she struck, cried out with the shock and pain as more nails broke, gasped with surprise as the severed tongues fell away and she heard Wrenden's screams of pain above her own as the spurting black blood sprayed them both.

Waves of green and red light run along his arm. The energy signature was clear. It was Qwelby reaching out to him, to them all, sending his healing love. Mentally, Wrenden tried to follow back the lines of energy and was met by soft, swirling white, making him think of snow. He was sucked in as if being taken to meet his elderest. The whiteness disappeared, leaving him with no clues as to where Qwelby might be.

As he tried to penetrate it, his mind started to freeze. Reluctantly, he pulled his awareness back to where he was and crashed down onto his sister's back and wrapped his left arm around her waist. He rested his badly bleeding arm on her back, watching the soft red and green energy soothing it.

'Qwelby. Where are you?' he thoughtsent. His vision was filled with the same swirling white wall.

Tamina eased her aching joints and let her feeling of success flow through to the others. She half smiled to herself. When they were much younger, her irrepressible brother had named them the "Fearless Four." At that age Tullia and Qwelby were inseparable, and always referred to as "The Twins." She and the not-twins had accepted the name. It gave them their own group identity as a way of finding the energy to balance that of the twins. *Perhaps we should resurrect the name. We certainly are earning it!*

At last the mist cleared and they found themselves plunging through a spiral made of millions of bright points of light. Stars! A whole galaxy swept past them and the harsh cold of inter-stellar space bit into them.

Tamina was drained. Her strength gone. She was the oldest of the four and Tullia's elderest. They were her responsibility. As the cold reached deep inside her and she felt the last vestiges of her energy draining away, she knew they would not succeed. Despair reached out for her. Here, between dimensions, there was no protective helmet. Its insidious message was overwhelming her, paralysing her hopes. She thought of all the times she had spent with Tullia, and with Qwelby. Their strength was their twinness. She needed that. *'Help me!'* she thoughtcried.

That was wrong. Tears sprang into her eyes. *It's me that must help them!*

'I'm here, Sis,' a quiet voice came into her head.

'And us,' Pelnmara added.

Mmh. She felt too weak even to speak. Soft waves of green and red light wrapped around the black Despair. Hope broke through.

A point of light appeared straight ahead. It grew in size, became a soft, beige colour radiating blessed warmth. She shot forward.

Something hard struck her stomach. Her attention was pulled back to the gallery. Together with the not-twins whose hands she was holding, she had pitched forward into the barrier. Fear gave her the energy to scream: 'Stand firm!'

Bracing her feet against the railings she tried to lean

backwards, felt herself being pulled over them. Panic took her. If their bodies were to follow them into the XzylStroem, then all was truly lost. Not only their lives. The twins would never return home.

She was in two places at once. Although her attention was back on the gallery, she knew her Self was still hovering over that beige patch. Here on the balcony wearing helmets, her mind could not reach the others. She was trying to pull Shimara and Pelnak towards her. If her brother sought balance by pulling them towards him, then she would topple over the balcony.

It wasn't a question of letting go their hands to save herself, she knew she would snap out of her body and would be sucked into that beige patch.

Death awaited her.

Fighting with her last scrap of energy, her stomach pressed hard against the top railing, she felt her brother's energy flowing into her, not much, not enough.

'If anyone can do it, you can, Sis.'

She lifted one leg up and put her knee against the top railing, steadied herself and saw Shimara and Pelnak copy her.

Safe!

Later, she was to confide to Lellia that it was her brother's faith in her that had given her the last drop of strength she needed to pull back and steady them all.

Peace!

All effort ceased as a tiny patch of lilac illumined the beige.

Tullia!

With all thought of the gallery left far behind, they descended as if lowered by Gravity Repulsors until they were hovering above a now large and strong sphere of purple.

Tullia was alive and well!

Little beads of pink and green energy flowed from them down towards the sphere. Purple petals opened and waved to them. A soft sigh rose up and a gentle smile appeared, hovering over the petals.

In the centre of the petals a series of images unfolded. Sun shining on a red desert. Dark-skinned men and women, morphing between being almost naked with some carrying spears and bows, and being fully clothed as if in the winter. Brightly coloured, rocky mountains under a hot sun. A round, thatched building that was set on a wide open, completely flat, grey-white expanse with a beautiful, large, tan-coloured cat loping along. In spite of the setting, the energy that came from the large hut clearly indicated it to be a cute little corner shop.

The scene quivered, blurred, cleared.

It was night-time. Brightly attired people were sitting around a large fire with nearly naked, dark-skinned men dancing. There was chanting and clapping. The flames reached high up as if they were the arms of many exotic dancers and bathed the friends in a warm embrace. Tamina almost groaned with envy at the sublime movement of bodies without joints, flames that truly were Salamanders, her own special symbol.

She was pulled down by the arms of the flame-people and invited to dance. She became one of them, a flame-wrapped Salamander. High above them, the moon cast its light across the whole scene. Swirling around in the midst of the fire it seemed to Tamina as though the flaming arms of the Salamanders reached up above her, pulled the moon down and enfolded its silver beauty. Tears fell from her eyes as an unbelievably magical moment flowed through her, making her at one with the fire and the moon.

'Sis, Sis, please...'

Flaming Xzarze, Eeky. Not now!

The vision clouded over and disappeared, leaving only blackness. A terrible sense of loss filled her.

'Ouch!' Something hard was pressing against her side. She opened her eyes. It was like looking through a waterfall. Her clothes felt uncomfortable. No it was her body, it wasn't fitting her like it usually did. Perplexed, she looked around. The scenery wavered, she felt herself shaking all over, then her vision cleared and she felt normal. She was on the interaction gallery, pressed hard against one of the struts. Inside her helmet, her brother's voice was urging her to wake up, get onto her hands and knees, and crawl back to the viewing gallery.

She passed out and came awake to the sounds of subdued whimpering in her ears and felt herself being undressed by... Cook? Looking up she saw she was in cosy room alongside the Cavern and that the other three were being helped by her First, Second and Third assistants, who, naturally, were called FAC, SAC and TAC.

'Simple m'dear,' Cook explained, as she helped Tamina lie face down on one of the sofas that had morphed into relax couches, alongside her brother from whom the whimpering sounds were coming.

'We prepare food with plenty of loving for your insides and,' Cook picked up a large bottle from the armrest that had become a side table, 'swathes of Tenderest Loving Care, my own mixture, for your outsides.'

Tamina felt easing balm spread over her right arm and hand as Cook 'tut-tutted' at the burns. And heard continued 'tutting' as more TLC was applied all over her Form.

'Soon have those long legs dancing again,' Cook said as she stoppered the bottle and moved away to check on what SAC and TAC were doing with Shimara and Pelnak on the other sofa-now-couch.

Tamina rolled her head around to look at her brother. FAC was spreading TLC over his back whilst Lellia seemed to be wrapping an energy field around one of his arms. Drifting on the edge of sleep, she could only look and wonder what Lellia really was doing.

'You saved me, Sis,' her brother said, his eyes half closing.

Tamina looked at her right hand, where TLC had been smeared over her broken nails and torn fingertips. She put her left hand alongside. A beautiful dancer painted on each nail in red and flame orange with highlights of white and turquoise. 'Look,' she said to no-one in particular, her voice cracking.

'Greater love hath no woman,' Lellia murmered.

'Tullia did these for me, just before...' Tamina said with a sob.

'I'm sorry,' Lellia said. 'We'll get them back. Both of them.' She bit her lip as she slammed her Privacy Seal shut over all her conflicting emotions, stopping them from colouring her energy field, and returned to healing Wrenden's many wounds.

CHAPTER 34

THWARTED

VERTAZIA

Ceegren was frustrated and angry, emotions to which he was entirely unaccustomed. He had just been defeated by what was to him a group of young children. Although possessing the abundant, dynamic and penetrating energy of their second era, it had never occurred to him that four inexperienced children could successfully oppose the solid power manipulated by himself, Dryddnaa and two much older Venerables, Gentian and Midnight.

The children were so inexperienced in the seventh dimension that they had not been able to use the energy of that dimension freely, but each had clung to their InForming Matrix: the energy model for their normal, physical body. Totally vulnerable, yet they had been able to call on the elusive energy of the sixth dimension.

They had not created that by themselves. Of that he was sure. Had that been done by the Arch Discoverer and his wife? Or. And Ceegren paled at the possibility. If it owed its existence to the accursed twins, that meant all six were part of a discrete energy entity. He had to know. In the meantime he would prepare for the worst scenario: that all six... he paused his thoughts...

youngsters... had created a discrete sixth dimensional energy matrix available at will.

Very little was known about the sixth dimension. During the chaos that had followed the severing of the links with Azura the knowledge of how to maintain the original Aurigan records had been lost. Even copies made with different technology had degraded. The general assumption was that using vastly superior technology the Auriganii had linked access to the records to the amount of activated DNA segments. As if saying to the Tazii that with only three segments they did not have the maturity to handle what the Auriganii needed twelve to create.

His memory threw up a recall of an HWFantasy series where the sixth dimension was used as a time corridor, enabling the actors to travel into the past and the future, and then step into another spatial dimension. Was there a neutrino of truth in that? If so, no wonder the Auriganii had ensured that secrets like that were concealed from the less advanced Tazii.

With a sigh he eased himself out of the lotus position, stood in front of Belayyel, his large crystal, bowed his head in thanks, and watched as its support base of black velvet petals closed over it. He removed his short, cream coloured mediation robe and donned his normal, full length robe of Gelele Silk, infusing it with his usual deep, sea green colour. He left his meditation room and settled in his study.

Since a young man he had dreamt of being in a position where he could enable the Tazii to recover their twelve segments and rebuild the wonder and beauty of the pure Aurigan life when all were, literally, of one mind. As he had risen rapidly through the ranks of Custodians, to his surprise he had discovered that the absence from Tazian culture of any form of leadership even applied to the long succession of Arch Custodians. As with the rest of Vertazia, everything was done by the incredibly slow process of consensus. If he was to achieve his dream, that had to be changed.

The violent attacks on their four friends had not been well

received by the members of the Senate whose energy had been drawn upon. He was concerned that he had gone too far in seeking to prevent any communication with the twins. Fortunately, his most loyal supporters, the much older pair-bonded Venerables, Gentian and Midnight, were steadfast in their support. They had seen the changes wrought in successive men and women when they emerged from their period if induction as Arch Custodian. Each one's energy signature clearly revealing that they were carrying a heavy burden, a burden which was never discussed. Nor had Dryddnaa flinched from her active part. He would seek to excuse what had been done as the reaction to an extreme emergency. Better plans would be implemented for the future and, he sternly reminded himself, he had to be more cautious. He eased himself back in his chair and reassured himself by reviewing what he had achieved.

He had always enjoyed his visits to the Custodians' meeting place at IndluKoba. It was an extensive country estate that attracted both Kumelanii and less committed Traditionalists to research, study and holiday in an atmosphere of beauty, peace and serenity. Apart from a small management group of much older Tazii, the majority of staff were in their second Eras. Most of them working part-time.

Many Tazii chose the centre of Traditionalist teachings for the three key rebirthday ceremonies. The presentation of the EraBand at age twelve, the attunement of the crystal at age fourteen, and at twenty-four the induction into the ethos of collective adulthood. Most parents accepted the offer of a Custodian to be present at such ceremonies. Ceegren had been accorded the status of Elder at the earliest possible age of one hundred and twenty. He smiled to himself at how the parents of the children he had carefully selected expressed their gratitude and feelings of being honoured when, with his exalted status, he personally offered to participate in a ceremony.

His conscience pricked him a little as he acknowledged that

what he had done had been a touch underhand. He had subtly introduced into each youngster's mind a commitment to himself. Although that was perfectly concealed, he had fully complied with Tazian values. The commitment was only to himself as The Embodiment of Traditionalist Values. Were Ceegren to depart from those values, not only would the link be severed, he would incur a negative reaction. The longer the link had been in place and the wider his divergence from those values, the greater would be the damage from that reaction.

Since his elevation to Arch Custodian twelve years ago he had taken one further step to ensure loyalty. Whilst attending the adulthood ceremonies of carefully selected youngsters he had inserted into their minds a discrete and perfectly concealed layer. That layer contained routines that allowed for the new adult's inner development to proceed in spite of the surface inhibitions. It also permitted him to remove those inhibiting routines at any time he chose, along with an automatic reinforcement of the adult's commitment to himself.

Had he been wrong to do all that? He shook his head. Leadership. Strong, determined, focussed leadership was essential if the Tazii were to pull out of their slow and otherwise inevitable journey towards extinction.

All he needed was a small group totally committed to him with the abundant dynamic energy of their youth focussed on communicating a simple message. That energy sweeping through the farthest reaches of the MentaNet would spread like a seed crystal dropped into a supersaturated solution. As that was happening he would remove the restrictions imposed on those adults he had selected. Their particular energy spreading through the MentaNet would enliven those older adults who had commitments to him buried within their psyches.

He nodded to himself. All that still held good. Yet his plans had received an unexpected setback. The Acolyte he had been training to become the youth leader so essential to his plans had been Xaala's older brother. In three years' time he would have been at the perfect age: approaching the end of his second era when he would move from being a twiyera to an adult.

Now, doubts crept in. His planning had been good, but he really needed those three extra years to condition more youngsters, more new adults, and find a charismatic leader. Although he would review the youngsters at IndluKoba, he already knew there was no-one suitable.

Should he ease back and wait until Tibor, his younger Acolyte, was ready? That would be another six or seven years and give him the time to condition many more youngsters and new adults. He rose from his chair, slid his hands into the wide sleeves of his robe and walked to the window. He quieted his thoughts by looking at the night sky with its myriad stars lighting the blanket of snow. Out of the corner of his eye he saw a flash of movement. Turning his head he saw a large, Horned Snow Owl rise back up out of the shadow of an outbuilding with a tiny animal in its beak.

He bowed his head as he thanked the All for the answer.

Could Xaala be manipulated? Did he have a choice? His Acolyte possessed many excellent qualities. Mentally and psychically the best he had ever trained she was totally committed both to him personally and to the teachings, and of her own free will. She was nearly seventeen years old. A little over two metres in height, with a figure more like a skinny boy than a girl, and a sharp mind, she was not his image of the sort of female to whom people would warm.

She would have to become more feminine. Fortunately, he had never interfered with her mind in any permanent way. To have the charisma, the personality of an inspirational leader she had to be natural. There could not be the slightest hint of any overriding mental controls.

Dryddnaa would have to prepare her, and that meant giving the Chief Readjuster an even more powerful place within his plans. It was clear that Dryddnaa had her own plans and was building a power base within the Inner Council of the Senate. This really was the Dance of Discovery. He was going to need all his skills to ensure he remained in command.

With his decision made he felt the tension drain from him. He was tired and needed to relax and have his energy level restored. Amongst her many skills Xaala provided an excellent aura massage. He would avail himself of her services and gently explore his, he indulged a smile, their, next step.

CHAPTER 35

A TALL STORY

FINLAND

Qwelby was having a nightmare. It had started as a pleasant dreamstate, riding a comet to Earth and looking at scenery from close-up, meeting an Earth boy and being taken to his home. But then he was sliding down an icy slope and attacked by a group of men. His eyes flicked open. Where was Tullia? He rolled over. She was not there. There was no other bed. This was not their attic suite. This was not... It had not been a dream! He was on Earth. He had been attacked. He had defended himself, feeling movements from Tamina's Body Dance.

He jerked up into a sitting position. That was not dancing! Well it was. But it was... halfway to a WarriorDance. He knew, had known, how to do a WarriorDance. So, the energy was being kept alive? No. Tullia had dragged himself and Wrenden to more than one display. There had been no overt combat sensation. Of course not! The perpetrators would have been dealt with, 'stamped on' was a thought that slipped across the back his mind, by the Readjusters.

'Ah!' He grabbed his head as it filled with pain. A constant stream of tiny explosions. He lay back, feeling too sick and dizzy to

252

move. The full memory of the previous evening returned. He was on Earth. Safe. Where was Kaigii?

Slowly, the pain lessened as the myriad of pinpricks in his brain reduced, leaving him with a dull ache. When that had gone, he got up and found the door locked. With all the feelings of being cared for that he had received the previous evening he thought that was nice: to stop him sleepwalking. He slid his mind into the lock. Exploring it was difficult. *Third/fourth dimension. Same quantum energy that underpins the whole of existence, but overlaid with slower and denser vibrations. This is going to take a lot of effort. But. A bonus. Not imbued with extra inertia as at home.*

Stepping out of the room he found what was clearly a washing room, washed, then dressed in the clothes that had been left at the side of the bed. He went downstairs and entered the kitchen just in time to hear Anita, who was just finishing explaining her dream, ask in a puzzled tone of voice: 'Why do I dream of a desert when I don't believe it is a desert?'

There was no reply as all eyes turned to Qwelby. In the silence that followed he had time to explore the Azurii's weak energy fields. He saw surprise, curiosity and an absence of any indications of violence.

'How did you open the door?' Paavo asked.

'With my mind,' Qwelby answered.

'How do you feel?' Hannu asked quickly to divert attention. What other tricks could "his Alien" perform?

'I not here,' Qwelby replied.

'What d'you mean?' Hannu asked.

'Tullia. Twin. Not in head. I not...' he gestured with his hands.

'Whole. Complete?' Anita offered.

Feeling bereft and lost, Qwelby nodded. His compiler had not translated the words, but Anita's mind had been clear with what she was trying to convey.

Seija got up, put an arm around Qwelby and guided him to a chair.

253

He smiled at her as he sat down. She had responded exactly as his mother would. It was to be a long time before he discovered that his strong thoughts and feelings affected the Azurii without their being consciously aware of it, and to the extent that most responded accordingly.

'Where on Earth am I?' he asked.

Stifled laughter made him frown.

'Oh, Qwelby,' Hannu said. '"Where on earth am I," is just what we'd say.'

Qwelby smiled. The more he was continuing to experience the same warm energies that he had felt the previous night, the more he relaxed. 'Where on Earth am I,' he repeated, mimicking Hannu's inflection.

'In Finland,' Hannu answered with a laugh.

'I not have bag,' Qwelby said. 'I have planet. It is Earth.'

Hannu leapt up from the table and dashed up to his room.

'Did you sleep well?' Seija asked.

'I dream. I wake. Head hurts. I good.'

'You must be hungry. Here, drink this whilst I get you something to eat.'

'Thank you.' Feeling so much calmer than the previous evening, he was able to take in her energies. Of medium height and a comfortable build, like her husband she radiated a practical energy. Caring and concerned, was the big feel he received. That she did not come across as harassed like his own mother made him feel sad. He would much rather have his mother fussing over him than be on this strange planet.

Hannu came thundering back downstairs, clutching the bag which he thrust at Qwelby in his excitement.

Smiling, Qwelby opened it, took out what looked like a child's multi-coloured ball and handed it to Hannu.

With excited exclamations, Hannu turned it around in his hands as Anita peered over his shoulder.

'It's a map of Earth!' Anita exclaimed. 'Look Qwelby, this is

Finland,' she said, pointing with her fingernail. 'And we live just about here, in the south.'

In between mouthfuls of what he was told was porridge with butter and raspberry jam, tastes not that dissimilar to what he might have had at home, Qwelby explained how he and Tullia had found the globe when it was inside-out.

'Did you know it was a map of Earth?' Anita asked.

Qwelby shook his head, swallowed and answered with a look almost of horror on his face. 'No! We not dare. Or be stuck inside.'

'What!' exclaimed Hannu, in an incredulous tone of voice.

'Oh, yes. Imagination very powerful in quantum world,' was the solemn reply. 'In my language, word for imagination is image-in-action.' He smiled, sadly. 'Translate into Finnish. I see does not work.'

'Mum would like that,' Anita said, thinking that her mother would want to meet Qwelby just as much as her father did.

'That's neat though,' Hannu said, telling him different words. 'It does work in English. That's a language a lot of people on Earth speak.'

'That's all very well,' interjected Seija. 'I've work to do. Shoo, upstairs you lot.'

Ensconced in Hannu's room, the three youngsters spent the rest of the morning looking at books, searching the internet and teaching Qwelby Finnish. Thanks to Gumma's compiler, he was soon able to communicate very well.

As he finally finished his explanation of how he and Tullia had left Vertazia, and he had arrived on Earth, the two Finns were stunned into incredulity.

Qwelby was feeling a lot happier. At least his new friends understood what he had told them. He didn't blame then for not really believing him, he scarcely believed it himself. What was equally good was the compiler that Gumma had given him was working. Not merely building a language database in his mind, but providing him with grammar and syntax.

Between them, the two Finns told Qwelby all about CERN, giving him every hope that his twin also was on Earth.

'Anita. Your father's here,' they heard Mrs Rahkamo call.

The three youngsters went downstairs to the kitchen to find both Rahkamos were there with her father.

'Hullo Anita,' Dr Keskinen said as he kissed his daughter, looking past her to the boy with the unusual face.

'Dad, may I present Qwelby who comes from a world called Vertazia. Qwelby, this is my father, Dr Viljo Keskinen.'

Qwelby offered his hand. Anita's father responded automatically, and was surprised to hear: 'Goood ev-en-ing, Faa-ther of An-ita,' said with a perfect, albeit musical, Finnish accent.

Hannu and Anita laughed. After all, it was exactly how they had taught Qwelby to greet Hannu's father.

Viljo let go of Qwelby's hand and frowned. The previous night he had been told that the alien looked like a human boy. Now, seeing him and hearing him speak, he was inclined to think that this was no alien but someone from the Far East, and his friends had been taken in by a cunning boy with a very tall story.

A timer bleeped to say lunch was almost ready.

'We must go,' said Viljo, looking at his daughter. 'You can come back afterwards if...'

Paavo cut him off. 'Please, both of you come back.'

'I hoped you'd say that,' Viljo said. There was a puzzle. He wanted both to solve it and help his friends.

Seija had just finished clearing away when Viljo and his daughter returned. She directed Anita upstairs and her father to join Paavo in the living room. The kitchen empty, she lent against a worktop to steady herself as everything that had happened in less than twenty-four hours welled its way through her mind. For a moment, she was at a loss what to do. She didn't want to join the men. Their talk would be all too technical and complicated. An intuition

256

popped into her mind, she liked it. She wrapped up warm and went out to visit Taimi Keskinen, Anita's mother.

'Qwelby, you've explained how you and Tullia left Vertazia. Please tell us about your friends,' Anita said as they entered Hannu's room. 'And Tullia,' she added with a shy smile.

As his rich baritone rolled around the room, Qwelby was soon back home, vividly describing his world as he took them on a guided tour and introduced them to the Fearless Four, wondering why he had used that old name. If Hannu and Anita noticed words in Tazian, they were too enthralled to ask for translation.

Eventually, Qwelby ran out of breath and leant against the wardrobe for support.

There was a long silence.

All Anita's senses were awhirl. It was so like the first snowfall when Hannu had invited her to his home. With both of them cold and wet, in typical Finnish manner, his mother had bundled them into the sauna, then given them hot chocolate whilst Anita's clothes dried.

Once up in his room, Hannu had paced around, telling her all about his dreams of space travel and meeting a race of peaceful aliens, and what humans could learn from them. Out of breath, he had finished leaning against the wardrobe.

Finding someone of her own age she felt an affinity with, she had confessed that she had always been a loner, more interested in her schoolwork or studying science with her father or more subtle energies with her mother.

Later, they had stood in silence at the window watching a heavy snowfall, his arm around her shoulders, her arm around his waist.

Just then his father had come home with some friends. Realising it was late, and daringly for fear of spoiling what had been a special day, she had given Hannu a quick kiss on the cheek, and gone home.

Now, Anita had the same lovely warm feeling as on that day, but was full of confusion. It was "their Alien" who was enthralling her. And in a way more powerfully than Hannu did.

257

'Your voice is so beautiful,' Anita said in a dreamy tone. 'Your purple eyes revolving round in their violet settings. They sucked me in. Then your singing took me there. I saw Tullia... then I was... I was her. Seeing your world through her eyes... It was so weird. I guess it was different, but seeing it as she does, it wasn't I ...'

She got up from the bed where she was sitting with Hannu and took both of the Tazian's hands in hers. 'Oh, Qwelby. I understand how much you miss her... how much she means to you... I feel it. Inside.' Looking into his hypnotic eyes, she wanted to take him in her arms and comfort him.

'Wow. That was something else!' Hannu said, breaking what had become a heavy atmosphere. It was only since meeting Anita that he had been introduced to meditation and what she called the Inner Worlds. And now...

'It was all so real. I thought... for a time... imagined... I don't know... I was seeing through your eyes... I felt as though I'd met Wrenden. He sounds a whole lot of fun.' He reached out, took Anita's hand and pulled her to sit back down on the bed.

'Violet is I am in tune with my Kore. Eyes revolving we call twirling. That's when I'm excited. Well, correct, but translation not good. Your word is energised,' Qwelby explained as he sat down on the chair, smiling.

It is true what they say. Azurii are human. It's just that their energy sensing is not so strong. But to thoughtwrap Anita so well that she was in Tullia and not me. Dragons Breath, I'm good!

But what is wrong with Hannu? That strong streak of jealousy? He's seen my world through my eyes. What's wrong with Anita seeing it through Tullia's?

'You said about time differences?' Hannu asked.

'NullPoints.' Qwelby said. 'You know space-time-consciousness is all one?' Hannu and Anita nodded. 'What we call a NullPoint Bubble has no space or time, just consciousness. How it works?' He shrugged his shoulders. 'Dad or Gumma would have to explain.'

With Qwelby saying that due to the higher energy frequencies on their world, Tazii grew taller and bigger than Azurii, further discussion ensued and the Finns discovered that Tazii often lived to two hundred and grew up emotionally a lot slower than people on Earth.

As Anita continued to look into Qwelby's gently twirling eyes, she felt she was being sucked in again, it was as though she was becoming a stand-in for his twin. Unaware that she was being energy linked to Tullia in what the Tazii termed share-bonding, her heart beat faster at the thought of being so close to a pair of alien twins.

CHAPTER 36

HUMAN MEETS HUMAN

FINLAND

Later in the afternoon Seija returned from her visit with Taimi Keskinen. She felt a lot more comfortable in her own mind after talking over the whole situation with another woman and mother.

She had had enough hot drinks with her friend, so she poured herself a glass of beer, took it through into the living room, sat down in an armchair and put the glass on the table with a bit of a clunk. The two men stopped talking and looked at her. Assured of their attention, she said: 'We are not going to tell the police, the army, or any other people like that about Qwelby. He is a lovely boy. He is lost and I don't care where he comes from. He needs our help and he desperately wants to find his sister. We are going to help him.'

She could not tell them how she felt about Qwelby. It had been difficult enough explaining to Taimi, another mother. There was an energy from him that seemed to be asking her to be 'mother,' not his mother, just 'mother.' And it felt good to respond.

For a while nobody said anything. Paavo, who had sat forward in his chair when his wife spoke, slowly sank back into his chair. 'Right,' he said at last.

Viljo nodded.

They remained sitting there in quiet contemplation, staring into the flames. The living room door opened and Hannu put his head around the corner. 'Mum, is it alright if we come in?'

She nodded, and Anita and Qwelby followed him. Paavo commented that he felt hungry. Everyone looked at their watches and realised just how much time had gone by. Seija headed out of the room, grabbing her husband and pulling him into the kitchen, leaving the others to sort out the furniture. Then she telephoned Taimi to come over.

The children chose the larger sofa so all three could sit together with Qwelby in the middle.

As her father sat down in the armchair next to Anita, she leant over and asked: 'You will help Qwelby, won't you?'

'We need to know more about him,' her father temporised.

'Please, Daddy, he's just got to find his sister.'

'Well...' he started.

Anita moved across to her father sat on his lap, hugged him and put her head on his shoulder. 'Please Daddy. He's so lonely. He's lost on a strange world and he must find his twin. We've got to help. Please promise you'll not tell anyone he's here?'

Ever since she could talk, Anita had been able to twist her father round her little finger. What his daughter was asking was difficult for a man in his position. But, whoever the boy was, he was in the Rahkamos' house. Those big blue eyes staring up at him, appealing.

'I promise. But remember this, Anita. He is a stranger. A very obvious stranger. Other people will see him, hear about him and his real story will come out eventually. You do understand that don't you?'

Anita kissed her father's cheek and returned to sit on the sofa as the Rahkamos and Taimi Keskinen came into the room, laden with trays. As soon as everyone was settled with food and drink, Anita and Hannu explained a lot of the things Qwelby had told them about his world.

Dr Keskinen was thinking it was all very interesting. A world of fantasy taken from a variety of science-fiction films by a very clever and manipulative boy. Well, Qwelby was in the Rahkamos' home. It would be a betrayal of friendship for him to interfere.

The two story-tellers paused.

'Qwelby, will you explain to me exactly how you came here,' Viljo asked as he leant forward.

'From finding what you call the comets,' Anita suggested.

With his compiler working well, Qwelby told the whole story right through to his rescue by Hannu. Once again the musical tones of his rich baritone enfolded his listeners and took then into his adventure. There was silence when he finished. Everyone was waiting for Dr Keskinen to comment.

Viljo dragged his mind back from wherever it had been. He had to admit that the boy was a born story-teller and had done his research. It was easy to understand why the children believed him. He would let them down gently.

'The facts are good,' he said. 'The Large Hadron Collider is a circle twenty six kilometres around. The buzzes are explained by the magnets placed at regular intervals all around it which hold the two streams of protons in opposite directions. They travel about ten thousand times around before crashing. Lots of different particles are given off when that happens. Qwelby is saying that they, along with all sub-atomic particles, are actually composed of these kuznii that have no mass. Then, like photons, they can travel at the speed of light. And we know that photons can slip through other dimensions where they can travel faster than the speed of light on this world.'

He could not help but smile. There was something fascinating about what the boy had said. Not the story itself. Even though he had not fully broken away from being enwrapped by Qwelby's voice, he knew that was obviously a load of bunkum. But the concept had appeal. 'Of course, there is the La Palma and subsequent series of experiments,' he added.

'What's that?' asked Paavo.

'Teleportation!' exclaimed Anita and Hannu together.

'Quantum entanglement,' the scientist corrected. 'But not for anything living,' he protested.

'It would explain how Qwelby got here, though, wouldn't it Dad?'

'Humans cannot be carried on photons.'

'Qwelby isn't human, Dad.'

An uncomfortable silence filled the room.

'Explain, please,' Qwelby asked. 'I do not understand.'

'We're humans and you're... an alien, from another race,' Anita said, feeling uncomfortable.

'Erm, well, perhaps not,' he responded. He took a deep breath. 'We're taught that we're really the same.'

A stunned silence ensued.

He cleared his throat. 'Aeons ago we, um, Auriganii as we then were, had all our DNA active. About one hundred and fifteen thousand turns ago, that's what you would call a year, we left our homeworld as the sun was going to become a white dwarf. It took about forty thousand turns to find this planet. It looked so beautiful from space that we named it Azura Yezi, the Blue Planet.' He paused. This was basic history to him, but to these Azurii?

'But you live on Vertazia?' Hannu queried.

'At first we settled here on the Blue Planet, living in many places including islands, mountain tops, and around an enormous lake in a fertile valley that split one of the continents in two. They were sort of bases, like the ends of a bridge between Earth and where we mainly lived in the higher dimensions. On Earth at that time there were several races of hominids. Some of us mixed with one particular group.'

263

Qwelby's voice had faded away and the ovals of his eyes had become completely pale violet.

Anita shivered as a cold draught swept across her. 'You're talking as though you were there,' she said in almost a whisper.

Qwelby's eyes returned to their normal large purple centres in pale blue ovals, and Anita felt the room grow warmer. 'I was,' he replied. 'Err, well, sort of,' he added, shaking his head to clear the dizzy feeling and wondering how that consciousness shift had been so easy when he was in the solid third dimension.

Then it struck him just what had happened. He appeared to have accessed a memory that was millennia prior to any such memories that were encoded in his genes. The room slipped out of focus as a tendril of thought arose from deep inside his mind, but slipped away as he tried to grasp it. The room came back into focus and he saw people were staring at him. He sensed a mixture of concern and some fear. *'Need friends,'* his Intuition said.

Doctor Keskinen nodded. Given that Qwelby was not talking in Earth years, what he was saying fitted in with more than one extreme theory of how human beings had developed. *The boy had certainly has done his research well for his preposterous story.*

Qwelby took a deep breath and calmed himself. 'We are taught that there was a terrible war amongst the humans that caused the Earth's crust to shift, an ice age to end and the seas to rise. Many of our bases were destroyed, and over a long time we lost the ability to move between what had become two, parallel worlds. That part of the Archives is so strongly warded that we, that's me, Tullia and our special friends all working together cannot access it.' He grinned. 'There are lots of areas that are heavily restricted to much older people which we do, er, access. But not this. We are told the event was so terrible that the record has been sealed forever.' He and Tullia had not been part of the SubNet culture for long enough to even think of asking if it might be possible to access that information.

'Whatever happened, the result was that we have three DNA segments active and you, two. The big difference between us is that we live at a much faster rate of vibration than you.' He turned to Dr Keskinen. 'And that makes us closer to the energies of the quantum world.'

'La Palma, Gran Sasso, then MonKiw. It was all over the internet. Quantum entanglement. And now across dimensions!' exclaimed Anita, looking at her father as if to say 'sorted!'

Her father opened his mouth. Where to start with demolishing her suggestion? CERN had been one end of both the ultimately successful Gran Sasso series and then the subsequent MonKiw trials. But not for anything requiring so much energy to transport, and definitely not for anything living.

'If at some distant time in the future we are ever to recover our original Aurigan nature with all twelve DNA segments,' Qwelby continued. 'We, that is you Azurii and us Tazii, have to join together. We need your energy and you need our third segment. And.' Was he telling them too much? There were mixed feelings flowing all around the room with strong encouragement coming from Hannu and Anita sitting either side of him on the settee. 'So, you see, we want, we need, to be friends with you.'

It had been exciting and a validation of their powers when he and Tullia had wormed their way into the ShadowMarket. There had been no way that they could back out when faced with demands for energy exchanges that tied them in to the SubNet. At times what they had discovered about the Azurii had been disturbing, but they had been able to isolate that discomfort as it clearly was all part of the lives of the Azurii. Now, he felt he was bearing a heavy burden as he had to make it clear the Tazii were totally unlike how the Azurii imagined all aliens to be.

There was silence as the adults tried to absorb the ideas. Taimi Keskinen was delighted. A Yoga teacher, she firmly believed in the world of energy and what could be achieved by working at what people called subtle levels. Could Qwelby see auras, she wondered. She would love to discuss that with him. Could he help her to increase her skills with energy healing?

Qwelby smiled at Taimi as he realised that she was accepting what he had said and was interested.

'A wormhole,' Viljo announced. Six heads swivelled, different expressions on their faces. With a smile he held up a hand to still their questions. 'Its existence is explained by Einstein's Theory of General Relativity. In fact I consider it is more likely to operate between dimensions than in the ordinary space-time of our universe...'

'We could use that to get him back home?' Hannu interrupted excitedly.

'No.' Dr Keskinen shook his head. 'I'm sorry. I got carried away thinking of one of Anita's favourite TV series: "Deep Space Nine". So far only small wormholes have been created under laboratory conditions and are unstable. It's just a theoretical explanation of how Qwelby could have got here across dimensions.' Keskinen gave Hannu an apologetic smile for having demolished the boy's suggestion.

'Consciousness,' added his wife. 'We explore that in my yoga group. It's pure energy. That also must be present in all dimensions.'

'Yes,' Qwelby nodded. 'So. Not carried on photons. Err...' Qwelby leant forward, his purple orbs disappeared and his ovals became completely violet. 'When an object reaches the speed of light, all the constituent subatomic particles expand to fill the whole of the universe. That is they all achieve coherence at exactly the same moment. Space, time and consciousness are one. When the consciousness element also achieves coherence, that determines the location of the object in space-time,' he said in a monotone as though repeating a lecture he had been given. Opening his eyes he continued in his normal voice. 'My consciousness must have been focussed on Hannu and Anita and the hillside outside your house. The multiple wave forms that all my particles had become collapsed back into particles, and I arrived.'

Qwelby sighed and slumped back. He knew how travel was said to have been achieved by those Auriganii who inhabited the ultra-fast vibrations of the ninth dimension. The thought that was how he and Tullia had travelled was mind-blowing, but still did not explain how he had slowed his vibrations so as to be on Earth in the solid, third dimension.

'Superpositioning, Dad! Everything all at one.' Anita was jiggling with excitement. 'It's how the Infinite Improbability Drive worked in The Hitchhiker's Guide to The Universe.'

Dr Keskinen was feeling bemused. Of course his daughter understood quantum mechanics. Until meeting Hannu and then his group of friends, her principal interest had been in dividing her time between himself and his wife, exploring their differing interests. But this boy. His family had to be scientists.

Qwelby said in a faint voice. 'Tired. Heavy. Energy loss.'

After the events on the day of the first snowfall, Hannu and Anita had quickly become good friends. Her few friends when living in Helsinki had all been girls. None of them very close as she had not shared their interest in clothes and dating, and was uncomfortable with the personal things they talked about: although she wondered how much of what they said was true. She had much more interesting things to explore: science and the world of the psyche. Time for the other stuff later.

With someone of her own age she could really talk with, Anita had came to the conclusion that either there was not a lot of truth in what the Helsinki girls had said, or they didn't have interesting boyfriends. But. Although they spent a lot of time in each other's company, she and Hannu never really were alone. They were either with their group of friends, her father in his laboratory, or working on a school project with parents around whichever house they were in.

For Hannu, Anita was easy to be with. Unlike even his best mate Timo, she didn't laugh at his ideas or daydreams. She was a good skier and fitted in well with his group of friends. Having had little success with the girls at school he was afraid he might ruin the nice relationship they had if he tried to take it any further. As she had not done or said anything, he had begun to wonder if she regretted that quick kiss she had given him on that first day.

Then, one evening working at Hannu's house, they had wanted to run an experiment using her father's laboratory. On the way there, Hannu took her hand. Thick gloves made it clumsy, and he was heartened when she slipped her arm through his.

Anita had begun to wonder if her feelings that first day had all been stupid, and he wasn't interested in her as anything more than someone to talk with. Then, when she slipped her arm through his, he put his other hand on top of hers. Instead of heading for the front door as usual, he steered them around the back. She was tingling with excitement. Surely, at last, he was going to? He did. And they had their first kiss. The first of many.

Ilta and Oona had immediately noticed the difference. Hannu had happily put up with the ribbing from his mates, and Anita had found herself no longer just 'one of the group', but 'one of the girls'.

Now, Hannu was uncomfortable. With Qwelby sitting in the middle, it was as though he was coming in between them. Yet at the same time he sensed more energy flowing between himself and Anita. That was nice. But he would rather they found that for and by themselves. Yet, some of those feelings were for the alien. And that was exciting – in a mental way.

Anita felt giddy and uncertain with a whole new rush of feelings for this alien. *Was this what it was like to have a brother? Or be his... alien twin?*

Seija checked her watch and broke the silence. 'This has been an incredible day, well, two days actually, and very tiring for everyone. I think it's time the young folk went to bed.' She turned to the Keskinens. 'If it's alright with you, it would be nice if Anita could stay for another night. Who knows how being here may help her dreams?'

Viljo felt his wife squeeze his hand as Anita asked pleadingly. He grunted, and his wife thanked Seija.

'He's very clever,' Viljo said once the youngsters had gone. 'That gets around the problem of Einstein's E equals MC squared, where an object cannot travel at light-speed because it would attain infinite mass. Hah!' He laughed. 'Anita's right. He's got that from The Hitchhiker's Guide.' Satisfied that he had demolished the boy's story, Viljo sank back in his chair and silence settled over the room as the two sets of parents sipped their drinks, watching the flames crackling around the logs. It had been a very strange time and they all felt the need to relax and gather their thoughts.

Viljo was troubled. He was aware of the work of Drs Kozyrev, Ginzburg, Larson and Tift, all in different areas of quantum mechanics which, if accepted, overturned Einstein's famous equation and meant the boy's explanation could be right – and a lot more. No. He would not go down that route.

'It's a fantastic story,' Viljo said. 'Part of me would like it to be true. And I found I was actually believing it as he was speaking. But, really, with quantum theory as it stands, it's just not possible. What concerns me is that he is so convincing. There's something there I can't put my finger on. We need to find out who he really is and where he comes from.'

'I'm not so sure,' Taimi said. 'I've always envied those people who can see auras. When he was telling his story I saw an energy field around him. It's like a strong heat haze. And it extends a lot further away than you see in those Kirlian photos.' She took a deep breath. 'I can't explain it, but when he was telling us about how he came here, more than just believing him, I felt he was telling the truth.'

Viljo accepted that all life exhibited electro-magnetic fields, but the chakras and auras his wife believed in, that was going too far. Not wanting to start yet another of their inconclusive arguments, he said nothing.

'I agree we need to find the truth,' Paavo said, nodding. There was something about the way the boy had trusted him that made him want to do what was right for him, and take the time to discover what that was. 'While we do, we need to explain why he's here.'

'Taimi, will you come round tomorrow and see if we can work out some sort of explanation?' Seija asked.

'Yes. I'd like to get to know Qwelby better,' Taimi replied. She was beginning to understand what her friend had been trying to explain to her earlier that afternoon about the feelings the boy engendered.

Their husbands remained silent. Unaware of how much he had been influenced by Qwelby's sincerity, Viljo was intrigued and content to let the matter be taken out of his hands. Paavo had no preconceptions as to what the truth might be. He had gone to the ski slope and seen how the boy's arrival could not be explained. Nor could he explain the feelings he had experienced when he had picked up the unconscious boy and put him into bed. A feeling of being trusted with a precious life had made him want to care for the stranger.

'Idiot!' Viljo exclaimed, slapping his forehead. 'There's the hole in his story. CERN's first run after the shutdown was late yesterday afternoon. But that wasn't announced until late this morning. Hours after he'd told that story to our children. He must have prepared it, what... over a week ago before the shutdown, and then missed the news that CERN had closed.' He hesitated; the full situation regarding the stoppage was still not to be revealed. 'It scarcely made the news. A minor glitch with some recording equipment, and the opportunity taken to advance a minor, scheduled maintenance programme.'

'When was that run?' Taimi asked.

'About four...' her husband's voice trailed off as he realised that was when Qwelby had arrived.

'So, not actually disproving his story,' Taimi said, with a teasing tone in her voice, knowing that her daughter would see that as definite proof that Qwelby was telling the truth.

'You're enjoying this, aren't you!' Viljo said, uncomfortable with his wife's teasing.

'What I am enjoying is that Anita is at last starting to have the fun that a teenager should. You know I've always thought her too mental, and spending too much time exploring our work and theories. For the first time in her life she has a group of friends. Good friends,' she added as the two mothers exchanged smiles. 'It's Christmas, let the children have their adventure.'

At first, Viljo had played along with the boy's story, waiting for him to make a mistake. What he had just realised about the coincidence of timing had rekindled within him what he had felt whilst the boy was talking. No matter how far fetched his story, there was the possibility that he had been telling the truth. A very faint possibility. As a scientist, he owed it to his friends to establish the truth: one way or the other. He would give serious thought as to how he might achieve that. 'Innocently' playing along with the boy?

Viljo raised his glass in a gesture of acceptance. As he received an acknowledging gesture from Paavo, the two flicked their eyes sideways to their wives and smiled in silent agreement to leave well alone. The women were happy with their scheming!

Viljo's smile concealed a disturbing thought. An inevitable consequence of the theory developed by Roger Penrose of twistors, 'particles' that were so small they did not possess any spatial dimensions, was that at that minimalistic point in space, matter and information became indistinguishable.

And what was matter anyway? Merely a vast amount of information: data about mass, spin, axis of rotation, location relevant to other data, rate of decay, and much more. And that held good all the way up to the incalculable amount of data that comprised any complex living organism. He left aside the question of what his wife called 'Soul', where their discussions often become heated. However unlikely it was, he preferred the Penrose-Hameroff superpositioning theory of consciousness to Aristotle and the discredited vitalism of a past era.

If what Qwelby called kuznii was in fact the ultimate 'particle', then it had to be pure information: data. And using photons, Earth scientists had successfully transported substantial amounts of data to the Moon and back.

Whilst Hannu and Anita were taking their time to say their goodnights, the object of Dr Keskinen's confused thoughts was trying to contact his twin.

Having adjusted the mirror in the wardrobe door, Qwelby stripped and sat on the bed in the lotus position facing it. He knew it was not Mirror, and was hoping that by blurring his vision and pretending the dark body and black hair of his reflection was his twin, it might help him to reach her.

His eyes opened and he looked around the room, slowly recollecting where he was and feeling as if all the energy had been drained from his body and he was made of heavy metal. He never fell asleep like that at home. This third dimension was so very different. He slowly got under the duvet.

But he had not been asleep. He had been... deepstate working? With a red and green Lulwanulay? What would that be in Finnish?

Sleep took him.

CHAPTER 37

ANGRY PARENTS

VERTAZIA

When the initial healing had been completed and the four friends had fallen asleep after their terrifying journey to connect with Tullia, Lellia had sent short messages to their parents assuring them their children were safe and asking them to come to Lungunu at five.

With only twelve ouers in a Tazian day, 'five' meant that everyone had arrived and was comfortably settled down by mid-morning of the following day in Lellia's Spherical Room, the optimum shape for complete thoughtshielding. The floor was a normal flat surface, this time of lush green grass, the rest of the globe presenting an image of distant hills and soft clouds drifting across a blue sky.

'The youngsters made contact with both twins' energies,' Lellia said by way of introduction, and went on to explain the full detail of that contact and the images that had been seen.

'The red sand, the appearance of the men and women, the way they were morphing, we think that they must be descendents of the Auriganii who remained on Haven when the rest of our forebears came here. As you all know, the planet that the Azurii call Mars is not like that in this dimension, yet the effects all four experienced as they returned, the waterfall sensation, bodies not fitting, all indicate time travel.'

Aware of the looks of incredulity, horror, then sympathy on the parents' faces, she took a deep breath before continuing. 'They are all certain that the healing, red and green energies were coming from Qwelby. Wrenden felt a clear connection telling him that Qwelby was all right, although he was prevented from reaching him. So we think we know both are well, but not when, and only where Tullia is.'

Otrodan, Pelnak's father leant forward. 'I know what the six XzylStroems do. But I don't pretend to understand how they work. What we do know is that you can reach him that way. Why haven't you brought him back? And without involving our children.'

'Yes. Why aren't our children here?' queried Yarannah, mother of Tamina and Wrenden.

Lellia was relieved to get away from her fear that the way the four friends had experienced Qwelby meant that he was in the NoWhenWhere and beyond any help. She explained why the children were absent.

'He's in a what!' Yarannah exclaimed in dismay, when told that his injuries were so severe that her baby son, as she thought of him, was resting in a bath of Tenderest Loving Care. And that the other three had all spent the night sleeping in the kitchen.

Aware they were in a completely Privacy Shielded room and were free to vent all their emotions without any spreading into the MentaNet, they did so, vigorously. Yarannah was in a ferocious mood.

'Why did you not give him all the energy healing he needed? Lying in a bath all night, children sleeping on a kitchen floor! This is absolutely outrageous. What are you? Monsters!' Her face had gone bright red, she was shaking all over and could not continue speaking.

'We gave them all the energy healing they needed,' Lellia replied with a touch of asperity in her voice. 'Their biggest pain is in their very Selves. Allowing their bodies to take time to heal helps their Selves to recover. The others are sleeping comfortably, NOT on the floor, because all three wanted to be with Wrenden. They refused to be parted.'

Again, it was the not-twins mothers who calmed everyone down. They did not have the genetic heritage that made Quantum Twins so special. Nevertheless, as identical twins themselves, they completely understood the strong need that Tullia and Qwelby had to be mentally reunited, and the youngsters' desire to help them.

Neither the twins' parents nor Pelnak's had been happy when the relationship had formed. Yet they had to accept that their opinions were irrelevant. "Esting" as the elderest/youngerest relationships were described, happened through the activation of genes in the third segment. No-one had ever been able to figure out why. It was accepted as one of the Aurigan legacies.

The bond was usually formed as the younger of the pair was approaching the end of their ninth year. It remained strong throughout the second era and invariably continued to be a life-long bond of friendship.

The elderest acted as a sort of caring older brother or sister, helping and guiding the youngerest through each phase. The ideal age gap was considered to be between ten and eighteen months. At almost sixteen months each, the estings between Tamina and Tullia, Qwelby and Wrenden were perfect. No-one understood why Pelnak had been chosen when he was only four months older, and Qwelby tended to overpower his elderest.

It was unusual to be both a youngerest and an elderst. It was the one beef between the twins. With Qwelby and Wrenden regularly getting into trouble, Tullia's oft expressed opinion was that Qwelby was far too irresponsible to be an elderest, whereas she would have been perfect.

Shimara had no such responsibilities, yet it was inevitable that with her twin-like relationship with Pelnak, she saw herself as a bit of an elderest to Qwelby, which he playfully teased her about.

Education on Vertazia principally consisted in children exploring as they wanted from an early age, guided by their families, and with regular meetings at colleges. The choice of the latter varied as they wished. The apparently lax system worked well as through to the end of their second era youngsters were guided by their annual hormonal release cycles, most especially during their second era from the age of twelve.

In the semi hive-like interconnection of the race there was an in-built incentive. In a world of energy there was no need for money. From a very early age children learnt that failure to study and explore, or provide energy to others in some way, meant they would not acquire energy for their own needs.

It was through meeting at college that the six had become good friends, years before Tamina had become Tullia's elderst. That had been three and half years ago and the relationship between all six had been irrevocably cemented when Wrenden had become Qwelby's youngerest two years ago. The boys shared the complaint that having two, bossy, big sisters was too much for any male.

The parents of Pelnak, Shimara, Tamina and Wrenden eventually accepted that it was that deep connection, not any failing of care, that had resulted in their children moving between dimensions.

Everything that needed to be said had been said, and then repeated two or three times. There was a lull in the discussion.

Jailandur, father of Wrenden and Tamina, leant forward, twisting his hands together.

'My son, our son, is lying in your kitchen the most injured of all.' He took a deep breath. 'At home we cannot fail to see how upset he is. And how Tamina has changed and is really caring for him. We know that all six call themselves XOÑOX.' He looked at his wife.

'I am ashamed at the feelings I have expressed. The anger that

I hurled at you,' he gestured to the twins' family, 'when our children have shown how much they love the twins.' He carefully made eye contact with the parents of Shimara and Pelnak, his wife refusing to meet his gaze.

'How can we throw anger or blame at others, when we ourselves have brought up our children to be so loving that they go and demonstrate that love by putting themselves in incredible danger to help their friends?'

He got up from his chair and walked to the server where drinks were set out. He gestured to a decanter containing a dark green liquid, which poured a generous measure into a tumbler. He took a large swig.

There was general movement, pouring of drinks and quiet talking whilst everyone took time for reflection. Except for Yarannah who marched up to her husband and started a heated discussion. Eventually, it was she who virtually commanded everyone to sit down, then set out her demands.

'My two children are involved in this. Both times Wrenden has nearly died. I do NOT want them to continue searching for your children. But it seems I have no choice!' She was shaking with fury. 'There WILL be strict rules. They will NEVER go into the XzylCavern again. They will ONLY search in ways that brook no danger. They will only do that when all four are together, and they will be properly supervised.

'I am not happy to say this, but the searching must be done from here. With all the science and esoteric stuff you have, Lungunu must be, should be, far more protected than any of our ordinary houses.' She spat out those words with angry jealousy. 'Neither of MY children is to do anything without MY approval.'

There was a stunned silence, and the not-twins parents slowly nodded their heads.

'Good. Now, I'm going to see my children,' Yarannah declared as she turned and headed towards the door.

Back home, having seen the state of her children, Yarannah was fuming. She felt cornered, trapped into an agreement she did not want to make. For a time she even considered going back on her word, but knew that the reverberations throughout the MentaNet would have serious consequences. Not just reneging on a promise, but one made to youngsters during the crucial second era of their development! She imagined the arrival of a Readjuster and being "Requested to participate in an in-depth discussion."

Why do we use euphemisms for the darker side of life? To be taken away from my children when they need me the most? 'Never!' she declared aloud.

Breaking into her thoughts, the sound of her husband's irritated voice as he argued with one of the GardenCarls about its programming reminded her of the last time that Lerinda and her husband had visited. Lerinda was a Junior Readjuster who did not agree with the more extreme views of the Kumelanii. But no. This was family.

A little while later, Yarannah was surprised when Lerinda contacted her. She was mortified to discover that after leaving Lungunu her anger and dismay had been so strong she had not been able to contain her feelings within her Privacy Shield. Yet there was the consolation that as she had thought of her friend at the time, her disturbed feelings had been directed towards Lerinda rather than being spread all across the MentaNet. When Lerinda offered to hear her concerns, as a friend, Yarannah felt a burden was being lifted from her shoulders.

A long time was to pass before Yanarrah was to discover how deeply and systematically that friendship was betrayed.

CHAPTER 38

DRYDDNAA PLANS

VERTAZIA

Dryddnaa was ambitious, but in true Tazian fashion she did not consider that was for herself, but for the whole race and its future. She had always been a tall and well built girl. A little gene modification had ensured that she did not have her parents' weight problem. Now, at two metres ten, she was rightly described as statuesque. Flaming red hair which, unusually for her age, she let grow waist long. Set in the palest of blue ovals, her grey eyes were her one regret. She could not bear the thought of being called 'Grey' or, worse, 'Steel', when she became a Venerable. She was already contemplating another genetic alteration.

From an early age she had wanted to help people, mentally, and that had lead her to becoming a Readjuster. As a youngster she was considered highly promising. So much so that in spite of carrying weak residual genes from Léshmîrâ Kûsheÿnÿ, known as the Reconciler, no personal development restrictions were imposed when she achieved adulthood.

Knowing her views, her great grandmother had given her two pieces of advice: 'Never do anything to make anyone question the freedom you have been accorded as that can be taken away from you. Wait to express your own, divergent views, until you are unassailable.'

Dryddnaa's divergence was that she considered the restrictions imposed on achieving adulthood had damaged Tazian society. She believed that there was need for more exploration and creativity rather than less, and that those carrying the Reconciler genes could act as a mediating influence provided they were carefully monitored – by experienced Readjusters.

Where she agreed with some of the restrictions, even those she considered were imposed too harshly, and far too few individuals were allowed to be free or partially free of them. Through tiny increments over millennia they had been steadily increased by the Custodians. It would take centuries of painfully negotiated, small steps, to reverse the policy. That could only start by obtaining the concurrence of the overwhelming majority the Senate. She was always very careful how and to whom she expressed: not her views, but what she described as 'tentative thoughts.'

As a Chief Readjuster she was acknowledged to be one of the best in her vocation. Having been accepted as an Elder at the earliest age of one hundred and twenty, Ceegren had shortly thereafter invited her into the Inner Council. When that was queried by Gentian, a much older Venerable who was one of Ceegren's key supporters, he had replied: 'Keep your friends close, and your opponents even closer.'

With all the contretemps flowing from the twins' departure, Dryddnaa sensed that Ceegren saw an opportunity to manipulate the situation. Although successful in the Spiral Assembly through his gentle and considerate approach, nevertheless he was a hardliner, taking a firm stance on the full implementation of what he considered to be Traditionalist ways.

In return for his patronage she had to ally herself to him. But carefully, if she was to turn the situation to her advantage. She was not unassailable. One false step and she might find herself caught in a trap of her own making, with little option other than to help put plans into effect that were inimical to her own way of thinking.

To succeed, she needed information. Information from within the circle of family and friends. The four adults in the family were mentally completely free. In addition, Mandara and Lellia were highly respected Elders on their way to becoming Venerables. Given their combined skills, Dryddnaa had no doubt that whatever was spread into the MentaNet was likely to be carefully edited, if not downright sanitised.

Taking the perfectly true stance of her great concern for the twins' wellbeing and their eventual return home when cured of the Violence Virus, she visited in person several carefully chosen Readjusters. She explained that her reason for not using normal thoughtsending was to keep clear of the MentaNet so as to spare the family the embarrassment of her interest becoming widespread knowledge. Not only that Readjusters were considering eventual treatment for their children, but also the inevitable inference that it had to be the family's fault and, no matter how elevated their status, 'sympathetic visits', as she phrased it, might be necessary from a team of Readjusters.

Naturally, she discreetly emphasised the team aspect and the need for discretion in providing any information that might be help her to understand the background, and how appreciative the Counsel of Readjusters and the Senate of Custodians would be for any help in resolving the unprecedented situation.

Although personal ambition did not feature largely in Tazian society, various gifts were available. Elevation at an earlier age than normal to the higher reaches of the Profession, to the status of Elder and even to the Coordinating bodies: "Governing bodies" being another concept that the Tazii did not accept. In a society without money, the substantial energy credits that followed were tempting.

She allowed herself a wry smile that the increase in energy credits only materialised if and when the individual made the contribution to the race that was required by their new position. She would have to be very careful that none of her selections backfired.

CHAPTER 39

DAUGHTER TO A GODDESS

KALAHARI

Tullia awoke with arms and legs so leaden she could hardly move. Slowly, she became aware of sounds, voices and some words she understood. She turned her head to the side and opened her eyes. Sunlight made a small patch of light on the reddish coloured sand of the floor. Shining through the open doorway of a grey grass hut the sun had to be high in the sky.

Yesterday! The boy and girl! Her visit! The red sand. This was the Red Planet! She was on Haven!! And without Kaigii!!!

Darkness closed in and a deep sleep wrapped her in its embrace.

When she next awoke it was with a jumbled memory of dreaming. There had been knocking on a door. But there was no door. Just a grey mist that swirled about. A mist that felt like syrup each time she tried to move through it to reach... what? A sensation. Colour. That's what it was. Little beads of pink and green flowing into her. Love and healing energy. From...?

Hearing a soft sound, she opened her eyes and rolled onto her side. The patch of bright sunlight reached far into the hut. Tullia's internal clock told her that her sleep had been a long one. She had slept right through a whole day until the morning of... what? Her third actual day here. Wherever 'here' was.

A shadow moved. She looked up. Tsetsana was peering though the doorway, the young girl's aura showed she was excited and nervous.

'Dumela, Mma Tooleear.'

'Busana Tsetsana,' Tullia replied. She replayed the words that Tsetsana had spoken, assuming 'Dumela Mma' meant 'Good morning.'

Slowly Tullia got out of bed and Tsetsana showed her the bowl of water just inside the entrance and a towel she was holding. The young girl stood with downcast eyes as Tullia slipped out of her night covering and had a quick wash in the very cold water.

As Tullia took the proffered towel she heard Tsetsana gasp. Looking up, Tullia saw eyes as round as saucers above a wide open mouth. She looked down at her body, and grimaced. Her body, arms and legs were a patchwork of bright red marks looking like flames. They seemed to be in the same places as the lilac patches on her bodysuit. *The journey through that tunnel. These red splotches look like radiation burns.*

'Hiechware?' Tsetsana asked.

Tullia looked blank. There was no translation.

'Hoachana?' Tsetsana tried naming another of the San tribes with distinctive reddish-brown colouring.

Again Tullia could not respond, except to shrug her shoulders and spread her hands.

Late morning and already the day was warm. Tullia realised that clothing was going to be a problem. Her bodysuit was much too warm. Normally when she arrived at Lungunu she would have taken it off. That day she had kept it on because it was new, the latest style and in her favourite colours.

With all the people in the village wearing lots of thick winter clothing, several also wrapped in blankets, she felt uncomfortable wearing what girls did underneath a bodysuit: hotpants and a little top. Her choice that last day had been an embroidered, turquoise, camisole top and hotpants. However much Quantum Twins needed to be alike, and often wore unisex clothing, she was a girl and they were in the era of establishing their own identities.

With gestures and Tullia learning new words, Tsetsana eventually left the hut to return with a collection of clothes of different sizes. Finally, Tullia was comfortably dressed in a pale blue tank top and a short, brown skirt: all she needed for what was to her warm weather. She sat down to eat in the shade outside the hut.

Tullia's stomach was telling her that it did not want much food. She thought that not eating it all might be the wrong thing to do, so was happy to offer to share with Tsetsana.

Recovering from her surprise, and scared of offending a Goddess, Tsetsana shyly accepted. As they ate in silence, she felt herself relaxing. The Sun Goddess seemed quite human. But for her heavily slanted and unusually coloured eyes, with her size and colour she could almost be a Himba, or an unusually large San.

They finished eating and Tsetsana took away the plate and water jug. When she returned she spoke a few words and spread her hands apart indicating the village.

Tullia thought she was being asked if she would like to look around. 'Kabona,' she responded, getting up from the upended tree trunk on which she had been sitting.

Hoping she was guessing correctly what Tullia wanted, Tsetsana took them around the village, not knowing what to say to a goddess who must know everything. Slowly, she realised that this Goddess did not know everything, and also was having to learn the language of the Meera. *Perhaps that's why she has come to us, to learn about us and our ways?* She felt a shiver of excitement run through her at the realisation that she, Tsetsana, was teaching a goddess.

Tullia was becoming increasingly puzzled why everyone seemed to be holding her at a distance, and glancing strangely at Tsetsana.

Walking outside the village, Tullia found a large hole and jumped into it, looking for what she thought was the entrance to a burrow. In response to her questioning gestures, her compiler provided 'big food' and 'we eat.'

The sand around the edge was very soft. She held out a hand for support as she got out, and felt a lovely, soft energy flow from Tsetsana, along with a strong feeling of amazement. That was so Tazian that Tullia dwelt on the sensation and decided the amazement was because she, so tall, was seeking help from the diminutive Meera.

Although the impressions were very weak, they were such a delightful similarity to Tullia's normal life that she continued holding Tsetsana's hand for the rest of their walk. The puzzle as to why she sensed pride and honouring as well as happiness added to Tullia's desire to learn their language quickly. She had so many questions to ask.

CHAPTER 40

A COUNCIL MEETING

KALAHARI

The man that Tullia thought of as Wiseman approached as the two girls returned to Tullia's hut.

'Mma Tullia, my name is Xameb.' He pointed to himself.

Tullia nodded and tried to repeat his name: 'Click-ameb,' feeling embarrassed as Tsetsana giggled.

Xameb gestured for them to sit, and patiently coached Tullia in what he said were called 'click sounds' that the San used. As he coached her in the first sound of his name, she decided it was like what she would use to say 'gee up' to a horse or donkey, but from both sides of the mouth at once.

Finally, Tullia pronounced the double 'click' sound correctly, which made the 'ah' sound follow on perfectly. She flashed him a big smile of joy.

Over the following days as her complier built the translations she discovered that the San had never developed a written language of their own. Experts from other counties had come and written down what they heard, using their own spelling and conventions for the 'click' sounds.

Yesterday, it had seemed to Xameb that Tullia was a young woman, several years older than Xashee's sixteen, probably a human being and not the daughter of the Goddess Nananana. Now he was confused.

Part of the time she seemed like a young girl, embarrassed, even shy. Yet now that she had got the pronunciation right and he sensed her relaxing, he was aware of a powerful energy flowing from her. Yesterday, he had dismissed the shimmering all around her as merely an effect on his eyes of her brightly patterned clothes. Now, wearing simple plain colours, he accepted he was seeing her aura, stronger than he had ever seen on anyone.

Even so, there was a strong sensation of youthfulness. He had never thought of a 'Daughter of the Goddess' as being just that. The concept of a young Goddess had never entered his mind.

As his thoughts returned, he realised that they were waiting for him to speak. Tullia had tilted her head to one side with a look on her face as though she was reading his thoughts. *Perhaps she can, if she is indeed the Daughter of the Goddess Nananana.* He smiled and broke eye contact. It had been a little unsettling.

With gestures and a few words, he invited Tullia to accompany him to meet with several other people.

He was thinking hard as they walked together. Whilst Siskas were the friendliest of all the extra-terrestrials, he had never heard of one that was this friendly and approachable. She had even responded to his healing touch as well as any of his villagers. In fact, when he thought about it, he realised that she had responded faster than any of his own people ever had.

And now she was already conversing a little in the language of their tribe. What age to put on her? Did that even matter? She could be a hundred years old, yet young for a Goddess. He had a lot to think about.

As with all the San tribes, the Meera did not have a council of elders, or any form of leadership apart from the village headman.

Ghadi had thought carefully about how they should treat such a distinguished guest and who should be involved. He had decided on a small group to include his wife Kotuma, Xameb and a few others who had specific responsibilities.

As Tullia reached the small group of men and women seated on colourful blankets, they all rose. Xameb invited Tullia to sit on a thick cushion. As they all settled down cross-legged, she smiled to herself at yet another similarity. Although not as bright as hers, they all had pink soles to their feet.

Again with gestures and words, Xameb introduced Ghadi and his wife. Tullia found herself relaxing as her initial assumption made from the shorter man's energy field that he was the leader was confirmed.

Ghadi began to speak. A stockily built man, a full head shorter than Tullia, as well as the leader he was also the tribe's most skilled and powerful healer. She was even more aware than at her first meeting that his presence and stature came from his innate nature and energy. That was a comfortable similarity to life on Vertazia.

Tullia started to relax as she understood the general sense of what he was saying. As well as some of his words being translated, she was reading his energy field. As that happened it seemed that she heard more of his words in Tazian. What was most reassuring was that the words matched the colours swirling through his aura. *So like at home!* She managed to choke back the tears that were threatening.

When Ghadi finished talking, Tullia went inside herself and ran through her mind the Tazian words she had heard, and recalled his energy flows. She was fairly confident she had understood that they considered her to be a very important visitor and were honoured by her arrival. *That explains the awe, but why the fear? I will keep this very simple and hope the compiler has learnt enough!*

'Thank you, your words, welcome.' *I think that came out okay.* 'I thank you, food and water.' She turned to Xameb. 'How say you name.'

She stopped. She could not think of what more to say that her compiler might be able to translate. She could see that they were taken aback by her use of their language. That was not the reaction she wanted!

'Where am I?' burst from her lips, as she struggled to hold back her tears of frustration. She saw the stunned expressions on their faces.

After what seemed like an age, Xameb replied. 'We are Meera tribe of San.' He gestured all around with his arm. 'We live in Kalahari which means "Land Of Great Thirst".'

She nodded, deciding that she would use their word for their planet: Kalahari. It was shorter and she liked the sound as the 'r' was trilled. In shock, her mind numb, she assumed the whole planet was a desert, was not Earth, and had to be Haven.

How? Where is Kaigii?

Struggling to control her thoughts and not break down, and with her strong aura extending well beyond her clothes, her excited energy field made her appear to be made entirely of flames. Taking a deep breath, she calmed herself and the flames lessened.

'You want know where Tullia from?' She saw a variety of different emotions flooding through their energy fields as they nodded. As she unwound her legs she discovered she was shaking. On hands and knees she crawled the short distance to the area of clear sand in the centre of the circle.

Using her long fingers, she drew a circle, on top of which she drew a hut and asked for the name of the village. Xameb wrote that down alongside the hut. Drawing in the soft sand was easy, but it was proving too difficult draw the two worlds in the same place. She settled for drawing the two planets separately, with lines radiating from one as she tried to explain that she came from there.

As she continued to draw, she was surprised at how easily they understood the concepts and started a discussion amongst themselves. They easily accepted that she came from another planet that wanted to be friends with the people on Kalahari. They discussed ancestors, and she explained that her people were not their ancestors. Then she remembered that the Auriganii had settled for a while on Haven, the fourth planet from the sun, and began to wonder whether these people were descendants of those Auriganii who had not moved to Vertazia.

The lifestyle of the Meera village was firmly rooted in the past. It served as a basis for research into the traditional lives of the San, for the San themselves as a way of maintaining their historic traditions, and as a tourist venue, with visitors staying in the nearby Tourist Village.

As a result, there were no physical reference points for language outside of the Meera's very simple lifestyle. Her compiler was struggling with the different syntax of three languages and, particularly as a result of the very different concepts inherent in Aurigan, mistranslations abounded. Amongst others, the Tazian for 'planet' became 'sun' in Meera. When Tullia later discovered that the word for 'sun' sounded the same, she was not surprised. Many Tazian words sounded the same as each other, the accompanying thoughts providing the appropriate meaning.

As they started to talk again, she held up her hand. They fell silent as she drew some more, explaining about Kaigii, her twin. 'He is with tall trees. And,' she wrapped her arms around herself and shivered.

The Meera nodded and smiled.

She drew them a picture of a tree which was totally unlike anything any of the villagers had ever seen before. With her compiler storing in her brain an ever increasing number of words, and their obvious interest and understanding, she tried to explain how she had arrived on Kalahari. She was amazed from their reactions that what appeared to be a simple, even primitive village community that was in the middle of nowhere and with no signs of any technology seemed to understand what she was trying to explain. She rationalised that it had to be their Aurigan legacy.

Fortunately for Tullia she was unaware of the impression she was creating. With her aura still very excited and the red, flame-like patches all over her constantly moving arms and legs, she looked as though she was on fire. Added to that were her hands. Compared to Tamina's dancer's hands, Tullia never considered her fingers especially long or supple, yet as she drew and gesticulated, to the Meera they appeared to be very flames themselves. And when her eyes twirled: a Sun Goddess with eyes of purple fire.

Scrabbling around on hands and knees, drawing in the sand with a look of fierce concentration on her face and her long, bright pink tongue waggling out of the corner of her mouth, smiling as she learnt more of their language, the Meera saw a happy child. A veritable Daughter of the Sun Goddess.

That was confirmation of what they had understood her to be explaining with the two circles she had drawn at the beginning, showing that she came from inside. Her mother was the sun and, as her daughter, naturally she had been born from within her mother's body. Now she was explaining how she had travelled on a ray of sunlight. And of course she came from another reality where she existed as pure fire.

Slowly and carefully Xameb explained that the hills of Behengo she had seen on her arrival were where the Gods had rested after they had created the whole planet. And that they still lived within those hills. It was as if Gallia was speaking from within Gumma's body. *Admittedly,* she said thought to herself, *a Gumma that was a lot slimmer!* Nevertheless, it was a comforting, Tazian quirk.

Tullia was fascinated. Her people knew how the multiverse was created through science. Thinking about their history of the journey through space looking for a new home, she nodded to herself as she guessed the ten great Tazian Heroes and Heroines, Uddîšû as they called them, had to be similar to what the Meera were calling ancestors or Gods.

Seeing Tullia nodding her understanding as though she knew the Gods; it was all so clear to Xameb. The Sun Goddess and the Sun God were the two halves of the sun: twins. Their children were twins who one day would be the two halves of the sun. And so on throughout all time.

There was silence. With a start, Tullia realised that she had closed her eyes. She looked up, feeling embarrassed.

Ghadi leant forward. There were no titles in the language of the Meera. 'Mma' was merely a polite form of address for a married or mature woman. He decided that was insufficient for a Goddess who he feared was about to burst into flames at any moment.

'Great Lady, Daughter of the Sun Goddess, we are honoured by your visit. We offer help to find the Great Lord Sun God Kaigii.'

Tullia's compiler was having serious problems linking appropriate words and concepts between the two languages. She was struggling to accept what she was hearing. Being addressed as 'KulaKesaa' as if she were a Venerable and referred to as the planet's Uddîsû. An image came into her mind of an WrapperEnactment. She had been the Aurigan Ambassador, wearing an outrageously gorgeous robe and headdress, the whole outfit flickering with changing colours. In front of her the planet's ruler was bowing low, holding out his hands and offering her a bejewelled goblet from which both would drink as a sign of friendship.

The compiler seized on the image and 'honoured by your visit' became 'Honoured Ambassador.' And the references to Qwelby were naturally translated as 'KosiKosuu' for a Venerable, and again as the planet's Uddîsû.

It was all too much. Tullia lowered her head as she sort to repress her smile at being addressed as if she were over one hundred and forty-four years old. The amusement relieved her tensions, and she dwelt for a moment in the comforting memory of the WrapperEnactment.

A feeling stole though her. She was receiving from the Meera a sensation as if she was in a KiddyLiveShow, where the young audience believed her to be the Heroine, and she had to act out that role. Looking up, she saw energies of relief and expectancy. Glancing around she saw that what looked like the whole village was clustered around the huts, and just far enough away not to overhear conversation at an ordinary level.

The Meera in the circle around her were relieved. Tullia's regal inclination of her head had told them that their leader's words were acceptable. And they saw that her energy had calmed and she no longer looked as though she was about to bust into flames and destroy the village.

Tullia realised that she was required to reply. Her head was bursting from all the language she was learning. Her mind went blank. All she could think of was the greeting she had given the previous day, and it seemed safest to return to them the words they had used.

Taking a deep breath and full of nerves, she sought strength by imaging that Ambassadorial role, stood up, brought her palms together in front of her heart, bowed her head and lifted her head back up. As she formed the Tazian words in her mind, she swept her arms down, unaware that her imaging and movement once again made it look as though she was on fire.

Feeling very much as if she was in a LiveShow, she remembered to speak clearly. In a steady voice which surprised her, the Meera heard in a beautiful, deep, rich contralto: 'I, Tullia, Great Kehsa Sun Goddess, Honoured Ambassador to Kalahari, thank you for your welcome and offer of help.' It was embarrassing to describe herself as if she were an Uddîšû. Had she known the compiler was translating that as 'Sun Goddess', she would have corrected that, very rapidly.

The group clapped their hands as they smiled and nodded.

Towering over them, Tullia felt as if she was receiving the audience's appreciation. She smiled with happiness that, once again, she had managed to say the right thing. Without thinking, she inclined her head as if on stage.

A sigh went around all the Meera, not only had they had felt the power in her imaging, unknowingly, they had absorbed it. Seeing her on fire again, this time they had realised that it was not threatening but a display of her natural power. Now, seeing the smile splitting her face from ear to ear and feeling her happiness, they knew beyond any doubt that she was the young daughter of the Sun Goddess. The gracious inclination of her head had shown that she had accepted her due and was dismissing them.

Why she was lost was a puzzle. And that was for their Shaman to solve, if and when the Goddess so wished. They rose, picked up their blankets, and moved off in different directions.

Tullia felt immense relief. She had played her part, the part they required of an Extra Terrestrial, the audience had applauded, and left. It was to be some time before she discovered that the applause had not been for any performance, but was the Meera's way of showing that she had touched their hearts.

With her head pounding, Tullia needed to be by herself and in the open. She walked out of the village and into the bush, noting the position of the sun.

It was some time before she saw the tops of very different trees, and made her way to them. The three Mongongos towered high up into the sky. She wrapped her arms as far as possible around the trunk of the largest tree.

'I must learn their language quickly and explain who I really am,' she said. 'Please help me find peace, or my head is going to burst wide open.'

At the foot of their rich, grey trunks was a small area bathed in sunshine and clear of spiky bushes. She settled down to meditate.

The clearing and especially what she thought of as Mother Tree was to become her favourite place for being by herself.

CHAPTER 41

CONFUSION

KALAHARI

Tullia awoke feeling relaxed and surprised. She never fell asleep when meditating! She got up, brushed sand off herself and her clothes, and rested her forehead against Mother Tree. *Thank you,* she thoughtsent. Although it was a windless day she heard the rustle of its leafless branches.

Checking the height and angle of the sun, she headed back to the village. As she entered the small gate by her hut, Tsetsana approached.

'You gone long time. I was worried, Great Kehsa,' was what Tullia heard.

'I sleep with big trees,' Tullia replied with a smile.

'How did you find your way back here?' Tsetsana asked, in a surprised tone of voice.

'The sun,' Tullia replied, gesturing to it. And wondered why Tsetsana went bright red and her aura flared with embarrassment. Not realising that the girl was cursing herself for her stupidity and, at the same time, Tullia was confirming the tribe's belief in who she was. Naturally, the daughter of the Sun Goddess had asked the sun.

Tullia walked on to the Shaman's hut. Xameb was sitting

outside on a blanket. He rose, gestured, and they sat down together.

He had spoken with Tsetsana about her morning with Tullia. Influenced in particular by what Tsetsana said had been Tullia's horror at seeing the flame-like markings all over her body, he felt he understood Tullia's mixture. She was a powerful Goddess who responded as such when approached formally. Yet, in her world she was a young woman and wanted the Meera to see her like that. He would approach her as it appeared she wanted, but carefully.

'Will you tell me how I may help you find your twin, or...' he gestured around them. 'As you are here, will you walk the path of my people?'

Relief flooded through Tullia. For once in her life she wanted someone else to take charge and tell her what to do. And she liked his energy field. He was not afraid of her, although she saw a strong measure of respect.

The more they talked, the more Tullia's excitement increased. As Gumma had explained, the compiler was reading her thoughts and memory recalls and associating them with Xameb's words. She hoped it was doing that correctly as she explained that her people had no knowledge of gods or goddesses, instead, they relied on quantum science and the sometimes almost human manner in which it operated.

'It seems to me the deep ways of our two worlds are very similar. We are only using different words to describe the same things,' Xameb said.

'I was thinking the same.'

'Please explore the Tsodilo Hills. If you open to a deep connection with energies of this land, you will have a strong base from which to reach out to your twin. You understand?'

'Oh yes. That is like at home. Anything to connect with Kaigii.'

'Good. I will speak with Xashee. He takes tourists there, knows the paths well and our history.'

'May Tsetsana come?' Tullia asked.

Xameb smiled and nodded.

The sun was setting as Tullia returned to her hut. She saw Tsetsana coming towards her, bursting with curiosity, but reluctant to come too close.

'Not now, Tsetsana, I'm tired.' *Neutrinos! I didn't mean to sound so sharp.*

Tsetsana immediately looked down on the ground. 'I am sorry. I did not mean to upset the Sun Goddess.'

Tullia frowned at being addressed as "Uddîšû." She gave a deep sigh as she accepted that she had been given various titles, and had to learn to put them on when other people used them. It was similar to the time she had taken several small parts in an KeyPoint LiveShow.

The contrast stopped her thoughts with a jolt. *This IS 'First Contact'. I AM an extra-terrestrial. I AM like an ambassador. If they knew about quarks, twistors, XzylStroems: and Ing! If I could tell them, they would think I'm even stranger than an Uddîšû.*

She gave another deep sigh and saw Tsetsana glance at her, and almost shrink inside herself. *She thinks this is all her fault. I can't cope with all this!* Her legs went weak. Drained of all energy she staggered and held out a hand towards the young Meera.

Tsetsana reacted instinctively and stepped forward. Being so much taller than the Meera, Tullia had to bend down to put her arm over Tsetsana's shoulders.

Inside the hut, Tullia flopped down on the bed and made faint gestures. Tsetsana was awed at what she was doing for a goddess and at the same time puzzled. She could see she was helping a woman much taller and bigger than herself, but it felt as if she was holding someone the size of her seven-year old sister, Nthabe. Eventually, she got Tullia into her night robe and tucked her into bed.

Too much was going through Tullia's mind to let her fall asleep. She knew the Tazian third segment structured learning cycles in a precise manner, most especially during the second era between their twelfth and twenty-fourth rebirthdays. As hormones were released in a very specific progression, so youngsters were able to access increasing inner awareness and delve deeper into the knowledge that was held in the Collective and their own third segment. Now, Qwelby and herself were in the fourth phase of their second era: exploring the wider meaning of home and roots.

She sat up, stifling a little cry with her hand. Was this it? 'The Mystery' as they thought of it. The reason for Quantum Twins? Was that why she was with the descendants of the Auriganii – in the third dimension – to link them with the Azurii through Qwelby? Restoring an Aurigan 'home' by spearheading the reunification of the two races? Tazii and Azurii. They would have to slide through dimensions. In their real bodies. And go home!

Forgetting, she reached for her twin and almost cried aloud at the fierce stab of pain through her mind. Clutching her head she fell back onto the bed and lay there looking through the open doorway, over the other huts and into the millions of stars twinkling in the night sky.

Steadily, she disciplined herself only to think about her twin and where he was as if he were a separate person. Their normal inner communication meant going to the empty corner in her mind. Too much pain. Trying to reconnect through meditation was different. That was outside their internal relationship. *If I focus first on Wrenden, then image Qwelby alongside him...* She smiled wryly at the idea of using Qwelby's irresponsible youngerest as a helper.

The energies here are so like at home, although much weaker, and there's a lot about their energy fields I don't understand, but I know that Xameb does understand. I feel it. I see it in his aura. He will help. As that knowledge steadied her and the pain in her head turned into its usual dull ache of absence, she rolled onto her side, curled up into a tight ball and fell asleep.

CHAPTER 42

A COVER STORY

FINLAND

School holidays, late nights, lots of excitement, the children slept late. By the time they came down for breakfast on Wednesday morning, Paavo was at work on the ski slopes, leaving his wife to explain.

'Last night all four of us agreed. We will not tell the police or anyone about Qwelby. Well, that is who you are or how you got here.' She saw him looking puzzled. 'And we need to find a way to explain you.'

'Why?' he asked.

'No-one must know you're an alien,' Hannu said, taking over the conversation.

Relieved of the responsibility, Seija got up from the table, telephoned Taimi Keskinen, and got on with her morning chores.

'But why?' asked Qwelby. 'You all know where I come from.'

'They'll want to take you away, experiment on you,' Hannu explained.

'They're not all like my Dad,' added Anita.

'But we won't let them,' Hannu said firmly.

'So, let's plan,' Anita added, tapping the table.

By the time that Paavo returned from work and the Keskinens arrived for lunch, the youngsters had prepared their plans. Viljo was reluctantly dragged into the planning by his daughter's suggestion.

'Mmh,' Viljo grunted, turning to look at Qwelby. 'Dr Jadrovic has just gone back to his home country. It was an opportunity that came up at the very last minute and was too good to refuse.' He took a deep breath, blew it out. 'Anita's right. We could say that a holiday had been planned and, as he didn't want to disappoint his son, you'd agreed he could stay with you.' He looked at the Rahkamos.

'He was planning to bring his family here', Taimi added. 'He'd asked me to speak with his wife and tell her what it's like. That's not happening now.'

'That's perfect,' Anita said. 'That'll explain why Qwelby's been learning Finnish. Ready to go to school here.'

'As he's on holiday, we'll have to take him round and show him all sorts of things,' Hannu added with excitement. 'Qwelby, you did say you've skied and skated on Vertazia?'

'Oh, yes. I like both.'

'Hold on a moment,' interjected Viljo. 'There's one thing you need to understand. All three of you. Whatever country you've come from, Qwelby, you are already speaking Finnish well. And with a perfect accent. If I understand what is happening, you will be speaking it better as each day passes?'

Qwelby nodded. 'Yes. I am already starting to understand Finnish.'

'You?' Hannu queried. 'I thought your translator...'

'No. It doesn't work like that. It just stores the words and the way of using them in my brain. A mixture of a dictionary and a grammar.'

'Think simply!' exclaimed Anita.

Qwelby looked at her. 'Ah, you mean like a young child?'

'Exactly!' Hannu said.

'All the time?' Qwelby looked unhappy.

'No,' Viljo said. 'With all of us here you can speak normally. But with everyone else. Speak simply.'

'Why?' Qwelby was very puzzled.

'We can't learn a language as quickly as you. There are many people here on Earth who will want to take you away and experiment on you to discover the truth about you.' Unaware of it, Viljo was reinforcing Qwelby's fear of 'The Authorities'.

'Okay, Viljo, it looks as though you have to fill Qwelby in with his background,' Paavo said.

'Dr Jadrovitch is Czech,' Viljo replied. 'I don't remember if he told me where he grew up.'

'That doesn't matter, Dr Keskinen,' Hannu said, seizing the initiative. 'We find a small village in a far corner of the Czech Republic. Search on the internet for some basic information. Qwelby talks about his home as if it was that village. The important thing is that Qwelby speaks so little Finnish he cannot say much.'

'All that I can understand,' said Seija with a smile. 'But Qwelby doesn't sound like a Czech name.'

'He can have 'Newman' for his family name,' proffered Anita. 'Obvious really, isn't it?'

Qwelby chuckled. 'I like it. At least that is true, in a way.'

'I know 'new man' is chelovek novy in Russian. But what in Czech?' asked Hannu.

'Člověknový,' was Anita's swift response. 'And Kopecký for his first name. It is a real name. It means Hill and he arrived here on a hill.'

Qwelby looked upset. 'But my name is Qwelby.'

'That's okay,' explained Anita. 'We can say that Qwelby is your nick-name. You've chosen it because you don't like being called "A hill".'

'You've got it all planned, haven't you,' Taimi said in admiration.

Anita smiled and nodded. 'Yes. I was thinking all last night.'

'Okay,' said Paavo bringing the attention of the three children back to him. 'You understand what Dr Keskinen has said. You, Qwelby, must be very careful how you speak to other people. And you two must remember he is Czech...'

'Right, Dad. Got it. Can we go skiing now?' Hannu interrupted.

Paavo looked at his watch. 'There's less than two hours of daylight left.' He glanced around the other adults. 'All right. And Qwelby, remember. Try not to speak at all today. Just listen. Okay?'

Qwelby nodded, his seriousness making him look a lot older.

'Your eyes!' Anita exclaimed. She had been watching Qwelby, fascinated by how he changed so much, telegraphing all his feelings especially through the shading of the colours in his eyes. 'You'll need to keep your ski goggles on all the time,' she explained. 'Shame,' she added at the thought of the almost hypnotic quality being shut away.

'I've got a pair you can have,' Paavo said. 'They're quite dark.'

'And you two,' Viljo said looking at the two Finns. 'Remember. Speak simply to him!'

'Yes, Dad, we understand!' Anita confirmed.

'Yes, Dr Keskinen,' said Hannu, trying to look serious as he jiggled with excitement. Who knew what powers "his Alien" had!

The two fathers shared a look, turned and nodded to their children.

'Thanks Dad,' the youngsters cried in unison, leaping to their feet.

'I've got an old pair of boots should fit you,' Hannu announced as the two boys ran up the stairs.

'Meet you there,' shouted Anita as she dashed into the lobby, heading for her coat, boots and home.

Qwelby's eyes lit up. As he followed Hannu up to his room the thought of action swept away his feeling of unhappiness at the deception, and put to the back of his mind the problem of how he could possibly talk about his home as if it were on Earth!

After dinner the three gathered in Hannu's room and they had a long talk about deception. Between them they agreed that Qwelby was playing a game. The rules forbade him from speaking his own language; he had to tell as few outright lies as possible and being 'economical with the truth' as Hannu put it, was a specific requirement. Even so, Qwelby was very unhappy as it was such a big conflict with the whole of his life and Tazian values.

Failure in a game on Vertazia would have little consequence beyond an almost certain and usually embarrassing forfeit, especially if Tamina had a chance to get her own back on himself or Wrenden for all the tricks they played on her. Whilst it had been made very clear that failure in this game could have very nasty consequences, he had serious doubts that he could consistently tell untruths for very long. On top of that was the worry about making an innocent slip of the tongue. Speak like a little child made sense!

'You must think about Tullia a lot,' Anita said.

Qwelby shook his head. *How to explain?*

His friends felt the room grow cold as Qwelby's purple centres disappeared and the ovals of his eyes turned pale violet. The room warmed as his eyes returned to normal. But he looked old and haggard.

'I'm only half here, on the surface of your world,' he replied. 'All the energy connections I'm used to. None of them are here.' He did not mention their auras, they were so weak compared with Tazian fields and a lot of the time he had difficulty understanding them. 'Without Tullia in my mind, I'm only half complete. So I'm only a quarter here. And that quarter is desperately trying to focus on functioning in your strange world.' He waved his hands.

'It's made worse by the fact that so much of the simple, solid stuff is what we've seen in flikkers, and is not a lot different from what we have at home. Knives, forks, cups, skis. For a moment my mind can blur and I think I'm visiting family who work with the Shakazii. They try to live more like you.' He sighed. There was too much to explain and without Tullia he did not have the energy.

'Not having her in my mind is like a permanent ache. I have thought about her a couple of times. Big mistake! I flick to her corner in my mind and that ache becomes a fierce pain.'

'Your parents. A rescue?' Hannu asked.

Again the room went cold whilst Qwelby thought.

'Skiing today has been totally different from at home because working with energy is not possible. I came down that simple, little hill, what you call a baby slope. My focus on what I was doing was so intense I was not aware of anything else. My vision a straight line to the bottom. Somebody could have crashed into me and I would not have known until it happened!

'At home I would know where everyone else is and what they are doing. I would not have to judge the quality of the snow and have to think of the difference that makes to how to turn and stop. I would know!'

He stopped talking as he realised he was almost shouting in his frustration. He took a few deep breaths to calm himself.

'My whole life here is like that. Focus on the here and now.' He paused, looking at his friends' faces and auras. He saw acknowledgement, if not understanding.

'Thinking of home, parents, rescue. That's like the other people on the ski slope. I dare not take my mind of the here and now. When we are together, then I, we, will be able to think of other things.'

Qwelby settled into bed later that night with mixed feelings. In spite of skiing being difficult, with everything so solid and unresponsive that he felt like a beginner, Hannu and Anita were becoming good friends. He could not even go to Kaigii's corner of his mind and share his deep concern with her. *Oh, Kaigii, where are you? I miss you.* He winced as pain stabbed through his head. If he told her that she would ask what was wrong with him. He could almost hear the scorn in her voice. He would give all his remaining years of energy credits from his studying to hear it!

Leaving the light on, he rolled over to go to sleep. He wasn't afraid of the dark itself but he didn't want to be plunged into a nightmare by all the thoughts that he knew were waiting in the shadows. The most worrying was an opposing mixture of fear of being attacked if he left the house by himself, the thought of how to make better use of what he had learnt when he and Wrenden copied Tamina's dance movements, and a scary sense that somehow he already knew.

Yet there was one consolation. He was aware that thoughtsending did not work like on Vertazia, but something did. As he was telling his story with passion and feeling, he had seen from the way their energy fields were responding that he was taking all his listeners with him. As he sank into himself his Intuition provided the answer. Through his voice they had received his thoughts, images and feelings. He was able to thoughtwrap Azurii!

He sat up with a jerk, wide awake. Was this it? 'The Mystery.' A clue to the purpose of Quantum Twins? Were they destined to live on Earth? Spearhead the reunification of the two races? Be a bridge to the Auriganii on Haven? Flying between the two planets would mean dimension shifting... and the ability to go home!

He reached for Tullia and almost cried aloud at the fierce stab of pain. Feeling sweat break out all over his body he held his head in his hands and sagged back against the pillows. A kaleidoscope of images assailed him.

Too much. Too much...

CHAPTER 43

TULIA
EXPLORES
KALAHARI

Tullia awoke to her fourth day with the Meera feeling muzzy from half-recalled dreams. At some point she was sure she had seen a girl with a pink face and long, blonde hair. As she tried to remember more, she had the strange feeling that she had seen the girl before. Then she remembered the plans for the day. She was going to visit the Tsodilo Hills with their interesting energy. The first step in creating a meditation link with Kaigii.

Before her mind took her thoughts to the empty corner of her mind, she pictured Wrenden. The two boys were inseparable, and forever in trouble no matter how much she and Tamina tried to organise them. Imaging Wrenden was good, because Kaigii would be in the background, safely outside her internal link with him.

Out of bed, a quick wash in cold water and into a tank top and shorts. Although it was still chilly, for her the day would soon become comfortably warm, whereas as she joined Xashee and Tsetsana they were dressed for what was to them another cold day.

Although the hills were not very tall, the highest being about four hundred metres above the desert, she found the paths were not easy with lots of rocks and boulders in the way. The more she was shown, the more she was in awe of the hundreds of paintings that covered the hills. She could not find words to describe them. Magnificent, stunning, beautiful, did not convey the energy they exuded.

'Lots of people from other countries have come here and dug up parts of the desert. They've made lots of measurements, trying to estimate how old the paintings are.' Xashee shrugged his shoulders. 'It doesn't matter if they are thirty thousand years old, fifty thousand, or some say seventy. The paintings were created by our ancestors to honour the Gods who created the world and everything that lives in it.'

As Xashee explained the various paintings to her, Tullia found the one of the whales and penguins the most amazing of all, in the middle of the desert, hundreds of kilometres from the sea and thousands of kilometres from the cold seas in which penguins traditionally lived.

Later that day she was taken to what was called the Female Hill. There, Xashee showed her a giant footprint, centimetres deep in the rock. 'That is the mark made by the Creator God as the first man was lowered onto our world,' he said. 'That's why the Hills are known as the Mountains of the Gods.'

He glanced at his sister, and gave a tiny shake of his head. He was not going to say anything about the Serpent or the Cave. Tullia either knew or she did not.

Tullia stood in the depression, wondering. Xashee had told her that the San had come to Kalahari about seventy thousand years ago, and outsiders had found what they needed in the way of evidence to prove that. What were then the Aurignii had arrived on Vertazia about seventy five thousand years ago, after staying on Haven for a time. She knew Time was very different in different dimensions, but not how that worked. Was it possible that these people were the descendents of the few Aurignii who had not left Haven? Goose pimples ran all across her skin and the red patches flared uncomfortably hot.

Tullia was in a dream as they made their way back down the hillside. On top of the energy of the Hills she had been absorbing all day there had been a special feel as she stood in the footprint. She did not know what it was, but was aware that it was triggering a response from deep inside her. She felt energy spiralling along the two channels either side of her spine.

The path was narrow and there was a long drop to the desert floor. Half of her mind was carefully watching where she was putting her feet and hands, the other half was wondering how she would answer if she was asked about her life as the Daughter of a Goddess.

She thought: *Tell the truth. They would never understand it!*

With a shiver and an empty feeling in the pit of her stomach, she realised just how far away she was from home and how different life here was compared to Vertazia. Worst of all, the space where Qwelby usually lived in her mind was still blank.

Determined not to cry, she stood still and took several deep breaths to calm her nerves. Resting one hand on the rock face at the side of the path she turned to look out across the land. On this side of the hills it was more like a desert than the bush. Switching her vision, she looked at the lines of the planet's magnetic field. A childlike sense of awe at the hidden beauty of the planet as she switched between the two visions took her back to when she was learning how to switch perceptions. Lost in thought, she ran the fingers of one hand through her long, black hair and flicked it across her chest, watching the green sparkles from the interplay with the magnetic field.

Now, she felt the land embracing her with its energy, and understood what Xameb meant by rooting herself into it so as to draw on that energy to help reconnect with Kaigii. The whole landscape shimmered as if with heat haze and turned into what she thought of as a real desert: great sand dunes like waves in the sea marching to the distant horizon. Deep within herself she sensed the new vision was calling to her. She shivered as the dunes disappeared and once again ran her finger though her hair, this time flicking it back over her shoulders.

Further ahead and below, her two guides had turned to see if Tullia was alright. As they looked up, they saw a tall and imposing figure standing very erect, her hand resting on the rock as though she owned the hills. Staring into space with her hair reaching down to her waist and framing her head against the pale blue sky, Tullia seemed to be reaching out to other Gods. As she ran her fingers through her hair, green lights flickered along its length.

Tsetsana trembled. It was her dream again. Shimmering green highlights had been in that Siska's hair. It must have been Tullia visiting her, foretelling her arrival. Not to Xameb their N-'om K"xausi, but to her!

What did it mean? Was she being asked to be a special friend to a Goddess? One day she hoped to be taken by Xameb as his student, and become a Sangoma. But now, surely she was too young, too inexperienced. Was that why in the dream the Siska, Tullia, had worn the traditional clothes worn only by older girls and unmarried women, as if to say that even though she was a Sun Goddess, she was similar to Tsetsana?

She wanted to tell her brother of her dream. Yet each time she had been going to, something had happened to prevent her. Should she tell him now?

'Walk on,' Xashee said. 'It's not right to look at the Goddess like this.'

All sound had stopped and the gentle breeze no longer tickled her skin. Tullia's consciousness was in-between time and space. *Am I one of their ancestors? They see me as one of the Gods who brought them here, living on a different planet?* Gods. It seemed as though fire sparkled in every cell of her being. Magnetic storms. A flood engulfing a valley as large as a continent. An island sinking below the sea. The whole world shaking. Terrible loss. Pain as though her heart had broken in two. Searching. A river. A pyramid. An indistinct image...

310

Sight returned to her eyes along with a feeling of panic. She looked out across the desert. It was not the verdant green valley of the flood she had just seen. But. She had to save her people. Bring them to the mountain top.

Careless of the uneven surface, she ran down the narrow pathway. Rounding a corner, startled as she almost ran into her guides, she tried to stop. A stone gave way beneath her foot. Her leg shot forward and she started to topple sideways over the edge of the path. In horror, her eyes focussed on the rocky outcrops all the way down the side of the hill to the desert floor, a long way below.

A cry of alarm escaped her lips as, unbid, here eyes switched vision in two stages, leaving her looking at the gravity waves pressing down on everything and which were about to send her crashing down the jagged rock face. Trying to regain her balance she flung her arms out wide and felt a hand grab her arm. Twisting round, she collapsed into Xashee. As they fell down on the edge of path she heard his cry of pain as she landed on top of him. Her momentum was rolling her off him, out over the edge. Her free hand scrabbled uselessly at the smooth rock face. There was nothing she could grasp to save herself.

Her legs swung over the cliff face and she dropped, feeling her arm slip through Xashee's hand until her fall stopped with a jerk as his grip held around her wrist. She could not help looking down the rock face. A picture from years ago flashed through her mind.

In a tantrum, she had hurled at Qwelby a special doll that Gumma had made for her. She had missed her twin and the doll had struck the corner of a piece of furniture and fallen to the ground with its head, legs and arms severed from the body. She imagined that was what she would look like if she were to fall.

Above her, she heard the sound of movement, scraping over rocks. She looked up. Xashee was lying face down on the very edge of the path. Tsetsana was lying across him, her hands gripping his waist.

'Other hand,' Xashee croaked, extending his other arm.

Tullia stretched, but her fingers were a few centimetres away from his. Her muscles straining, she had to ease them and try again. As she lowered her arm, she swung, heard Xashee grunt as he slid dangerously closer to the very edge. Sweat broke out across her forehead and trickled into her eyes. She took a deep breath, and with panicked thoughts running through her mind, feet scrabbling helplessly on the rock face, again reached for his now blurry fingers. They met, gripped and curled together. She relaxed the tension in her shoulders and her face banged against the hillside.

Please let this be Vertazia where I can thoughtsend to my sandals, asking the fastenings to come undone so my toes might find the smallest of cracks.

It was as though the Mountain Gods heard her plea. One of her feet found a purchase. Pushing down, looking up, she lifted her body, uncurled the fingers of one hand, stretched her arm and watched almost like an independent observer as their two hands made a wrist grip. Her sigh of relief was echoed from above as she relaxed and rested her check against the rock.

With his sister pulling him, and his legs scrabbling on the path, Xashee managed to move backwards, hauling Tullia painfully halfway over the edge of the path.

Movement stopped.

'Hold on,' Xashee said.

'I don't plan on letting go!' Tullia thoughtsent. Then realised life on Haven did not work like that. She was finding it difficult to breathe with her chest and stomach squashed over the cliff edge, her feet unable to find any purchase.

With a massive heave and a cry of pain from Xashee, she was hauled back to safety, scraping her body and bare legs against the rock. He let go with one hand, grasped her thigh and heaved for a second time, pulling her on top of him as he wrapped his arms around her.

Dazed, winded, hurting all over, Tullia lay there sucking in lungfuls of air. Mentally she burrowed into the comfort of the strong arms, reminding herself that Kalahari was a dangerous planet where her Tazian energy skills did not work.

She heard a groan from beneath her. Putting her hands on the rock either side of her saviour, she carefully pushed herself off him. He gave a stifled cry. She saw blood on his leg, and that it was awkwardly twisted underneath him.

She blinked her eyes and shook her head as she recovered her senses, pulling herself upright by a hand on the cliff face, taking in the dust, scrapes and blood oozing down both her legs. She pushed her hair away from her eyes and saw Tsetsana was helping her brother to get his arms out of the straps of the backpack he had been carrying.

'We help you to stand,' Tullia said.

As the two girls got him upright it was clear he was not able to put any weight on his injured leg. He leant back against the cliff face, his sister supporting him. Tullia knelt and looked at the wound, blood trickling down. It was long and deep but looked clean. She looked at the ground. A piece of rock broken off the cliff face with a curved, sharp edge had been the cause. She looked back at his leg, concerned for the dark pulsating aura around his inner thigh.

Xashee was trying to take his sweater off.

A picture came into Tullia's mind. She was five years old. She had been practising thought-control in the garden with Qwelby. It had been difficult to balance thoughts with actions. She had tripped, fallen, and gashed her knee. He had taken his top off and was about to wrap it around the cut when their mother appeared from the house.

She remembered the scene clearly. Her mother had held up a hand and strongly thoughtsent: 'No! The wound must stay clean.' What was odd was that she was remembering the scene as if she was her mother. She heard her own voice say: 'No! The wound must stay clean.'

Xashee heard a strong command and obeyed.

'We need to take you to lie down,' Tullia said.

'It's not far to the bottom,' Xashee lied through gritted teeth, not daring to question the Daughter of a Goddess.

Bending over, Tullia put his arm over her shoulders and supported him as he hopped down the path, blood splashing onto the rocks.

Wearing the backpack, Tsetsana followed, awed by the actions of a Goddess.

CHAPTER 44

HEALING POWERS

KALAHARI

At last they reached the sandy ground. 'Lie down,' Tullia said with a feeling of relief in her voice. It had been a difficult descent.

She gently straightened his leg as he groaned through clenched teeth. She held out a hand and Tsetsana handed her a bottle of water. She offered it to Xashee who drank and managed a grim smile.

'Clean cloth?' Tullia asked.

Tsetsana shook her head.

Tullia looked down at her tank-top. Ripped and dirty, that would not do. She felt soft cloth thrust into her hand and smiled her thanks to Tsetsana who was pulling her thick jumper back over her head.

Wetting the cotton shirt, Tullia gently washed Xashee's cut. Then, with his leg still between hers and careful not to touch him, she focussed all her energies into the centre of her body. She was aware from the dark, throbbing colours around his thigh that the injury was serious.

She carried the genes of Rrîltallâ Taminullyya, a great healer who had lived during the time the Auriganii were travelling through space. She had already decided that when she was an adult she wanted to be a healer. She needed those energies now.

Taking regular, deep breaths, she sank into her Kore. Speaking Tazian she said: 'I, Tullia Rrîl'zânâ Mizenatyr call upon you, Rrîltallâ Taminûllÿâ Uddîšû, great Healer. Help me heal this young man who has saved my life... please.'

She brought her hands to either side of Xashee's thigh, palms facing inwards, lowered her head and started to hum very softly. As she heard the music of the colours flowing, so she changed the tone and pitch of her hum, manipulating the flow with her long and supple fingers. The existence of a sixth finger on each hand was so natural she did not question it.

As she worked with the energy flow, a corner of her mind was wondering at the power that was flowing into her back, coming in from both sides. The sensation reminded her of the feeling of her wings when she had been very young and dressed as a winged unicorn for a KeyPoint LiveShow.

Her forehead started to itch. It grew stronger. Tears fell from her eyes. She bent her head over even further until her forehead was aimed directly at the top of Xashee's thigh and her tears were falling on the torn muscles that her inner vision showed her inside his leg. Her necklace had swung free from her tank top and she saw the purple crystal pulsing brightly.

Tsetsana had heard the Goddess singing. Now she saw a shimmering surround her, looking like heat rising from sun-drenched rocks. Combined with the red patches on her skin flaring, Tsetsana saw the Sun Goddess on fire.

As the sunlight grew stronger behind Tullia's back, Tsetsana bit her knuckles to stop from gasping aloud at the sight of what had to be the Mother Goddess herself infusing her daughter with power. Then her eyes widened as she saw what had to be golden tinged sunlight spiralling from Tullia's forehead and pouring into

Xashee's body, as all the time green highlights were flickering throughout her long hair.

The photons flowing from Tullia's forehead achieved coherence.

Time stood still.

Time returned. Tullia remained bent over, dizzy from the energy that had now ceased flowing through her, and very excited. She had channelled so much power and so gently, and so many years before it was expected. Was it Xashee's need? Was it being on Kalahari with its slower vibrations? Or was the Tazian structured pattern of growing up not really necessary?

'The secret is always inside... little QeïchâKaïgïi.'

Startled, Tullia sat back on her heels, opened her eyes and looked around for the source of the whisper. No-one had joined the three of them. As she took deep breaths to steady herself, fingering her crystal and thanking Kanyisaya for its help, she became aware of the silence surrounding her. It seemed all the deeper because of the far-off piercing call of a bird: uip uip uiiiio. A gentle breeze brought a momentary chill. It broke the spell. She gave a deep sigh and smiled at Xashee.

He pushed himself up on his arms, staring at Tullia. Her eyes were their usual soft purple. He was sure the ovals had turned the lavender colour of Nthabe's favourite t-shirt, and the purple orbs had been revolving.

Starting to rise, Tullia trembled, drained of energy. Arms reached out to steady her as brother and sister helped her sit back down.

There was a long silence, broken only by deep breathing from Tullia and Xashee. Slowly Tullia's head cleared and she felt some energy returning.

'Is that what you do on your planet?' Xashee asked.

Tullia nodded. 'Yes. I ask for help from...' Her compiler was not proffering words in Meera for what she wanted to say. 'My ancestor...'

317

Brother and sister saw the purple orbs of Tullia's eyes disappear as the ovals became completely violet.

'I channel her energy through me and into you in the form of photons, light,' Tullia said in a voice that sounded like an echo. 'The photons are a vibration. Like the vibrations in air a sound makes to reach your ears. Except it is in a different dimension, as the energy is not going to your physical body but to a deeper part of you that we call the InForming Matrix. I think you might call it a Spirit Body. If, deep inside... here.' Tullia placed a hand over her heart. 'Your Self wants the healing, your body hears the music of those photons and, like people singing together, wants to join in. To make the waves that will make the same music, your body has to heal.'

Tullia's head dropped onto her chest. A few moments later she looked up, blinking her eyes and looking puzzled. She was aware she had spoken in Meera using words her compiler had not yet learnt.

Her companions were staring at her in awe. She had sounded just like Xameb when the Great Serpent was speaking through him in the sacred cave at the foot of the Hills.

Embarrassed by their looks, Tullia quickly broke the silence. 'This first time I need so much power.' She smiled. 'You saved my life, Xashee. Very nicely.'

The teenager looked down at the ground, embarrassed. He tried to say to himself that he had pulled her into his embrace only to prevent her from rolling over the cliff edge again. But he knew that was not the whole truth. 'I'm sorry.'

'Sorry for saving me?!' she exclaimed.

'For holding you,' he replied,

'Oh, no! Please not be sorry!' Tullia begged.

Xashee glanced at her, then lowered his head again. He was churning inside. Holding her must be forbidden. She was the Daughter of a Goddess. And he had never experienced such a strong feeling from touching another person. And then her healing energies. Like from the tribe's own healers, but so much stronger. Wanting to describe the feeling as a way of remembering it, he found only one word: love.

'Please,' Tullia wailed. 'I'm not a Goddess. I'm a girl like you!'

All three laughed as Tullia had been speaking directly to Xashee.

'Was it bad saving me?' she asked Xashee.

She saw him relax, a faint smile still hovering around his lips. 'Not really.'

'Thank you, Xashee.' She leant forward and gave him a brief kiss, full on his lips.

Tsetsana's hand flew to her mouth as she gasped in surprise. Xashee flinched away and his eyes went as round as saucers.

Tullia jerked back. 'What I do?'

'We don't do that,' said Tsetsana.

'Only when...' added Xashee.

Tullia was about to burst into tears. What she had done was so normal on her world. That she had offended the only two people who were becoming her friends was awful.

Xashee was distraught. *This is a Goddess. About to cry? And it's my fault!*

Tsetsana was becoming accustomed to Tullia's changes in mood and manner, from Goddess to almost child-like when with the young children. 'Please, don't cry. You haven't hurt us. We were surprised.' She looked at her brother, who was blushing madly. 'It's just that what you have done is... very friendly...' she finished awkwardly

'Oh! I'm sorry,' Tullia said, beginning to understand. She smiled and felt herself also blushing with embarrassment. She lowered her eyes. When she looked up again, Xashee was still blushing but no longer looked shocked.

For the first time the two Meera realised just how lonely Tullia must be. And how human she was in her own, very different way. It was not easy. She came from the sun. She looked like a Siska.

She sang with a rich voice rather than talked. She had special powers. Her healing powers had been yet another confirmation that she was a Daughter of a Goddess.

Unaware of the impression she had created earlier, Tullia did not know whether it was the healing or the kiss or both that had opened up a gulf between her and her companions. It hurt, far more than the cuts and bruising to her legs and the burning of the red patches. Without her twin even in her mind, she was desperate for friendship and acceptance. She took a deep breath.

'We have had a lovely day in hills. You are the first people I met. Can we be friends. Please?' She gave Xashee a shy smile.

Xashee had fallen under Tullia's spell the first time they had met. He was embarrassed. Being with her so closely for the day, watching her, seeing her almost child-like wonder at the paintings, hearing the beauty in her voice, and now feeling the powerful energy flow into him, he was totally captivated. 'I would like that,' he replied softly. And blushed again. She seemed even more beautiful now he knew that, at least at times, she was as human as himself.

Tullia felt warmth spread across her face and wondered why.

Tsetsana squeezed her shoulder and softly giggled. The three of them hugged, awkwardly as they were still sitting on the ground. Tullia felt such a joy and a release. *Human at last!* It was such a relief to feel her own age.

They got to their feet and walked back to the village

Xashee kept looking at his leg. He was sure from the pain when Tullia had landed on top of him, and again when he had tried to walk, that he had torn some muscles, yet now he was walking with only a slight limp. And the deep gash had healed well. Leaving a long, faint, pink scar which stood out clearly on his dark brown skin.

It was dark by the time they reached the village. The Meera slowly gathered as they noticed Xashee limping slightly, but all eyes were for Tullia who seemed to be glowing from inside.

320

Nlai heard a grunt and turned to look at her friend. Kou-'ke was scowling. Puzzled, Nlai looked back, switching her gaze from Tullia to the two Meera. This time she saw the look of adoration on Xashee's face that was directed not towards Kou-'ke but to the Goddess.

Seated around the family fire a little later, Xashee and Tsetsana started to explain what had happened. Milake, their father, soon gestured to them to stop and went to speak with Ghadi. The leader agreed, Xashee and Tsetsana were to relate the events for the whole tribe.

When the big, communal fire was burning well and the whole tribe gathered around, the two young Meera told their story. To start with, they were subdued. As they got into the relating, their natural abilities took over and they brought the events alive.

Tullia learnt for the first time the impression she had given when she was standing on the hillside that afternoon. It made her uncomfortable. Yet again she was being pictured as a Goddess. When it came to Tsetsana showing how Tullia had fallen on Xashee, wounding him badly, there was a general murmuring of his wound being a sign of his manhood.

The long, bright pink mark was easily seen in the firelight. Murmurs of surprise ran around the Meera. They looked at Tullia with awe. Healers were very important in the lives of all the San tribes. Not only had she healed him, she had not needed the ritual of the dance to do so.

It came as a shock to Tullia when the enactment finished. She had been so wrapped up in the saga that she had felt as if she was watching a scene from the tribe's history, not a portrayal of herself.

She was relieved that the enactment had stopped with the healing. She realised it would be too much for the youngsters to portray friendship with a person whom everyone else thought of as a Goddess. But that saddened her again, although she was happy that the kiss had also been omitted. She blushed as she thought of it. She sensed all eyes upon her and buried her face in her hands.

Feeling an arm around her and sensing the compassion flowing from Deena, she was content to be led to her hut, helped into bed and left alone.

Seated around the fire, Kou-'ke turned to her best friend with a grimace on her face and shook her head. Nlai understood. Kou-'ke and Xashee were almost engaged. The two fifteen-year-old girls did not need to be able to read energy fields to know Xashees's feelings towards the visitor. Kou-'ke feared that the powerful goddess had come to steal a human mate and worried that she had already chosen Xashee and bewitched him.

Was any man safe? Nlai wondered, thinking of K'dae. And how to compete with a Goddess?

Whilst the tribe accepted that she was the untouchable Daughter of the Goddess, they also saw a powerful young woman of marriageable age. Knowing that feelings have lives independent of the mind, Nlai and Kou-'ke were not the only ones to talk about Tullia's impact as, grouped together as normal, the young women of the tribe settled down for the night in their several huts. For differing reasons, there was a general hope that Tullia's developing friendship with Tsetsana indicated that the Goddess was not interested in men.

Like all Tazii of her age, as yet Tullia had no special feelings towards boys. With her comparative immaturity, she was totally unaware that the jealousy she noticed in the girls' auras was directed towards her, and thus unable to prevent the disastrous events that later were to follow what was supposed to be a joyous celebration.

She was aware of the mixed feelings coming from both Tsetsana and Xashee and worse, the feeling of awe from the whole tribe. She was existing on a knife edge. Without the link to her twin she was only half her self. To make it worse, although a lovely people, the Meera were pushing her away by treating her as if she was a Venerable at the peak of her powers and some great Uddîšû.

Please, the little girl within begged the Multiverse. *I don't want to be a Goddess. I just want them to see me!*

Aware that she was still in shock and that if it was allowed to surface she would be enwrapped in total paralysis, her mind created a cocoon of safety by concentrating only on essentials. Striving to mange with a lifestyle vastly different from that on Vertazia, learning their language and having to cope with being treated as a Goddess was all she could cope with.

Her times with the young children were a blessing. Even if they called her 'Goddess' or 'Daughter', those were just names they used whilst they treated her as big sister. That gave her the strength to reach out to the young women and men, asking them through her energies and actions rather than words to accept her as what they called a teenager, and a young one at that.

She did not have the energy to cope with thoughts of family, friends or returning home and also maintain the protection of her cocoon. Her internal focus was on soaking up the energy of the land so that Xameb could help her reconnect with Qwelby. She felt like a butterfly trapped in a chrysalis. Reconnect with her twin and she could emerge into the sunlight, whole again and be ready for new awareness, thoughts and actions.

Enwrapped in her own thoughts she slipped into her memory and returned to the top of the hill from where in all directions the land looked exactly the same as far as she could see. The realisation that Kalahari was their name for Haven, meaning she was in the same sun system as Vertazia, was a reassurance she clung to as surely as she had clung to Xashee's hand.

'The life forms on Haven in the fifth dimension are very different from what I am experiencing. Life here is slow and solid and similar in those respects to what I've seen of Earth at the Elmits. My mental powers do not work like they do at home. That confirms I am in the third dimension.' Satisfied with her reasoning she continued muttering to herself.

'Xashee has told me of other tribes of San who are red like me. Of course, those names Tsetsana asked me must be for Red San tribes. Her memory replayed the two words "Hiechware" and

"Hoachana." The peace and ease I have with the Meera. Their ability to understand where I come from and how I got here. Perhaps the San are like the Tazii, pure Auriganii descendants? To be anchored in the third dimension their DNA must have degraded to only two segments, like the Azurii.

'That explains so much. Especially the loss of memory of their true origins. Yet those survive in their simple lifestyle that honours all life and takes from nature only the minimum needed. So unlike the violence amongst the Azurii.

'Conclusion. Kalahari is to Haven what Azura is to Vertazia. Our forebears travelled countless light years across the galaxy. If Kaigii is on Azura. I must be able to take the short step to my next door neighbour!'

It was to be a long time before memory of the inexplicable images she had seen from the mountain top was to return.

CHAPTER 45

XAALA HOOKED

VERTAZIA

Freed from her duties, Xaala was relaxing in her room. She had slipped out of her customary thigh length, cream tunic and wrapped around herself an equally short robe in soft shades of the ten colours of the rainbow. She had scarcely believed the multi-level message she had heard a little earlier. She had been lost in relaxing Ceegren's tensions, her hands moving with accustomed skill through his energy field a little above the soft robe he wore for treatment.

'I need your help,' he had said, at the same time transmitting images on more than one level.

Involuntarily, her hands had stopped moving as she absorbed it all. His request was genuine. The fast energy spectrum of her second Era was needed. Was essential. To him and thus crucial to the future of Vertazia. Almost buried in case it should frighten her, was the picture that she would be working with others of his level.

She continued to bask in the thrill of that moment. At last, Teacher actually needed her for the high level skills which had been the focus of her training. It was nearly five years since the LifeLines of her parents and older brother had been terminated in a freak

Omnitor accident and she had been orphaned. He had taken her in as his junior apprentice two years earlier than the customary age. Since then he had been like a father to her. More so than ever her real father had been.

'You have great potential.' Ceegren had said on her arrival. 'I can help you develop that. But only if it is what you want. To know if you want that, you have to find your Self. Explore. Everything. If you so wish.'

Necessity had forced Xaala to learn much earlier than most children to hear the thoughts that others considered were hidden by their Privacy Shields. Although clouded, the images accompanying his words had been clear. The three segments of her DNA like a ladder reaching into the sky, with a few dark clouds scudding across. A beautiful sunrise at the top of the ladder. Later, she came to realise that Ceegren's underlying message had deliberately been half hidden, and he had been testing her.

She had explored and made mistakes, yet never been criticised. Each had been used as a lesson. She knew he loved her but could not show it, because he was Teacher and a hard task master. He demanded the best, yet in such different ways that she always strove willingly to comply. She longed to repay him for his faith in her.

Now she was relaxing, reinforcing in her unconscious the energy signatures of both twins that she had extracted from the MentaNet. 'They need to be your own copies, as you perceive them,' Ceegren had said when she had suggested that surely he was far more skilful in providing such images.

Mixed groups of senior and junior Custodians were monitoring all possible communication wavelengths. Their principal duty being to block all communication until Ceegren was able to act. Her duty was to make her unconscious aware that it needed to be permanently open to any other trace of the twins' signatures in the quantum field. When discovered, she was to reinforce her images of them and, trace by trace, establish their location with increasing accuracy.

'I expect the energies to be so subtle that what I am asking you to do can only be achieved by a youngster operating on the same wavelength. That is in the same, second era, as the twins,' Ceegren had explained. 'That you are little more than eighteen months older than them is perfect.' He had smiled. 'Think of yourself as an elderest, looking after their best interests.'

This time the accompanying imagery was clear. All Tazian life was precious. He was inviting Xaala to help to save them. Carrying an infectious disease, they needed to be kept away from Vertazia, both mentally and physically, until an effective means of isolation was established and suitable treatment devised.

It happened. There was the slightest vibration. It partly matched to Tullia. Carefully storing the impression as if wrapped in cotton wool, she walked through to Ceegren's suite and, unusually, knocked gently on the door. She felt a quick flick across her mind. Door opened and her Teacher beckoned her to sit on her usual meditation cushion.

Seated, she relaxed and felt him slide into her mind. To Xaala it was like being stroked. Had she been a cat, she would have purred.

'Analysis,' Ceegren requested when he withdrew.

'Very faint. Very far away. And also not the full signature.' Xaala hesitated, this was very new ground for her, Quantum Twins being unlike anybody else. She licked her lips. 'What I did not detect was any impression of Qwelby. My conclusion is that they are not mentally connected.'

'And the energy?'

'Healing?'

'Excellent, my child.' Ceegren waved the fingers of his right hand at her.

Xaala blushed, rose and returned to her room. Normally he would have thoughtsent her dismissal. To Xaala, a gesture like that was as intimate as if her had kissed her cheek. Which he never did.

Ceegren's thoughts were pulled in opposite directions. He

knew Tullia carried the genes of the great healer of the Aurigan journey. Good. Xaala could track her. What was disconcerting was that Tullia's personal signature indicated she had to be very far away, yet she was handling energy as if she were on Vertazia. And without her twin's participation.

If the boy were to demonstrate the same power it would be almost impossible to prevent them reconnecting. Once that happened, and if all six youngsters truly had created an energy construct in the sixth dimension, how on 'Tazia was he going to prevent the Abominations from communicating with their young friends?

His mind presented the inevitable conclusion: Reincarnation Rescheduling. He buried that disconcerting thought deep behind his impenetrable Privacy Shield.

CHAPTER 46

AN OATH RENEWED

FINLAND

Romain had flown into Helsinki-Vantaa airport and then on to Jyväskylä, picking up his rented car late on the thirtieth of December. On settling in his room in the Scandic Hotel he had made a secure connection with his assistants back on the island. A brief exchange and they had confirmed that there was still no news about any of the expected EM interference around Kotomäki, or anything else out of the ordinary.

A long sleep and a late breakfast was no hindrance to his plans. For those he needed full daylight. So it was a little after ten thirty on the following day that he set out. Driving the ubiquitous black Volvo, he headed south on the E63, then turned off onto the road that led to the small town.

As he reached Kotomäki his GPS confirmed what his equipment on Raiatea had indicated: that the location of the event was on the edge of the local ski slope. He parked his car near a small row of shops and walked back to the pavement that ran along a row of houses that backed onto the bottom of the slope. Even through his binoculars he was unable to see any signs of disruption to the area indicated by his equipment.

Without a drag lift, skiers had to tramp sideways uphill. They had made paths on each side of the slope alongside the trees that formed the boundaries. Carefully walking up the slippery path on the left-hand side, Romain discovered and followed tracks leading through a strip of trees and out into a small snowfield.

Although there had been a heavy snowfall since the twenty-seventh, from the still obvious disturbance of the snow it looked as though a lot of people had been searching a large area. Back in amongst the trees he found a large hole had been dug right down to the frozen hillside. Someone had seen something arrive that was so definite it had been worth a lot of effort to search for.

With the confirmation that his equipment was as accurate as he expected in determining the location of the event, he walked into the town centre and enquired at the police station. To his surprise, there had been no reports of any strange event. In response to his request it was agreed that he could return later that evening to speak with the night-shift duty sergeant.

When Romain duly returned, Sjöström listened to his explanation. She confirmed that apart from the well publicised extreme display of the Northern Lights, there had been no notable events of any sort, neither on the twenty-seventh nor around that date. No meteor falls, not even odd weather features or anything else so minor that did not warrant a formal report. She said nothing about the brief communications blackout that had occurred on the twenty-seventh. That was an internal matter and confidential. Besides which, it had been ascribed to the unusual display of what the wags were describing as the Southern Lights.

Romain left the police station feeling perplexed. All the indications from his equipment were that it had been a major event likely to have caused electro-magnetic effects across a wide area. Whether it was the massive amount of data 'dropping off' that had apparently ruptured his Python, or the arrival of an actual physical object, he had expected there to have been obvious signs. Lights, sound, something akin to a whirlwind looking like the Aurora Borealis reaching down to the ground. But something so minor that it had only been seen by one person, perhaps a group of friends? If it had been an object, it must have been very small as there had been no signs of any braches being broken on the close-packed trees.

A thought was elusively hovering at the back of his mind. Something to do with the road at the bottom of the slope. He made his way back to the road and walked along the houses. It was not a thoroughfare. Who would have been walking along it at that time? Schools were closed and it had not been the end of the working day.

A patch of light appeared on the snow. He looked up as someone closed the curtains of an upstairs room. That was it! The view from that level was clear across to the area that had been searched. Had someone been upstairs, looking out at the crucial moment?

He turned round and started walking back to his car. Still puzzled at what seemed to be the minimal effects, nevertheless he felt satisfied that at least he had an idea of how whatever had happened had been seen.

Some way ahead two figures appeared, walking towards him. From their gait he assumed two young men, hoods pulled up against the cold. He had almost reached a streetlight as they passed under it, talking animatedly. One white face, one black. *No, Romain thought to himself as he walked on. Around here I've seen only white faces, pink cheeks and blonde hair. Just a trick of the light.*

He did a double take and stopped. A house opposite the slope. Two young men. He turned back. There were a good distance away and walking quickly. He would have to run to catch them up. 'Steady David,' he muttered to himself. 'Lost in thought, staring at the ski slope, you don't know even know for certain they came out of one of these houses.'

He stood for a moment looking at the houses and the ski slope. Despite his burning desire to find whoever had seen, and possibly found, whatever might have arrived, he knew that a stranger calling at houses in the dark and on New Year's Eve was not a good way to start his enquiries. Besides which, still feeling jet-lagged, he needed another good night's sleep. Returning to his car, he drove back to his hotel in a contemplative mood.

Romain had staked his career and a considerable, hard earned fortune on his belief in the experiments that the rest of the scientific community derided. He had to succeed. It was not just for fame and glory and the confirmation of his erstwhile impressive reputation. Success would establish him as one of the leading scientists of all time, ranking along with Copernicus, Newton and Einstein.

He saw a glowing future. The certain award of the Nobel Prize for Physics followed by his appointment as the first Director-General of the newly established Trans-Dimensional Research Institute. Possibly even the Romain Institute. 'Professor Sir David Romain CH, FRS,' had a nice ring to it.

Back in his room in the hotel, he took a small bottle of wine from the refrigerator and poured a glass. He needed the cold bite of the Chardonnay to help settle his nerves. Now, on the brink of the most important discovery of his life, it looked as though someone else was about to beat him to it. If someone had found an object, what would they do with it? Show it to family and friends then, curious at to what it might be, take it to the museum in Jyväskylä?

He gritted his teeth. No-one was going to steal from him the fruits of all the years of hard work, isolated from the majority of his fellow scientists apart from holding a Visiting Professorship at a minor university unknown outside the USA.

His mind went back to an evening in the early years of working by himself.

Disappointed at another failure of one of his key series of experiments, he had gone to his suite of rooms, showered and changed into pair of black trousers, a very fine black polo neck, socks and shoes. All to match David Niven in what was one of Romains' favourite films: playing Sir Charles Lytton in the Pink Panther series

With his suite of rooms on the top floor of the complex of laboratories high up on the mountainside, looking across his patio he had a marvellous view of the ocean. Where the pale blue sky met the dark blue sea, the curved horizon was sharply defined. For a moment he felt he was standing on a flat, round planet, looking at World's End.

Believing in what he called the multiverse, comprising the whole of everything, as essentially alive, he stepped out onto the patio and raised his glass of Martini to the scene in front of him and promised: 'I will prove that you are the true reality.' He thought of all the work he had done over the last few years and added a heartfelt plea. 'I just need a little bit of help.'

Determination filled him. 'I will do anything, anything at all to succeed.' The stem of the glass snapped in his fingers. He looked at it, bemused. Blood was trickling from a cut. He gave a grim smile. Tracing his family back through the ages he had discovered a Norse heritage with the original family name being Reginsen, corrupted over the years to Rolandson, which he had changed to Romain along with changing his birth name of Desmond to David.

'With my Viking heritage, this looks like a blood oath,' he murmured.

As it dipped onto the horizon, the sun mirrored the dark red colour. Carefully holding the bowl of the glass with his cut hand he raised it to the sun and drank the last drops of his Martini.

'Well, *Reginsen?*' A voice echoed from the past.

He looked at the little trickle of blood and, beyond it, the sun seeming to taunt him with the same colour. The sun, the giver of life to the whole solar system.

He felt his body tremble with the force of the commitment he was being compelled to make.

'I promise I will do whatever it takes to prove the existence of other dimensions.' He raised his hand to his lips and licked up the blood.

'*Well done, Reginsen.*'

In his hotel room, with the windows closed and the central heating on, he shivered as a chill breeze swept over him, through him, raising goosebumps and temporarily numbing him. He had the weird sensation that he was his equipment detecting a disturbance in the quantum field.

He stepped to the window with the glass of wine in his hand. He had not drawn the blinds and he looked up into the dark night sky and the bright, full moon. A new energy pulsed from deep within, bringing images of a Viking longship ploughing through storm-tossed waves. He was both manning the steering board and standing in the prow, holding the carved warhead as he peered into the mists.

Feeling that he was committing himself to a partnership with that inner voice, he softly repeated his oath.

'I promise I will do whatever it takes to prove the existence of other dimensions.'

He tossed back the remains of his drink in one gulp.

'Whatever it takes!'

He felt a sense of satisfaction deep within that seemed to come from another person, Rekkr Reginsen as he named what was becoming his alter ego. The old Norse "Rekkr" meaning both "man" and "warrior."

Later that night as he settled down to sleep he felt optimistic. He would start his enquiries the following day with the row of houses facing the ski slope. He was sure that was where the answer lay.

CHAPTER 47

DECISION TIME

KALAHARI

The day after almost falling to her death, Tullia awoke feeling deeply disturbed. *Why?* Her Memory replayed her dreamstate.

She saw herself watching a figure that had to be Xashee lying on a path, blood pouring down the mountainside like a waterfall. The flow stopped, he shrivelled up and disappeared. She went skipping down the path like a happy child. At the bottom she saw her crystal. As she bent down to pick it up, it turned into a tiny heart, bleeding. Her heart!

Then she saw an enormous Goddess astride a mountain. Reaching to the ground, her hair formed a bright green robe through which golden light radiated from her body. In her hand she held a staff that reached to her shoulder. It was tipped with a facsimile of a winged rainbow-coloured Unicorn's Horn. For a moment she wept at the beauty and power of what had to be Rrîltallâ Taminullyya.

As she took in that everywhere across the desert floor people were kneeling or prostrating themselves, she realised with a shock that she was the Goddess. She wanted to scream and deny it. She turned to the people around her and begged them to stand up.

Then she was in the sky, level with the Great Healer who faded in and out, alternating with a series of men, women and children, all radiating joy. She did not see him, yet she knew that Kaigii was amongst them.

She dropped to her knees on the mountain top, tears flowing uncontrollably, wanting to deny the image, the message, yet unable to deny Kaigii. They were one.

The replay finished, she swallowed and licked her lips. 'Me?' she said softly as understanding reached her. She had a gift, and a choice to make. The gift she knew. It was her genetic inheritance from the great Healer Heroine. The choice was clear.

Better to be seen as a remote Goddess, sharing my gift of healing with anyone who needs it, than...

She slipped off her night robe and splashed herself with cold water, wishing she had Mirror and could talk with Image.

Whistling airhead! Image-into-action!

She bent over the bowl of water and focussed. A few moments later Image appeared. She stared at the surprisingly youthful face with the ovals of its eyes entirely a vibrant purple, rimmed with silver and green highlights sparkling in its long hair.

Remember you heritage, Tullia. And be who you are,' Image said.

Her mind whirling, Tullia gripped the bowl for support as she felt herself flying through space on the back of Trellûa, the Great Healer's own Unicorn.

In the distance she saw the Dragon Kèhša astride Zhólérrân. Understanding reached her of the complex reasons that had made the man take the Dragon's name as his own. And what she had done. Why was that not recorded in the Archives?

'Yes, Rrîltallâ Trellûa Taminûllÿâ,' Tullia solemnly replied, as the recollection of "what she had done" faded rapidly from her conscious memory. Image smiled and disappeared and Tullia was looking at her own reflection. She shivered at the power of the connection, and the promise she had made. She felt unsettled and needed to feel relaxed and able to centre for what she wanted to do. She explained her need to Tsetsana, saying she would find her young friend when she returned from her special place amongst the Mongongos.

CHAPTER 48

A NIGHT TO REMEMBER

FINLAND

After the day with the snowman, so happy to have found someone he could really talk with, Hannu had introduced Anita to his group of friends. One of them had mentioned the fun they had had for Hannu's sixteenth birthday treat at the laser dome in Jyväskylä. She had mentioned it to her father. He had acquired various items of equipment and, happy to see his daughter making friends, roped the two, willing youngsters in to help him create body packs and adapt toy rifles they bought.

Ilta and Oona, the other girls in the group, had been amused when Anita had joined the boys in testing out the laser packs to make the early part of the longest night celebrations. Ilta was sixteen and going steady with Timo. Fourteen-year-old Oona liked Hannu, but he was not her idea of boyfriend material. The whole practice evening had gone well and Anita had been accepted as a member of the group. She had seemed to be more tomboy than girl.

Wednesday afternoon and Qwelby was again practising skiing on the slope on the edge of Kotomäki. It was getting late, his muscles were aching from adjusting to the different conditions on Earth and he was taking a rest, watching Hannu and Anita descending the slope, when his vision blurred. Thinking it was from being tired, he closed his eyes. It seemed that the very land was calling to him. The ground that lay under the snow. Before he had time to analyse what was happening he heard voices calling out. Looking up, he saw a group of teenagers in bright jackets and trousers with two wearing colourful ski suits coming in through the entrance off the road, arms waving. Panic filled him as he recalled his arrival on Earth and what he had seen from inside the snowman when a group of boys had attacked Hannu.

Moments later he heaved a sigh of relief as the newcomers slid into their skis and he saw their energy fields were full of curiosity and friendship. He guessed it was the group of friends Hannu had mentioned. He skied down to them and was introduced, with Hannu explaining that his friend needed to keep his goggles on as he had delicate eyes. When, from their blonde hair and pink cheeks. what appeared to him to be four brothers and sisters wanted to know about his unusual colouring and looks, asking if he was a Red Indian, and then to know where he came from, he could not help but massively radiate feelings of happiness and companionship and seek their friendship. Feelings which each of the new arrivals unknowingly accepted and thus reciprocated.

By the time their initial curiosity had been satisfied, with Hannu answering most of the questions as Qwelby spoke so little Finnish, it was getting dark and time to go home. Nils pointed out that their new friend wasn't going to enjoy a typical New Year family get-together on Friday, unable to talk with a group of people he didn't know anyway. He suggested another night with the laser rifles. No-one questioned his assumption that Qwelby had been accepted as a member of their group.

Happy to feel included, Qwelby was even happier when Hannu and Anita said they would take him out that evening to practise with the lasers. Coming from a world where the people related as much through their energy fields as thoughtsending or speaking, and having to concentrate hard on trying to decipher what was to him the confusion within the weak Azuran energy fields, it never occurred to him how much his feelings were influencing the Azurii and reinforcing their initial reactions to him, for good or bad. And that they were completely unaware of that.

As they all headed for their various homes, Oona quietly confided to her older brother's girlfriend: 'He's cute.'

Ilta smiled. "Cute" was not how she would describe him after having felt herself being sucked into his sparkling, purple eyes.

'It is the solstice on Friday?' Qwelby asked as the three of them walked to Anita's house.

'No. That was last Tuesday,' Anita replied.

Qwelby stopped, staring, his mouth wide open. Even under the street lights the two Finns saw that he had gone very pale. Taking an arm each they guided him to Anita's home and up into her bedroom.

The room was a perfect girl's haven, decorated in pinks and lilacs, with posters of what he assumed were teenage idols on the walls: singers, musicians and a bare-chested man lounging over a motorbike. A total contrast to Hannu's room. It was such an Azuran similarity to Tullia's section of their loft suite that Qwelby was pulled two ways. Part of him feeling the pain at the reminder of his separation from Kaigii, and part of him so relaxing in the normality that he did not think of teasing Anita for being so girly.

Once settled there with his favourite hot chocolate drink, Qwelby explained. 'Think of Vertazia as a sort of invisible shell around Earth, fixed in position. It occupies the same space. In a way like thousands of neutrinos are passing though this room, our bodies, yet we are unaware of them. The only time difference is due to levels of vibration. Our days are longer. What we call KeyPoints and you solstices and equinoxes, are the same. We left the day before the solstice. I am in the same hemisphere. So I arrived.' He shivered as he hesitated. 'Seven days later.'

The two Finns felt the cold as the ovals of the alien's eyes turned completely violet. There was a long silence.

'That helps explain why I can't reconnect with Tullia. Not only are we millions of kilometres apart, we must be time separated.'

'Where were you for a whole week?' Hannu asked.

'I don't know. Massless particles do not experience time. That just proves what I said to Dr K. That Tullia and I were reduced to Kuznii, the fundamental particle of all existence.' He got up from where all three were sitting on the bed. 'I'm sorry. I need to be by myself.' He held up a hand as the others rose. 'Please. I know where my coat and shoes are.'

Later, as soon as he had eaten with the Rahkamos, he made his excuses, retired to his bedroom and again tried to reach Tullia. As long as he tried to mentally link with her outside of himself as he would with any of his friends, he was alright. It was only when he forgot and flicked into her corner in his mind that pain stabbed through him. As he unsuccessfully reached out, he was taken back to the impressions he had experienced on the ski slope, when the arrival of Hannu's group of friends had cast it from his mind. On the top of the snow covered slope he had been about to ski down a massive sand dune. As he had looked up to see who was making the noise, through the snow he had caught sight of a vast array of dunes marching into the far distance. They were calling to him.

If that's where Kaigii is, why do I not reach her?

He felt himself sucked into a funnel that turned into a spiralling tunnel. Miniature spirals were revolving on the walls interspersed with zigzag lines and strange hatchings looking like chess boards without borders. Out of a mist a pair of human feet emerged. As they walked towards him he saw it was clearly a man; then equally clearly a woman; then another shock – the head was that of a baboon. Even as he tried to decipher the image the baboon grew a long curved beak and a birds head, the name "Ibis" came into his mind, was superimposed over that of the baboon. Slowly and definitely the head shook from side to side as the sand dunes collapsed and Qwelby was left rushing down the spiralling tunnel into oblivion.

The following day, the three youngsters again spent the daylight hours on the slope opposite Hannu's house. Qwelby was withdrawn. Half his mind was concentrating on accustoming all his reactions to the slowness and solidity of Earth, the other half continuing the desperate search for any clue that might be hidden in his memory of his weird experiences as to when Tullia might be.

As they were stepping out of their skis that evening Qwelby asked if he could try the laser pack before dinner, adding: 'After dinner, will you meditate with me? Help me try to connect with Tullia?'

Anita was excited. She had learnt to meditate years ago.

'Err. You mean we, I, just sit and... think of Tullia?' Hannu asked.

'Yes. As simple as that,' Qwelby replied. Glancing at Anita he saw the glow in her aura, and grinned, aware that his eyes were twirling with anticipation.

They made their way to Anita's house where all three kitted up with packs and rifles and made their way into the woods. When Qwelby had learnt the rules and mastered the equipment they returned the kit to Dr Keskinen's laboratory and the boys went home. After dinner, Anita walked round to join them and they congregated in Qwelby's bedroom.

Qwelby explained that all he wanted his friends to do was to sit quietly and think of Tullia, holding an image of her in their minds. 'I will talk you into our time together,' he explained. 'I'll describe Tullia a little and then leave it there. After a time, about twenty or thirty minutes, I'll speak softly to end the meditation, and say a few words to make sure you feel back in this room.'

342

'Don't worry Hannu,' Anita added. 'You won't have gone anywhere. It's just to help your mind feel settled.'

When the meditation finished half an hour later with no contact, Qwelby declared himself happy. 'I was not really expecting this to work on our first attempt. We need to do this several times to align our very different energies. What is good is that I felt that was happening. You were just there, Hannu. And it was easy to sense you, Anita.'

'You have a very strong energy field,' Anita said, almost in awe at what she had felt. 'It wrapped around me.'

As Anita left to go home, Qwelby again noticed shades of yellows, oranges and dark greys flickering through Hannu's aura. They puzzled him. He couldn't make any sense of them.

Qwelby having declared himself ready for more challenging skiing, on Friday the whole group skied cross-country to the resort at Muurame. There, Qwelby went down the green run and then successfully tackled the two blues. During a break for lunch, and with Hannu and Anita helping him as he had to maintain a pretence of having limited Finnish when others were present, he managed to explain that his looks were due to something unusual in his DNA. *Which is perfectly true*, he thought to himself.

That evening, New Year's Eve, Hannu, Anita, Jarno, Nils and Qwelby gathered in Dr Keskinen's workshop. Gone were the bright colours of skiing, now all were well wrapped up in well padded, dark jackets, trousers, hats and gloves. When the last pack had been strapped on and tested, Anita reminded them of the rules. 'Qwelby doesn't know the woods like we do. So he walks straight into them for two minutes. You three run home and touch your front doors. I'll leave here in exactly two minutes.'

Seven o'clock. The sun had set long ago. A full moon threw the whole landscape into a stark contrast of black and white. They had deliberately chosen an area that included the end of the village around the doctor's house where the street lights were well spread out. Amongst the trees it was much darker, but for a short way the players would still stand out against the snow.

On his practice night Qwelby had been able to detect Hannu and Anita at a short distance. With two more days skiing, concentrating hard on developing his energy skills, he was hoping for more. After two minutes of leaving a straight line of clear tracks, he moved sideways and settled down behind a tree. It was not long before he detected an energy field moving slowly, then one more, then all four. *Dragons Breath! This is like playing HideNSeek on 'Tazia.*

For a moment, his memory drifted back to their last game of HideNSeek with Tullia's mini-twistors in the barn at home on the chaotic day that had ended with him here, on Earth. He pulled his mind back from that train of thought. Back to the Earthly game. In spite of his sadness, he smiled. Here he was, kneeling on earth on Earth.

As he came out of his reverie, he realised he had lost the others. *Time to really play a Tazian game!*

He easily slipped back into his steady breathing rhythm, focussed within himself, then opened to the energy sensations he had felt previously. There. And another. Someone was nearby on his right. He moved carefully and was rewarded a few moments later with the dark shape of one of his friends crouched behind a tree. He lifted his rifle and fired. With a grin on his face, he rolled behind the tree as he saw his target light up and an eerie screech reverberated through the trees.

That felt so good. His innate abilities were returning. Right now they were weak, but they were not lost. The first step on the path to reconnecting with Kaigii was to strengthen them.

The game moved further and further into the darkness of the forest. Although hiding became easier, there were an increasing number of flashes and screeches from successful hits on the packs.

Red LEDs had been fixed around the muzzle of each rifle. Mimicking the flash from real guns, they gave away the shooter's position by lighting up when the rifle was fired. Not only was someone an excellent shot, successfully scoring off players who thought they were well concealed, there was no sign of the shooter's muzzle flash.

The four Finns were fairly certain they knew roughly where each other was, but not Qwelby. He had to be the shooter. They had just started to call softly to one another seeking to agree to gang up on him when, with a shock of vibrating air shattering the silence came the unmistakable sound of a police siren. Through the trees the lights of a car travelling fast came into view, followed by the rooftop flashing lights of the police car.

A squeal of brakes and tyres as the leading car took a sharp corner. Headlights swung around in a circle followed by a sickening crash and the wailing of a car horn. More squealing brakes as the police car shuddered to a halt. Voices, cries, shouts, the sound of hammering, smashing glass, a cry of rage followed by the crashing of bodies through the trees.

Then sirens and flashing lights from another police car arriving from the opposite direction. As the siren wailed into silence a voice called from the road.

'We've got your driver. Give up. You're finished,'

A string of expletives was shouted from the edge of the forest.

CHAPTER 49

DANGEROUS TIMES

FINLAND

Seeing the fugitives run into the woods and disappear amongst the trees, the youngsters used owl hoots to gather together and offer a mixture of conflicting suggestions.

Qwelby was on a high. It was true, not only were Azurii slower physically and mentally, their energy sensing abilities were massively underdeveloped. 'We catch them,' he said.

'How? We can't see them,' Nils objected.

'I can,' Qwelby answered, putting all his certainty into the tonal inflection of his rich baritone voice.

'Go for it, Q!' Hanno said, thumping him on the shoulder in his excitement at feeling "his alien's" certainty as though it were his own.

'Vumelaxqibell!' Qwelby said, raising a fist in the air

'What?' Hannu asked.

'Comply or... Die!' Qwelby replied, laughing. That was what he and Wrenden would chant when they submitted to being told how to behave by Tullia or Tamina. A literal translation was:

"Comply or Be Readjusted", but Qwelby thought "Die" was what Hannu would say.

Their attention was taken by the sound of police sirens and flashing lights as two more cars arrived and stopped, cutting their lights. One was a very long way off on the opposite side of the forest to the crash. The other far away and almost straight ahead.

Without looking back, Qwelby set off on a course to intercept the two figures that were cautiously moving through the trees, their energy signatures clear to his sight. Settling into a typical Tazian game and knowing that the targets were energy blind, he was really enjoying himself. From their excited energies, he also knew exactly where all his companions were. *So like at home. I'm almost beginning to feel normal.*

Soon, he detected a line of figures moving through the woods from the direction of the road. They had to be what his friends called police. He stopped and hooted like an owl, adding a thought of 'come to me,' gestured, then waited as the others silently made their way to him.

'Police?' he said, almost whispering as he pointed to the right and behind.

The others nodded.

'Targets.' He pointed ahead and to the right. 'I go that way.' Pointed ahead and left. 'You make a line after me.' He extended his arms out in front then brought then together. 'Squash!' he announced triumphantly as the others grinned and nodded.

A few minutes later Qwelby cursed silently. The targets had veered to their right. He looked for Hannu who was well behind him, hooted softly and gestured. No response. He shook his head. If he waited for Hannu to catch him up, the lines would meet all right but the targets would not be caught.

He called up a mental picture of the map he had been shown when they had been planning the evening. The targets were headed for Puolivalintie. It was a long road and only one police car had

347

driven along it. The "targets" could easily slip across, unseen.

He had no option. If he had to tell Tullia that in the woods on a dark night he had been outwitted by two Azurii who had no energy sensing: he would never hear the end of it. Even Wrenden would rightly laugh at him! *Not on your roaring life!*

He took a deep breath, then another, then a third. He forced the air into the base of his spine. 'Zhó'zânâ!' he spoke his middle name quietly, evoking his genetic inheritance from Zhólérrân, the Dragon Kèhša. Would it work on Earth?

He grunted. He didn't even know if it would work on Vertazia! That power was not supposed to be his until his twenty-fourth rebirthday at the earliest. But from his short time on Earth he was already beginning to wonder just how it was that youth development of his homeworld was so strictly regulated

The targets were walking one behind the other and with quite a gap between them. Taking as long a stride as possible, Qwelby matched his footsteps to those of the nearest target, hoping to conceal the soft susurration through the deep snow. It worked.

'You are caught,' Qwelby said, tapping the man on the shoulder.

The man swung around, uttering words Qwelby did not understand, and threw a punch straight at his face.

Qwelby was taken by surprise. At home, in a game, when you were caught, you just stopped. Taking him on the side of the head as he ducked, the blow added to the momentum of his move and sent him sprawling onto the snow. The man turned away.

Driving his feet through the soft snow and onto the frozen ground, Qwelby threw himself forward and grasped a leg. The man measured his length in the snow. As Qwelby got onto his hands and knees, a vicious blow from a boot slammed into his chest pack. Attacked when he arrived on Earth, now assaulted by a man who did not follow the rules of the game. This was too much!

As his assailant started to get up, Qwelby heaved himself forward and grabbed a foot. The man fell to his knees and lashed out with his free leg, his boot catching Qwelby a stinging blow in the face. He cried out with pain. Rage filled him. 'Zhólérrân!' he cried, a corner of his mind wondering why he had used that name. Dragon energy erupted. He heard himself roaring like a wild animal and hurled himself forward, wrapping both arms around the man's waist.

A fist repeatedly struck his head. He heard the welcome sound of footfalls through the thick snow, only to find his arms seized as a man tried to pull him away. Qwelby hung on as he was kicked in the side, freed one arm and tried to grab the leg, missed and was kicked in the side again. Shouting nearby and further away. Hands seized his free arm and tugged as another kick landing painfully on his hipbone made him cry out.

Dark figures rushed up from behind as Hannu, Jarno and Nils piled into the mêlée. Cries, shouts and swearing filled Qwelby's ringing ears. As his assailant let go of his arm, Qwelby wrapped it around the recumbent man's waist and tightened his grip. With torchlights shining, more dark figures arrived and piled into the fray, arms and legs flying everywhere. Authoritative voices called out telling the boys to let go. As the fighting ceased and the man he had been hanging onto was pulled to his feet, Qwelby found himself rolling off and landing on something hard. He heard the sound of metal snapping on metal and saw rings being placed around the man's wrists.

As he got onto his hands and knees and felt around he discovered a large, heavy bag. As he heaved it up out of the snow, something rolled down away from him. He bent over the bag and grasped what felt like a rock about the size of his fist. It vibrated, sending tremors through his arm and filling his mind with images. Amongst his favourite WrapperFantasies were those of Aurigaini stranded on Earth after the Great Schism War and struggling to get to Vertazia. Surprised by the reality of that feeling, much stronger than being Wrapped in an Adventure, he pulled his hand away. The images faded and he became aware of animated talking going on all around him. He tasted blood trickling into his mouth and felt it running from his sore nose and a cut lip. Then a shock

349

hit him. The thieves: people stepping outside the acceptable norms of society. Very bad people! Readjusters. Police. "The Authorities!"

'What have you got there?' a woman's voice asked, as she shone a light on what he now saw was a large backpack he had been exploring, one zip partially open.

Feeling panic welling up inside, Qwelby looked up and to the side. His friends were grouped there together with Dr Keskinen, all just behind the woman who had spoken. In the torchlight her dark blue clothing and cap with its variety of white badges standing out clearly marked her the same as the men: Police.

The light in the policewoman's hand swept up to shine on his face. Instinctively, he raised a hand to shield his eyes and, remembering he was not wearing sun goggles, lowered his head whilst strongly thoughtsending an indication of respect.

'Err...' he mumbled as he grabbed the stone and fought the river of images long enough to pull himself off the pack and drop the stone into his coat pocket.

'He's on holiday. Doesn't speak much Finnish,' Hannu said, stepping around the sergeant.

'Wait,' Sergeant Sjöström commanded as Hannu reached Qwelby. She stepped forward and knelt down, giving the boy with the black face a long look before feeling the backpack.

'I'll be damned!' she exclaimed as she unzipped the main compartment. 'Proceeds from the burglary.' She looked back up. 'Name?'

'Qwelby.'

'How d'you find it?'

Earlier, the sound of her voice had told Qwelby that she definitely was in command. Now he heard a softer tone and could tell she was happy. Mentally thanking Hannu for his words, Qwelby pointed to the ground. 'I lie,' he said.

Out of the corner of his eye, he saw Sjöström smile. 'A lot was taken,' she said speaking slowly as she thought. 'Two men escaped the car. The other one must also have a bag.' She rose to her feet, gesturing to one of the constables to take the pack, and looked around the group of people.

'Yess,' Qwelby said, recalling the images he had stored in his memory when he had started to follow them. Helped by Hannu he got to his feet and leant on his friend as he swivelled his head to the left and right, stopped, nodded and pointed with one arm. 'Approximately fifty yurdii.'

'What?' exclaimed Hannu.

'About eleven times my height,' Qwelby replied.

'Okay,' Sjöström nodded to a constable, then turned to the Doctor who was kneeling alongside Qwelby. 'Is he all right?' she asked.

'A bit dizzy, that's all. We'll get him home and my wife will look after him,' he replied.

The sergeant nodded and spoke some more with Keskinen.

'The only way the police can give you all a ride home is to bring round the two cars from by the crash,' Keskinen explained. 'Those officers will have to walk back to get them. Almost to my house,' he added to reinforce his suggestion. 'It will be quicker if we all go to my home. Hot drinks and...'

'That's all right, Dad. We'll walk back. Won't we?' Anita said, stepping close to Qwelby and putting an arm around him.

Carrying two large and heavy packs the three police constables set off followed by Keskinen in conversation with Sergeant Sjöström.

'We'll follow in a moment. He's still dizzy,' Hannu said to Nils and Jarno, who waved and headed for the Keskinens' home.

Relieved to be away from the police and the searching looks that the woman had kept on giving him, Qwelby stepped away from his friend. 'Dank oo Annu,' he said.

It was plain for anyone to see that his friends liked each other, Qwelby thought. Yet he was puzzled. Their energy fields were a mish-mash of conflicting emotions. Worse were the dirty streaks of yellow in Hannu's. They needed to have time together. And he had so much to process that he needed to be by himself. 'Need be alone,' he said. He made a "go on" gesture with his arm as he added: 'I follow.'

CHAPTER 50

CAPTURED

FINLAND

After a few moments, Qwelby started to follow his friends, running the night's events through his mind: cataloguing, tagging and filing them in his memory. The emotions he would explore later.

He had become so hot that he was sweating. He unzipped his coat and cardigan as far as the laser pack, and undid the top buttons of his shirt. As the cold eased his chest, he realised how hot his crystal had become. He held it between his fingers. 'Dank oo, Drakobata,' he murmured.

A sensation of hurt and pain reached him. As he opened to it, other feelings appeared. Feelings so dark that he did not want to explore them. Focussing on the sense of pain, he wandered off to the side, away from the direction in which his friends were headed.

The sensations were getting stronger. Someone needed help, but he could not see an energy field: frustrating but not surprising.

Closing his eyes to concentrate better, he continued to walk towards the sensations, trying to compare Azuran and Tazian energy fields to estimate how far away the man was.

Suddenly, he was grabbed and swung around. A hand clamped across his mouth and something hard and cold was pressed into the side of his neck.

'Make a sound n'I'll cut yer,' a harsh voice growled in his ear. The man's breath stank. The hand was removed from his mouth and that arm wrapped around his chest above the laser pack.

Qwelby felt himself being half dragged, half pushed sideways. The rifle was banging against their legs, in danger of tripping them up.

'Pick it up,' his assailant snarled.

Jolted out of his reverie, his thoughts scattered in all directions, Qwelby did as instructed. Aware that he was being dragged further and further away from his friends, he started to struggle. This was no game.

A knife dug into the side of his neck.

'Don't be stupid, boy,' the rough voice snarled.

What was wrong with this world? Attacked for no reason the moment he arrived on Earth. Now assaulted by a man he wanted to help! With his frustration building he struggled again. He had to get away. Be by himself. No! Be reunited with Tullia. Desperate to reconnect and to have the additional power that would bring, he sent out urgent thoughts, forcefully summoning his twin. Drakobata was throbbing at his throat.

'Stop that!' his captor ordered as he became aware of a red light pulsing up into the boy's face.

'You're cutting me,' Qwelby said.

Arttu was in no mind to hear excuses. A big, heavy man, dark hair and a swarthy complexion, his face was set in a permanent scowl. He had rejected his given name and chosen Arttu, meaning bear-man. He grimaced at the thought that today he was not living up to his name.

Everything had gone wrong from the very moment they had broken into the jewellers through what he had been assured was an unalarmed skylight. Disoriented by the ear-splitting noise of the alarms he had dropped awkwardly onto the floor, spraining his ankle. Downstairs, he had tripped, fallen and smashed the glass in cabinet with his head. Getting to his feet he had gashed a hand on the broken glass and discovered he had sprained his wrist in that fall. Then the final disaster, his stupid driver losing control on a sharp bend.

At last there had been a measure of luck. Not only had the air bag saved him further injury, it had hidden him from sight as he had slipped down during the crash. He had managed to reach down, slide a knife out of its sheath on his ankle and puncture the airbag. The side door had been flung open. He had rolled onto the ground and crept into the safety of the trees. Since then he had liberally helped himself from his flask of maali.

Now this black boy was the last straw. Juju or voodoo or whatever was not going to stop him: Arttu the Bear-Man!

'Yeow!' Arttu exclaimed as pain shot through his knife-hand. 'What yer doin' yer black...'

Qwelby was unfazed by not receiving a translation of whatever else his captor had said. He had finally pulled himself together and was discovering that some aspects of life on Earth worked like they did at home. Rejecting his pain was causing that to be returned through the knife to his attacker, and magnified by the fear that went with it. But he needed to take more positive action.

Always before when either twin was in serious trouble, they would call on the energy of the other. With the knife cutting into his throat and an arm squeezing his chest, Qwelby could not take three deep breaths. Reinforcing his plea to Tullia, he sucked in energy through the top of his head, sending it spiralling down the two channels that twisted around his spine. As he focussed that into the base of his spine, was he fooling himself, or did he really detect purple and lilac swirling amidst the predominance of red, green and brown?

He felt a hand grasp his crystal through his thick cardigan.

'Zhólérrân!' he shouted as he sent the energy shooting through his central spinal column. He heard a roaring sound like a space rocket taking off. His throat hurt, it was burning. Flames sprouted from his mouth. His wings unfolded, thrusting his captor' arms away.

He lifted his right leg and drove it backwards into his captor's knee, heard a crack, a scream and felt the knife cut into his neck again. A deafening thunderclap set his ears ringing as a flash of light as bright as the midday sun illuminated the surroundings. Propelled forwards by the momentum of his kick, he did not know whether it was a trick of the shadows or whether the light had actually revealed Hannu and Anita nearby, and the afterglare that made him think he had seen a bare mountain top.

His shout was stifled as he fell face down in the snow. Pain was shooting through his neck. He staggered to his feet, clutching his head where he sensed his crown had burst open. Feeling he was about to burst into flames, he pulled his gloves off and grabbed the straps at his sides. Yanking them free, he pulled the laser pack over his head and threw it down. His coat followed. He wrestled his cardigan and shirt over his head and threw himself down onto the cooling snow.

KAIGII! I need you.

CHAPTER 51

DRAGONFLY

KALAHARI

It was afternoon by the time Tullia and Tsetsana reached the footprint on the Female Hill. Tullia slipped off her clothes. 'Look,' she said to Tsetsana. 'Red marks are gone from my arms and legs, but still bad on my body. I want to do a lot today.' She smiled. 'So I told Xashee to rest.'

She saw Tsetsana smile her understanding.

Tullia stood there, drinking in the warmth. 'Today is my fourth day here. Only this morning I know Kaigii must see and feel the same sun. The energy in the footprint is very strong. I will stand in it and in the sun.' She hesitated. There were so many words to learn, no written language and few reference points. 'My people. We drink energy from the sun. Important.' She put her hand to her heart. 'I ask, please, I find him.'

Tullia smiled as Tsetsana nodded, amazed that the girl seemed to understand, not realising that amongst the several errors as her compiler created the dictionary in her mind, one of the consequences was that the Meera considered her to be a Sun Goddess, and thus her twin a Sun God.

'Ahhh. Siyakiti. Donselangi. Lulwanulay,' Tullia cooed, holding out her hand palm down for a large flying insect.

'I've never seen a dragonfly that large,' Tsetsana said as it settled down, its body extending the full length of Tullia's hand. Every part was a deep, rich red except for its two pairs of wings with their centres looking as though they were made of green lace.

'We call it "Whirlingwings",' Tullia said. Slowly she brought her hand nearer to her face. 'Hullo, Dragonfly,' she whispered. She was conscious of its legs, almost as thin as an individual strand of her hair, yet griping her finger with amazing force from what she assumed were tiny suction cups. Two pairs of multifaceted eyes stared at her for what seemed like an eternity. Once again she experienced a sensation as if each cell in her body was being delicately brushed with a feather. She felt her finger released, the wings blurred, her visitor hovered for a moment, then rose into the air and flew away.

'Dragon-Fly,' Tullia whispered to herself as she banished a momentary sense of sadness, turned and stepped onto the footprint and faced the sun with her arms at her side, palms facing forward. She lifted her head and closed her eyes. Settling into a slow and steady breathing rhythm she sank deep into her Kore, pulling the sun's energy into her. When she felt filled, she called forth a memory of the last time she had sunbathed on Vertazia to charge her solar energy quotient.

She sank back into that day on the banks of the river near her home. Qwelby and the other boys had gone off somewhere to play, leaving her alone with Tamina and Shimara, sharing a lovely girly time. But that was not right. Kaigii was not there. Then she remembered.

Kaigii and Wrenden had persuaded quiet Pelnak to join one of their silly pranks. Swimming underwater they had leapt up shrieking like banshees and splashing water over the girls and their neatly folded clothes. She had been furious. 'You're supposed to set an example to Wrenden!' she had shouted.

That was no good. She wanted one of their companionable

times together. The right energy for a connection. Memory returned of the scenes revealed by the Lantern. The images on that morning. The desire that both she and Kaigii had to explore their Aurigan heritage... as a way of understanding their future? A sudden wind sprang from the desert floor. Rushing through the rocks it sounded like the beating of mighty wings...

CHAPTER 52

RAINBOW

VERTASIA

Xaala jumped as a sting on her wrist accompanied the chirping of the Temporal Message Alerter embedded in her bracelet. She ran through the house on her bare feet and into the Receptor Room where her practised fingers rapidly accessed the controls. She removed the Messager from the Receptor and ran to her Teacher's meditation room, knowing he would have translocated there.

As she turned the corner of the corridor she saw that Door had complied with her thoughtsent request to open. Ceegren was already seated in the lotus position on his meditation stool, facing his crystal, Belayyel, which rested on the altar a couple of metres away.

There were two cardinal rules when working with Time: Speed and Ultimate Respect. She had run as fast as the wind, now she landed on both knees at his side, bowed her head and lifted the Messager up to him with both hands. As Ceegren removed the Messager from her, Xaala lowered her hands and took a deep breath to still her racing pulse.

'Look into my eyes,' Ceegren commanded, breaking into her reverie.

With the power that all Venerables possessed, looking into those two ovals of deep sea green was highly dangerous without permission. Xaala raised her head, wondering at an honour that was usually only bestowed as part of his deep teachings.

She felt him slip through her mind and into her Kore.

A flick of his fingers reinforced his thoughtsent command to take her place on a mat on the floor, facing Belayyel.

The message had been one word: 'Spelling.' Xaala had immediately deciphered that. 'Spelling' meant 'ABC', and that meant Abomination Contact. The Quantum Twins, whose flight to Azura was causing so much consternation amongst the Kumelanii, were trying to reconnect. Ceegren had explained to her why that had to be prevented. Her heart beat fast. She was to participate in a meditation crucial to the whole of Vertazia.

She was a little short of her seventeenth rebirthday. *Admittedly the last four months of any phase is its most powerful and I am at the end of my fifth phase of creativity. But this is only my second Era. It's not as though I am even a young adult in my third Era.*

'Precisely,' Ceegren said. 'The abominations are twiyeras. Your own second Era energies are necessary in order that the advanced level energies of myself, Dryddnaa and Gentian will be brought through to their fast vibratory level.'

Gentian, another Venerable, Xaala thought. *But Dryddnaa. She must be a very powerful Chief Readjuster for her to be involved instead of a third Venerable.*

'Now. Surrender,' Ceegren ordered.

With the rigorous training she had received from Teacher, Xaala easily emptied herself of all thoughts and emotions, settled into the lotus position and focussed on Belayyel. She knew she was to be a passive channel. At some time afterwards, Ceegren would require her to access her Memory and relate in detail everything she had seen and heard, together with the thoughts and emotional responses that she had not been aware of at the time.

Energy built up and took control of her. Far away in the mist she perceived two columns of light a long way away from each other. As she flew towards them, the columns grew stronger, brighter, longer. The energy in her jetted out, turning into two roiling black clouds that blotted the columns from her vision.

Tullia shivered as a cold wind struck her. Opening her eyes she saw a dark cloud hurtling towards her. She was alone, standing on a narrow, bare mountain top. As the cloud reached her it changed into thin streamers which wrapped around her, painfully piercing her body where they gripped, and tried to drive her backwards. *Backwards! Over the edge to my death far below on the desert floor.*

Bending her knees, she half crouched, flailing with her arms, tearing the strips away and flinging them over the side of the mountain. They squealed. *Squealed?!*

Gyrating, she tackled more streamers as they tried to encircle her body, their tips constantly striking her bare flesh, pushing her backwards. Wings sprouted from her shoulders. They shielded her back, beating at the dark streamers, knocking them to the ground. As her hooves stamped on them they dissolved into dust with almost human sounding squeals.

Wings? Hooves!

As she kicked the last one away, the remaining cloud coalesced into a menacing, grotesque blob. As it flowed around her, it felt soft and squashy. For a moment it seemed comfortable, easing away the pain from the many cuts. As she started to relax, it pressed closer. Her mind cleared. It was trying to crush her to death. With an effort, she raised her arms. *Arms? Legs!* Her hooves thrust it away from her body.

The Blob extended thick tendrils, trying to curl them around Tullia's legs. Fast and furious her tail whipped left and right, again and again. As the pressure eased, she dropped onto all four legs, stamping on the wriggling tendrils and kicking them over the edge of the mountain top.

A misshapen face appeared, one glaring yellow eye above thick, dark red lips pulled back in a snarl revealing pointed black teeth. Growing a long neck it lunged towards her. She tossed her head, slashing her horn through its neck. With a ghastly spurt of black blood that sizzled where drops struck her body, the head toppled over, its forked, slime-green tongue reaching for her.

Tullia spun around and kicked out with her hind legs. She felt her hooves strike the gruesome head and watched from between her legs as with an ear splitting shriek it toppled backwards over the far side of the narrow mountain top.

Her hooves slipped on the smooth rock and she crashed to the ground, looking with horror over the edge to the desert floor kilometres below. Something soft was spreading over her legs and up her back. There was no comfort this time, the feel was revolting, cloying. Her hind legs were trapped. She beat hard with her wings as she tried to turn and use her forelegs, her horn, anything. The cuts on her legs and body were stinging as the slimy morass inserted thin tendrils into her bloodstream, slowly paralysing her.

'KAIGII!' she thoughtsent with the last of her remaining strength.

Qwelby felt himself cooling. He lifted his head and carefully covering his mouth with his hand, took a few deep breaths. His head slowly cleared and the pain in his neck lessened. He brought his hands together by his shoulders and started to push himself up. Darkness descended all around as heavy weight landed on him. It felt like a trick Wrenden had played, dropping a duvet-cover full of water on him. Then, all he had done was to use his stronger power to negate his friend's imaging of water contained in the duvet. This was different. This was not a simple trick. And the power behind it was strong.

He was on Earth, in the third dimension, or really the fourth as he was amongst people who also had the power of consciousness. He would just use physical force. With effort, he forced himself up onto hands and knees. He could see light creeping in under the edge of whatever was weighing him down. He got a foot out and with a mighty effort of arms and legs rolled over, heaving the mass to one side. He wriggling out quickly and crouched into a defensive position. And saw the dark mass fade away. The only resistance had come from its size and weight. It had not been empowered with the slightest degree of sentience.

As he stood upright, dark figures leapt at him. Red, orange and yellow they passed though his body. All the colours were dirty and smelling of evil. As the forms solidified he saw three, four legged beasts with wide open jaws full of long pointed teeth, saliva dripping from their mouths, now turning back to face him again. As the first leapt to attack he shifted consciousness, trying to thoughtblock its path. He saw his tail lash out and the beast explode in a flash of light. A second beast leapt for his throat. He seared it in mid-air with a burst of flames from his mouth. The claw on his hind leg shattered the back of the third.

From above the trees a flock of beasts descended on wings like those of giant bats. They had animal bodies with heads and beaks like prehistoric pterodactyls and long front legs ending in wide spread talons.

The dragon grew, rearing up above the trees, flamed the first beast, ducked and grabbed two more by their tails, hurling them into the night sky where they exploded in showers of incandescence. Flaming another, he lifted a hind leg thicker than any of the trees and crushed a beast that had landed behind him. He heard the boy shriek with pain as a beast landed on his forearm and stabbed him in the shoulder. He closed his massive jaws on it, ripping its head from its body. Another landed on his other arm but the next wave was upon him before he could rip that one away.

A great gout of flame spewed from his jaws swamping his attackers and they exploded in balls of fire. But the flames died before all had been vanquished and he felt the claws of the one remaining beast dig into his thigh. He sank his jaws into the body of the beast on his arm, ripped it free and swung his massive head to one side and then back again, smashing the one in his mouth against the one on his thigh and saw them both explode. Roaring defiance into the night sky he echoed his Rider's cries of pain.

I'm not a dragon, I'm a DragonRider.

The thought hung in the air.

'I'm not a Dragon or a Dragon Rider,' the boy said aloud, clutching his bleeding left shoulder. 'I'm...'

A creature like a lion with the head of a bull landed in front of him and reared up on its hind legs, as tall as the dragon. Confused with the different levels of consciousness, different dimensions interacting, he did not react fast enough and the lion's claws raked down across his chest. The boy howled with pain. Too close to flame his attacker, the dragon leapt into the air. Briefly steadying himself on his tail he brought his hind legs up in front and bore down with all his weight, slashing down with the claws of both feet. The bull-lion screamed and exploded in a blaze of light that ripped open a tunnel though the forest.

In the distance Qwelby saw a unicorn.

She was beautiful in all her splendour. Her body was silver, her long and flowing mane gold, her silver tail was gold tipped. Slashing her head from side to side, her horn was vibrant with all the colours of the rainbow as she beat at her attackers. Qwelby felt his heart burst open.

'TUUULLLIIIIAAAA,' he roared, and lifted into flight.

As the darkness thinned, Xaala saw the columns of light spring up and join together, creating a rainbow of bright, pulsing colour. The two ends on the ground were vibrating, alternately becoming thinner and thicker, the colours seeming to run back and forth throughout the whole arch.

She was propelled into the rainbow. Dizzy, she became aware

the energies she was channelling were pouring out through her head and feet, a swirling mixture of dark greys and blacks, dirty reds, oranges and mustards. She felt nauseous as jolts of energy rebounded back into her body and seemed to be fighting within her very Self. She hung there, alone in Space and Time, wracked with ever increasing pain. Was she strong enough? Was it ever going to end?

A cruel laugh filled Tullia's ears as the numbing sensation spread along her spine, creeping towards her head. She heard the sound of strong wings beating. Whatever evil was attacking her, she was about to be carried away to its lair. Her last few moments alive. *Oh Kaigii. I am sorry. I do love you.*

She forced herself to look up. She would look death in the face. High above, circling down towards her on enormous wings, half hidden by dark mist was... what? As it passed overhead she saw the long tail, the large rear legs, the smaller front ones. A dragon! But not just any dragon. It was a rich dark red, glowing with streaks of emerald green and sun-kissed yellow, bright violet sparkling from its wingtips, all tinged with turquoise. A magnificent golden crest atop its head.

'QWELBEEEEEEEEE!' she cried, as the dragon circled around again and flew straight at her. She dared not watch and keep her horn pointing up at him. She lowered her head and felt a great rush of air. She screamed with pain as the vile grotesque was wrenched from her body, every single one of her cuts on fire as its penetrating tendrils were torn away.

Gasping for breath, she managed to turn her head sideways and watched as the dragon rose high in the air then dropped the struggling grotesque, dipped his wings and swung around, searing it and its wriggling tentacles with blazing fire. With an unearthly scream the monstrosity burst into flames and fell out of sight.

The dragon rose high into the sky, flamed again and gave a

mighty roar that shook the mountain. The monstrosity destroyed and his triumph displayed, Qwelby swooped down and landed in front of his twin. He enfolded the beautiful unicorn in his forelegs, and with a great down stroke of his wings he lifted her up and carried her back.

Tullia dug deep into her inner reserves and found the strength to rise on all four legs. Hooves clattering on the rock, she actually pranced up to her twin. He deserved all the honour she could bestow. Careful of her sharp horn, she lowered her head to his side, arching her neck, nuzzling him, whistling a melody through her fluted horn.

The dragon dropped onto all fours, exhausted. With a gentle whinny, Tullia turned around, sliding her neck under his wing, softly whistling to him to let her support him. As her forelegs stepped out of the depression of the God's footprint, she slumped to the ground, her arms stretched out in front.

Pushing with her hind legs she felt tremors run through her torso. Looking down she saw her ordinary body. But she was cut off at the waist. Beyond that there was nothing to see of anything. Looking across to her twin she saw his head and shoulders and one arm draped over her back. Nothing more.

'Sizangi!' she called. When Tsetsana did not reply Tullia remembered to switch to Meera. 'Help me!' she called again, looking at her friend who was sitting with her back to the rock, eyes and mouth wide open, one hand half raised.

A NullPoint Bubble! Tullia realised.

Again, Tullia pushed with her legs, pulling herself forward with her hands, ignoring both the pain and her twin. Completely out of the intense energy field of the depression, she was her normal self. *If normal includes dozens of burning cuts!* She took hold of her twin by his shoulders and helped him move forward, watching the rest of his body and legs appear as if out of nowhere, blood trickling from many cuts. As he shuddered and shook himself like a dog coming out of the water, she noticed large, dark bruises curved around each of his shoulder blades.

With a jolt, he fell on his back on the snow. As he rolled over and onto his hands and knees he saw Hannu and Anita a few paces away, running towards him. No! They were frozen like statues.

A *NullPoint Bubble!*

Tullia was lying a few paces away.

Qwelby crawled to his twin and pulled her into a tight embrace, ignoring the stinging pain from all his cuts.

On the mountain top, Tullia pulled her twin into a tight embrace, feeling warm blood trickling over her from his wounds and ignoring the sharp pain from her wounds as he put his arms around her and pulled her tightly to him.

'KAIGII!!' they exclaimed.

'Trust you to get lost, Kaigii,' Tullia said fondly, running her fingers through his thick, long hair.

Qwelby just grinned and snuggled into her embrace. Being told off by his twin was a reassuring return to normality. She always wanted to look after him. Right now if felt good.

As his pain eased, he looked up. Their eyes met, twirling, faster and faster. They had always looked after each other. She, a unicorn-riding Healer, he a dragon-riding Warrior protecting her from the attacking Solids. And before that in peaceful times when he had led a small team to create the HomeSphere, and she had led the equally small team that had persuaded all the Auriganii to live in and around it for their search for a new homeworld.

Each saw the other's eyes stop twirling and the purple orbs pulse with inner fire. Fine silver rims appeared around the orbs, then around the blue ovals. They remembered seeing each other's eyes like that as they were given the honour of launching the HomeSphere on its journey. Then seeing depictions of those eyes on all the levels of the HomeSphere. Feelings emerged, unbelievable feelings.

'I Am You,' each whispered to the other in wonderment.

Speechless, they looked at each other as they understood what made them unique.

<*But how??*>

Smiles spread across their faces as they realised that their mental connection was restored.

Memories of Space Wars and Dragon and Unicorn Riding were all logical. Through careful pairbonding over the millennia, very strong Uddîšû genes had been preserved and passed down to both of their parents. The twins' own uniqueness had increased that strength. But to have such definite memories back to Auriga itself. Memories not encoded in their parent's genes.

<*More genes?? Another segment?? Hidden by Aurigan energies??*>

Open-mouthed, they stared at each other. Had they solved part of The Mystery, and why they were "identical" but very obviously a boy and a girl – gender in a fourth segment?

<*An explanation. But why?? That, is the real mystery*>

Realising there was little strength in his arms around her, Tullia cuddled him, rocking him gently. Seeing her twin's energy field vibrating as powerfully as hers had done ever since arriving on Haven, she gave a little grunt of relief. *So vibrating like that is normal for being in the third dimension.*

Each eased their grip on the other and leant back to get a good look. Each was soaked in sweat and smeared with blood. As they moved, each saw the other's muscles ripple and the sun's rays turn each body into a host of tiny sparkling rainbows. Images tumbled through their shared minds.

He was standing on a landing shelf on the edge of the HomeSphere, lifting the exhausted Healer down from the back of her unicorn and carrying her to a RelaxCouch. She was bending over the Warrior's wounded body, the six long fingers of each hand guiding the healing energies that spiralled from her forehead.

'Oh, Kaigii,' each murmured. 'You do need looking after.'

They laughed, at each other, at themselves, at their laughter. No matter how much they competed and tried to best the other, one thing would never change: underneath it all they cared. They were Kaigii.

<Qeïchâ Kaïgïï>

Something was wrong.

Tullia half thought she could see the rock through his body. *'Don't be daft. It's the sun. Heat haze. That's all.* But where her arm curved around his shoulders, she saw faint grey markings. Through her arm!

Qwelby could faintly see the snow through her body. He lifted one of his arms. Looking at it he could just make out the shapes of trees – through his arm!

'Logical,' their Intuitions said. *'You both are in two places at once.'*

Looking at each other was confusing, there were four of them.

'A NullPoint Bubble!!' they exclaimed. 'One of us to the other.'

'I'm on Earth with good friends, the boy and a girl with the snowman. They want to meet you,' Qwelby said.

'I'm on Haven with the tribe of hunters. They will welcome you,' Tullia replied.

'The girl's father is a scientist who will help us contact home.'

'My tribe accepts me as coming from another planet and want to help us be together.'

'Four days on this planet and I have been attacked three times...'

'These people are like us. I think they're descended from the Auriganii...'

Riddled with pain and feeling sick to her Kore, Xaala's conscious mind was shouting at her. The rainbow was changing. The colours had grown stronger and brighter and now were coherently flowing in one direction. Through her feet, along her spine and out through her crown poured cascades of bright pinks and greens, shot through with violet and white. It was beautiful. She welcomed the sense of peace and the cessation of pain that awaited if only

369

she would let herself go and be enwrapped in the feelings of...

NO!!!

With a wrench, she tore her mind free and thoughtsent: '*Abominations connecting. STOP!!!*'

'YEEOOW!!' the twins yelled as they were deluged by what felt like a river of icy cold water as a bolt of brilliant light shot between them. A great rent in the landscape opened, ripping between them. Qwelby was in the snow and Tullia on the hill, each looking at the other from a distance.

'KAIGII!' each yelled as they rose up and went to throw themselves across the widening gap. No Dragon. No Unicorn. Just a boy and a girl.

There was a blinding flash of light and a massive thunderclap that shook snow from the trees, rattled the loose rocks and threw Xaala half way across the room.

When their eyes cleared and the twins could see again: each was alone. They threw back their heads and screamed their despair to the multiverse. Each had the same sensation: that the Darkness had attacked them out of fear for the consequences of their being reunited. Each flicked to that special corner of their mind where the other lived. No pain! No strong contact, but no pain. Truly, once again, they were mentally connected.

As Xaala's eyes cleared, she found herself lying on her back, staring at the ceiling. Instead of the usual soft pastel colours, it was splotched with a mixture of angry reds and mustards and shot through with streaks of black, as if there had been an explosion in the room.

CHAPTER 53

HEROES ALL

FINLAND

Qwelby was in shock and felt himself trembling all over. Earth was so violent. And now people from Vertazia? He wanted to be with Tullia. Their twinergy would give him the strength he desperately needed. He heard the scrunch of footsteps in the snow and sensed people kneeling. He turned and reached, not so much for Anita, but for the female energy. Except when they were very young and had been fighting, the twins always turned to each other for support. They were one. Kaigii.

Anita saw a totally black face. Where were his bright eyes? She felt her energy draining away.

Qwelby eased away from her.

'Thank God!' she said, as his eyes appeared in the dark. 'I thought you'd gone blind,' she added as she removed her white scarf and tenderly wrapped it around the several cuts on Qwelby's neck.

'That was Tullia?' Hannu asked in a voice almost of disbelief.

Distraught at having been parted, Qwelby just nodded.

'Wow, she's...' Some second sense stopped Hannu from saying what he was thinking as Anita voiced her own thought: 'So beautiful.'

Feeling Qwelby's intense need for Tullia took Anita back to the day she had felt that she was looking at Qwelby's world through his twin's eyes. Helping him into his shirt, half Anita, half Tullia, she brushed aside his fumbling hands, helped him into his cardigan, zipped that up and then into his coat and zipped that up. 'You are so alike,' she said in a quiet voice.

The scornful reply that started in Qwelby's mind did not find its way to his mouth. He was picturing not his annoyingly bossy twin, but the brave and wounded young woman he had just been with, wondering what it all meant. Then it dawned on him. His friends had seen Tullia. It had not been a fantasy or an exaggerated deepstate! What more had they seen? He gripped Anita's arm.

'Don't tell. Please. No-one. And Hannu, I tell you later,' was what he tried to say as he forced the words out through teeth clenched from the burning pain in his throat.

'I promise,' Anita replied after a pause, feeling excited that she had grasped his meaning through his feelings, even if not too sure about the exact words. 'And for Hannu. We won't tell anyone.'

Qwelby gave her a crooked smile, happy that she had understood his mangled words.

'There's a man here. Says you've broken his leg,' Hannu said in a tight voice from a short distance away. 'He's drunk!'

'Oh. Ah. Yess,' Qwelby said. 'Dank oo,' he said in a croak to Anita, before crawling on hands and knees to where Hannu was standing.

As Qwelby's compiler stored several unknown words from his erstwhile captor, flagging them for later attention, he could see that the man was in a lot of pain, and the aura around his right knee was flaring brightly.

'Hold shoulders. I heal,' he croaked. He knelt down with the man's leg between his own, putting his hands on either side of the broken kneecap, little flickers of green running through his sholder length hair as he focussed his energies.

Apart from continuing to mouth obscenities, Arttu did not resist. He was too drunk and in too much pain to try to stop what was happening to him. Besides which, it felt good.

Flashing lights of police cars and the wailing sirens dying away broke into Qwelby's concentration. Panic flared within him. *Can't stop. Not Healer like Kaigii. Take longer.*

Moments later he was aware of torchlight, then voices calling. He heard Anita and Hannu shout back.

Qwelby was petrified. He had had one escape. It was pushing his luck to hope for another. But he had broken the man's knee. He had to heal it. Not just wanted to. Had to.

The lights came closer and swept across the scene.

'What on earth?' the sergeant exclaimed.

'Man hurt. I heal,' Qwelby said in a hoarse voice, keeping his head lowered and his hands either side of his attacker's knee. He was aware that Anita was at his side, trying to shield him.

He sensed three policemen standing around, holding torches and looking at him. Their energies were different from anything he had ever experienced on Vertazia. He guessed they must be similar to the Persuaders, the nearest the Tazii had to any sort of police force who only operated in the Shakazii's homelands. The word that came to mind was 'Enforcer'. They had plenty of determination and were curious. When skiing, he had seen a policeman and had learnt that they carried guns. And they were used for killing. Glancing up, he saw each of these policemen had a gun.

He wanted to swallow but his mouth refused to cooperate. He was dribbling!

'What was that noise and the light?' Sjöström asked.

Qwelby couldn't help it. He had to look at her. Strong concern, definite authority and a lot more curiosity than the others.

Unable to speak, he gripped Anita's arm and looked at her pleadingly, before returning to his healing.

'That man held him. He had a knife. It must have touched the laser pack,' Anita explained, recalling what she had seen in the bright flash.

'Are you three all right?' Dr Keskinen asked, having accompanied the police and wanting to interrupt the sergeant's questioning. 'We came as soon as we heard what sounded like an explosion.'

Definitely a NullPoint Bubble, Qwelby confirmed to himself as he saw the sergeant's feet moving around. He lowered his head even more, trying to brush away the dribble on the collar of his coat.

He felt a gloved hand under his chin, firmly lifting his head up. He closed his eyes, ostensibly against the torchlight, looked inside at his expanding panic and feverishly tried to push it back down into his belly before it erupted and his legs carried him away.

'We must get you to the hospital,' Sjöström said. 'Your face needs treatment and blood is seeping through that bandage.'

'NO!' Qwelby exclaimed, glancing at her. 'I heal good.' His throat hurting less, he added strong conviction to his tone of voice and an image of him smiling, relaxed and unhurt.

'It's all right, sergeant. My wife will look after him,' Keskinen said, reassured by Qwelby's certainty and only too anxious for there to be as little official involvement as possible.

Sjöström knew she was in enough trouble for letting a group of children get involved in the night's events, even though there was no way she could have prevented it. To have to report that one had been badly injured... nevertheless, she was an experienced police officer. She took a long look at the black stranger and realised that what she thought was blood was just a shadow on the silk scarf he was wearing.

But his eyes. She had only seen them briefly. They seemed to be larger than usual and ... shining? Sjöström had never met a black person. She remembered her brother telling her of a film he had seen. Set in Africa, one white man had said to the other something like: "Don't shoot until you see the whites of their eyes." So, it was true.

Healing finished, Qwelby had to move. He wanted to get away from the policewoman and her probing questions. But he was afraid that the very movement of getting up would free his panic and he would run away, be caught and taken away to be used in experiments.

'Where does he come from?' Sjöström asked.

'From Czech,' Anita answered from where she was kneeling by Qwelby. 'My father's helping him with some experiments.' Realising that whilst that was true, it had not been the best thing to say, she hastily added: 'His father's a scientist.'

As Anita was answering, Qwelby made a 'come here' gesture to Hannu. He had been moved a few feet away by the two policemen who had come to stand by Arttu, and were now gazing at Qwelby. 'Help. Hold. Hide,' he said as Hannu reached him.

'His family comes from Mongolia... originally,' Hannu added as he bent down. Qwelby had dropped his pretence as he had reached out to his friend, and in the stark torchlight Qwelby's dark and battered face resembled a character in a film Hannu had seen about Genghis Khan.

As Hannu helped him up, Qwelby tucked the damaged side of his face against his friend. He heard the sergeant's soft footfalls as she walked around and again shone her torch on his face. He knew his eyes were twirling with lots of colours. He kept them firmly closed. He felt a touch on the shoulder.

'Are you all right?' Sjöström asked.

'Yess, dank oo,' Qwelby said slowly, trying his best to speak clearly out of his badly bruised mouth. 'I good.' He used his last drop of energy to put as much conviction into his tone of voice as possible. 'Need sleep.'

The sergeant lowered her torch. A Mongolian. She had seen a film about Genghis Kahn. He had been very dark. Yes, she could see that. Kotomäki was a small town but not so large that Sjöström

375

did not know everyone, she knew Dr Viljo Keskinen and that there were several scientists from different countries working at the Research Institute in Jyväskylä.

Qwelby was hanging on to Hannu, feeling outright panic welling up. His legs felt rubbery as though they were going to collapse. At the same time his emotions were telling them to run away. He heard the muffled sounds of the man he had hurt being helped to his feet. He felt Hannu's heart beating, a throbbing pulse against the side of his hurting head. He was waiting for his hands to be seized, pulled behind his back and metal rings snapped on.

Time stood still.

He heard the sergeant move. The torchlight left his face. He tensed, waiting to be seized.

'Right,' Sjöström said briskly.

A stifled moan escaped Qwelby's lips as he went rigid with fear.

'You three take "Bear Man" to the station. I'll meet you there,' she continued. 'After I've taken the Doctor and these children home.'

Qwelby's legs turned to jelly with relief. He clung on to Hannu as to a lifebelt in a storm-tossed sea.

'Put him in an interview room, give him coffee, and don't say anything to anybody about what's happened in the woods. U.n.d.e.r.s.t.a.n.d!' Sjöström ordered.

Intuition told her that there was more to the situation with the black boy than met the eye. 'In more ways than one,' she said to herself. But this was neither the time nor the place to explore that. She needed to keep a lid on what had happened. Her curiosity she would satisfy later.

A few minutes later Sjöström pulled up outside the doctor's house. As the three youngsters got out, Hannu turned to Qwelby. 'You sure?' he asked, showing the stone he was holding.

Qwelby could not speak. He desperately wanted, needed, to keep it. But the energy consequences of doing so without permission were unthinkable. Internal disruption and, at home, that would summon the terror of a visit from Readjusters.

With a shrug of his shoulders, Hannu handed the stone to Sjöström with an explanation, and Qwelby's request.

Keskinen remained in the car for a discussion, which was quickly concluded to the satisfaction of both. Her report would keep the children's involvement to the minimum. No mention would be made of Qwelby's injuries on the basis of Keskinen's assurance that Qwelby would be taken to hospital if there were any problems and she would be advised immediately. The Doctor would go to the station the following day to make a formal statement.

'Shit! You do look awful,' Hannu said to Qwelby as they entered the hall with its bright light.

'Upstairs, quick,' Anita said.

Once in the bathroom Qwelby stripped to the waist.

'What the... happened to you?' Hannu exclaimed, cutting short his expletive as he remembered that Anita was there.

Looking in the mirror, Qwelby was shocked by the state he was in. His lip had swollen, dried blood was splattered all over his face from that and the nosebleed. He could see a bruise forming below one eye. There was a big bruise in the centre of his chest, several nasty gashes over his arms and torso and blood was trickling from a wound in his shoulder and three long gashes running the full length of his chest and stomach.

As he collapsed onto the side of the bath he noticed rips in his trousers, stained red with blood. 'That was really real,' he said in an awed tone of voice. 'In your world.' He had been on the verge of dismissing what had happened as having been an ultradeepstate. But seeing the torn trousers, he knew if they had been caught in that groundquake rather than separated by it...

His head swimming and his heart pounding, Qwelby groped for Hannu and clung onto him, breathing heavily as images cascaded through his mind.

Anita was standing at the basin holding a wet a flannel.

'Tank you, tank you, tank you. Bot of you,' Qwelby said, as he pulled away and sat back on the edge of the bath, his face almost grey with shock. The bruising was already easing and his words coming out a little clearer.

Anita handed the wet flannel to Hannu and carefully unwound her bloody scarf from Qwelby's neck. She told Hannu to clean Qwelby's face and neck whilst she found and then applied a dressing and a bandage to his neck. That done she took a towel and started to dry Qwelby.

'I do tat,' he tried to protest, his still slightly slurred pronunciation clearly saying he was not well.

'You need looking after,' she said as she continued to dry him, needing something to do as she was feeling very shaky from the night's adventures.

'Your neck was bleeding a lot,' Hannu said, wanting to break up the intense energy he felt flowing between his girl-friend and the alien.

'Yess. Healing tat man help me,' Qwelby replied, wincing as Hannu wiped the wounds on his arms.

Satisfied that they had dealt with Qwelby's face and neck, Anita gently wiped what had looked like a deep wound to his shoulder and the long gashes on his torso. 'They're already closing!' she exclaimed. 'And not bleeding.'

'Seventh dimension injuries. Kaigii. Identical. Have healer's genes like Tullia,' Qwelby said. 'This one real your world. Hurts more,' he added as he touched the bandage around his neck.

Qwelby's need for connection with his twin was so strong that Anita was fully enwrapped in the energy. 'Trousers,' she said. 'You're still bleeding.'

Qwelby stood up and undid his trousers. Seeing how much blood there was on his torn boxers, he removed trousers and boxers.

Anita gasped at what she saw, or rather didn't see.

'Tazii different from Azurii,' Qwelby said. 'My male, third leg we call it, inside.' He pointed to a small opening between his legs.

'It won't come out until my Awakening. Hannu tells me there's something a bit similar with Azurii boys.'

'I've told him to make sure he keeps a towel on when we're sharing a sauna. Religious inhibitions or something,' Hannu said.

Carefully washing then drying the two long gashes in Qwelby's thigh, and seeing the edges of his flesh knit together, Anita realised just how alien was the handsome young man with the magnetic eyes.

Trousers back on, boxers in the waste bin, Qwelby sat back down on the side of the bath as Anita picked up his shirt. Before he could stop her, she had got one arm in and slipped the shirt round behind him. He heard her indrawn breath, then felt her fingers gently tracing long curves by the shoulder blades.

'You see anything... strange?' he asked.

'Heavy raised bruising...'

'Saw you fighting, leaping in the air like in one of those oriental movies. Almost like you were flying. What more do you want?' Hannu said brusquely. Once again uncomfortable with how Anita's was treating the alien in such a personal and caring way, as though they had become more than boy and girlfriend.

'You saw me?'

'And Tullia. How the devil... ?'

'Don't know.' Overtaken by dizziness, Qwelby slumped forward to be caught by Hannu. Hanging onto his friend he waited for his head to clear. Instead his vision was assailed by images of burning, then a Salamander made of living flames sinuously gyrating.

'Attribute,' he muttered as his mind cleared. Tamina had wanted to know why her mother refused to honour her genetic inheritance from the Heroine Rrîltallâ Taminûllÿâ, and would not talk about it. The Twins had tried to find an answer through their recent access to the ShadowMarket. What they had been prepared to offer by way of energy exchange had not produced an answer. But they had discovered that the Heroine had what was called an Attribute: an energy form she could adopt at will - a Salamander.

Seeing their interest, and trying to get them to offer a better exchange, their source had hinted that other Uddîsû might also have possessed Attributes.

It was obvious. The Dragon-Riding Hero would have a Dragon as his Attribute, the Unicorn-Riding Heroine, a Unicorn. But why then had his friends not seen his Dragon? Dimensions, levels, rates of vibration. Somehow, he and Tullia, their rates of vibration had slowed so their bodies were as solid on Earth as the Azurii. But their other levels were still working. How? Not with only three segments, otherwise Tazii would be able to visit Earth in their ordinary bodies. He and Kaigii must have a fourth segment, taking them closer to their Aurigan heritage. Content he had found a logical explanation, Qwelby pushed himself upright and attributed the soft buzz in Tullia's corner of his mind to dizziness.

'This just like at home,' he said a few moments later with a lopsided smile as Anita finished helping him into the shirt and sweater. 'Tullia take charge and... sort me out.' *LAIM Boy!* he thought to himself as he slipped into her corner in his mind. No thoughtsharing, but the corner was occupied. He was whole again. And so was Kaigii.

Anita trembled and reached out a hand to Hannu for support. 'I'm feeling Tullia like I did the other day,' she whispered, as he put his arm around her. He pulled her tighter to him than he intended. He was uncomfortable with how much Anita was wanting to care for Qwelby, and starting to fear that he was loosing her to the alien.

'Is everything all right?' Taimi Keskinen called.

Not now, Anita-Tullia thought, aware that the room was awash with conflicting emotions. *I've got two boys to look after. And I don't know who I am right now.*

'Coming, mother,' Anita called back, and grimaced.

Each lost in their own thoughts, they descended to the kitchen where everyone was seated around the big table with steaming hot drinks.

'I've said that we'll leave telling the adventures until later,' Dr Keskinen explained as they sat down. 'There will be plenty of time when we gather at the Rahkamos, and everyone there will want to hear the story. But one celebration is in order. Qwelby. You scored more hits than all the others put together.' The Doctor held up his hand to still the exclamations. 'I have checked. The muzzle flash on his rifle is working perfectly. How on earth did you do it?'

"How on Earth" is a very good question! Qwelby thought. 'My eyes are different from yours. They give me a big advantage,' he said as he looked at the Doctor's wife, aware that he was playing a dangerous game. What he had said was perfectly true, but it was no part of the answer.

Taimi Keskinen felt the pale blue and shining ovals of Qwelby's eyes pulling her into the purple centres as a voice inside her head seemed to say: 'Explain later.'

'You okay?' Qwelby whispered, leaning close to Anita. 'I borrow lot of energy.'

'Borrowed?' she asked. 'Taken' had felt more like it.

'Yess.' He gave a lopsided smile. 'Now I borrow all. Anoder time I lend.'

'The same people you borrow from?' Anita asked, no longer whispering.

'No. Who need,' he replied, remembering that with Nils and Jarno present he had to keep to simple Finnish.

'Is this only for your healing?' Hannu asked.

'Now, yess. Tomorrow. Anyting,' he replied, knowing he would have to explain better when Hannu's other friends were not around.

'And then you give, lend, to someone else?' Anita asked as she used a tissue to wipe away the hot chocolate that was dribbling from the corner of his mouth.

'Yess.' Qwelby smiled, his eyes gently twirled and he saw her cheeks redden.

'It's late,' Taimi said. 'Time we all got ready for midnight.'

As everyone moved, Qwelby leant across to Anita. 'I sorry. I thought you Tullia. I took lots.' He glanced at Hannu. His aura was flickering with dirty yellow and both of their auras were swirling with feelings of discomfort Qwelby did not understand.

'You lot energy now,' he said to Hannu. 'You know how give your energy.' Then felt uncomfortable for a reason he could not fathom.

As they rose from the table, Hannu and Anita glanced at one another, looked away and blushed.

Ah, I understand. Azurii do not hug and hold hands like we do. So they can't share energy when they need it. Qwelby was satisfied that he understood what he had come to think of as "their problem".

As the boys filed out of the door, Dr Keskinen held Qwelby back. He had an idea of how to prove the boy a fake.

'I've been thinking of how I could get a message to your home world. My first idea is to try to add another transmission to one of the TV programmes you and your friends watch. I'll do some work on that and we'll talk another day.'

'I'm sure that swelling is going down already,' Taimi said in a surprised tone of voice, one arm round her tired-looking daughter.

'Yess, I borrow lot energy.' Qwelby gave Anita a smile of gratitude.

Qwelby saw Mrs Keskinen's eyes searching him. He gave her a faint smile and saw the look in her eyes. *She understands!*

'Come on Qwelby!' called Hannu in a grouchy voice, poking his head back through the doorway. 'Let's go home and party.'

Stepping out through the back door, Qwelby stumbled and almost fell onto Hannu. The two boys made their way back to the Rahkamos' house with Qwelby's arm draped over his friend's shoulders. Hannu's mixture of jealousy and fear of losing Anita waned as he felt Qwelby's need for more than just physical support. Biting back his desire to ask for an explanation of what had happened, he concentrated on supporting his now very obviously alien friend.

Qwelby used the time he spent washing and changing to store in a small room in his mind those experiences that were not to be shared during the celebrations. Drained of all his energy, he did not have enough strength to turn it into a seamless box, and had to be content with hoping that he had been able to safely lock the door.

Sjöström knew Arttu from her time as a constable in Jyväskylä. When she reached the station, the discussion with him was brief and to the point. His statement would be that he was badly hurt during the burglary, had tried to hide in the woods, and got drunk. His metal flask had come into contact with the laser. Her report would not mention that the boy had several nasty gashes on his neck: so no charge of GBH.

There had been children playing in the woods that night. Naturally they had been attracted by the commotion of him and his cronies being arrested. Any mention of them actually being involved would be laughed off as pathetic attempt at bravado, as though to say eight police officers could not manage Arttu and his cronies by themselves. And one of her constables had a black eye coming that was going to look good when photographed the following morning.

Arttu understood Sjöström's unspoken meaning. No pig was ever fair, but. On the other hand, she could stitch him up if she wanted. He agreed. He had no choice. As the sergeant left the police surgeon arrived to remove the knife still stuck to the melted flesh on his hand.

Arttu vowed that once that had healed he would make the boy regret revealing his hiding place. Seriously regret!

Much later than planned, the Rahkamos' house was full of a boisterous crowd. As well as the Keskinens, Nils and Jarno were there with their families, also Oona. Previously, she had asked Hannu if she could come, and his parents had been happy to agree.

Oona's father had forbidden her brother to join in the laser game for fear of damaging his ankle again on the uneven ground, hidden by the thick snow. To Oona that had meant a boring evening at home as the odd one out between her parents and her brother with his girl-friend, Ilta.

After everyone had left the Keskinen's, Anita had called Hannu on his mobile and told him to keep Qwelby upstairs until she arrived so she explain her idea of a story to account for his eyes. That his family originated in Japan and over generations had migrated across Asia, intermarrying with Mongolians. It was an unusual genetic occurrence. All his family were the same.

Qwelby was content. The last part was true. He would nod when she said that, and just not comment on the other part. He was the hero of the night. Exhausted, and with his sore throat and mouth, he was happy to let the others explain as much as possible of the evening's events.

When Hannu and Anita had realised that Qwelby was not following them, they had gone back to look for him and seen him seized by Arttu. They had followed, hoping for a chance to rescue him. Qwelby was sure that they over dramatised the story and was very happy when they both kept the promise Anita had made and did not mention seeing Tullia, nor any dragon. He had promised them he would tell them the whole story when they were alone.

The flash and scream? Some weird connection of knife, laser pack and the torc around his neck was all that Qwelby could offer with a shrug of his shoulders. He let them examine his EraBand, made of interlined rectangles each of three coloured metals. The gold and platinum were recognisable. 'Black is Xzyliment. Very strange metal,' he said, happy to keep to 'baby talk', and not try to explain that it was produced by the XzylStroems, and was thought to come from the Shadow World as it had a much higher concentration of anti-matter than was normal.

The sound of fireworks heralding midnight and the New Year interrupted their talking. Normally, they would have gone to the edge of the village to watch. Now, it would take too long to get dressed for the cold and walk that far, so they all trooped upstairs to watch the rockets bursting in the sky.

Back downstairs Qwelby headed for the sofa where he had been sitting with Hannu and Anita, to discover Oona sliding in at the end next to him.

With all four youngsters seated, Qwelby found himself squashed between Hannu and Oona, arms awkwardly trapped in front. Oona was much smaller than him and he moved one arm to rest along the back of the sofa behind her. As he did that he saw her blue eyes looking at him from her pale face with her small, red lips and rosy pink cheeks framed by long blond hair. It was such a contrast to sitting next to his twin or any of their friends at home that he could not tear his eyes away. And there was something else.

He became aware of a warm feeling, more than just the heat of their bodies touching. This feeling was inside. He was puzzled.

'You look uncomfortable. With your arm like that,' Oona said.

He saw her little pink tongue flick out across her lips and a look in her eyes he was unable to decipher.

Feeling embarrassed as he realised he had been staring at her, he grinned sheepishly and let it drape around her shoulders. She was right. That was more comfortable.

As conversation restarted, Qwelby was happy to let his friends continue to do most of the talking for him. Soon, Oona's head was resting on his chest and one of her hands on his thigh. The contact and the warm feeling were very relaxing. He gave a deep sigh and saw Oona look up at him with a question in her eyes.

Fatigue overtook him. He was aware that she was concerned for him, in a different way from his twin. It was nice. So much had happened that night that he didn't have the mental energy to explore the new sensations he was feeling, or those he detected in Oona.

'Mmh' he mumbled as he smiled at her and, without any conscious thought on his part, his arm pulled her a little closer.

Oona snuggled her head back onto his chest and he felt her hand give his thigh a gentle squeeze.

A knock at the door stopped conversation. A few moments later Paavo ushered Sergeant Sjöström into the room. Saying that she was off duty, she was happy to accept the offer of a drink to celebrate the New Year and also, she explained, the good news she brought. Appraised of the official version of events, and she emphasised "official", the owner of the jewellery shop was offering a small reward to the children without whose actions his property almost certainly would not have been recovered. The news about the reward could have waited until later, but Sjöström had felt impelled to satisfy her curiosity about the stranger. And she had a good excuse. She asked after the children, finally turning to Qwelby.

'Good. Thank you,' he replied with a smile. From deep within he summoned up the energy to add to his accompanying thoughts total conviction of having recovered from nothing more than a sight bump. He wished he could shake her hand and transfer that thought to her as a strong feeling.

Sjöström nodded and smiled, relieved both by his words and what was now his clear pronunciation. Seeing him clearly, the description of "Mongolian" sounded logical. His unusual eyes were half closed, giving an impression of tiredness. The happy atmosphere in the room and the way one young girl was snuggled up to him told her that all was well. It confirmed the holiday arrangements that Dr Keskinen had explained to her earlier as they had sat talking in the police car outside his house.

'Qwelby. Your piece of rock,' she said as she took it from her coat pocket. 'Mr Nykänen says it's just a piece of meteorite he uses to prop open a door. Probably used to smash the glass cabinets which is why it ended up in the backpack.' She held it up so all could see the wedge shape. 'He says you are welcome to keep it.'

There were murmurs at its beauty. A mixture of ambers and oranges with dark green threads.

'Meteorite be flamed!' Qwelby almost said aloud as he stood up, certain that its Aurigan energy signature was part of the explanation for his arrival in Finland.

The room was crowded and it was going to cause too much trouble for the sergeant to reach Qwelby. She had to content herself with handing it to one of the adults and watch it being passed around to Oona. The boy had his head slightly lowered, half hiding his eyes. He placed his left hand over the centre of his chest and bowed his head even further.

'Kabona, KuluLlaka.' It sounded as the rich baritone had sung the words as Qwelby used the polite form of address for an adult female. Sitting down, he turned to Oona and gestured for her to keep the PowerObject in her hands.

'TransDimensional Temporal Synchronicity,' he murmured to himself in Tazian. He had heard Gumma talk of such a theoretical possibility. He grinned at Oona's questioning look.

'It is beautiful,' he added, once again mesmerised by her bright blue eyes.

Sjöström explained what she meant by the "official" version of events: downplaying the children's involvement. She eased their disappointment by reminding them that they were to receive the reward. She finished by checking with Dr Keskinen the time they had agreed for him to go to the station later that day and make a formal statement.

As she left, Viljo looked at his watch. His surprised exclamation made everyone check theirs and discover that the fireworks had been a lot longer ago than they had realised. With thanks all round for the food, drink, and an exciting and exhausting evening, the youngsters agreed with Hannu as he declared: 'That was the best New Year's Eve ever!'

As everyone was getting ready to leave, Anita said she needed to use the toilet. She said quick goodbyes and winked at her mother as she slipped upstairs rather than forcing her way through the crowd of people in the lobby. When she came back downstairs a little later, Oona together with Nils and Jarno and their parents had gone. She grinned at everyone patiently waiting.

'Right, Qwelby. Explain how you are such a good shot,' she demanded.

Qwelby returned her grin. Her father was not going to believe the explanation.

'I persuaded the photons to play a game. You know that a beam of light sent from a planet at the edge of the universe eventually returns to its starting point, thus showing that the photons travel in a circle?'

All heads nodded.

'All I had to do was to estimate the distance from where I was hiding to my target and calculate the required radius for a section of a circle that would join the two points, then leave the rest to the photons. Each time they slipped through the dimensions to find a very, very small universe of the appropriate size. Likâbâlkitâ-Eh!'

'What's that mean?' Hannu asked in the silence that followed.

Qwelby felt himself blushing furiously and was glad that he was fully clothed, otherwise his friends would have seen his bright red colouring spreading all down his chest.

'Erm... It's what the Uddîšû said when they descended from higher dimensions to fight off our... attackers,' Qwelby mumbled, relieved that his compiler had provided "attackers" and was unable to translate the Aurigan overtones of "despicable troglodytes of lower dimensions."

Taimi took a firm grip on her husband's hand to still all the questions she knew were bubbling up. 'Tomorrow,' she said firmly, smiling at him. 'Home,' she added as she rose from her chair and looked at her daughter.

Anita lingered for a moment on the doorstep.

'Tullia. Tomorrow. Promise,' Qwelby said softly, looking from her to Hannu.

'You bet,' she said as Hannu grimaced. Not only was he longing to hear about whatever invisible enemies Qwelby had been fighting, away from Anita he wanted to ask Qwelby a lot more about the stunning young woman he had seen, impossibly illuminated by sunlight.

CHAPTER 54

TULIA
RECOVERS

KALAHARI

Tullia eventually stopped sobbing, looked up and saw that Tsetsana was no longer frozen. She stretched forth an arm, and gratefully accepted the young girl's arms around her as she staggered a short way and sat down.

Tsetsana took a bottle of water from the backpack and gave it to Tullia, then took another for herself. She pulled her thick jumper over her head, removed her shirt, bunched it up, wetted it and started gently cleaning Tullia's body and legs.

Tullia relaxed back against the smooth rock, both it and her body warmed by the sun. She was in deep shock from losing her twin. They had been in each other's arms. He had been coming to join her. Then they had been ripped apart.

In a daze, she watched Tsetsana caring for her. The young girl was so competent, just like the way she looked after her two younger sisters. Looking at Tsetsana's slight frame, Tullia realised just how big she was in comparison to the Meera. *What would they think if they met Tamina?* she wondered, wryly.

Realising that whilst she was warm, Tsetsana would not be, Tullia found the courage to speak.

'Tsetsana, you must be cold,' she said, relieved that she had not whinnied.

'I was not cold. I was frightened for you,' the girl said, sounding old beyond her eleven years. She leant to the side, retrieved her sweater and pulled it on. Then continued wetting her shirt and gently sponging Tullia's wounds.

'There's a bright red patch on your forehead, like a burn,' Tsetsana said.

'My horn,' Tullia replied, her thoughts miles away.

Noticing Tsetsana slowly nodding, Tullia stared at the girl as she realised what she had said.

'When you healed Xashee, I thought I saw a column of golden light coming from your forehead, twisting around,' Tsetsana explained, shyly.

Tullia did not know what to say. Her eyes had been closed. She had felt her forehead throbbing and had assumed it was from concentration.

'Can you stand?' Tsetsana asked after a while, holding out a hand.

Tullia took it and levered herself to her feet.

Tsetsana washed the dust off Tullia's legs. Wetting a clean part of her shirt, she carefully washed dust away from an aeeay of nasty wounds across Tullia's back and buttocks. They looked like marks made by large claws. She had seen Tullia on hands and knees struggling against something Tsetsana had not been able to see, then a sudden violent wrenching and blood spurting from the back of the fighting Goddess.

She licked her lips and continued her gentle sponging, eventually finding her voice.

'You have a nasty bruise here,' she said, gently touching a long mark. 'You have another on this side. They curve around your shoulder blades.'

'My wings,' Tullia said. Once again her thoughts were miles away as she absorbed not just how much Tsetsana had seen, but how simply she accepted it.

'Like the marks and the wounds on the Lord God Kaigii,' Tsetsana whispered.

'Yes,' Tullia answered, realising that her compiler never translated "Kaigii" when she used it instead of his name. The Azuran 'Twin' did not carry all the nuances of the Tazian word.

'Let alone the complexities of QeïchâKaïgïï in Old Aurigan', a voice inside whispered.

Any thoughts Tullia may have had about that were swept away by a startling realisation. Feeling dizzy and unsteady, she swung around and collapsed against the rock face, staring. 'You saw him?!' she exclaimed.

'Oh, yes! He's magnificent!' Tsetsana said, her eyes shining, thinking of the many bleeding wounds he had suffered, in, as she saw it, rescuing her Goddess. Frustrated that she still had not become a woman, she knew her feelings for him were not those of a child.

Magnificent? Kaigii! You need your head examining. The words never made it through Tullia's mouth as another shock hit her. She had been in a NullPoint Bubble with Tsetsana frozen outside, unaffected by Time, she thought. She looked up at the sun. It was a lot lower in the sky than when she had stepped onto the footprint. She stored that away as a puzzle for another time.

Looking back at her friend, Tullia saw a range of colours flaring through the girl's aura. The rich pinks and soft greens of love. The sort of love she felt for her parents and family and shared with her friends. *Even Kaigii at times!* There was more: a rich streak of orange. She had noticed the colour before with the Meera, mainly the young men, and especially strongly from Xashee yesterday.

'Of course. The healing! How would I feel if I were injured and Rrîltallâ Tamínûllÿâ came to heal me, the great Healer Heroine herself. I would be... gobsmacked! And seen through the eyes of the Meera, an

honoured ancestor. Whistling Xzarze, I don't want that. But at least I am
beginning to understand how Azuran energy fields are different from ours.

'Are you all right, Tullia?' she heard Tsetsana ask. 'Your eyes are going round like they did yesterday.'

'We call it twirling,' Tullia said, pulled out of her reverie and seeing Tsetsana kneeling by her, looking concerned. She took the girl's hands in her own. 'We eat. I try to explain.'

Tullia did not want to get sucked back into the feelings of what had happened, especially losing her twin, so she asked Tsetsana to say what she had seen. After patient coaxing she was amazed to discover that not only had the girl seen far more than Tullia had expected, she was even able to help Tullia understand how different what had happened was from a WrapperAdventure.

There, any Tazian experienced the Adventure as if they had become the chosen character, be that a person or an animal. This time Tsetsana had seen Tullia and a tall and well-built man as if through a sort of mist. And that mist seemed to be made of strange, winged shapes which were much larger than both people, especially what she assumed was an enormous bird that had arrived carrying the man inside itself. Yet she had not been frightened.

'I felt safe. I knew I was outside. You were protecting me. And,' Tsetsana bit her lip and looked down. 'I have The Sight. I had hoped Xameb would train me. I am too old now,' she finished on a sad note.

Tullia was excited. It seemed that Gallia was right with her theory about the interplay between the third and fourth dimensions. And probably most if not all Azurii lived in what the Tazii defined as the fourth dimension, that was the three physical plus consciousness. 'My Great-Great Aunt explains Life like we are born inside a really large onion.' Using her hands, she described the many layers of that vegetable. 'And as our consciousness, our awareness grows, so we see more and more layers. Those impressions you had of Kaigii and me being inside animals with wings, that's seeing another layer.'

393

Respecting both Tsetsana's hope and what she had seen, Tullia offered what she thought was a plausible explanation. Finding no translation for 'Dragon', she explained that Kaigii – *Lord Kaigii! Twin an Uddîsû?* – had take the form of something like a winged, fire-breathing lizard, and she, a stripeless Zebra with a single horn. Because Gods and Goddesses adopted special forms for protection when they were travelling in different worlds.

How Tullia wished that were true! In an WrapperAdventure one could enter the Form of anything, usually a person but also anything animate. Like all children, the twins had explored everything. This experience had been totally different: the deepest deepstate ever! Yet it had all felt so real. Annoyed she could not explain it to herself, she ran her fingers though her hair, the sun's rays producing green flickers akin to miniature flames dancing.

Dancing. Tamina. Flames. Salamander. Attributes. She nodded as she understood what had happened. She was relieved that she had not transmogrified into a unicorn, merely acquired the protective energy form of her inherited Uddîsû. And as all such energy projections worked, she had powered that from her own inner resources. Hence the marks on her physical body. *To have that power, I, we must be a step closer to Aurigan energies. A fourth segment makes sense. So, a little Mystery solved. Now for the big one. Why us and what for?*

A soft buzz in Qwelby's corner of her mind went unnoticed as a chilly breeze swept across the hilltop, telling of the late hour and that it was time to return to the village. Tullia dressed whilst Tsetsana put everything into the backpack.

'Your aura is very strong, Tullia,' Tsetsana said. 'I have sensed it faintly before. Now it's brighter but smaller.' She held out her two hands, fingers and thumbs spread out, thumbs touching.

Tullia smiled. That was so like at home. 'Yes. Concentrated on me for my healing.' She thought, slipped inside herself and decided. Taking Tsetsana's hands in hers she leant forward, placed her lips on the young girl's forehead between her eyes and a little above, and gave her a long kiss, both girls unaware of the green light that was flowing through Tullia's hair. She focussed all her energies onto the gift she thought she was able to offer, silently asking Tsetsana if she wanted it.

'Kabona. Twana-Udada,' Tullia said as she drew back from the kiss, watching her friend's energy field sparkling and her eyes go as round as saucers.

'Thank you. Little-Sister,' Tsetsana whispered, as Tullia laughed with joy and pulled her friend into a big hug.

'Xameb, our Shaman, we say N-'om K"xausi, changes into an eland when he travels in the otherworlds,' Tsetsana said as the hug ended. 'I have never seen that as clearly as I did today...' The young girl's voice trailed away as she recalled the images that had appeared before her eyes when Tullia had kissed her forehead. Swirling spirals seeming to flow away from her down a tunnel. A tunnel whose walls were made of many patterns of cross-hatched and wavy lines. Those images had started to appear towards the end of the tribes' last few healing and trance dances as she fell asleep, or so she had assumed. Then, they had been faint and frightening. Today, not only had they been strong and clear, there was welcome reassurance in that they had been a gift from the Goddess, enhancing her gift of The Sight.

Tullia's smile turned into a big grin as the words gave her great hope. Clearly, she was correct with her analysis that the Meera on Haven, or Kalahari as they called it, were direct descendants of the Auriganii. Having only two DNA segments was not a barrier to travelling in the fifth dimension. And Xameb, she struggled as she tried to say his correct title to herself, no wonder he was offering to help her!

Tullia: statuesque, imposing, exotic, desirable and with an energy drawing people to her as she asked for friendship. An untouchable Goddess desperately needing ordinary human friendship and delighted that Tsetsana had wanted to accept her gift. Innocently unaware of the conflicting emotions she was arousing in both men and women. Not wanting her Goddess status to be reinforced by being compared to the tribe's respected Shaman, Tullia focussed her gaze on Tsetsana's eyes.

'Please do not talk about this,' she said in a firm voice. Not having heard the Meera word for 'secret', she wrapped her arms around herself and added 'Hold.'

What Tullia had done for Tsetsana was so natural to a part deep within that it was to be a long time before she questioned what she had done, how and why she had even thought she might be able to help Tsetsana on the way to unlocking her innate abilities. And then add that as another possible clue to unravelling The Mystery.

Tsetsana nodded gravely. She still had not shared her dream with Xashee and now that also would remain a secret. She understood that Tullia was married to the Sun God, Great Lord Kaigii, yet for her visit wanted to be treated as a young Meera woman. And from what she had just witnessed it was clear that both God and Goddess were powerful N-'om K"xausi, whose inner worlds were only to be spoken of by themselves.

Tsetsana was certain that the Sun Goddess had chosen to be her friend because she had The Sight, and now had made her Little-Sister. Her heart almost bursting she vowed that she would do anything to help bring the Goddess together with her God.

If only Tsetsana had been allowed to speak of seeing the Lord God Kaigii, the obvious love he and Tullia had for each other, and how she had heard what she thought was them singing in their own language of that love. If only.

Once again it was dark by the time they returned. Tullia went straight to her hut and quite naturally slipped into long trousers and a thick sweater for the evening. Seated around the little cooking fire, she explained to the family that she had gone into a deep meditation whilst Tsetsana remained on guard for any wild animals. They accepted Tullia's need to be quiet as they ate.

'You sad, Tully,' Tomku, the four-year-old daughter of the family, said as she crawled onto Tullia's lap. She had quickly discovered that the big girl made a comfortable seat.

Smiling, Tullia started rocking the young girl. Talking Tazian in almost a whisper, Tullia told Tomku of life on her world and the games children played. To the Meera it sounded as though Tullia was singing a lullaby.

Tullia loved her time with the children who treated her as just another tribal sister. Especially the younger ones calling her by what was like a nickname. Her turbulent emotions slowly calmed as she relaxed into being what she was, a youngster enjoying the role of being a big sister. She even had a little chuckle at the thought that to them she was indeed a "big" sister.

Deep inside other and much older emotions were stirring.

CHAPTER 55

∗

X A A L A
R E C A L L S

V E R T A Z I A

Feeling sick in every fibre of her being and with a splitting headache, Xaala rolled onto her hands and knees. *I have failed. It's all my...*

'*Not so!*' Ceegren's thoughtsending was sharp. '*It was my error.*'

Xaala could not believe her ears. Teacher making a mistake? No wonder he sounded so weary and energy depleted. She looked up at him and was startled. His robe, which would normally be infused with a deep rich green, had faded to the palest shade. His face usually looked like it had been carved from a block of shiny walnut. Now it was just a plain dark brown.

He gestured.

She crawled the short distance to his side before settling into her normal position with her legs tucked underneath her, back erect, hands folded in her lap and head slightly bowed. She noticed that her skin had changed. It had lost its lustre, no longer a rich creamy coffee colour but so dull it was little darker than the creamy colour of her normal Acolyte's tunic.

As he placed his hand on the top of her head, she felt her crown open and gentle energy infuse her energy centres. A tear started in the corner of each eye. She held back the flow. She knew he loved her but could not show it.

'You have done very well, my child,' he said in a gentle voice.

She was stunned by his praise. That was the highest accolade he ever bestowed on her. 'Teacher,' she replied, bending right over to touch her forehead to the floor. She could think of no other way to show her obedience. She hoped he understood that was because of her love for him, so different from what she had ever felt for her parents.

'Go. Rest. Recover. No more today.' As Ceegren spoke, Xaala felt a hand on her arm. Looking up, she saw twelve-year-old Tibor, the new junior apprentice she was training.

Gratefully, she slipped an arm over his shoulders and allowed him to help her to her feet.

'I am to take you to your grandmother,' Tibor said as they left the room. 'She is preparing food and drink.'

Xaala could no longer hold back her tears. Although she knew he was exhausted, Teacher had still thought to care for her by summoning Tibor and sending instructions to her grandmother, who served as Cook and Housekeeper.

Having eaten and used the neutron shower to freshen her Self and her clothes for the following day, Xaala slipped into the short robe that she used when meditating. It had been a gift from Ceegren on her twelfth rebirthday. Its pale, silver-tinged, electric blue was intended to protect the open energy field, whilst not inhibiting deep contact. It had been the first time that she had channelled more than just her Teacher's energies and she was eager to see how different the experience had been.

Sitting in the lotus position she faced Mirror. Her crystal of dark grey-blue Xalulan was a heavy piece that in both looks and name was suited to a male. Even her name was a variation on Xallan, a boy's name. With the strong male genes that she had inherited, no wonder she looked like an overly tall, lanky boy! Was that why she had never found favour with her parents?

'Xaala! Stop snivelling,' she berated herself. 'In a few weeks time I will enter my sixth phase of integration. I will never be pretty. But Ceegren does not want a pretty airhead. He wants me to be mentally and psychically the best. And I do excel at everything for which he trains me.' Through Mirror she looked at her crystal. 'I am sorry, Xalulan. You serve me well. And at least my HorseMane hair is my own, unique, girly style!'

Gently caressing her powerful crystal she asked her Memory for a composite replay. If any further tagging and cataloguing was required, that would be done when she recalled for Ceegren. Relaxing through her breathing, she sank into her Kore.

She felt her whole self expand as the power of three Tazii flowed through her. She swelled even more as she realised it was her power that was leading the way like a bright torch piercing the dark night. She held herself in place high up above the planet, the apex of a triangle of which the base was formed by the Abominations.

As the dark energy flowed down to them she realised that they were fighting back with an energy far greater than had been expected. The third dimension was acting as an amplifier. Worse, even as the fighting progressed, what had seemed a beautiful rainbow was in fact a message of disaster. They were connecting! And she was being pulled into it. But she needed to be there, in the centre, acting as the channel for the energies that were seeking to keep the twins apart.

She sensed their great need to be together. What were those strange feelings flowing through her? Angrily, she thrust aside the MemoryTag that said 'love', cursing herself for wondering. Abominations like that could not know true love, what she felt for Teacher.

As the fighting continued, it was clear that the boy and girl had been infected with the Azuran Disease. Otherwise, how could they so viciously attack the dark clouds that were seeking to block them, and then unfairly forcing Teacher and the others to send ever more threatening images.

She knew that the powers of Quantum Twins were supposed to be great, and that the only previous pair had been of no use to the race as adults because they had became impossibly introverted. This pair felt different. And what was worse, not only had their four friends risked their lives trying to make contact, they also had possessed the power to fight through all attempts to prevent that.

She realised that there was a special energy between the twins and their friends. It reminded her of the stories of the beauty of Aurigan times. What was not beautiful was that the way their friends had fought had shown that were already half infected. If the twins returned they would connect with those friends and the Disease would spread at a terrifying speed across the whole planet.

A strong energy infused her, sending terrifying creatures to cauterize the twins' mental receptors, and cut them off forever from each other and the MentaNet. Even as Xaala felt pride that her thoughts had been received and were being acted upon, she screamed with pain as fire ripped through her and the creatures were flamed out of existence.

But why the vitriolic energy? Xaala asked herself, sensing that was not directly related to the fear of the twins reconnecting. Instead, it seemed to come from a foul Darkness. An eons old mixture of overwhelming shame and guilt that... fed the Custodians?

Her thoughts were brushed aside as a new sensation rippled through her. Dragon energy was flowing through her feet and being sucked out of her head by the welcoming embrace of Unicorn energy. The Abominations would connect!

Just in time, Xaala pulled herself away. When Ceegren required her to recall, he would see that it was on the Unicorn that the energies must be concentrated. Although equally strong, the Dragon was vastly more aggressive.

She went into the bathroom and splashed cold water on her face. Dry, she returned to her bedroom and settled down to calm her mind by meditating on the words of the Great Traditionalist, Insûmâne Haa-Zeyló.

CHAPTER 56

THE MANTRA

KALAHARI + FINLAND

Although Tullia was exhausted from the battle with the dark forces she was in too much pain to sleep, and although mentally reconnected, as yet there was no thoughtsharing. Having poured all her love into her twin she had little energy left for herself. She knew she should go out into the bush and bathe in the moonlight to help restore her inner reserves. But with being so viciously attacked and physically forced apart by what had to have been Tazii, she needed to think. She sat on the pile of blankets that served as her bed and sank into her Kore.

In front of her a young man lay on a medcouch. One of the DragonRiders, his body horribly burnt by the primitive but effective particle beams used by the Solids. One part of her mind was in his, shutting down his pain receptors, another part was analysing the damage.

Keeping erect the four long and slender central fingers of each hand, she folded over the two slightly shorter, opposed, outer ones until they were touching the centre of her palms, then folded down the other four to meet them. Having activated the interstitial energies of the sixth dimension she opened to the needs of the

Rider. In great swathes from either side she felt healing energy flowing into her Kore. Golden energy flowed out through the centre in the middle of her forehead to combine with the streams of green energy flowing from her sensitive fingers which she manipulated around the areas needing healing.

It had been another long battle, fighting off the attackers in the third dimension. Throughout the fighting she had been flying astride her winged unicorn in close contact with the warriors, the two of them tending to minor wounds of Riders and Dragons. The fighting had ended long ago and she and her fellow healers were now working with the most seriously injured as they were brought out of stasis.

Her body longed to be free of the tight ultralilac skinergysuit without which her tired energy field would have lost its focus and she would have slipped into the higher, formless reaches of the seventh dimension. Although she could heal from there, and with less energy expenditure, she knew the physical presence of the Unicorn Kèhša was an inspiration to all her healers.

There was another pair of hands, seemingly inside her own. They only had five digits. Long though, they were shorter than her six. How was it possible for anyone to heal with only five digits?

Five fingers! Tullia felt dizzy as she slipped back and forth between the two scenes with their one link – the power of the energy flooding into her through her shoulder blades as if wings were joined there, and then out through her forehead as if through her horn. She tried to argue that she was not a winged unicorn but a Healer who rode on them. With tears running down her cheeks her protests were stilled as she was increasingly immersed in the beauty of the flow of healing energy, and amazement that she must have accessed the seventh dimension as she had given Xashee healing. With even Mandara saying that the eighth dimension was no longer accessible to the Tazii, it had never occurred to her just how deeply she had gone in connecting with her Uddîšû genes.

And her life, in spite of the heart-aching absence of her twin: she felt more freedom than ever before. Was it possible that in some ways life on Mars amongst the descendants of the Auriganii was better than life on Vertazia?

A soft buzzing made her look up. It was the dragonfly. Its red body and tracery of red and green wings clearly visible in a patch of starlight at the edge of the open doorway. Seeing her twin's favourite colours took her back to the time they were in each other's arms, and then to the previous occasion in the stairwell. Thoughts, realisations, tumbled through her mind.

The children they had seen with the snowman. The Meera on Kalahari. Gumma trying to restore Aurigan technology. The strength of their Uddîsû genes. Doubled because of their twinergy, their power so strong that they had stopped played games against their friends as they always won. Instead, it was always girls against boys. Tazii DNA was Azurii plus one. Quantum Twins just had to be Tazii plus one. A step closer to Aurigan twelve segments. As she opened her eyes and looked out into the night sky, a faint buzz in Qwelby's corner of her mind accompanied the extra bright twinkling of a star

'Oh, Kaigii, why do we have to be away from Vertazia to discover what we are?' With no sense yet of thoughtsending working, she continued to speak aloud. 'Freedom? Freedom from a mental and psychological blanket of excessively structured development? And Gallia says that's even imposed on many adults!'

She stared at the myriad twinkling stars, momentarily imagining each one was an Aurigan looking down on her, encouraging her to take the next step in her thinking, to discover the real reason for her and Kaigii to be as they were.

'Enquire. Explore. Experiment. We WILL Succeed!' she tried to thoughtsend as sleep finally captured her.

* * *

405

Qwelby closed the door to his room as Hannu left. He stood for a moment gazing at the PowerObject that his friend had placed on the bedside cabinet, before collapsing on the bed, exhausted physically, mentally and emotionally. If the images he had received were true, and not merely memories from WrapperFantasies, then there were four more to be found: to create their best hope of being rescued.

Gingerly, he reached out a hand and rested three fingers lightly on the smooth face. It was warm. Unnaturally warm. Energy flowed up from deep at the base of his spine as images appeared. Five points of light marking the five points of a pyramid. He knew without a shadow of doubt that the additional fourth segment that he and Kaigii possessed was the key to tuning in to the PowerObjects. They had needed to find the first to trigger the sequence. A soft buzz in Tullia's corner of his mind drew his attention.

'Of course, what we saw from the stairwell, there must be one where Tullia is. That's why we are where we are. I must thoughtsend her. Then three more to find.' He withdrew his fingers and rolled onto his back.

He did not know how long he lay there before awareness of his surroundings returned. With limbs feeling like lead, he undressed. Catching sight of his reflection in the full length mirror on the wardrobe door, he stood there examining his wounds.

His sense of pride was replaced by a feeling of revulsion at the level of violence he had exhibited. His reflection shimmered and it seemed that there was a much taller figure clad head to toe in a single, tight fitting, multicoloured garment. He was not on Vertazia. The other could not be Image, yet it seemed that the newcomer was speaking to him.

'An Aurigan Warrior fights only in defence. You have no need to feel regret or sadness at what you destroyed. They were only energy constructs. You are right to be proud of your wounds. They were honourably incurred.'

A picture came to Qwelby of Oona's upturned face, her bright blue eyes wide open with admiration. She had rested her head on his chest. That had hurt. But he hadn't minded. He knew that feelings for girls were not supposed to awaken for at least another eighteen months. Yet being with her had been nice. For a moment he felt her there again with his arm around her.

Wanting to experience those warm feelings again took him back to the very different feelings he had experienced as he and Tullia had clung to each other.

As he climbed into bed, wishing she was in her own bed next to him, tiredness pulled him into a deepstate. He was flying through space, seated on a magnificent Dragon, its wing-beats stirring the stellar winds as they approached a planetary system at the edge of a pair of galaxies shaped like a butterfly.

He felt his muscles straining against the tight fitting, iridescent scales of his dragonsuit. Watched as his six long fingers lovingly caressed his mount's sensitive ear ridges as they headed towards home. Home, a beautiful sphere composed of a fine tracery of multi-coloured light, slipping though space and time. The home that he and Kaigii had created, and that they were now sworn to protect.

A great swathe of stars disappeared. A space rift had formed, its centre a black hole extruding from another universe. Stretching across millions of kilometres it looked like an ultra thin pair of lips. The top lip was the crashing of red and yellow waves on a sea shore, the bottom lip the reflection of the upper one. It was roiling its way towards him with the HomeSphere directly in its path.

He did not have time to wait for any warriors to join him. Thoughtsending an alert he mindmelded with his Dragon. Zhólérrân folded his wings and together they plummeted down towards the very centre of the black hole.

'Wait! Dragon Kèhša.'

The Unicorn Kèhša's appeal filled his heart with regret. He would never see her again. She was not a warrior. Did not, could not understand. 'A man has to do what...'

Fighting to prevent the intense gravity from crushing him was taking all his strength. Yet he needed more if he was to insert the right mixture of energies that would destabilise the black hole and allow it to be sucked back into its own universe.

A pair of eyes appeared in the distance. Ovals of straw yellow with unusually large emerald green orbs. They flared and hurled bolts of lightning at him, enwrapping within her energy that of all his warriors. And the healers!

'¡Fight! ¡Warrior Kèhša Of All Dragons! ¡Fight!' the accompanying Aurigan symbols demanded.

Wondering why the eyes were like Tamina's... a tapping sound brought him out of his deepstate. Looking around, he found the source of the noise. Flapping its wings as it tapped on the window was what had to be a baby Horned Snow Owl as it exactly fitted Hannu's description of what he had seen in the woods that night. With its two ears standing up on either side of its head, the unusual tuft of hair between them looked just like a miniature horn. No-one else had seen it and Hannu had been teased that all he had seen was one of the owls common to Finland.

About to dismiss the incident as overexcited, Tazian image-into-action, the persistent tapping made Qwelby focus his vision acutely. Between the owl's ears he very clearly saw a miniature horn, complete with spiral striations. The effort required to focus his fifth dimension sight through the slow vibrations of Earth drained the last drop of his energy. As he slumped sideways onto the pillows, trying to thoughtsend *'Together soon'*, he felt he was hallucinating as he fell asleep hearing Tullia's voice.

'Enquire. Explore. Experiment. We WILL Succeed!'

CHAPTER 57

ÓWEPPÂ
SIGNALS

VERTAZIA

As Tamina entered her bedroom that evening she glanced at the Talisman, frowned, and walked over to it. She was right. The reds in the twin's two segments were brighter. As she picked it up she noticed a dark mark on the pale wood of the stand that Pelnak had made. It had the same twelve sides and looked as though it had been burnt into the wood.

With Óweppâ in her hands she sat on her bed feeling old and tired. This was all too much. She wanted to tell the others and share the burden with them, but not before she had tried to understand what it might mean for Wrenden's sake. Not only was he her young brother, now that Qwelby was no longer with them she felt a second sense of responsibility as he was Qwelby's youngerest.

'I don't need protecting!' Wrenden said angrily from her doorway. 'Your thoughts are leaking,' he added, in a tone of disgust.

Tamina grimaced as she realised that she had been betrayed by her subconscious. Yet she felt relief as she acknowledged that "her little Eeky" was growing up, and proffered the Talisman. As he took

409

Óweppâ and examined it, she got up, took down the stand and held that out to him as she sat down.

Wrenden joined her on the bed and the two of them sat looking at the two objects, trying to find a positive meaning in what they saw before activating their wristers to call the not-twins.

'We've got to rescue them,' Wrenden said, looking at his sister.

Surprised by the firm tone in his voice, Tamina looked up, and was surprised even more as she took in the energies flowing through his aura. Gone for the moment was the irritating little pest. She was looking at a... mature young man, who had nearly died trying to save his elderest.

'Whatever it takes,' he added, in a tone that brooked no contradiction.

Thoughtsending that she had detected behind Mandara's words that the four of them stood the best chance, was his opinion that due to the sixth dimension connection they were the only chance the twins had of making contact, she took a deep breath.

'Whatever it takes,' she said, matching his tone of voice.

Looking deep into each other's eyes they held their hands up and made the XOÑOX symbol with both hands.

CHAPTER 58

BROKEN
BRIDGES

VERTASIA

As Xaala withdrew from her meditation and settled down to sleep, the full realisation came to her: the Abominations had to remain on Azura - for ever. From their intense need to be together it was obvious that if they were reunited they would only live short lives, like the other pair. Even that could be another twenty years. She was well aware of the fear that if they did succeed in reconnecting they might return to Vertazia.

They were sister and brother. She had had a brother. Her parents had not wanted a girl but another boy, yet forever were complaining that she looked like a boy! There had been no love, only expectations. Yet no matter how hard she had tried she was never good enough for them.

Her grandparents who worked on Ceegren's estate, they loved her, but it was not like her experience of the twins' love for each other. Xaala shook herself in disgust. That was not love. Abominations could not love. Yet their friends had risked their lives to rescue them. If that was not love, what was?

What would her parents say if they were alive and could see that she had progressed to being better than her brother had been at the same age? It was all so unfair. Five years ago she had lost her family in an accident. If not for that, might she now at least have had her parent's respect?

An accident.

If the twins met with an accident...

But an accident was just that. She knew it was possible to travel to Azura through using the seventh dimension. But that was only in energy form. She would not be able to affect conditions there.

She gasped in horror at where her thoughts were leading. The unthinkable! That had to be caused by her contact with the twins' energies. That beautiful, powerful, rainbow bridge between them. Their energies flowing though her had been sublime.

'No! Stop!' she cried aloud, putting her hands over her ears in a vain attempt to stop the barrage of conflicting thoughts. She had no fear of her cry being heard as she kept her room permanently shielded, except for receiving incoming messages.

Weaving around the back of her mind was the unavoidable fact that if the twins were to meet with an accident, a serious accident, that would be the perfect solution. Again, the unthinkable! Throwing back the covers she swung her legs over the side of her bed and sat looking into Mirror. 'Help me!' she pleaded.

Her mouth dropped open as her reflection changed to nothing like she had ever seen before. She was wearing a tight fitting, ankle length, flame-orange sheath dress that left her shoulders bare. In her right hand she held a long rod with what looked like a large flower bud at the end. Mirror shimmered as though flexing.

As everything cleared she saw that her head had been replaced by that of a lion, with what appeared to be a circular hat standing upright on it. The figure was standing in a desert. Behind it a strange bridge to nowhere. A gently curved, stone arch supported on a pillar at each end.

Looking for clues, Xaala focussed on Image and was drawn to the lion's eyes. She felt its rich, chestnut orbs mocking her insipid brown ones, challenging her. She licked her lips and gripped the rod firmly, holding it diagonally across her body as though in answer to the challenge. As she did so, one of the pillars flexed and as if in slow motion the arch slowly crumbled from that end until it had completely collapsed all but for the other pillar which remained standing, erect and isolated.

The connection between that bridge and the rainbow bridge between the twins was obvious. But the rest? The techniques that created Mirrors were faint remains of long-lost Aurigan technology. They seemed to generate a form of auto-hypnosis, revealing an individual's inner state of being, and much more at times. Sadly, analysis of the Aurigan overtones was difficult due to the lack of records from those times.

Mirror opaqued and cleared to reveal a normal reflection. Xaala found herself standing up with her arms in position as if still holding the rod. A kaleidoscope of thoughts tumbled through her mind. Shocked at their content her whole body broke out in sweat. Breathing heavily she sought control as she went into the bathroom.

Standing under the natural shower she imaged each drop of water carrying away all the negative energy she had manifested. Dry, she returned to the bedroom where she sat cross-legged on the bed and concentrated all her energy into shutting away, irretrievably deeply behind her Privacy Shield, the thoughts she had experienced. The image of herself as that woman she tucked away in a corner of her mind, sealing that place securely. She wanted to explore that, carefully and in her own good time.

Calm at last, she slid back beneath the covers and fell into a deep sleep.

CHAPTER 59

EXPOSURE

FINLAND

Anita was quiet on the walk home, trying to sort out her feelings. Hannu was her first boyfriend. They had only been together for a few weeks, yet they were so easy together, whether that was by themselves or with their group of friends. Was she in love? Real, true love, whatever that was?

Earlier that evening Qwelby had sucked energy out of her, then used it to heal a man's broken knee. Although he had kept his hands very close to the man's leg, she had seen his palms glowing with golden light radiating from them. *And he says he's not as good a healer as Tullia!*

Exhausted after the exciting night, Anita headed for her room as soon as she got home and collapsed into bed. She lay on her back, thinking. Since Qwelby had arrived she had been in a whirl with a whole new range of emotions flowing though her. She didn't feel about him the way she did about Hannu. Yet the feelings were stronger for Qwelby. At times he seemed so very grown up. He said he hated it when Tullia tried to look after him. Yet she sensed he liked it when she had been attending to his wounds. Touching his velvet like skin, she had wanted to stroke him.

With a sigh she rolled onto her side, in her imagination cuddling the alien. 'Tullia's right. You do need looking after,' she whispered as she ran her fingers through his thick, shoulder length hair. And fell asleep.

Downstairs, her parents were relaxing with a quiet nightcap. Viljo was feeling decidedly uncomfortable. He could not explain why he had allowed himself to involve the Institute through the story about Jadrovitch, nor why he had made such a crazy offer to Qwelby. It was clear from the boy's explanation about his shooting skills that he was seriously deranged. What was the term. Psychotic? Schizophrenic? Staring into the flames of the wood burning stove he took a sip of his Maali.

'You remember when MonKiw became fully operational, and running the combined experiments with CERN finally proved that photons can travel faster than the speed of light, and therefore must have slipped through other dimensions?' Viljo asked, rhetorically.

'How could I forget!' Taimi replied with a laugh. 'You, and I think every scientist in the world, were so excited.'

'While that boy was talking, once again I found myself almost believing him,' Viljo said, shaking his head. 'Inventive or what! And I have to say he is a great storyteller.'

Qwelby was the first person whose aura Taimi had seen. That night she had slipped into a meditative state. Watching the scarcely visible fluctuations of soft colours she was convinced that when Qwelby spoke he was telling the truth. She could not tell her husband that. He would dismiss that as women's intuition!

Viljo swirled the brandy in his glass, staring at it as if he might find the answer there. He swallowed it one gulp, coughed and shook his head. 'With the police involved tonight, someone in authority must be told about Qwelby.'

'Who?'

'Immigration is the easiest choice. Then it's up to them if they want to explore his mental state.'

'It's the weekend. And the New Year. All the offices will be closed. You'll have to leave it until Monday. And you will have to speak to the Rahkamos first,' Taimi said, temporising, as she really wanted to talk with the boy about the subtle forms of energy.

'Mmh. You're right. Let's not spoil the last two days of the holiday,' Viljo replied. After the events of the night his fear about what the boy might do had been assuaged and, anyway, his daughter was safely tucked up in bed upstairs. 'I'll discuss it with them Monday evening, after work.' He sighed, imagining his daughter's protestations and the travails that awaited the likeable stranger.

Later, sitting at her dressing table having just finished cleansing her face, Taimi gave her reflection a long look. She was feeling exhausted. She was not yet old, and not unattractive, but she did look different with her hair pulled back and her makeup removed compared to what she had seen on her last look in the mirror before leaving for the Rahkamos.

'Image,' she murmured. 'Like a mask.' She thought on what Qwelby had said at the end of the evening, and that took her back to his other explanation. As her husband had said, he was an excellent story-teller. And, she sighed, impossibly inventive. She had to admit that she wanted to believe him, especially when she felt herself sucked into his world.

She recalled the way her daughter had been with Qwelby that night, the three youngsters on the settee with Qwelby in the middle. She shook her head. She had seen from Hannu's reactions that trouble was brewing there.

Taimi had established a successful Complementary Health practice in Helsinki. She was a Yoga Teacher, Reiki Master and CymaTherapist who used Electrophotonic Imaging to measure the human chakras and diagnose ailments. Giving that up had been a wrench.

Seija had been enthusiastic in helping Taimi to establish her Yoga courses. Added to Paavo's friendship with her husband, that had eased their family's way into acceptance by the close-knit community, and given Taimi hope that eventually she would again be able to deploy the full range of her skills.

She had enjoyed teasing her husband, but he was right. And she owed it to Seija to return that help. She would go with Viljo on Monday night. She was sure that between them they could persuade the Rahkamos to go to the authorities. Perhaps someone local would be best. The sergeant who lived in Kotomäki and had, however briefly, met Qwelby.

See you!
Dje'eymey
Sala sentle
Bye nyt

As a reader of Sci-Fi, I guess you know that Einstein's theory of General Relativity establishes the existence of parallel worlds.

But did you know that humans had been around for about 350,000 years, when between 50,000 and 40,000 years ago there were rapid changes into what we are today. No-one knows why that happened; and it is true that even today only some three percent of our DNA is active.

Could the Twins be telling the truth?

You can tell us what you think via the website
www.quantumtwins.co
where you can read more about them and their world,
along with maps, photographs, notes on quantum science and
the world of energy.

The Twins' adventures continue in:

417

HUNTED

He jerked awake. A figure was standing in the doorway. Short and wide. Not an Aurigan. He reached for his stunner but his hand sent objects crashing off the side table and onto the floor. Unarmed, he rolled out of bed into a crouching position, ready to defend or attack.

Still no laser beam flickered. 'Thank the stars these solids are so slow,' he said to himself.

'Qwelby?' the solid said.

'Unkh!'

'You all right?'

He knew that voice.

'Hannu?' he asked, straightening up but keeping his hands poised.

'Who'd you think it was?' Hannu asked.

Qwelby heaved a sigh of relief and sat on his bed. 'I was on the HomeSphere. I thought you were a solid. Attacking.'

'Solid?'

'People like you who live in the third or fourth dimensions. Huh. Daft. I'm solid in my world.'

'Bad dream?'

'Yes. No. Timeslipping through past .... memories. When we lived in higher dimensions and our... bodies were... flexible.'

Qwelby's shoulders slumped. There was so much to explain. 'Effects from last night.'

'Yeah. Last night. You promised.'

'Later. All together.'

'Ah, come on Qwelby,' Hannu wheedled as he sat on the bed and put an arm around his alien friend. 'At least tell me what your twin's like, how she got here and why... well...' Hannu had seen a tall, naked and beautiful young woman in his friend's arms, impossibly bathed in sunlight in the pitch black night of the snow filled woods. Then she had simply disappeared

'Irritatingly Bossy. Wants to be a healer. Seventh dimension. I was there with her at the same time. On Mars in a hollow on a bare mountaintop in bright sun. She'd been absorbing the sunlight and the mountain's strong energy.'

'But what's she like,' Hannu insisted.

Qwelby's shoulders slumped. 'When we restore our full mental connection I'll take you to meet her,' he said in a sad voice.

'Yeah. That'll be good,' Hannu said, knowing how real the experience was when his alien friend thoughthwrapped them, as he termed his vivid descriptions. 'Come on, let's get dressed and go to Anita's,' Hannu said as he got off the bed and switched on the light as he left the room.

Missing the warmth of Hannu's arm around his shoulders and thinking of his twin, Qwelby was swamped by a flood of emotions.

Sadness that they were still apart. Anger as he blamed himself for not having ensured they were reunited. Pride that he had fought well against heavy odds and saved his twin's life. And determination.

His homeworld had always been full of peace and harmony and totally non-violent.

Until last night.......

If he had to fight his way to his twin, and then back home..... he would. To succeed he needed her support - their twinergy.

***

419

Tullia awoke feeling comfortable and warmly snuggled, arms wrapped around her.... not her Comfort Doll but Tsetsana!

Horrified, yesterday's feelings ripped though her. The fear of the vicious fight in the seventh dimension and the heart-rending pain as her beloved twin was wrenched from her arms. Even now the inner pain was far worse than the cuts and bruises all over her body.

Pouring all her emotions into a Comfort Doll was fine. That was what it was for. But not another human being! It would have been bad enough had it been Tamina with all her Tazian energy skills. But this lovely, eleven-year-old girl! How much damage had she done?

Tsetsana stirred. Her lips curled into a smile as her soft brown eyes gazed adoringly up at Tullia. 'You all right?' she asked.

'Me? Err.... yes. But are you all right?' Tullia asked, slipping inside her friend's mind to look for signs of disturbance.

'Mmh,' Tsetsana murmured as she frowned in concentration. 'I'm still sleepy but feel more awake than ever. Inside, I mean.' She blinked her eyes several times. 'You hurting last night. Give me lots of energy. I feel.... different. Nice.' She grinned. 'Like Little-Sister,' she added, savouring both what her Sun Goddess friend had called her yesterday and that she had intuitively understood the three words spoken in Tazian.

Tullia sighed with relief, more at what she had mentally detected than the words. 'Thanks be to the Seven Sisters!' she thought to herself. 'She has not absorbed my negative emotions but received the power. And what a powerful outpouring that was! She has more than just "The Sight".'

Tullia lowered her head and kissed Tsetsana on the lips, just as she would her BestFriend Tamina. Then gave a little gasp as she remembered the reaction when she had briefly kissed Xashee, Tsetsana's sixteen-year-old brother.

Tsetsana giggled. She had come to accept the strangeness of being a guide and teacher to the tall and beautiful young woman who the whole tribe considered to be the daughter of the Sun Goddess. Happy to reassure Tullia, she reached her hand up and placed her small fingers on Tullia's lips. 'Okay for girls to kiss,' she said with a smile.

Why not girls and boys? Tullia thought. That made her think of her twin, and that took her back to earlier the previous evening when she had lain with him wrapped in her arms and blood from his many wounds trickling over her. Her heart had gone out to him.

Never before had she felt like that. It was more than confusing, the depth of her feelings for her twin puzzled and worried her.

And there was the violence - from her own world! She was a healer, and able to channel far more power than ever before. Yet to return home it appeared they would have to fight against their own people. She could not face that prospect. It was a betrayal of all she believed in. She would rather remain living with the Meera, as long as the two of them were together.

ABOUT THE AUTHOR

Born in Cheltenham, Geoffrey Arnold moved around the country during his career as one of HM Inspectors of Taxes - better known then by his full name of Geoffrey Arnold-Pinchin, and for his bright ties; which included The Scream, he likes all sorts of art; Tom & Gerry, he prefers silent cartoons; The Pink Panther playing tennis, his favoured sport; part of the score of Finlandia, he likes a wide range of music; and an 'in your face' saxophone.

He lives in Birmingham with his wife and near his children and grandchildren, which means he only has to wait for one person to leave the house before he retreats to his insulated, neighbour-friendly loft with his saxophones and clarinet. The other half of his family lives in Somerset, providing him with a perfect writing retreat amongst more youngsters.

Before young children came along, he spent many years working with youngsters, then in amateur theatre and politics.

Now, he is a Medium, Astrologer, Counsellor, NLP Master Practitioner, Life and Business Coach, and very occasionally a Tax Consultant - gamekeeper turned poacher!

He says that meeting the Twins has made a major impact on his life, not least in trying to keep up with the science behind the stories they tell him. More of that on:

www.quantumtwins.co

where he would love to hear from you.

Geoffrey's personal website:

www.geoffarnold.co.uk